LILA & Ecco's Do-It-Yourself COMICS CLUB

Willow Dawson

D0507376

Kids Can Press

To the future cartoonists of the world! A special thank-you to the amazingly talented youth in my comics workshops; to Laurie Dack, who inspired the character of Lila's mother; and to my niece Gabrielle, whose beautiful art inspired Lila's drawing style.

Acknowledgments

The Ontario Arts Council, Writers' Reserve Program

Ray Cammaert, Singer / Songwriter, Pink Moth

Emily Pohl-Weary, Author, *Violet Miranda: Girl Pirate,* Founder of the Parkdale Street Writers

Brian McLachlan, Cartoonist, Creator of *The Princess Planet*

Scott Hepburn, Cartoonist, Creator of *The Port*

Kalman Andrasofszky, Illustrator, DC Comics and Marvel Comics

Ramón K. Pérez, Cartoonist, Creator of *Kukuburi*

Andy B, Cartoonist, Creator of *Bottle of Awesome*

Shannon Gerard, Poet, Cartoonist, Illustrator of *Sword of My Mouth*

Claudia Dávila, Illustrator, Graphic Designer, Creator of *Luz, Girl of the Knowing*

Karen Li, Editor, Kids Can Press

Katie Gray, Designer, Kids Can Press

Julia Naimska, Designer, Kids Can Press

All the other fantastic people at Kids Can Press, including Karen Boersma, Sheila Barry, Naseem Hrab and Lisa Tedesco

Shayla Dawson, Assistant

Jenn Woodall, Intern

And members of the Jimmy Olsen Club

Text and illustrations © 2010 Willow Dawson

Kids Can Press acknowledges the financial support of the Government of Ontario, through the Ontario Media Development Corporation's Ontario Book Initiative, and the Government of Canada, through the BPIDP, for our publishing activity.

Published in Canada by
Kids Can Press Ltd.
29 Birch Avenue
Toronto, ON M4V 1E2

Published in the U.S. by
Kids Can Press Ltd.
2250 Military Road
Tonawanda, NY 14150

www.kidscanpress.com

Edited by Karen Li
Designed by Kathleen Gray

This book is smyth sewn casebound.
Manufactured in Buji, Shenzhen, China, in 5/2010 by WKT Company

CM 10 0 9 8 7 6 5 4 3 2 1

Library and Archives Canada Cataloguing in Publication
Dawson, Willow
    Lila and Ecco's do-it-yourself comics club / Willow Dawson.

Ages 8–12 years.
ISBN 978-1-55453-438-8

1. Comic books, strips, etc. —Technique—Juvenile literature. 2. Comic books, strips, etc. —Authorship—Juvenile literature. 3. Bookbinding—Juvenile literature. I. Title.

NC1764.D39 2010   j741.5'1   C2010-900789-1

Kids Can Press is a **Corus**™ Entertainment company

Contents

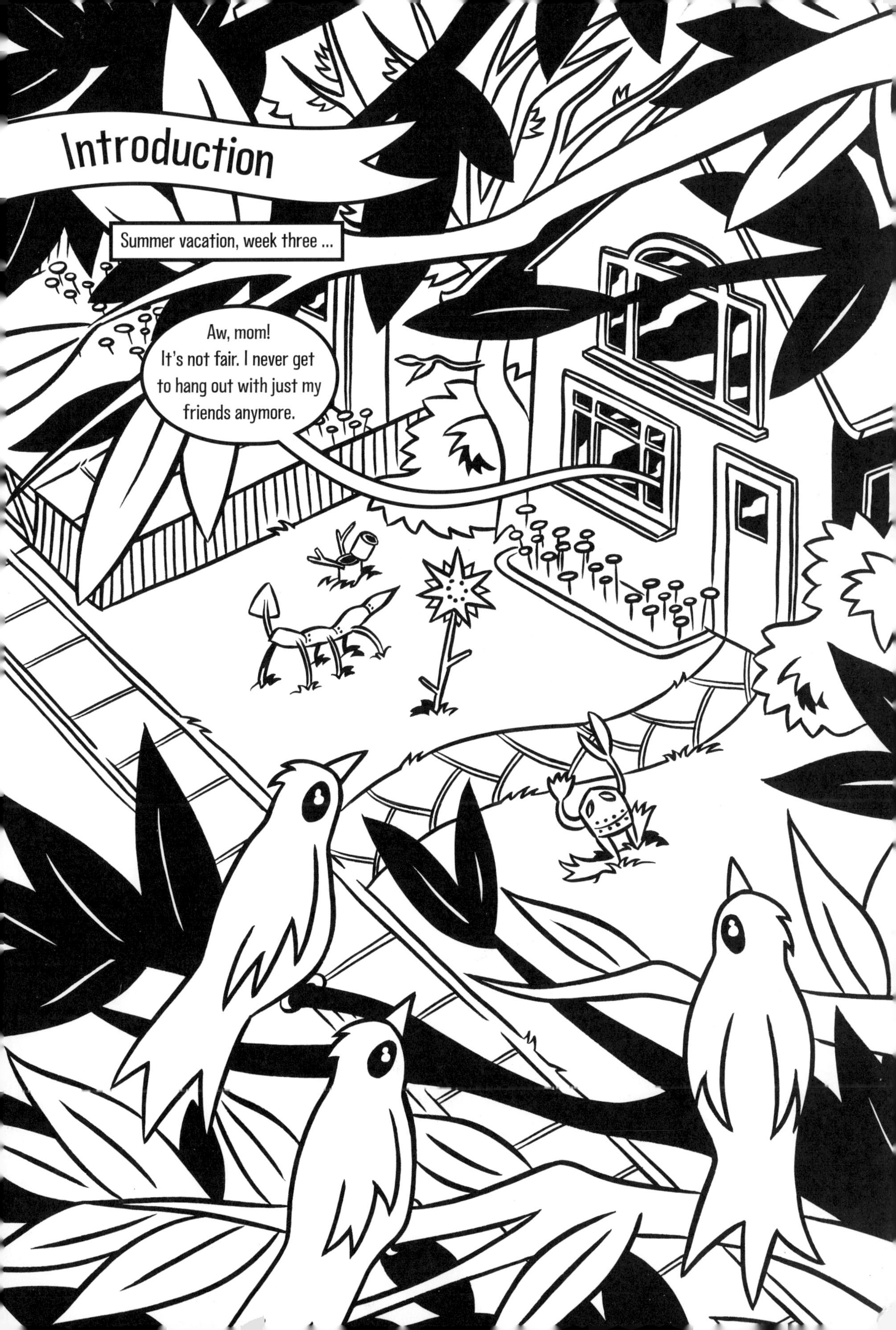
Introduction
Summer vacation, week three ...
Aw, mom! It's not fair. I never get to hang out with just my friends anymore.

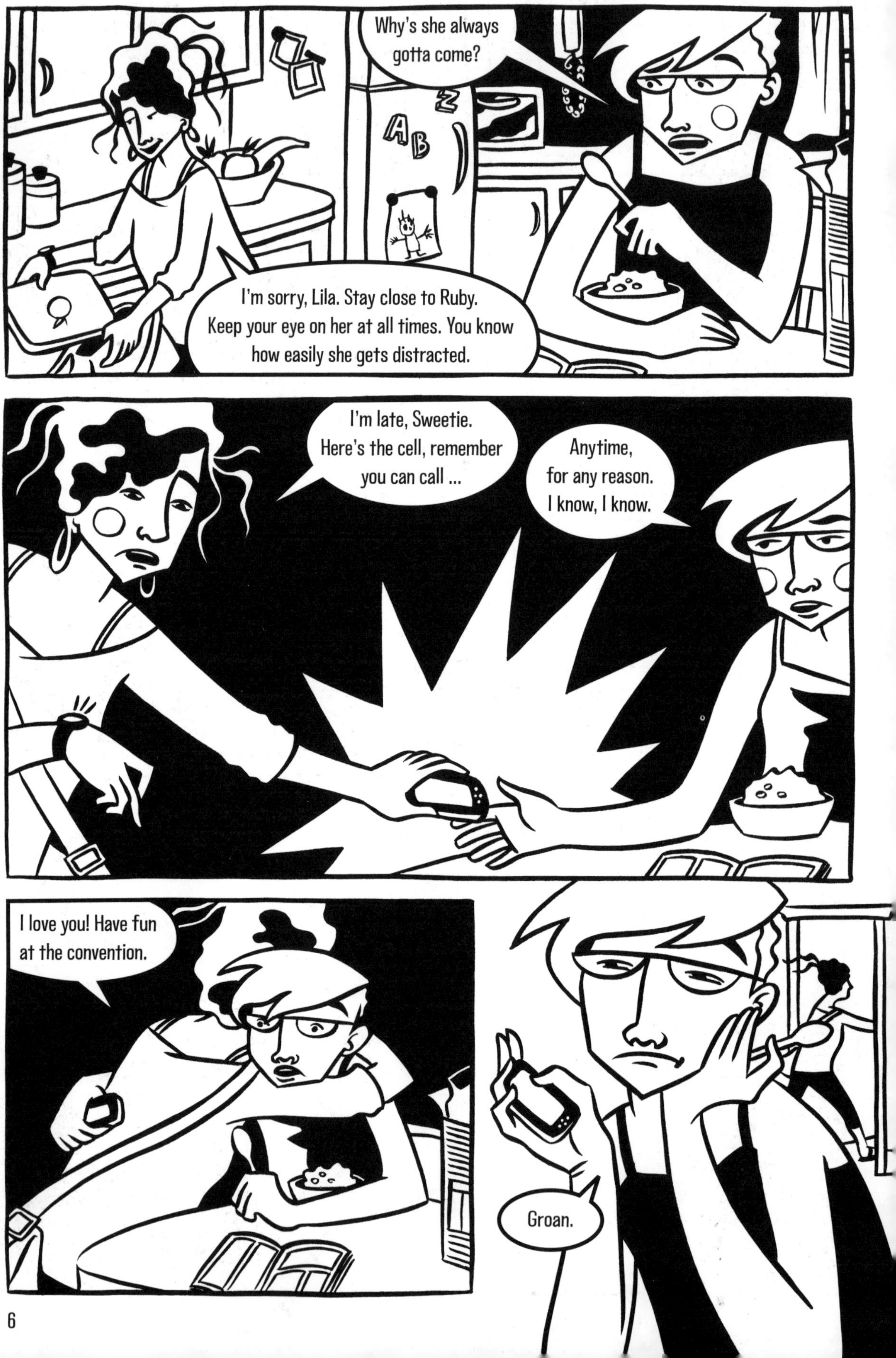
Why's she always gotta come?
I'm sorry, Lila. Stay close to Ruby. Keep your eye on her at all times. You know how easily she gets distracted.
I'm late, Sweetie. Here's the cell, remember you can call ...
Anytime, for any reason. I know, I know.
I love you! Have fun at the convention.
Groan.

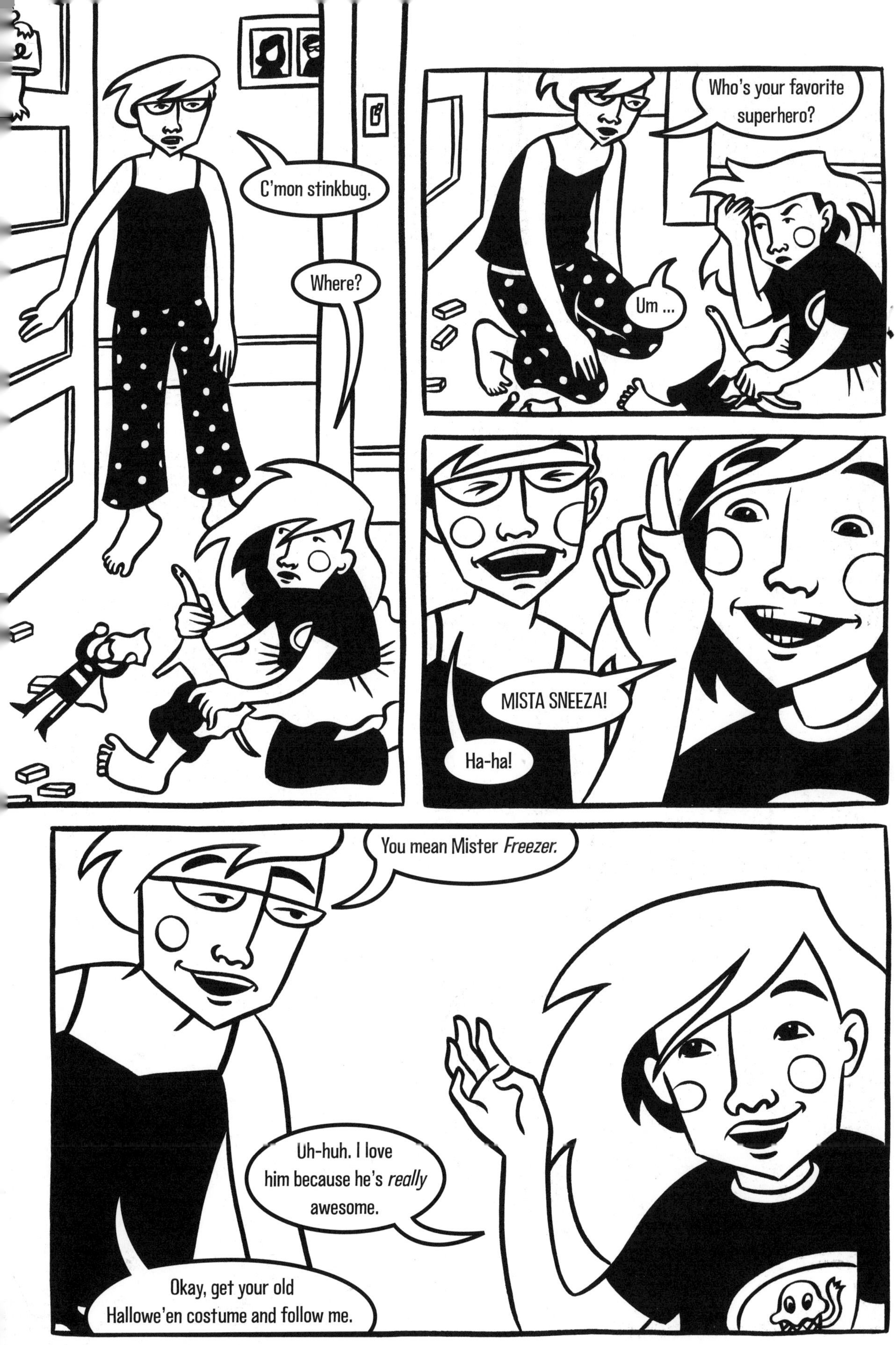
C'mon stinkbug.
Where?
Who's your favorite superhero?
Um ...
MISTA SNEEZA!
Ha-ha!
You mean Mister *Freezer.*
Uh-huh. I love him because he's *really* awesome.
Okay, get your old Hallowe'en costume and follow me.

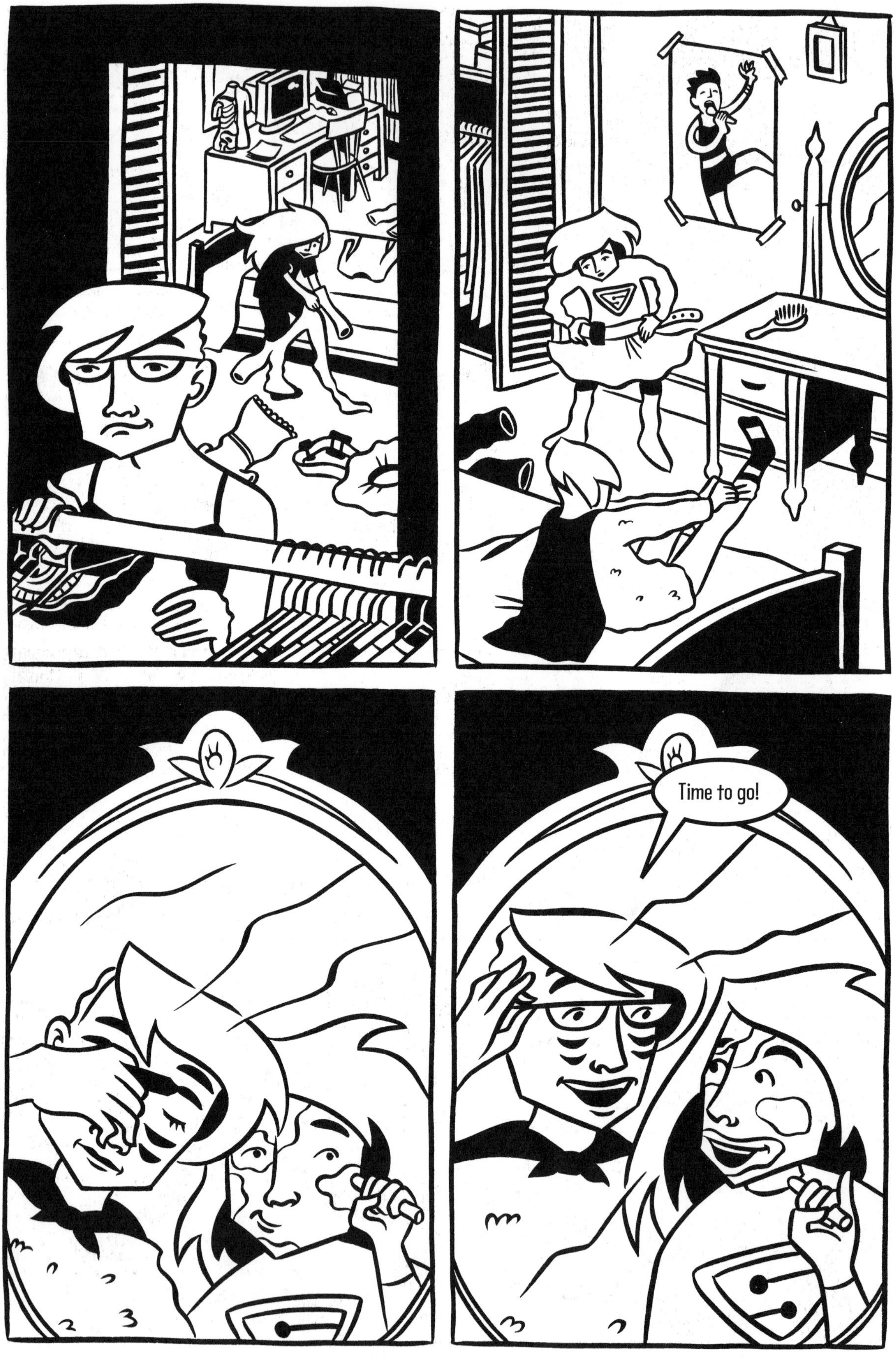
Time to go!

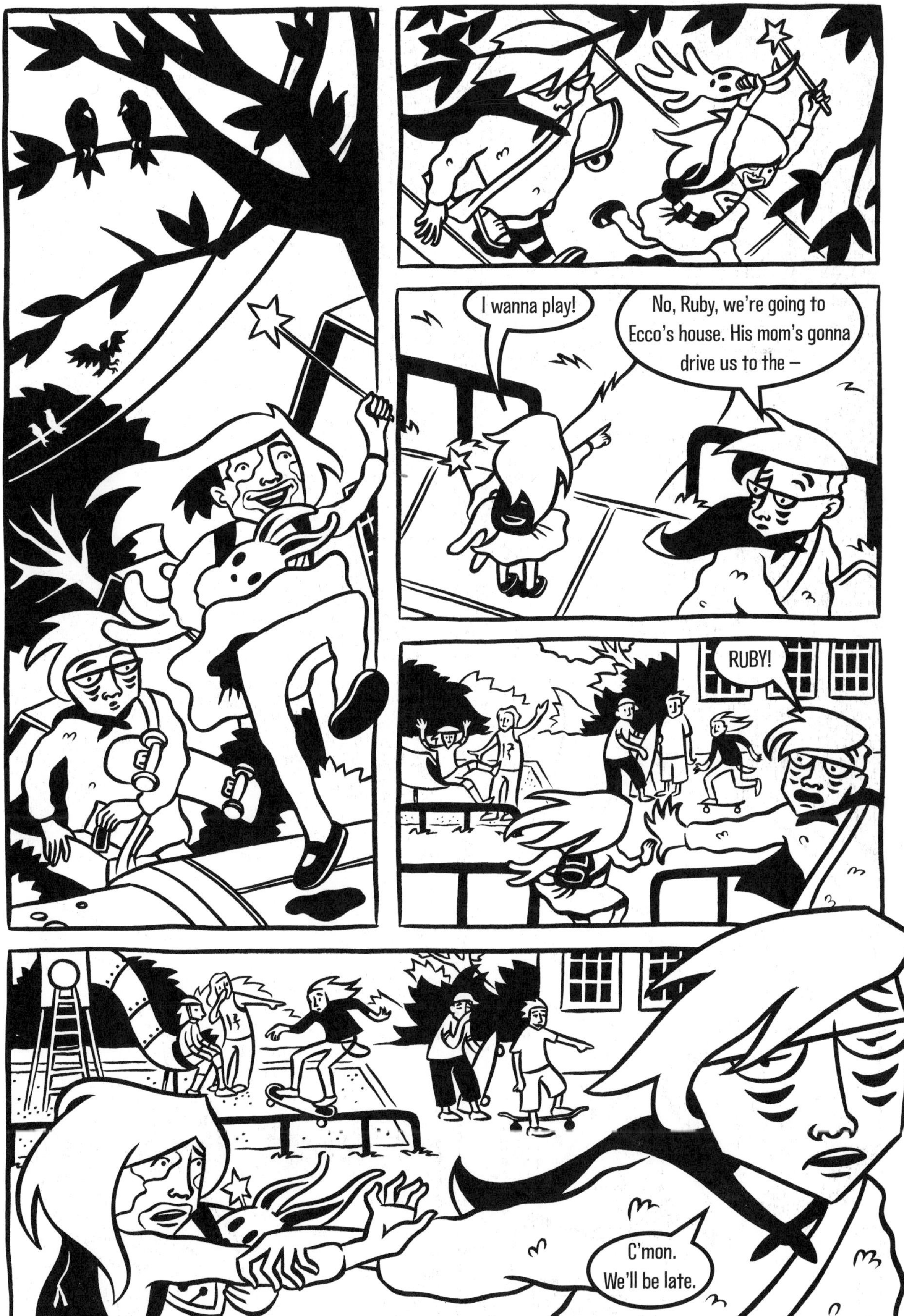
I wanna play!
No, Ruby, we're going to Ecco's house. His mom's gonna drive us to the –
RUBY!
C'mon. We'll be late.

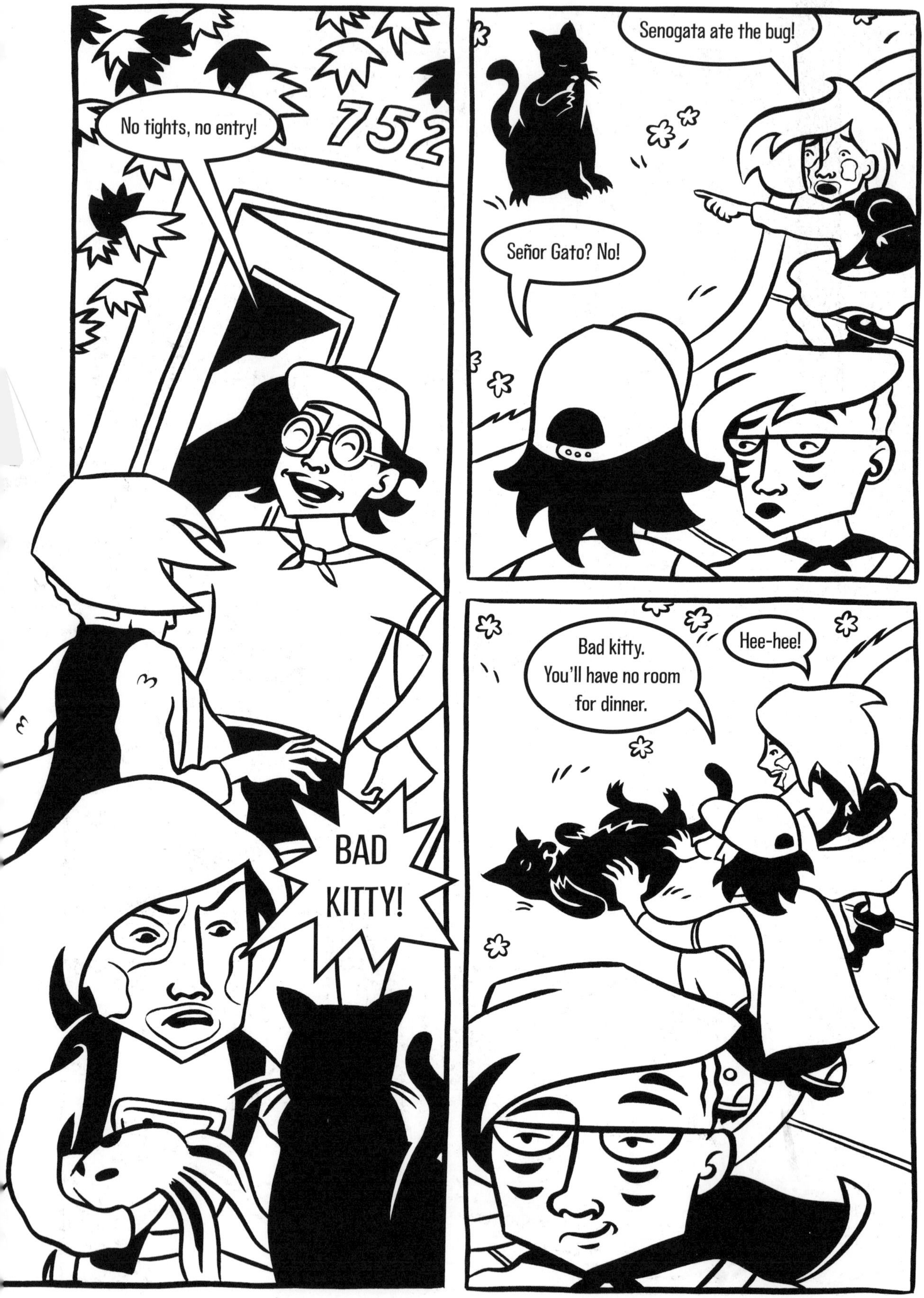
No tights, no entry!
BAD KITTY!
Senogata ate the bug!
Señor Gato? No!
Bad kitty. You'll have no room for dinner.
Hee-hee!

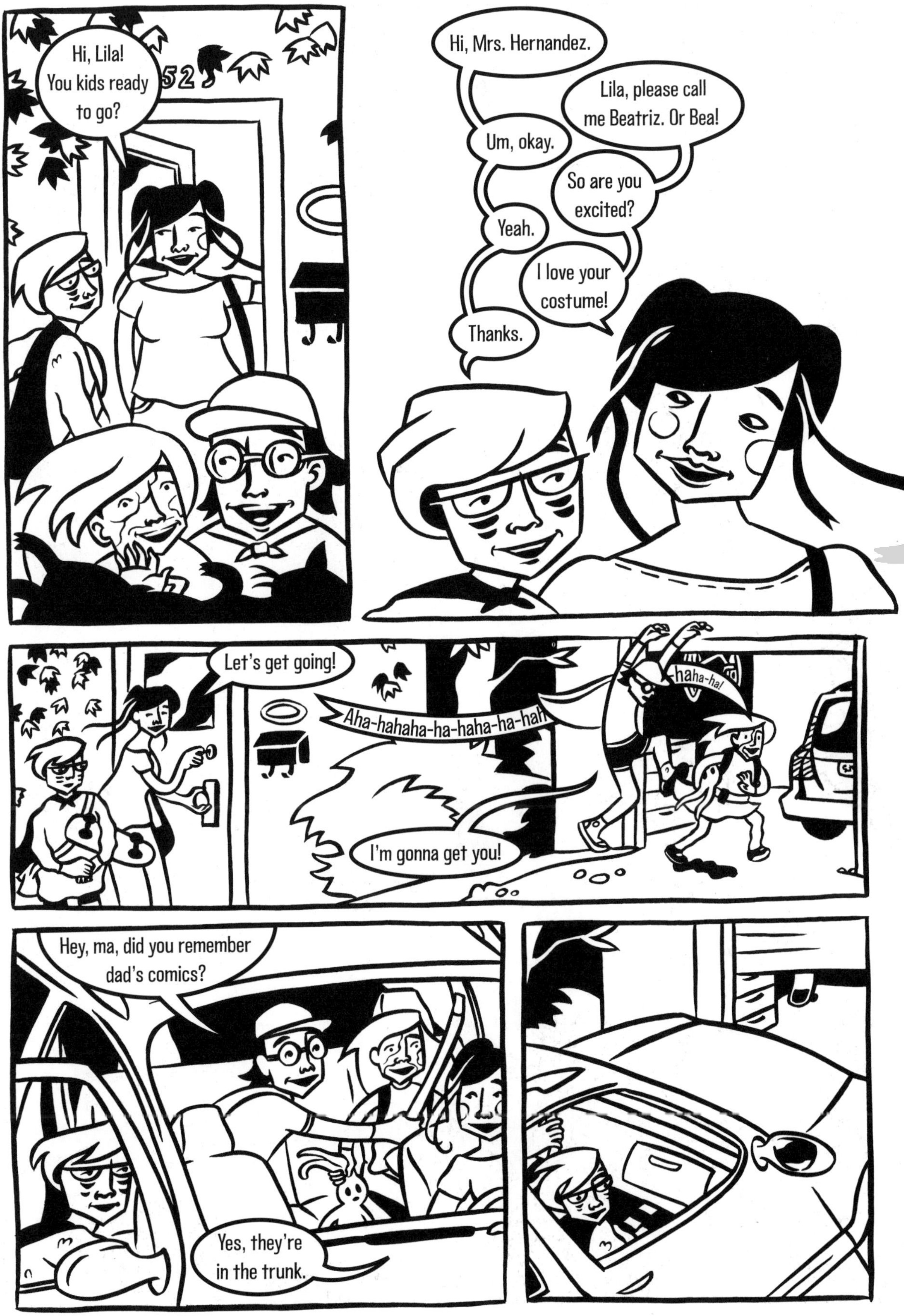
Hi, Lila! You kids ready to go?
Hi, Mrs. Hernandez.
Lila, please call me Beatriz. Or Bea!
Um, okay.
So are you excited?
Yeah.
I love your costume!
Thanks.
Let's get going!
Aha-hahaha-ha-haha-ha-hah
I'm gonna get you!
haha-ha!
Hey, ma, did you remember dad's comics?
Yes, they're in the trunk.

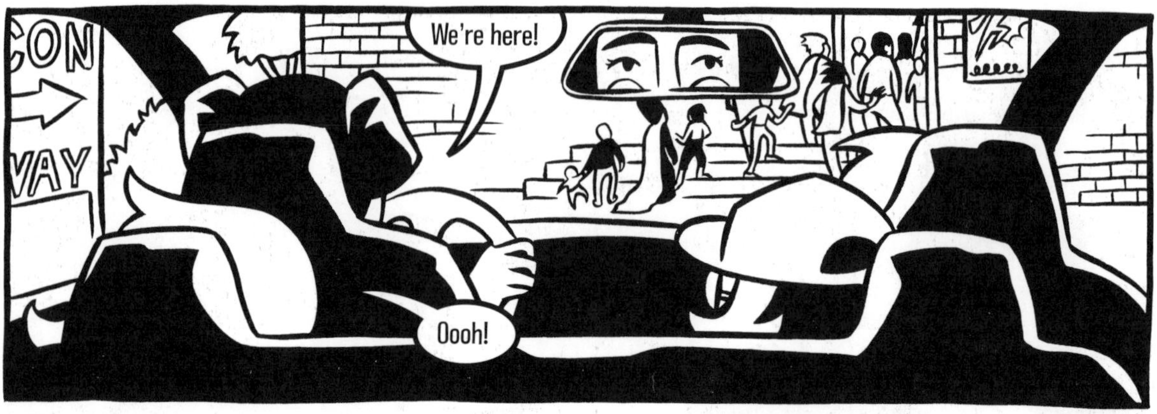
CON
WAY
We're here!
Oooh!

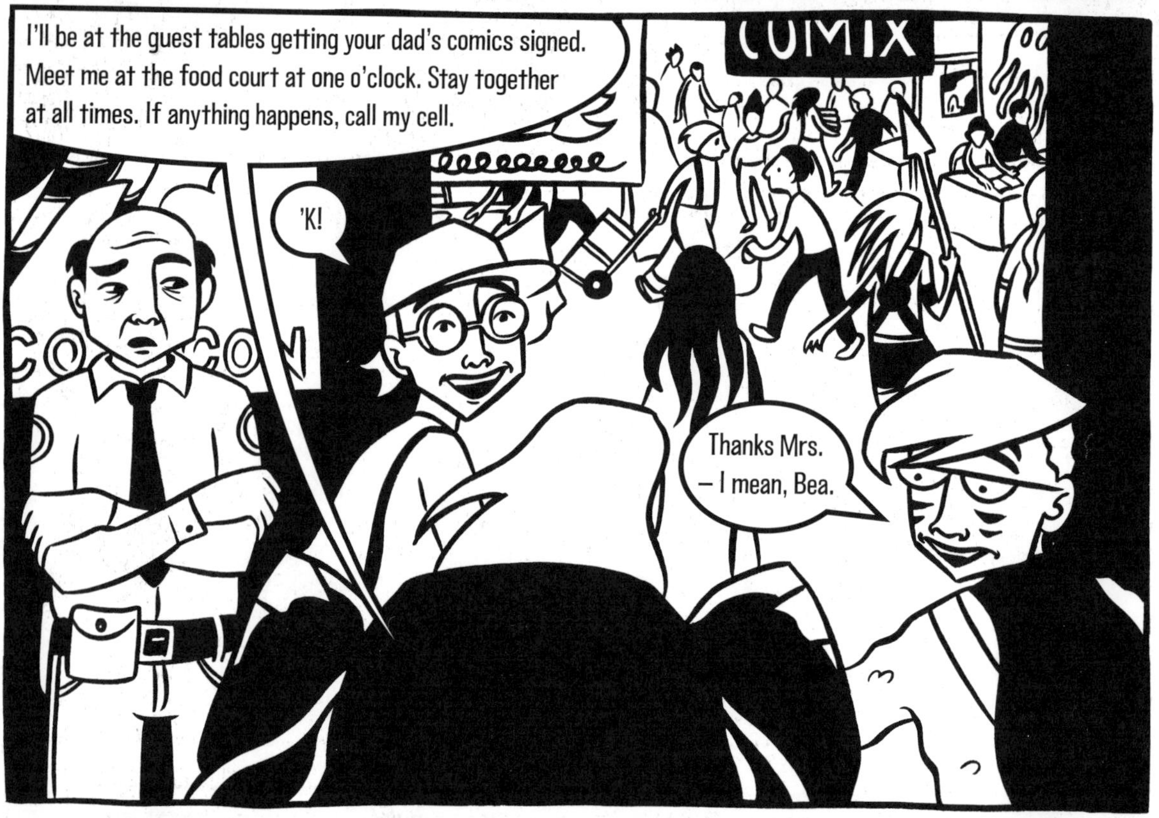
I'll be at the guest tables getting your dad's comics signed. Meet me at the food court at one o'clock. Stay together at all times. If anything happens, call my cell.
COMIX
'K!
Thanks Mrs. – I mean, Bea.

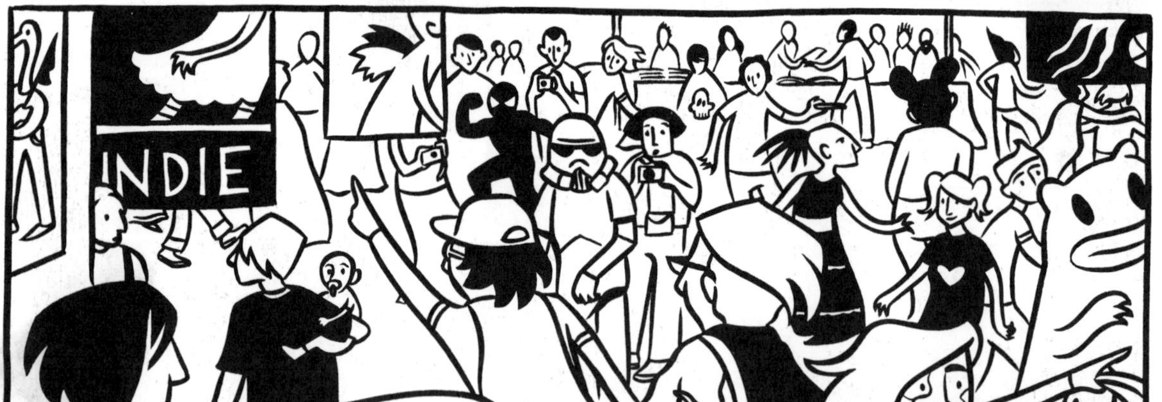
INDIE

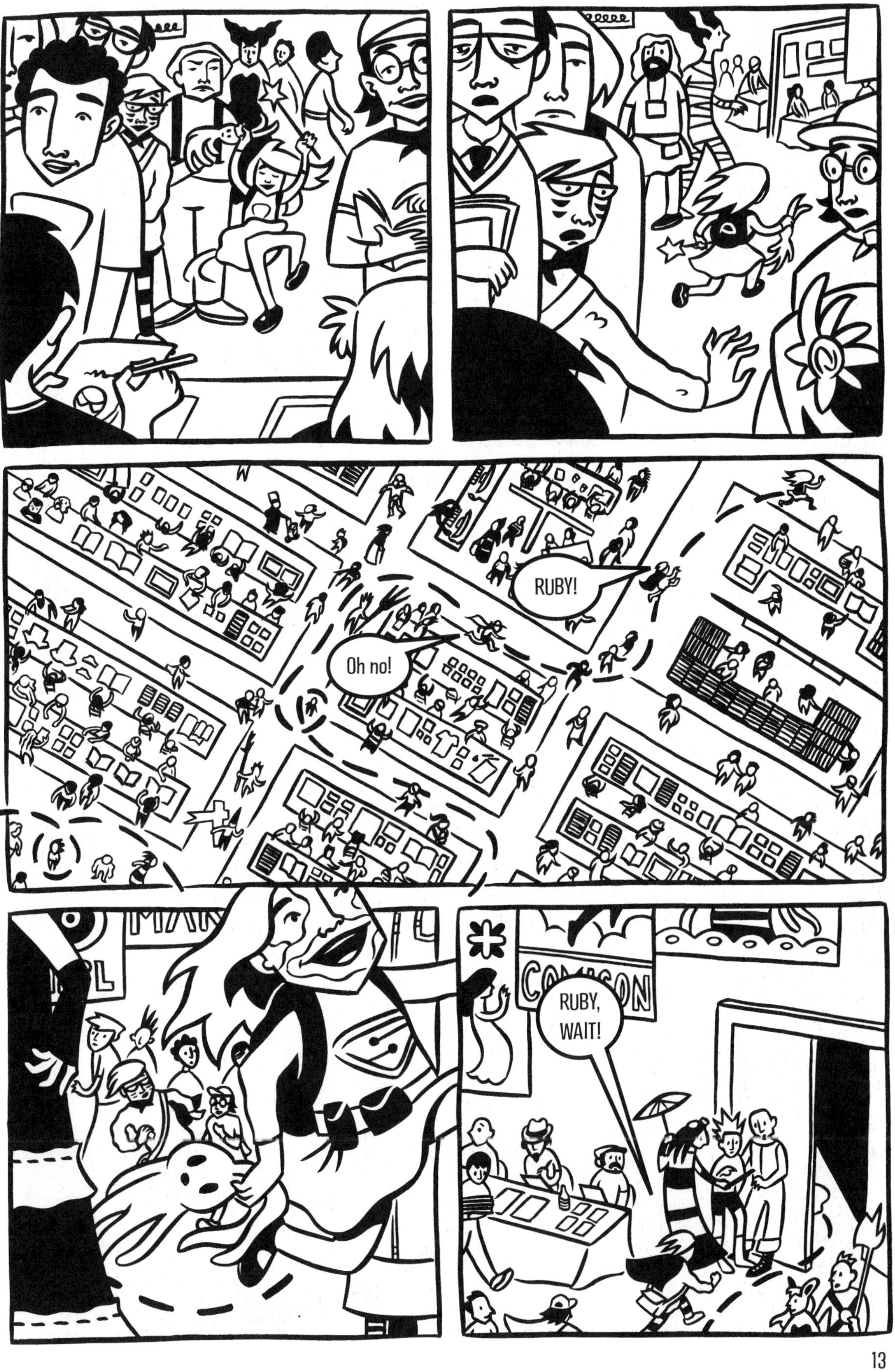
RUBY!
Oh no!
RUBY, WAIT!

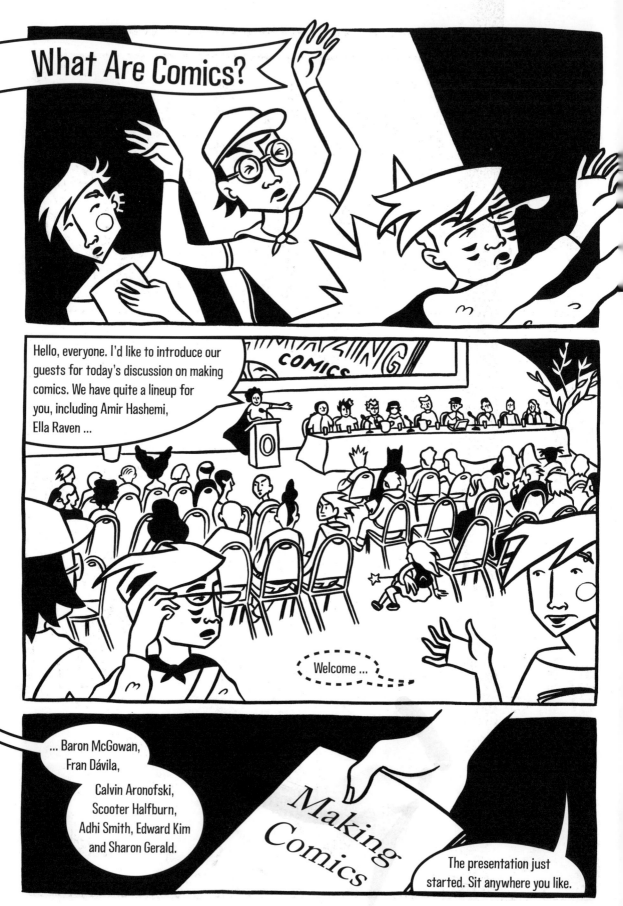

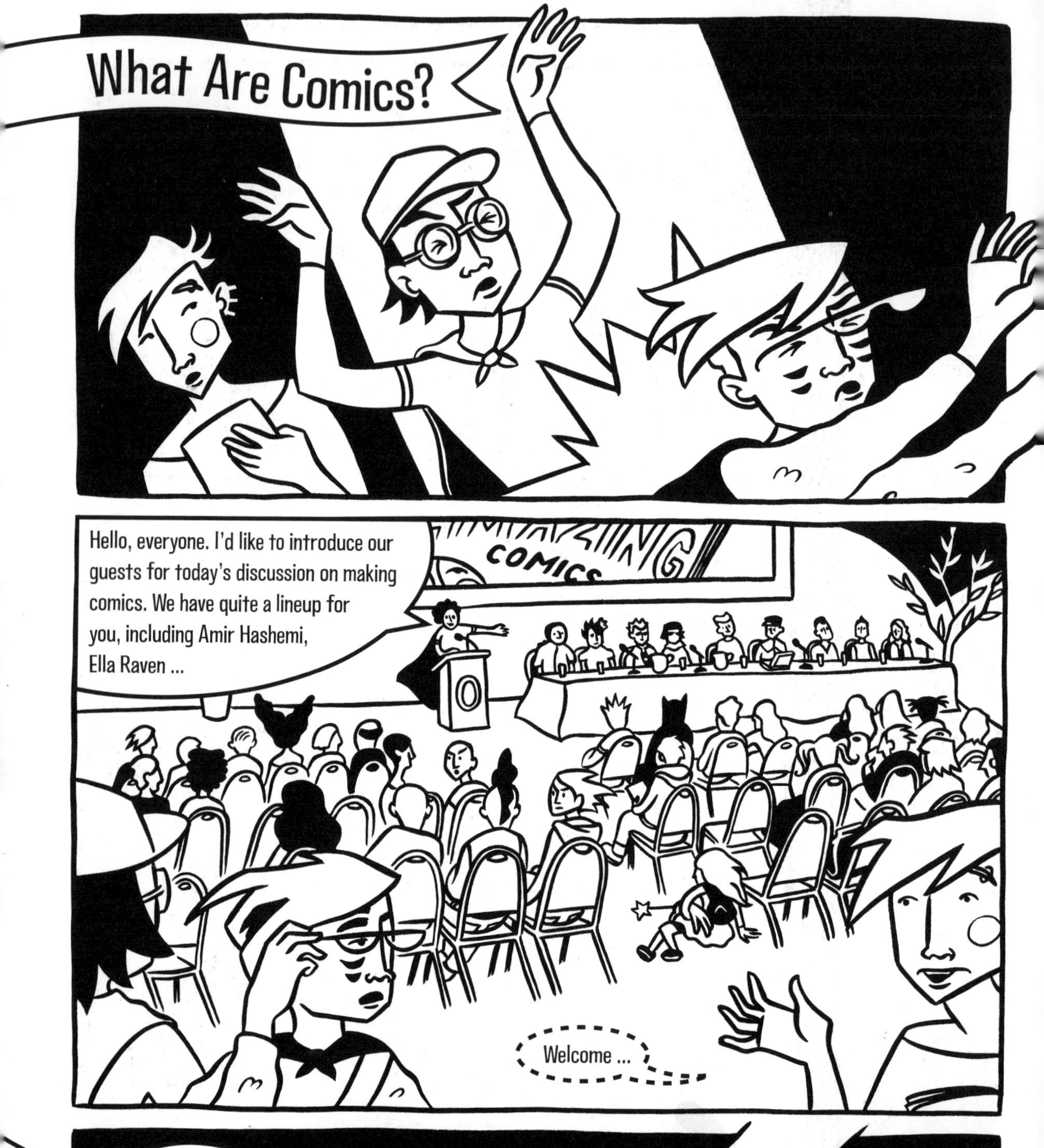
What Are Comics?
Hello, everyone. I'd like to introduce our guests for today's discussion on making comics. We have quite a lineup for you, including Amir Hashemi, Ella Raven ...
COMICS
Welcome ...
... Baron McGowan, Fran Dávila,
Calvin Aronofski, Scooter Halfburn, Adhi Smith, Edward Kim and Sharon Gerald.
Making Comics
The presentation just started. Sit anywhere you like.

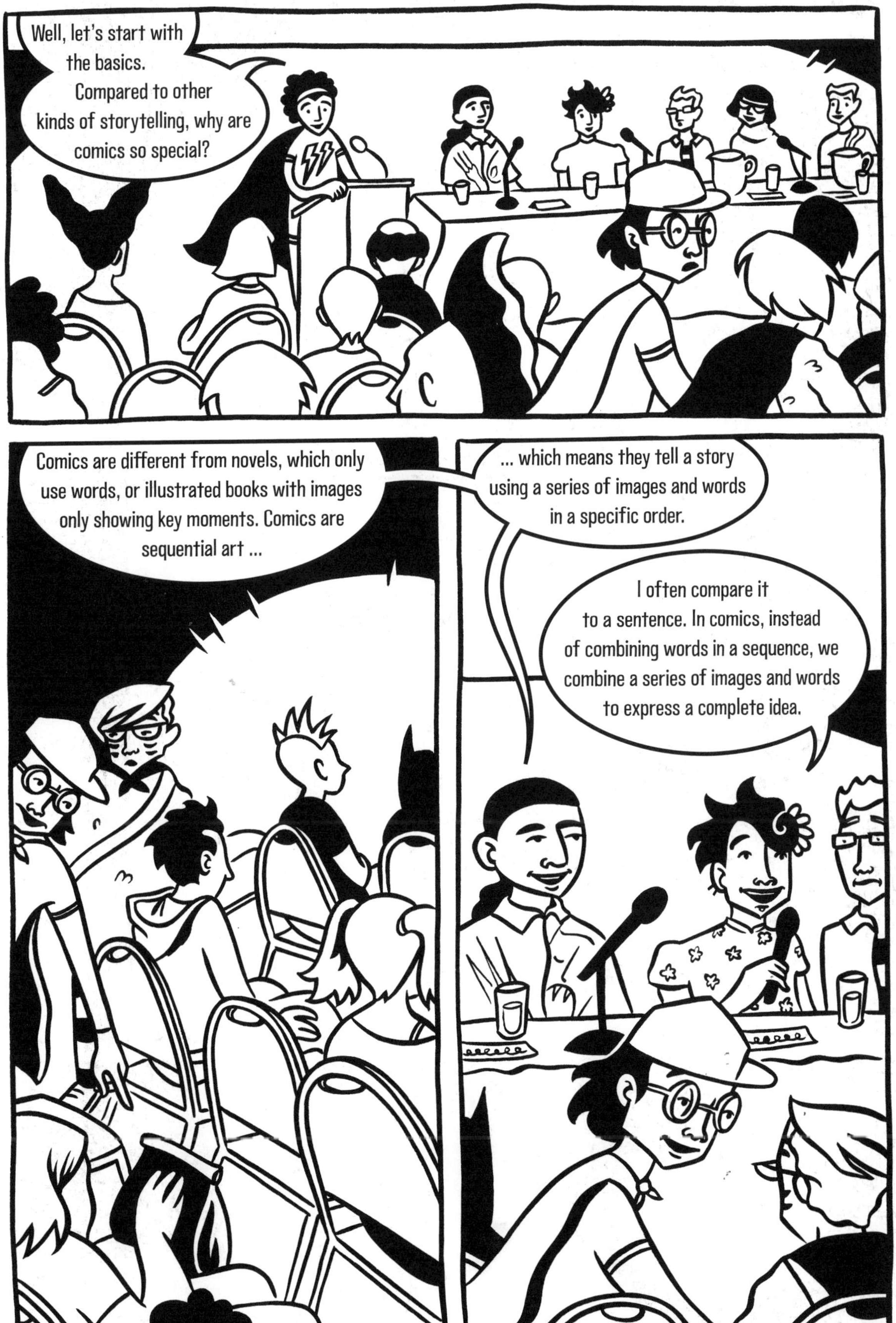
Well, let's start with the basics. Compared to other kinds of storytelling, why are comics so special?
Comics are different from novels, which only use words, or illustrated books with images only showing key moments. Comics are sequential art ...
... which means they tell a story using a series of images and words in a specific order.
I often compare it to a sentence. In comics, instead of combining words in a sequence, we combine a series of images and words to express a complete idea.

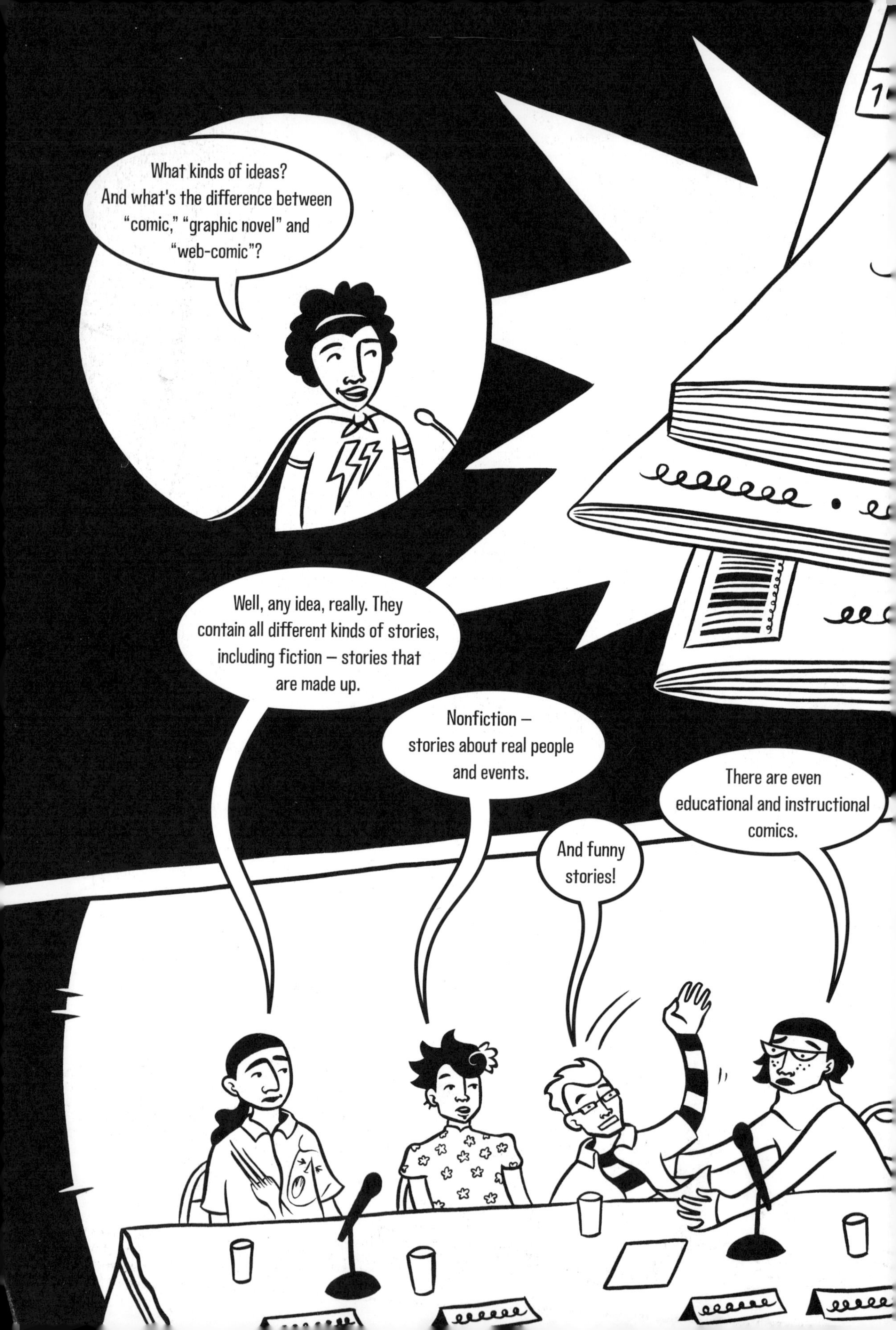
What kinds of ideas?
And what's the difference between "comic," "graphic novel" and "web-comic"?
Well, any idea, really. They contain all different kinds of stories, including fiction – stories that are made up.
Nonfiction – stories about real people and events.
And funny stories!
There are even educational and instructional comics.

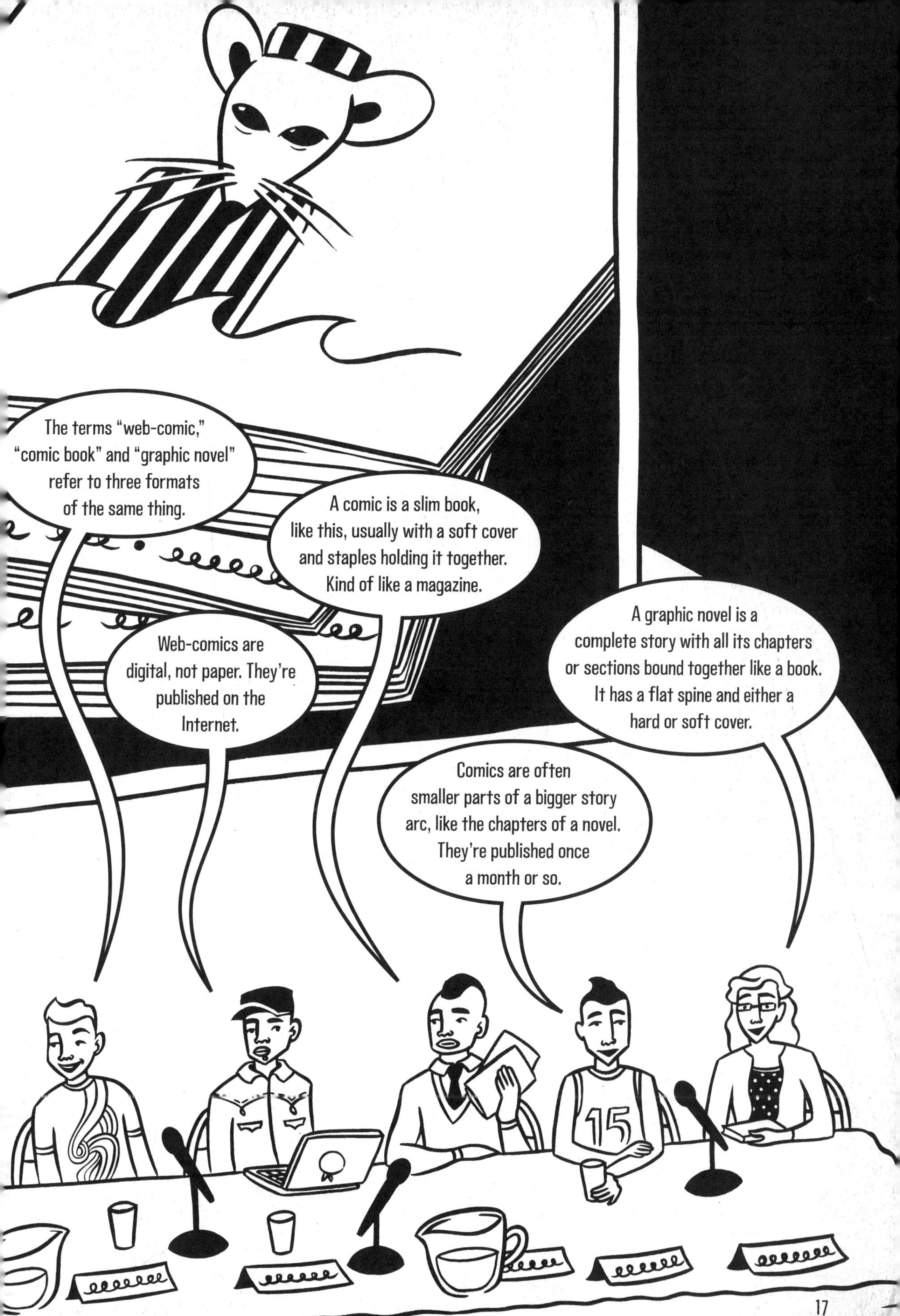

The terms "web-comic," "comic book" and "graphic novel" refer to three formats of the same thing.
A comic is a slim book, like this, usually with a soft cover and staples holding it together. Kind of like a magazine.
Web-comics are digital, not paper. They're published on the Internet.
A graphic novel is a complete story with all its chapters or sections bound together like a book. It has a flat spine and either a hard or soft cover.
Comics are often smaller parts of a bigger story arc, like the chapters of a novel. They're published once a month or so.
15

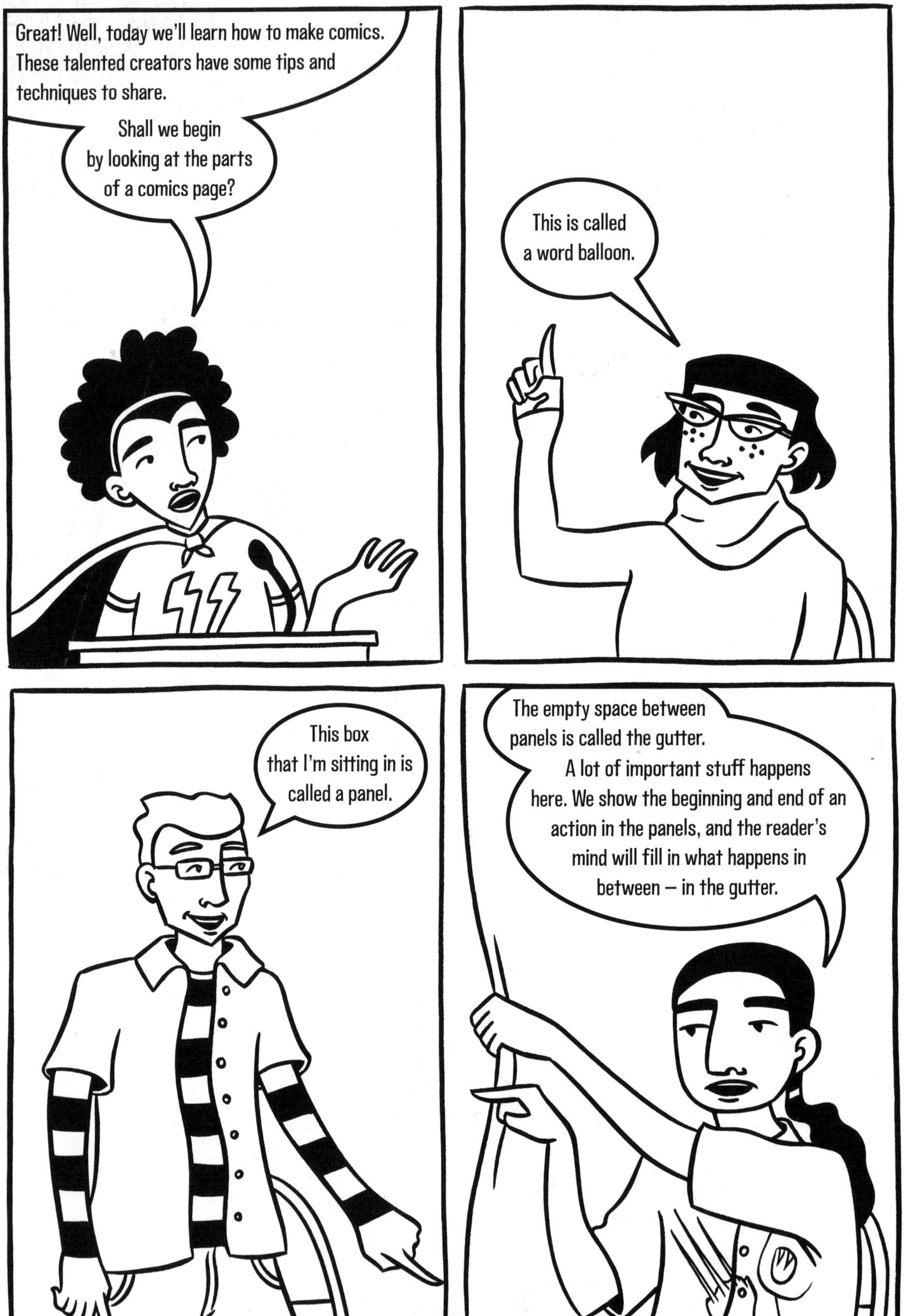
Great! Well, today we'll learn how to make comics. These talented creators have some tips and techniques to share.
Shall we begin by looking at the parts of a comics page?
This is called a word balloon.
This box that I'm sitting in is called a panel.
The empty space between panels is called the gutter.
A lot of important stuff happens here. We show the beginning and end of an action in the panels, and the reader's mind will fill in what happens in between – in the gutter.

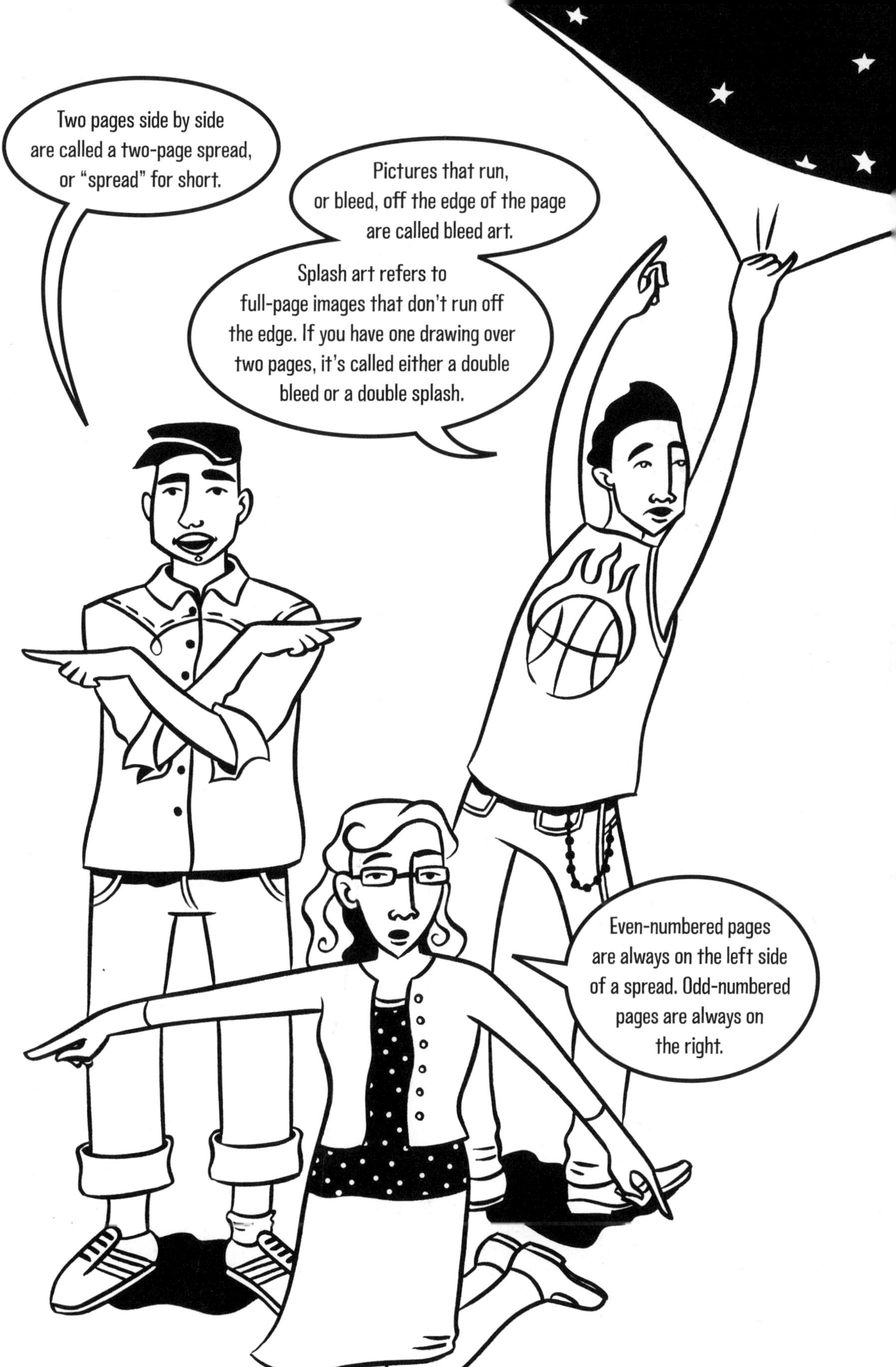
Two pages side by side are called a two-page spread, or "spread" for short.
Pictures that run, or bleed, off the edge of the page are called bleed art.
Splash art refers to full-page images that don't run off the edge. If you have one drawing over two pages, it's called either a double bleed or a double splash.
Even-numbered pages are always on the left side of a spread. Odd-numbered pages are always on the right.

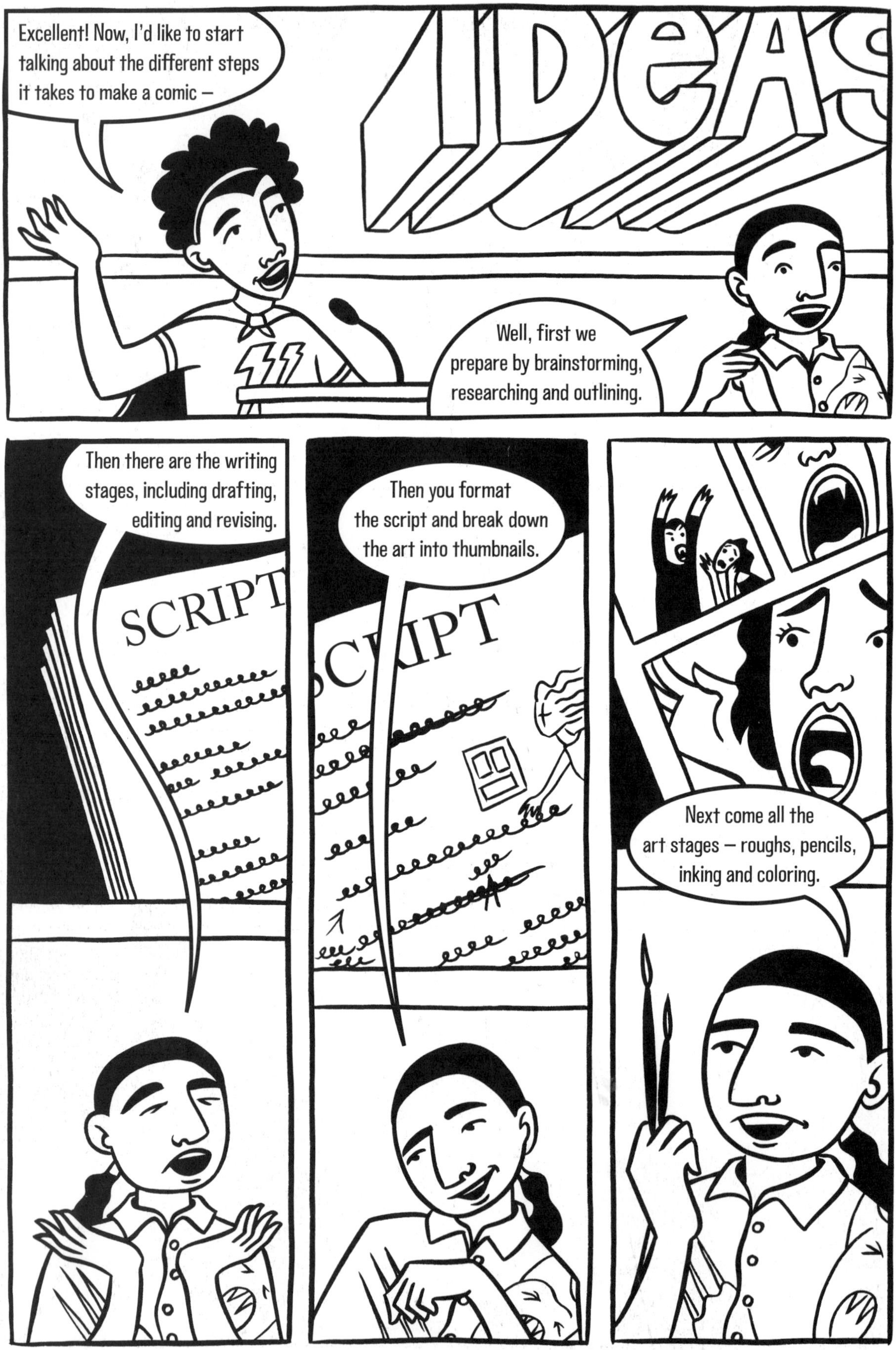

Excellent! Now, I'd like to start talking about the different steps it takes to make a comic –
IDEAS
Well, first we prepare by brainstorming, researching and outlining.
Then there are the writing stages, including drafting, editing and revising.
SCRIPT
Then you format the script and break down the art into thumbnails.
SCRIPT
Next come all the art stages – roughs, pencils, inking and coloring.

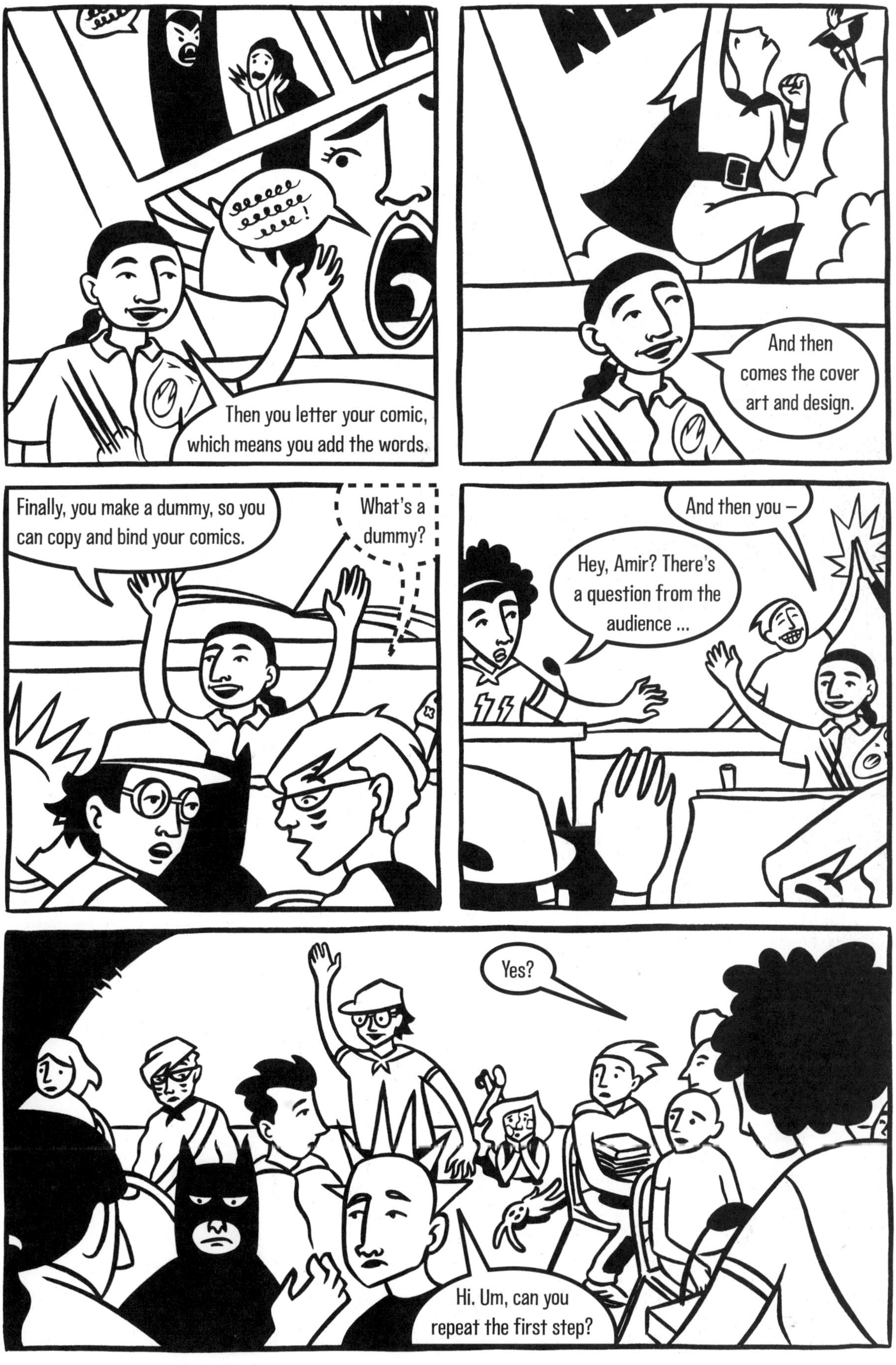
Then you letter your comic, which means you add the words.
And then comes the cover art and design.
Finally, you make a dummy, so you can copy and bind your comics.
What's a dummy?
And then you –
Hey, Amir? There's a question from the audience ...
Yes?
Hi. Um, can you repeat the first step?

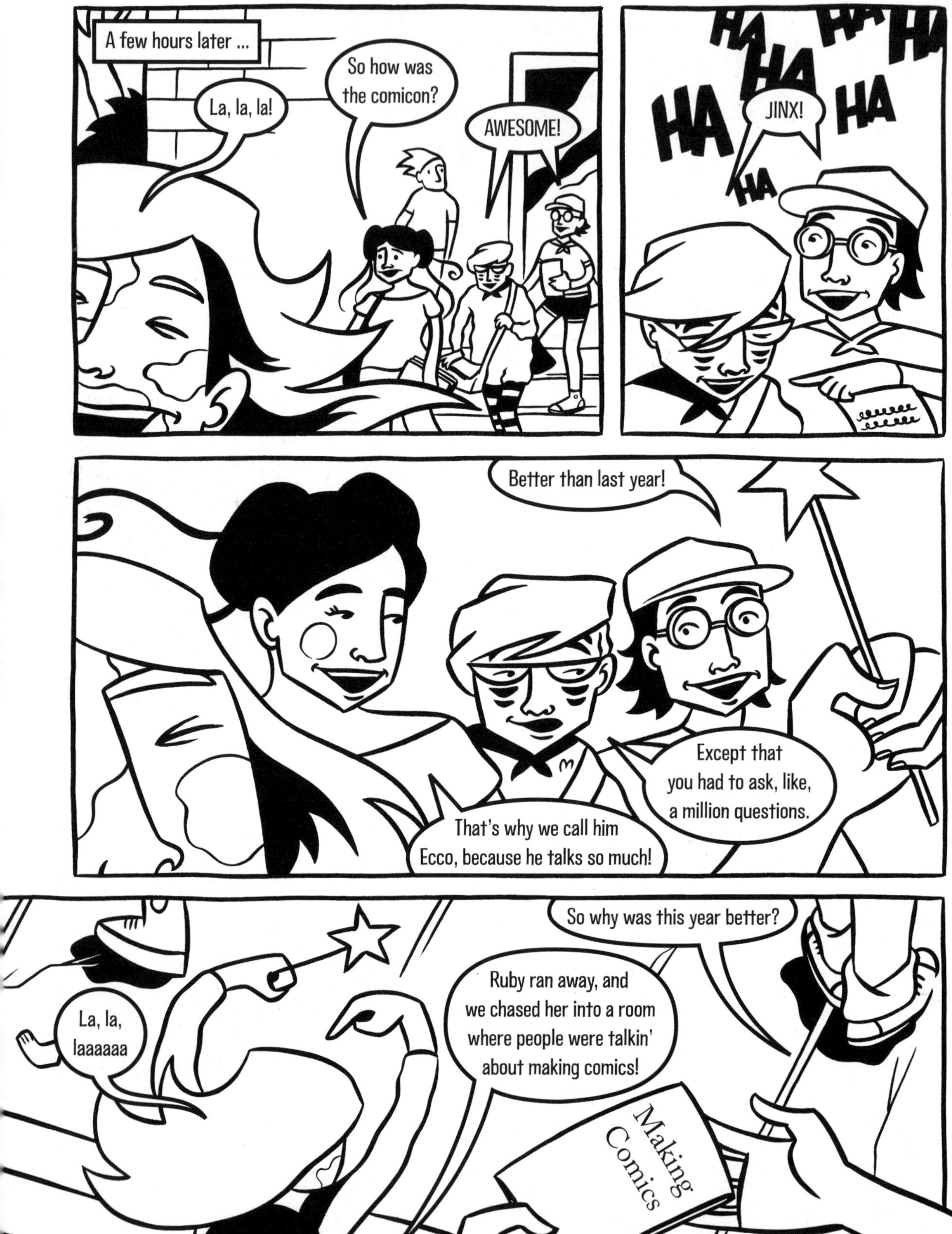

A few hours later ...
La, la, la!
So how was the comicon?
AWESOME!
HA HA HA HA HA HA HA
JINX!
Better than last year!
That's why we call him Ecco, because he talks so much!
Except that you had to ask, like, a million questions.
So why was this year better?
La, la, laaaaaa
Ruby ran away, and we chased her into a room where people were talkin' about making comics!
Making Comics
Oh, neat!

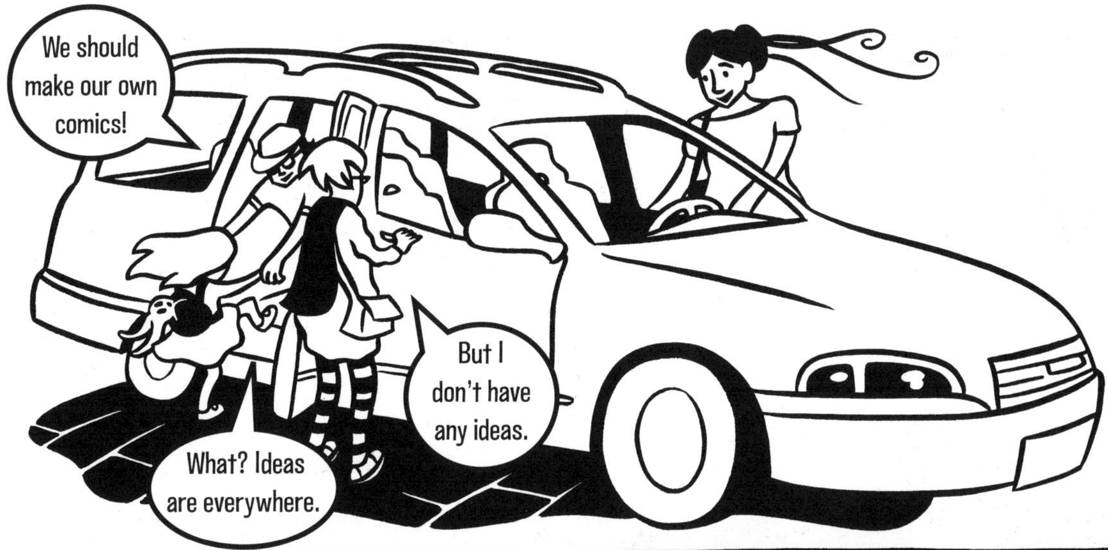
We should make our own comics!
But I don't have any ideas.
What? Ideas are everywhere.

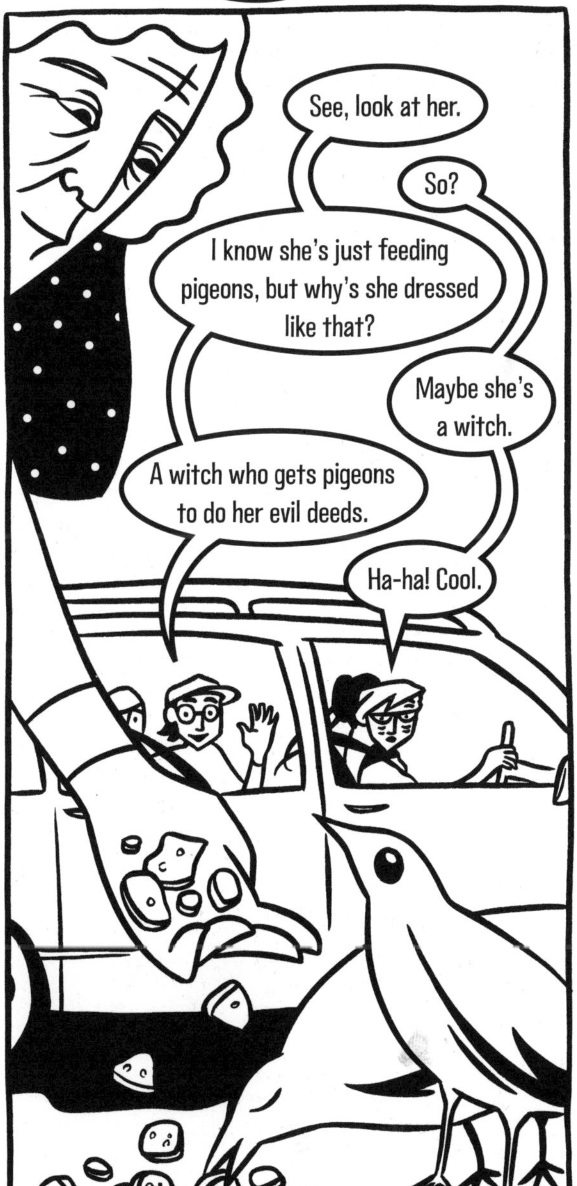
See, look at her.
So?
I know she's just feeding pigeons, but why's she dressed like that?
Maybe she's a witch.
A witch who gets pigeons to do her evil deeds.
Ha-ha! Cool.

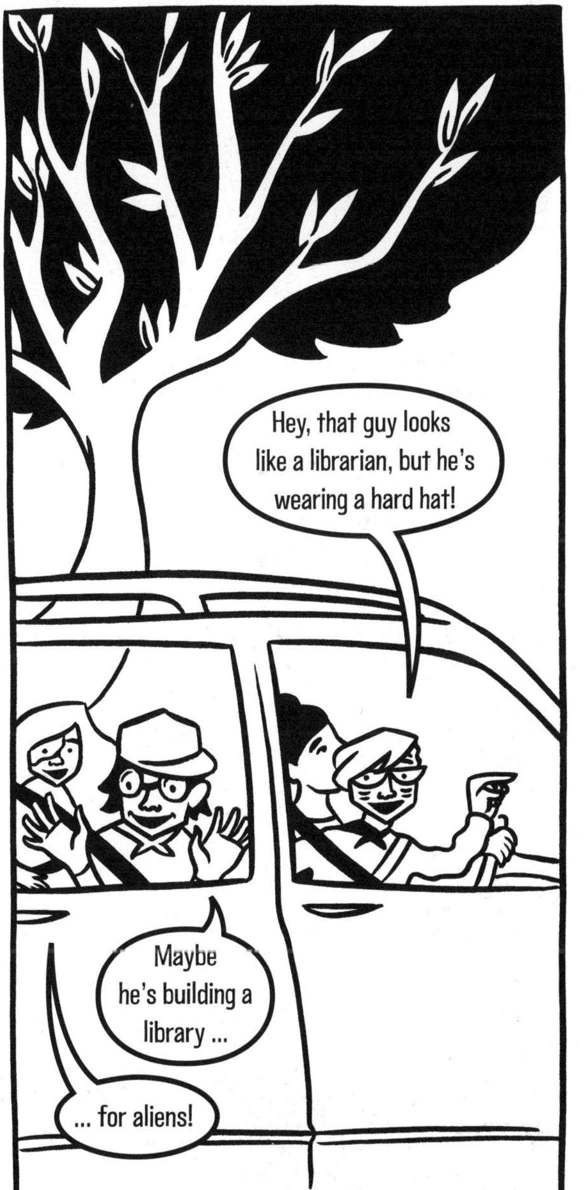
Hey, that guy looks like a librarian, but he's wearing a hard hat!
Maybe he's building a library ...
... for aliens!

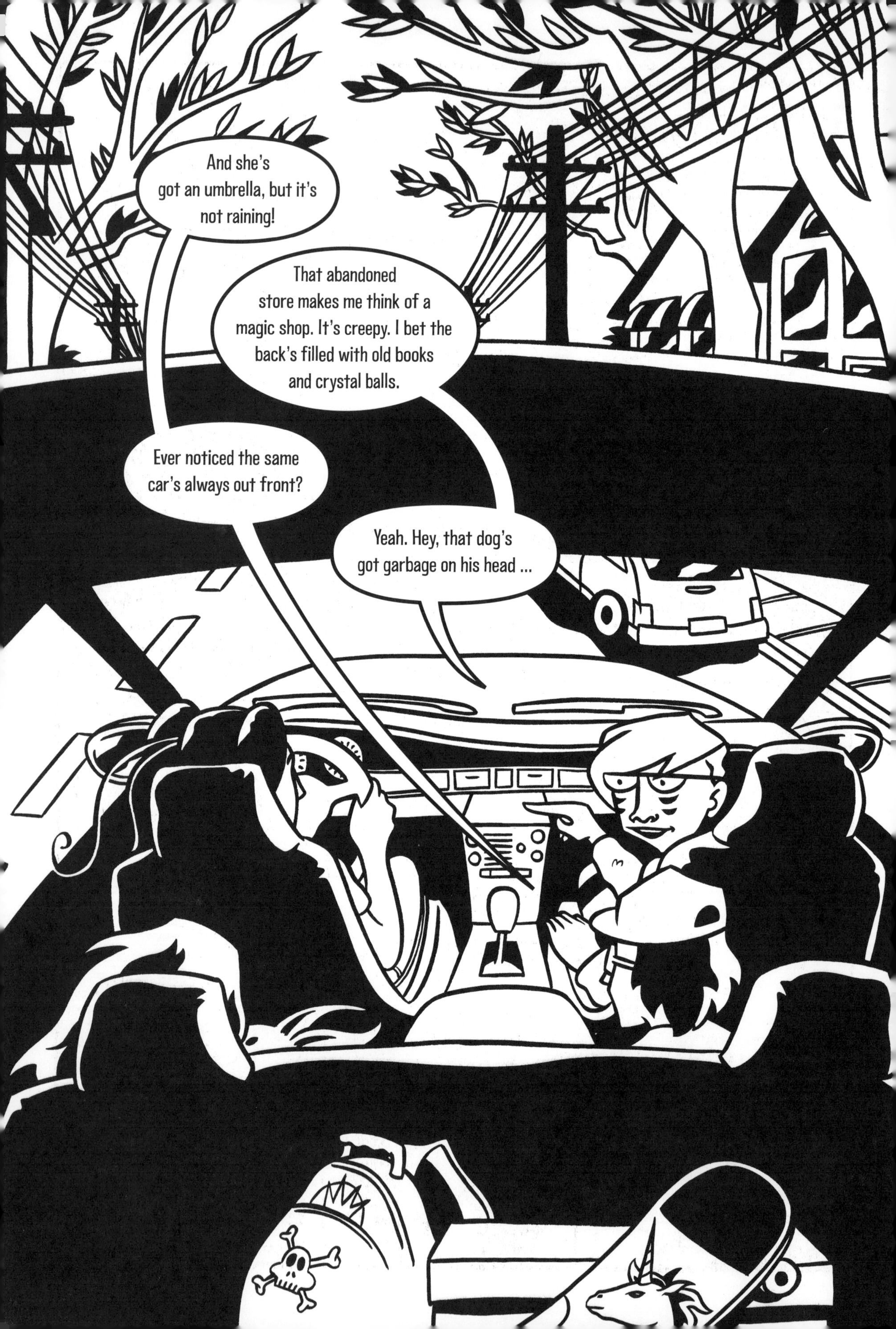
And she's got an umbrella, but it's not raining!
That abandoned store makes me think of a magic shop. It's creepy. I bet the back's filled with old books and crystal balls.
Ever noticed the same car's always out front?
Yeah. Hey, that dog's got garbage on his head ...

Getting Started

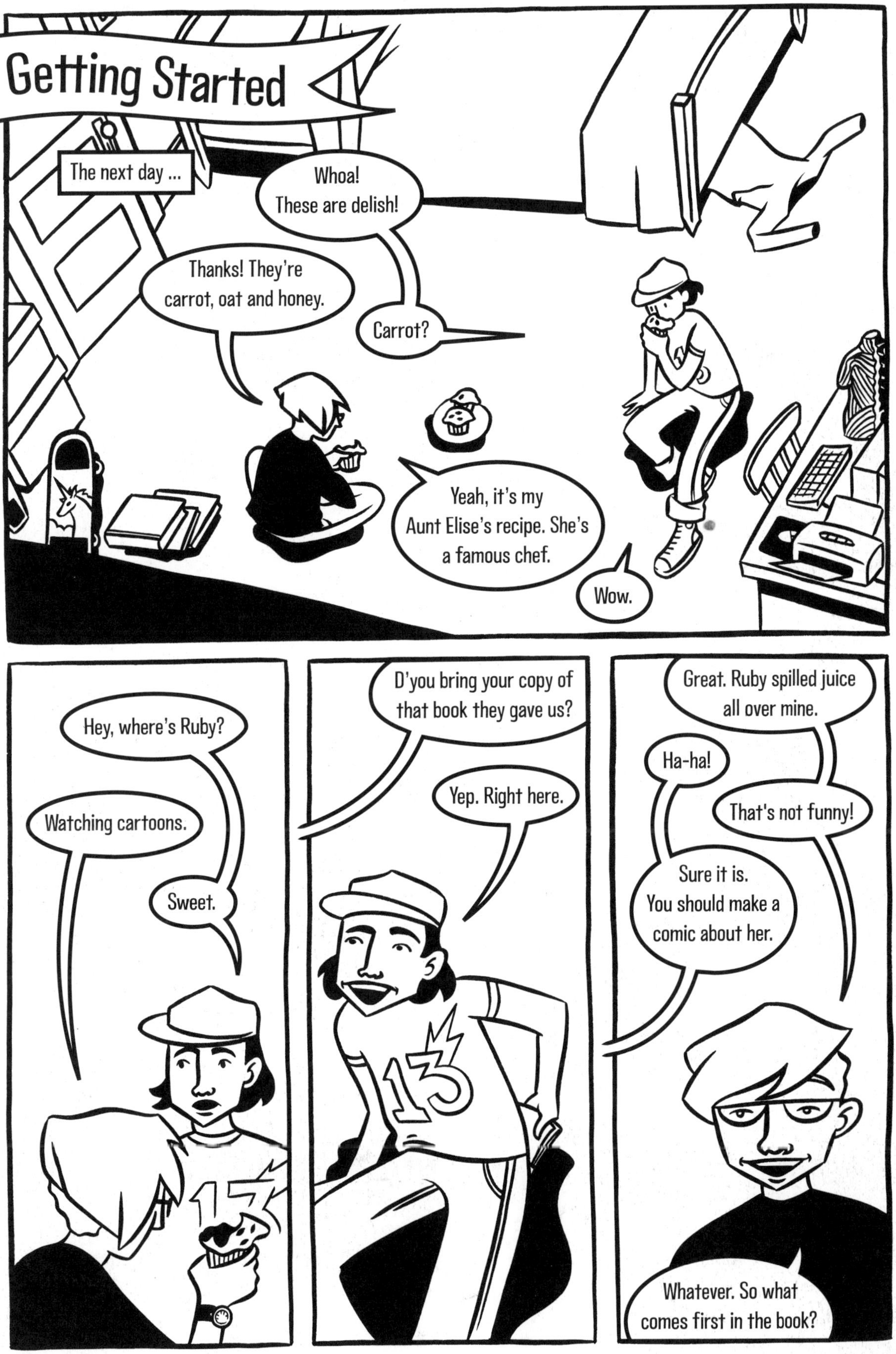

The next day ...
Whoa! These are delish!
Thanks! They're carrot, oat and honey.
Carrot?
Yeah, it's my Aunt Elise's recipe. She's a famous chef.
Wow.
Hey, where's Ruby?
Watching cartoons.
Sweet.
D'you bring your copy of that book they gave us?
Yep. Right here.
Great. Ruby spilled juice all over mine.
Ha-ha!
That's not funny!
Sure it is. You should make a comic about her.
Whatever. So what comes first in the book?

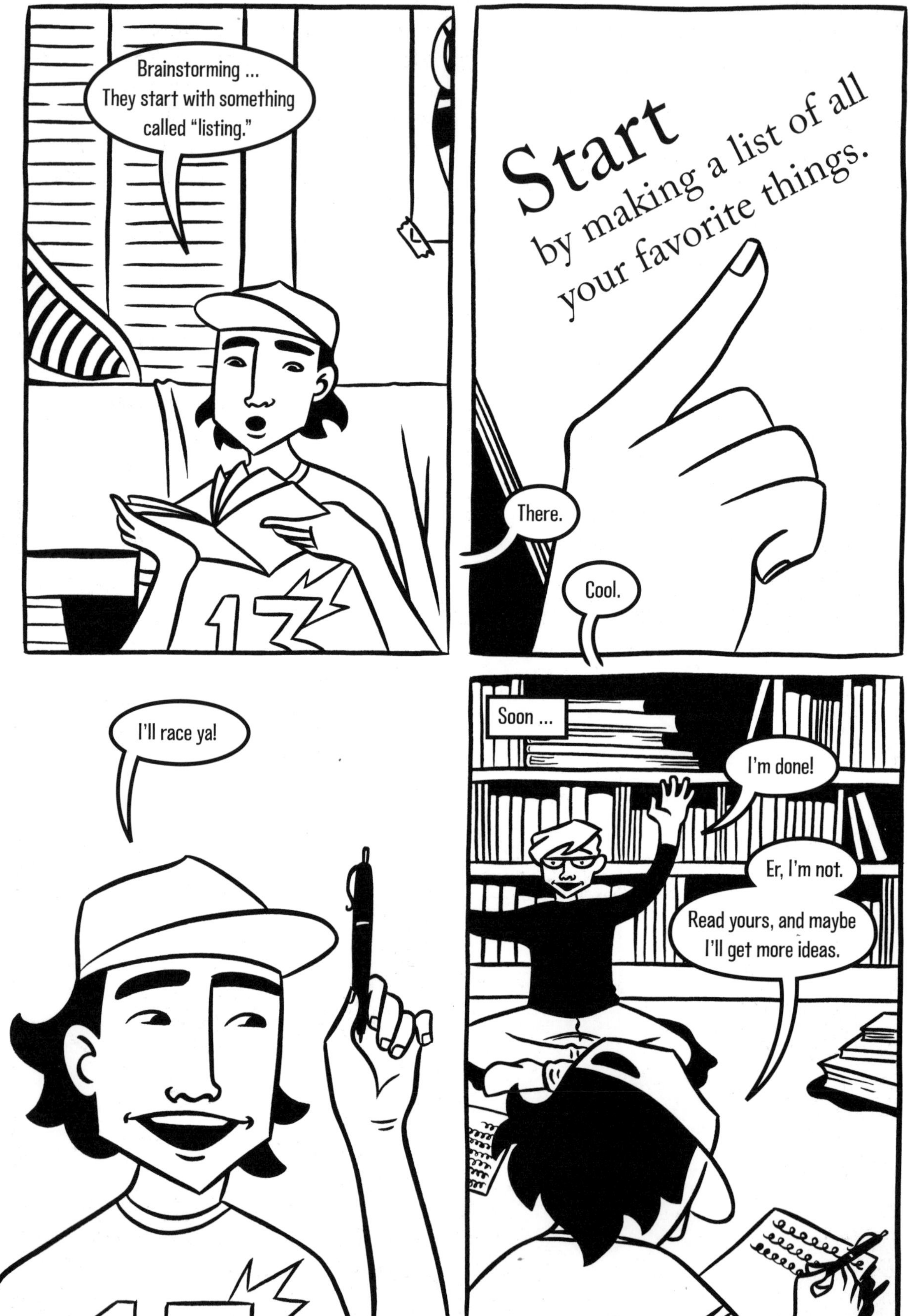

Brainstorming ... They start with something called "listing."
Start by making a list of all your favorite things.
There.
Cool.
I'll race ya!
Soon ...
I'm done!
Er, I'm not.
Read yours, and maybe I'll get more ideas.

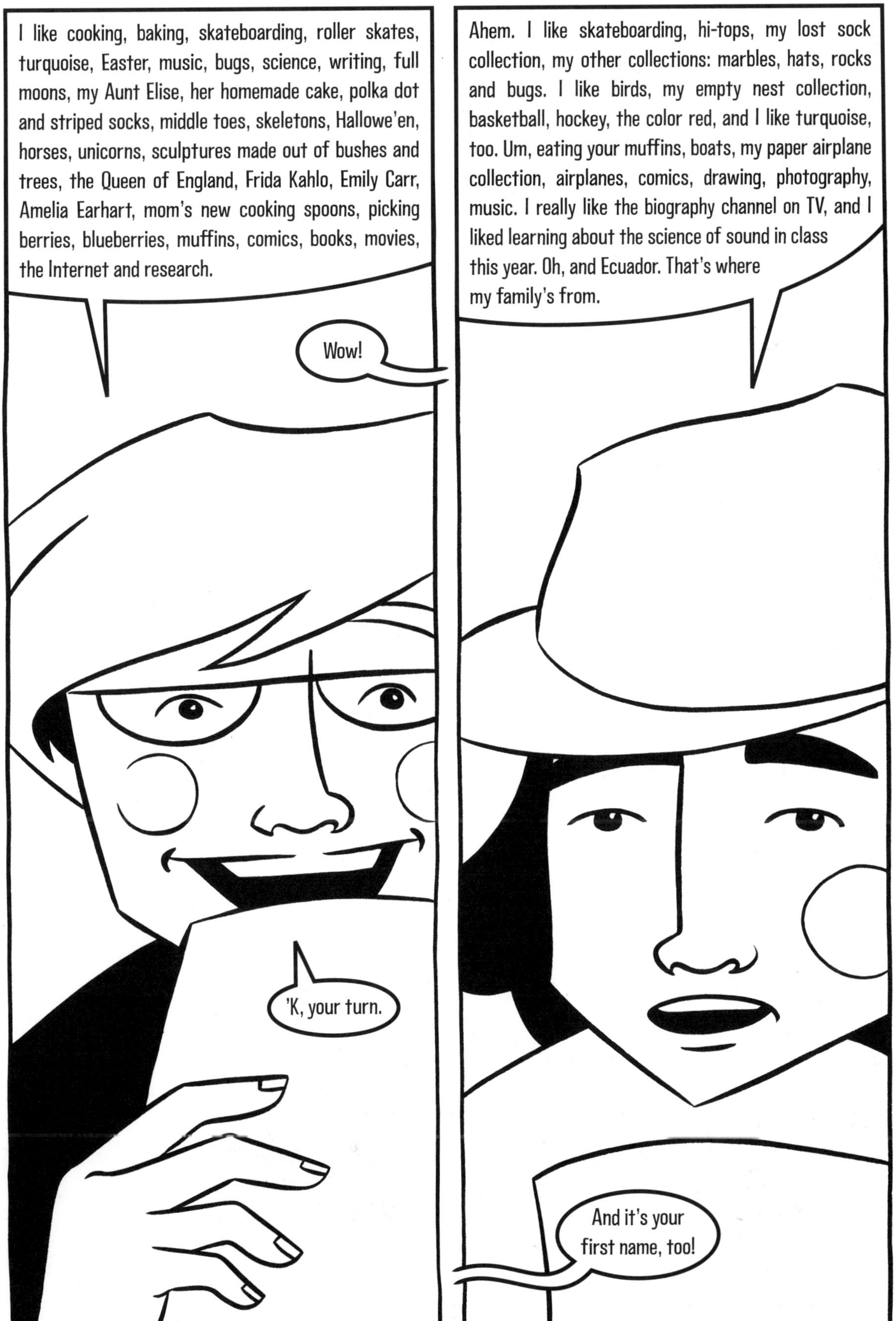

I like cooking, baking, skateboarding, roller skates, turquoise, Easter, music, bugs, science, writing, full moons, my Aunt Elise, her homemade cake, polka dot and striped socks, middle toes, skeletons, Hallowe'en, horses, unicorns, sculptures made out of bushes and trees, the Queen of England, Frida Kahlo, Emily Carr, Amelia Earhart, mom's new cooking spoons, picking berries, blueberries, muffins, comics, books, movies, the Internet and research.
Wow!
'K, your turn.
Ahem. I like skateboarding, hi-tops, my lost sock collection, my other collections: marbles, hats, rocks and bugs. I like birds, my empty nest collection, basketball, hockey, the color red, and I like turquoise, too. Um, eating your muffins, boats, my paper airplane collection, airplanes, comics, drawing, photography, music. I really like the biography channel on TV, and I liked learning about the science of sound in class this year. Oh, and Ecuador. That's where my family's from.
And it's your first name, too!

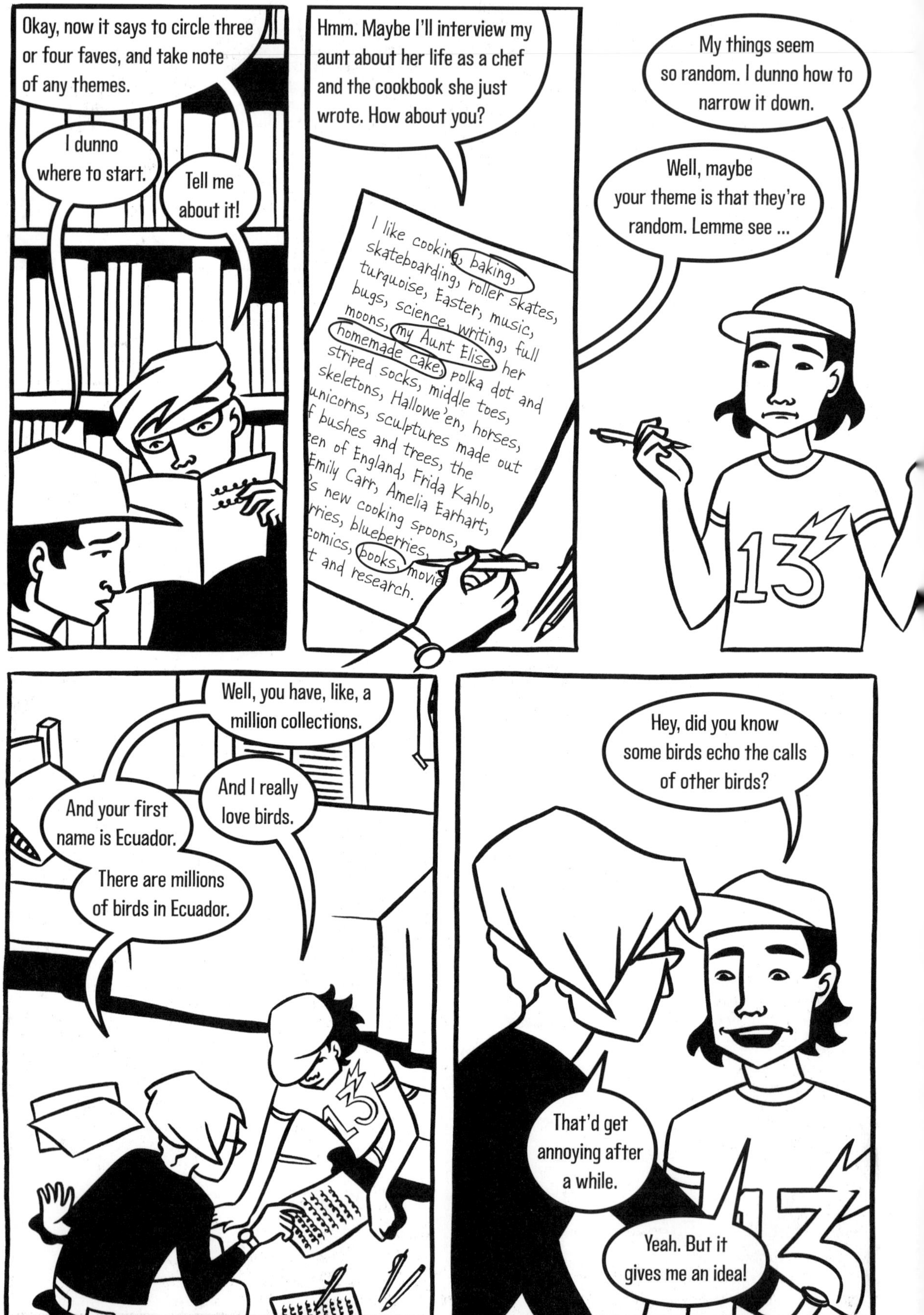
Okay, now it says to circle three or four faves, and take note of any themes.
I dunno where to start.
Tell me about it!
Hmm. Maybe I'll interview my aunt about her life as a chef and the cookbook she just wrote. How about you?
I like cooking, baking,
skateboarding, roller skates,
turquoise, Easter, music,
bugs, science, writing, full
moons, my Aunt Elise, her
homemade cake, polka dot and
striped socks, middle toes,
skeletons, Hallowe'en, horses,
unicorns, sculptures made out
f bushes and trees, the
een of England, Frida Kahlo,
Emily Carr, Amelia Earhart,
s new cooking spoons,
rries, blueberries,
comics, books, movie
t and research.
My things seem so random. I dunno how to narrow it down.
Well, maybe your theme is that they're random. Lemme see ...
Well, you have, like, a million collections.
And your first name is Ecuador.
There are millions of birds in Ecuador.
And I really love birds.
Hey, did you know some birds echo the calls of other birds?
That'd get annoying after a while.
Yeah. But it gives me an idea!

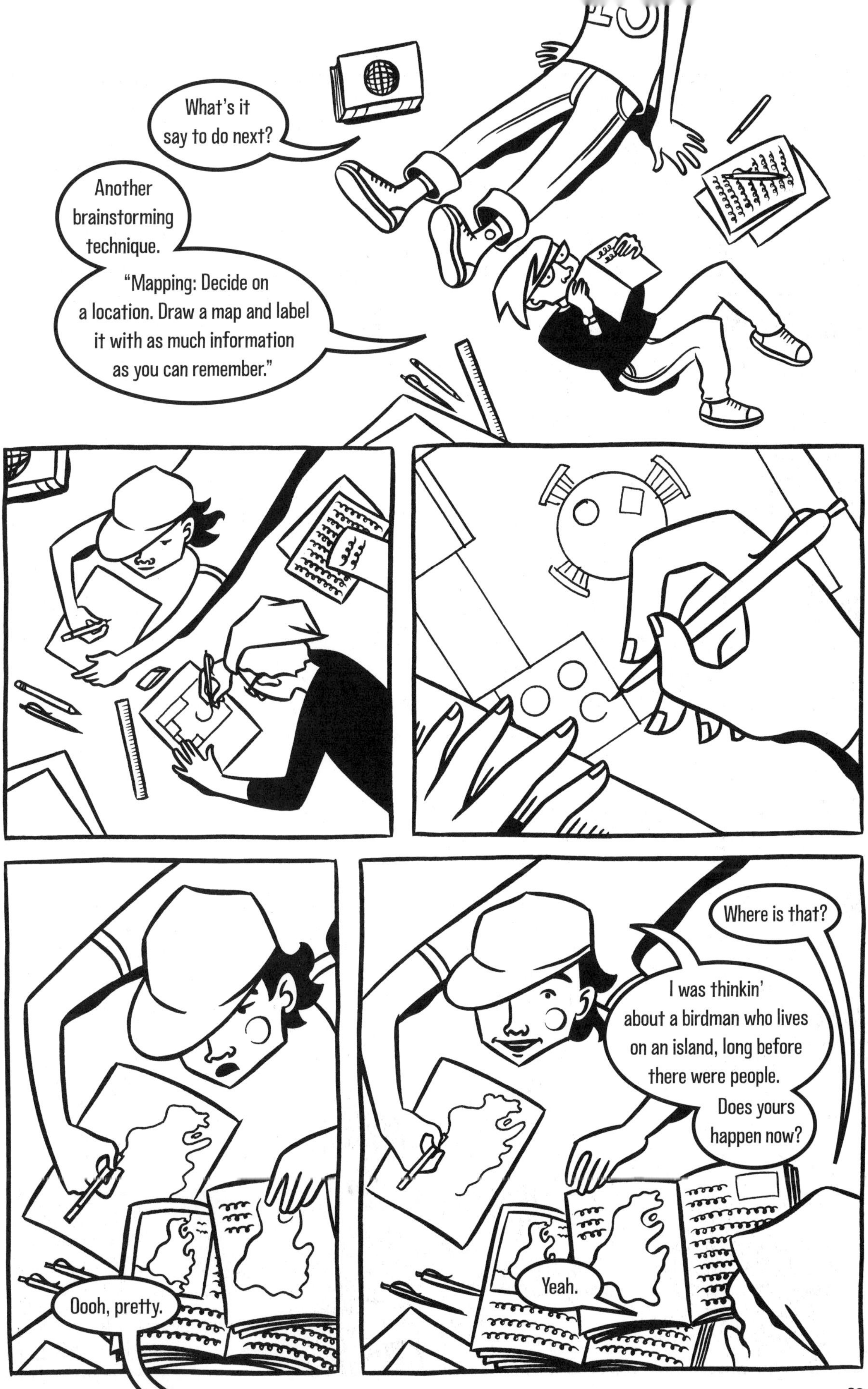
What's it say to do next?
Another brainstorming technique.
"Mapping: Decide on a location. Draw a map and label it with as much information as you can remember."
Oooh, pretty.
Where is that?
I was thinkin' about a birdman who lives on an island, long before there were people.
Does yours happen now?
Yeah.

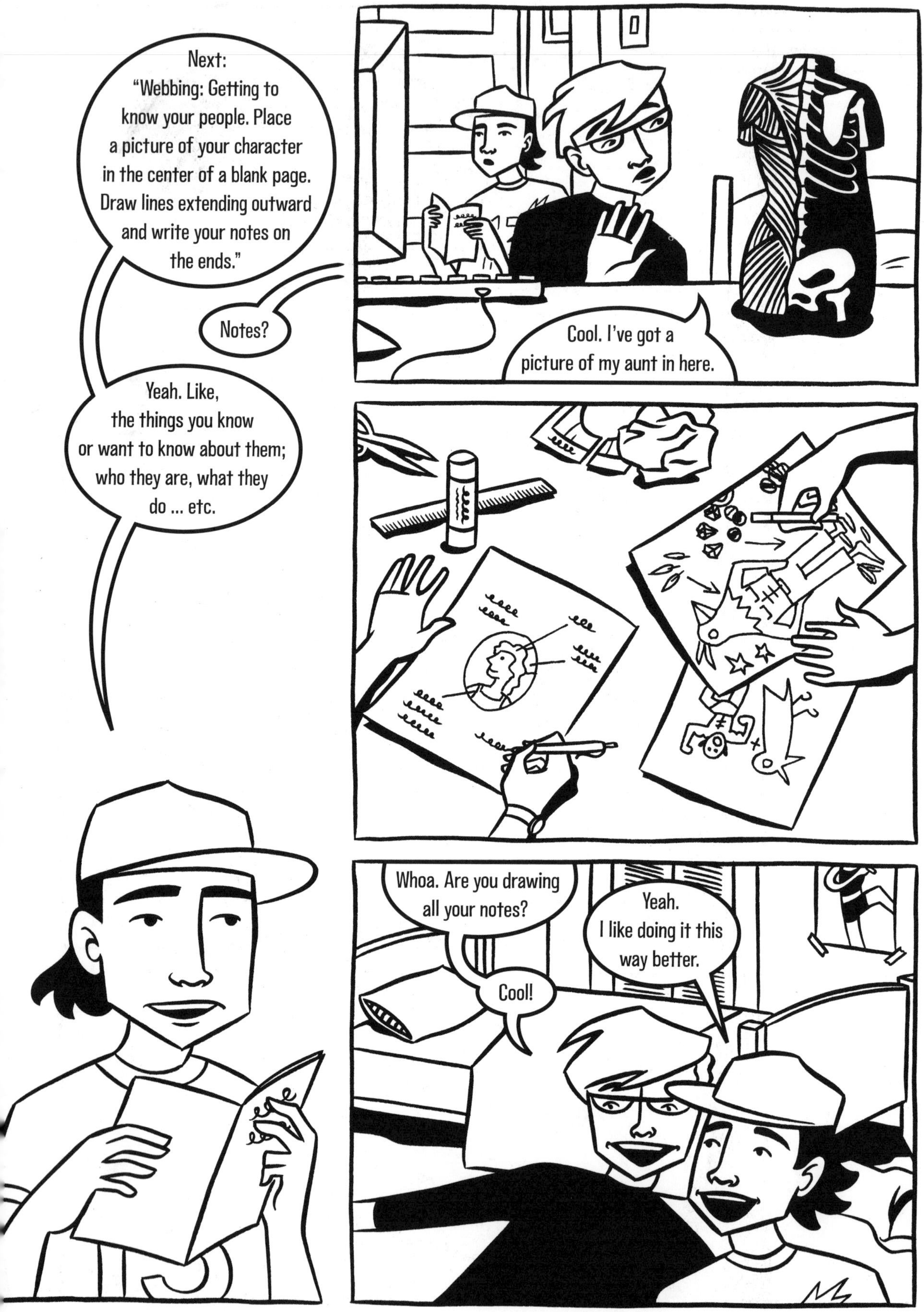
Next: "Webbing: Getting to know your people. Place a picture of your character in the center of a blank page. Draw lines extending outward and write your notes on the ends."
Notes?
Cool. I've got a picture of my aunt in here.
Yeah. Like, the things you know or want to know about them; who they are, what they do ... etc.
Whoa. Are you drawing all your notes?
Yeah. I like doing it this way better.
Cool!

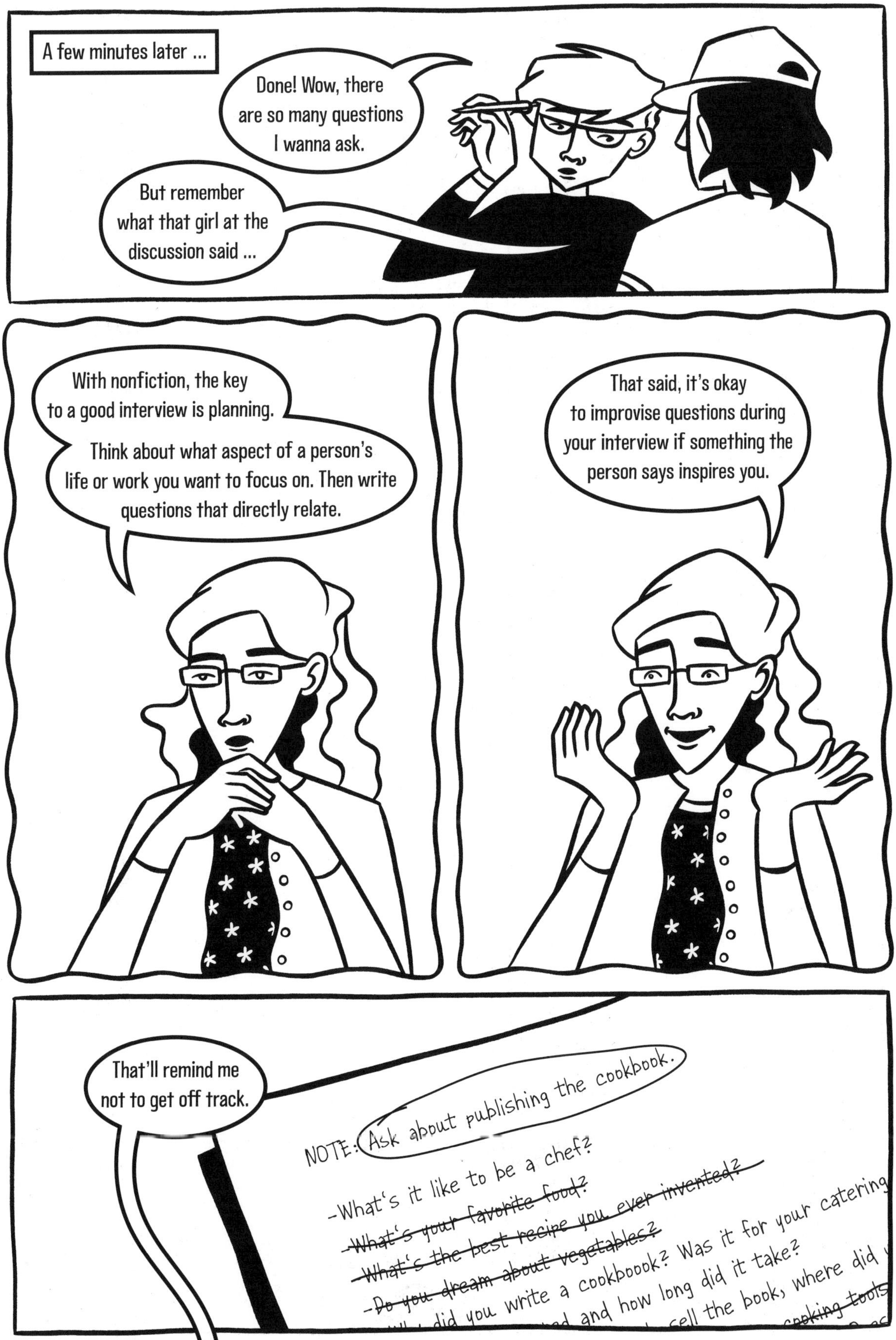
A few minutes later ...
Done! Wow, there are so many questions I wanna ask.
But remember what that girl at the discussion said ...
With nonfiction, the key to a good interview is planning.
Think about what aspect of a person's life or work you want to focus on. Then write questions that directly relate.
That said, it's okay to improvise questions during your interview if something the person says inspires you.
That'll remind me not to get off track.
NOTE: Ask about publishing the cookbook.
-What's it like to be a chef?
-~~What's your favorite food?~~
-~~What's the best recipe you ever invented?~~
-~~Do you dream about vegetables?~~
did you write a cookbook? Was it for your catering
and how long did it take?

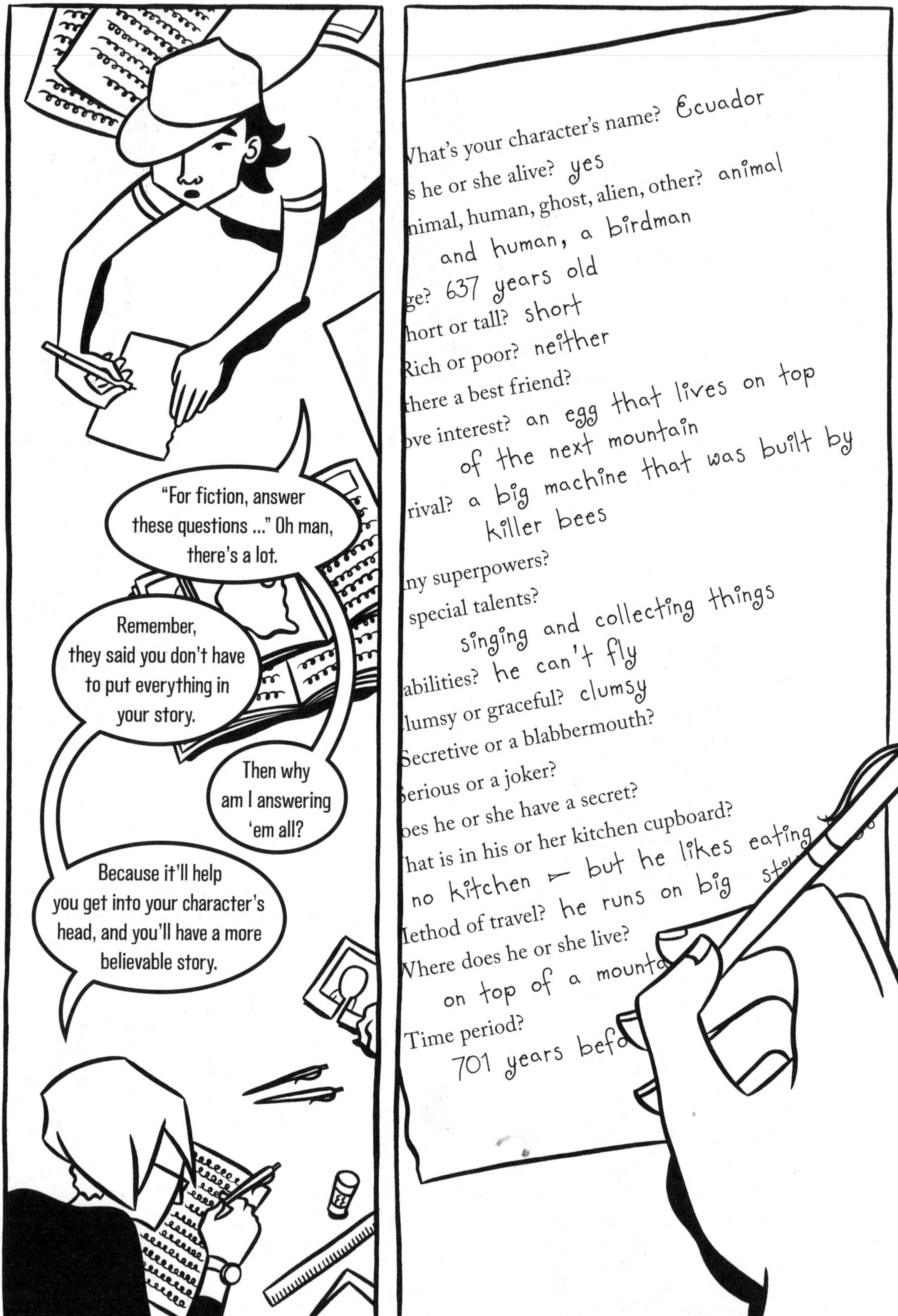
"For fiction, answer these questions ..." Oh man, there's a lot.
Remember, they said you don't have to put everything in your story.
Then why am I answering 'em all?
Because it'll help you get into your character's head, and you'll have a more believable story.
hat's your character's name? Ecuador
s he or she alive? yes
nimal, human, ghost, alien, other? animal
and human, a birdman
ge? 637 years old
hort or tall? short
ich or poor? neither
there a best friend?
ove interest? an egg that lives on top
of the next mountain
rival? a big machine that was built by
killer bees
ny superpowers?
special talents?
singing and collecting things
abilities? he can't fly
lumsy or graceful? clumsy
ecretive or a blabbermouth?
erious or a joker?
oes he or she have a secret?
hat is in his or her kitchen cupboard?
no kitchen – but he likes eating
ethod of travel? he runs on big
Where does he or she live?
on top of a mount
Time period?
701 years befo

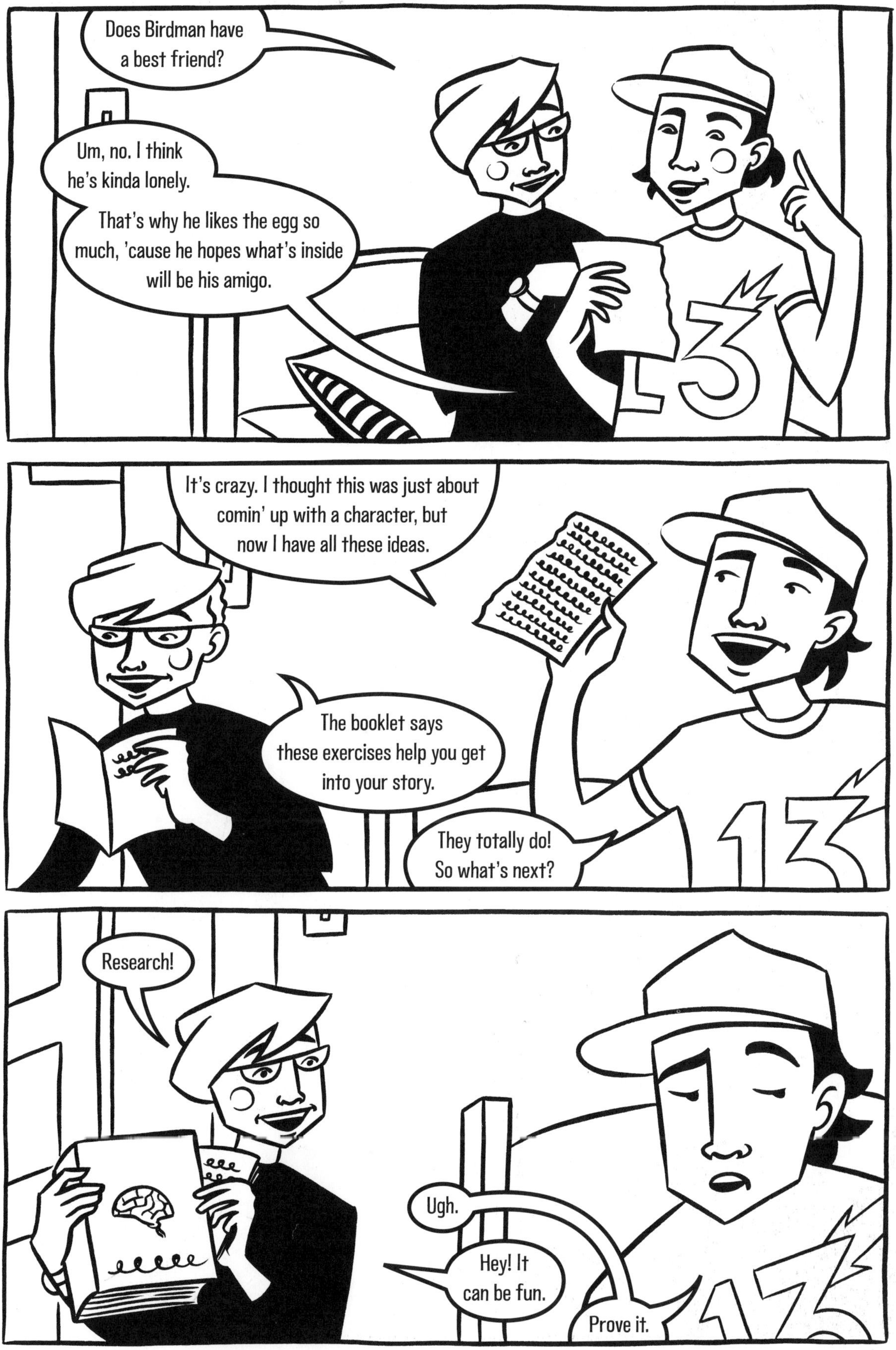

Does Birdman have a best friend?
Um, no. I think he's kinda lonely.
That's why he likes the egg so much, 'cause he hopes what's inside will be his amigo.
It's crazy. I thought this was just about comin' up with a character, but now I have all these ideas.
The booklet says these exercises help you get into your story.
They totally do! So what's next?
Research!
Ugh.
Hey! It can be fun.
Prove it.

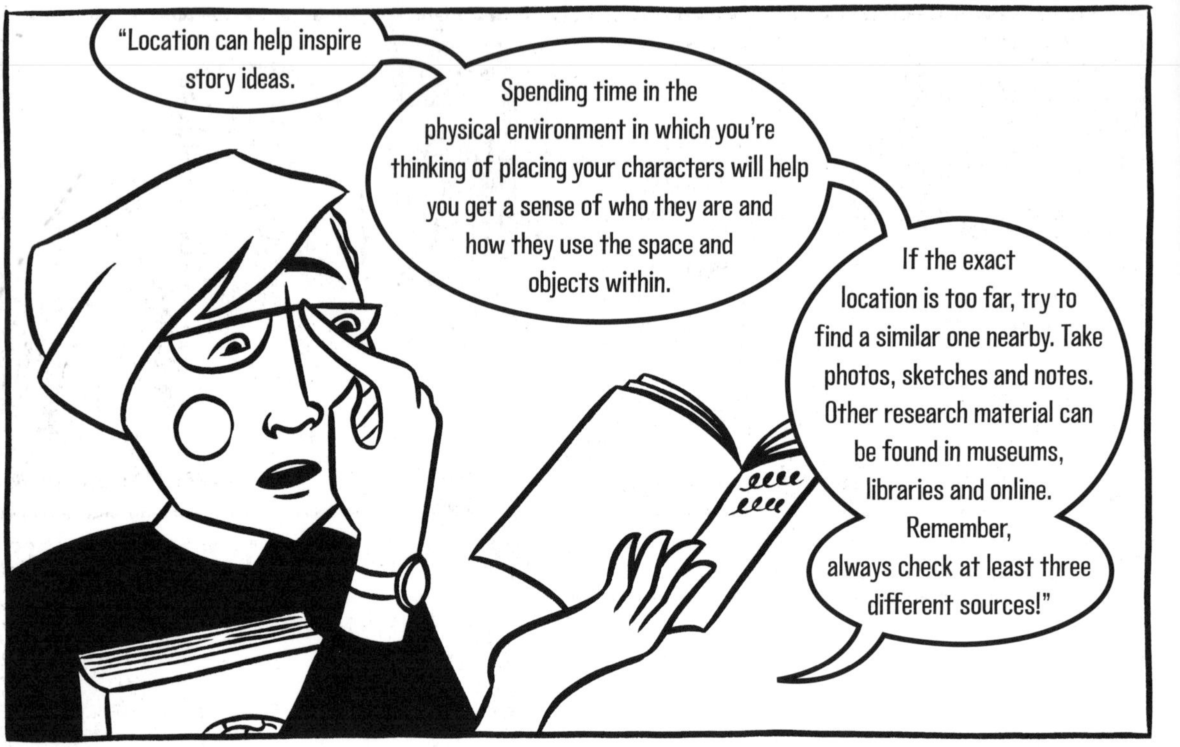
"Location can help inspire story ideas.
Spending time in the physical environment in which you're thinking of placing your characters will help you get a sense of who they are and how they use the space and objects within.
If the exact location is too far, try to find a similar one nearby. Take photos, sketches and notes. Other research material can be found in museums, libraries and online. Remember, always check at least three different sources!"

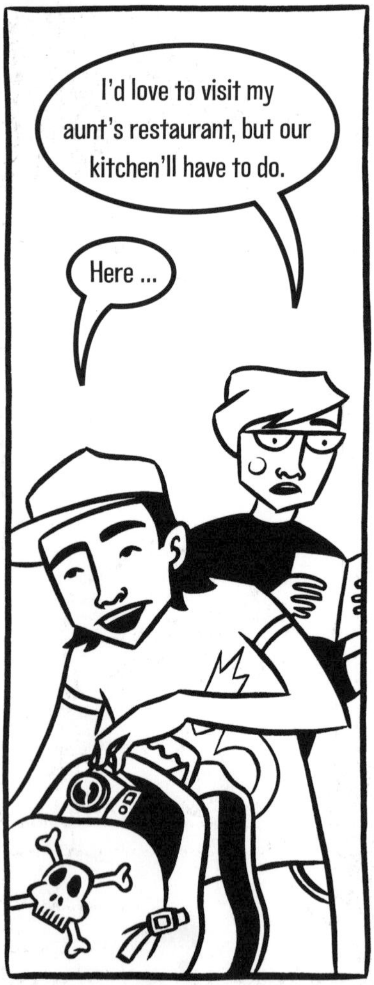
I'd love to visit my aunt's restaurant, but our kitchen'll have to do.
Here ...

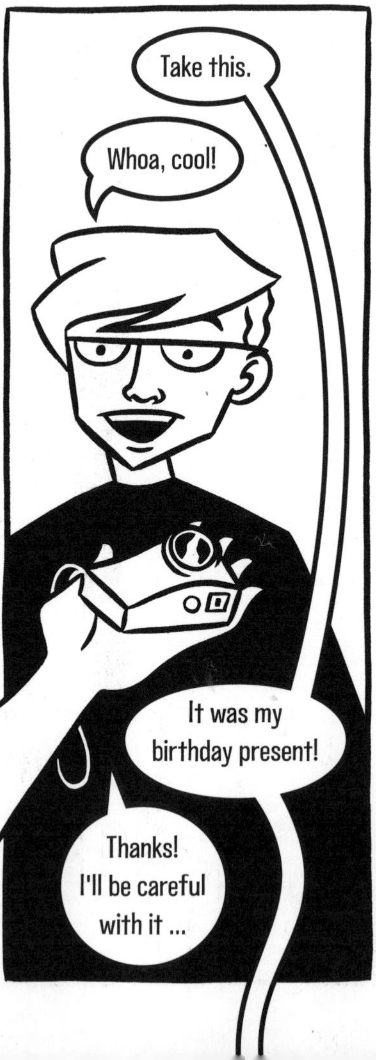
Take this.
Whoa, cool!
It was my birthday present!
Thanks! I'll be careful with it ...

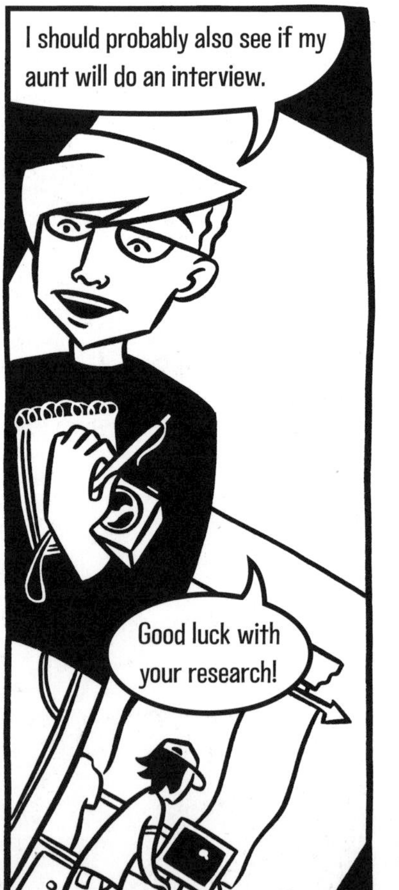
I should probably also see if my aunt will do an interview.
Good luck with your research!

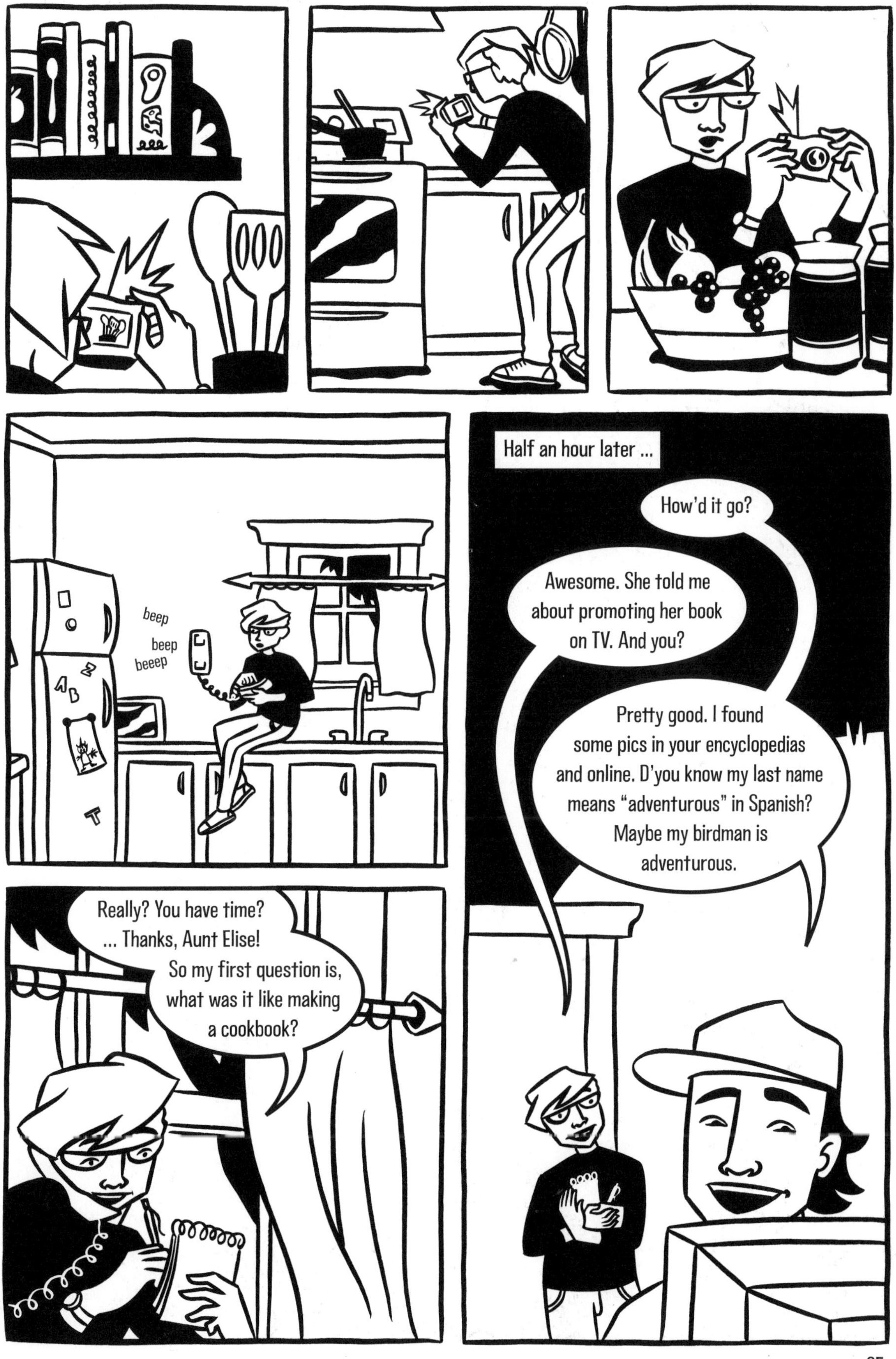

beep
beep
beeep
Half an hour later ...
How'd it go?
Awesome. She told me about promoting her book on TV. And you?
Pretty good. I found some pics in your encyclopedias and online. D'you know my last name means "adventurous" in Spanish? Maybe my birdman is adventurous.
Really? You have time? ... Thanks, Aunt Elise!
So my first question is, what was it like making a cookbook?

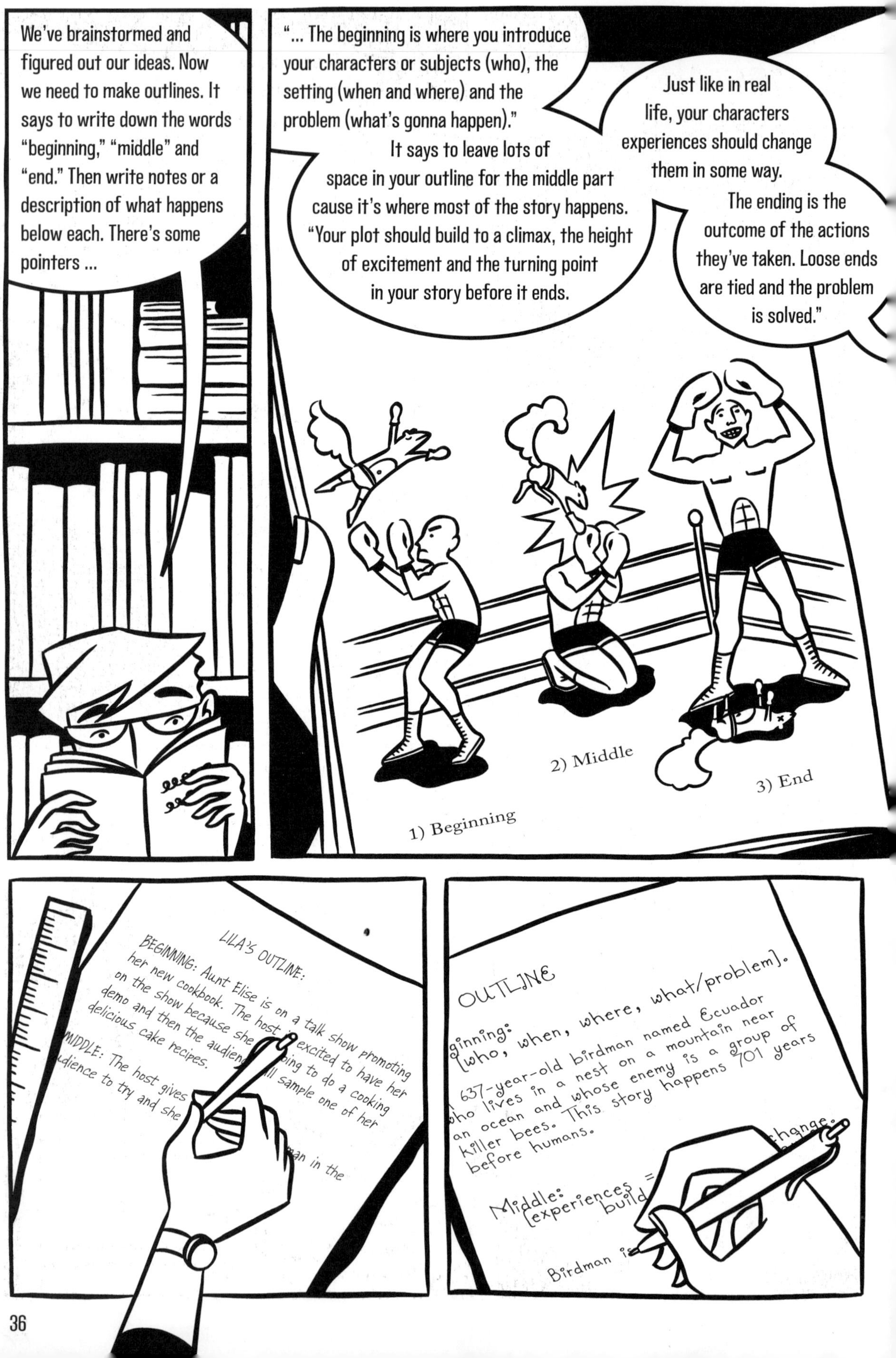
We've brainstormed and figured out our ideas. Now we need to make outlines. It says to write down the words "beginning," "middle" and "end." Then write notes or a description of what happens below each. There's some pointers ...
"... The beginning is where you introduce your characters or subjects (who), the setting (when and where) and the problem (what's gonna happen)."
It says to leave lots of space in your outline for the middle part cause it's where most of the story happens. "Your plot should build to a climax, the height of excitement and the turning point in your story before it ends.
Just like in real life, your characters experiences should change them in some way.
The ending is the outcome of the actions they've taken. Loose ends are tied and the problem is solved."
1) Beginning
2) Middle
3) End
LILA'S OUTLINE:
BEGINNING: Aunt Elise is on a talk show promoting
her new cookbook. The host
excited to have her
on the show because she
ping to do a cooking
demo and then the audien
ll sample one of her
delicious cake recipes.
MIDDLE: The host gives
udience to try and she
man in the
OUTLINE
ginning:
[who, when, where, what/problem].
637-year-old birdman named Ecuador
who lives in a nest on a mountain near
an ocean and whose enemy is a group of
killer bees. This story happens 701 years
before humans.
Middle:
[experiences = change.
build
Birdman is

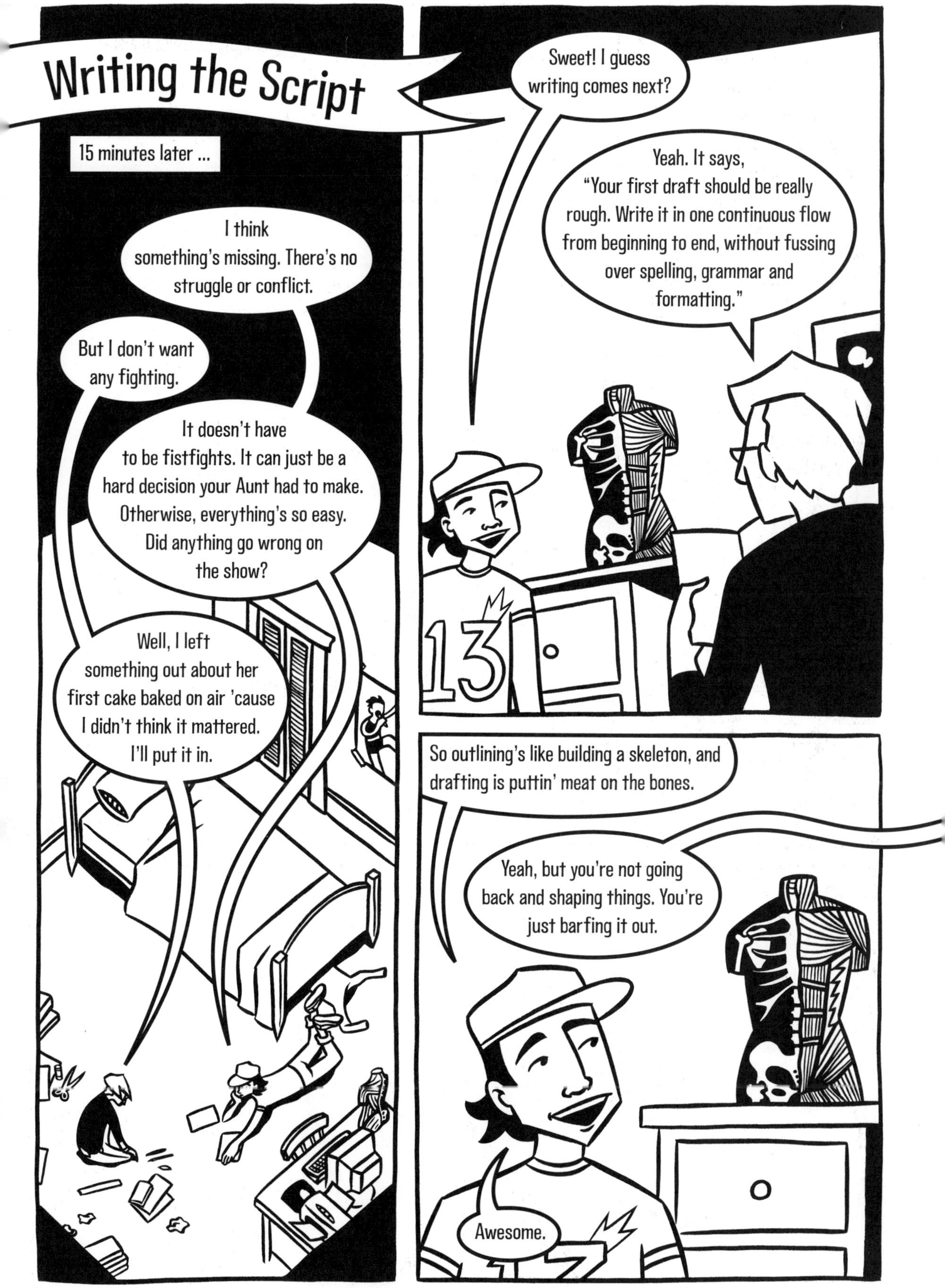
Writing the Script
15 minutes later ...
I think something's missing. There's no struggle or conflict.
But I don't want any fighting.
It doesn't have to be fistfights. It can just be a hard decision your Aunt had to make. Otherwise, everything's so easy. Did anything go wrong on the show?
Well, I left something out about her first cake baked on air 'cause I didn't think it mattered. I'll put it in.
Sweet! I guess writing comes next?
Yeah. It says, "Your first draft should be really rough. Write it in one continuous flow from beginning to end, without fussing over spelling, grammar and formatting."
So outlining's like building a skeleton, and drafting is puttin' meat on the bones.
Yeah, but you're not going back and shaping things. You're just barfing it out.
Awesome.

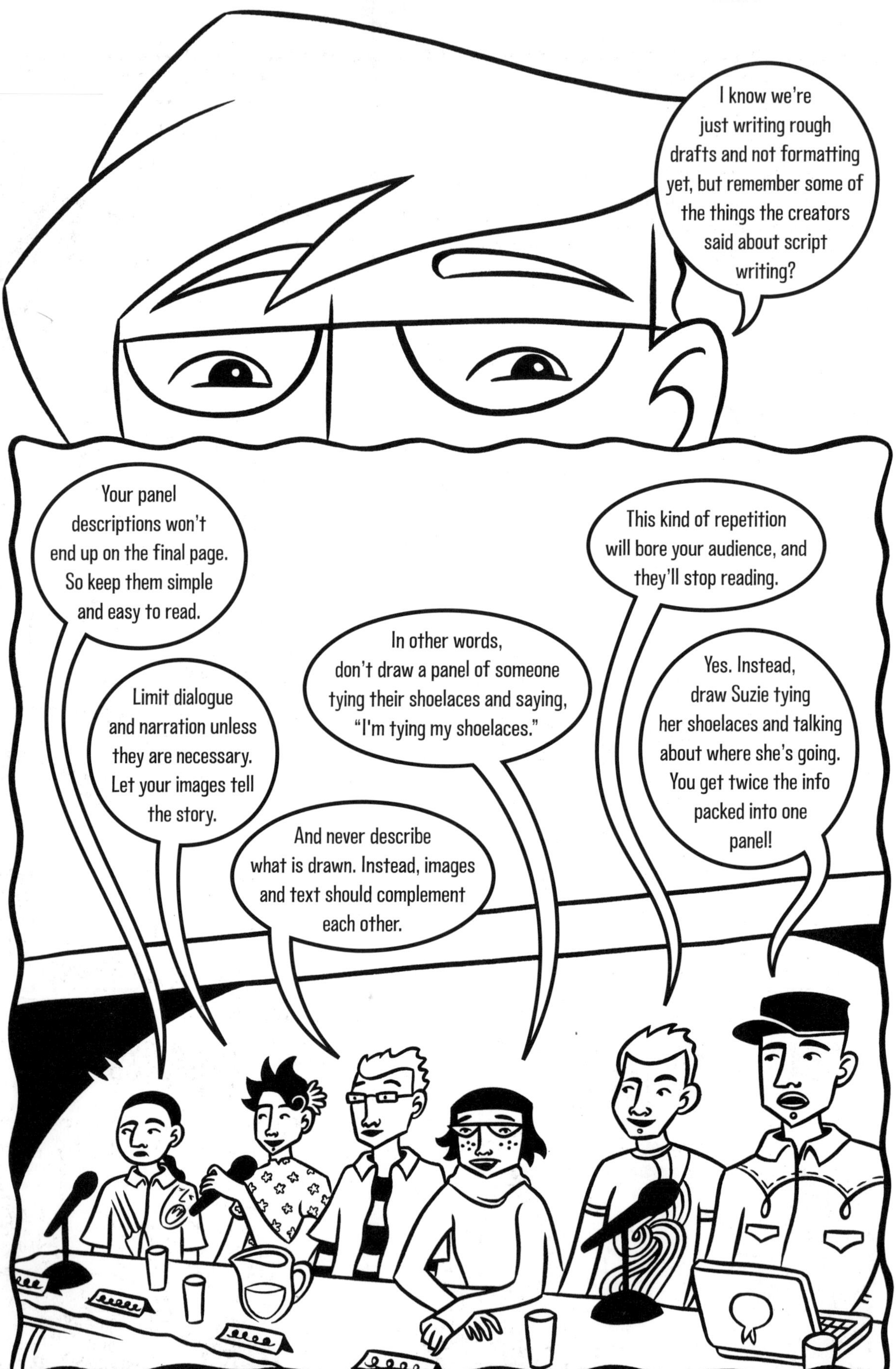
I know we're just writing rough drafts and not formatting yet, but remember some of the things the creators said about script writing?
Your panel descriptions won't end up on the final page. So keep them simple and easy to read.
Limit dialogue and narration unless they are necessary. Let your images tell the story.
And never describe what is drawn. Instead, images and text should complement each other.
In other words, don't draw a panel of someone tying their shoelaces and saying, "I'm tying my shoelaces."
This kind of repetition will bore your audience, and they'll stop reading.
Yes. Instead, draw Suzie tying her shoelaces and talking about where she's going. You get twice the info packed into one panel!

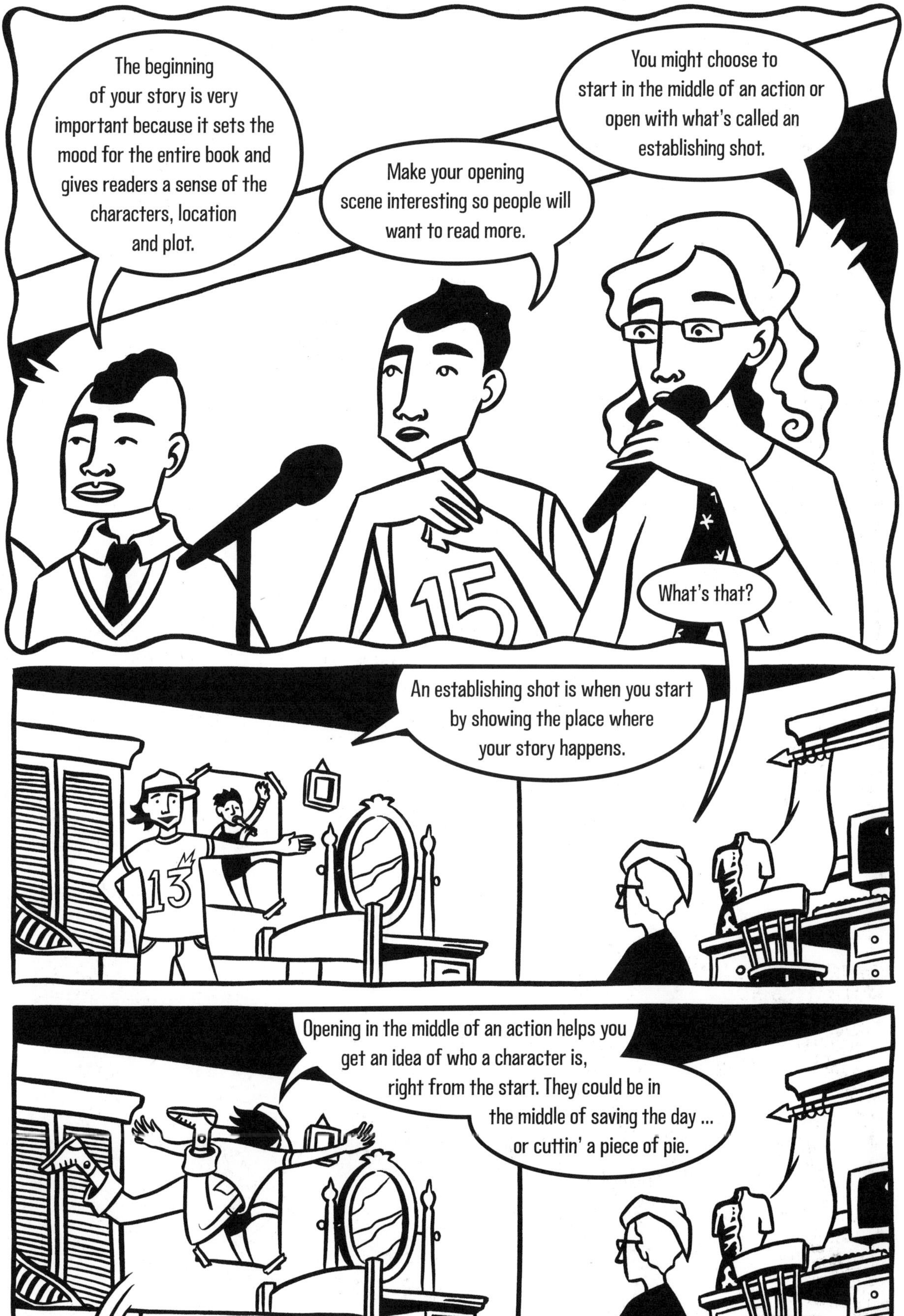
The beginning of your story is very important because it sets the mood for the entire book and gives readers a sense of the characters, location and plot.
Make your opening scene interesting so people will want to read more.
You might choose to start in the middle of an action or open with what's called an establishing shot.
What's that?
An establishing shot is when you start by showing the place where your story happens.
Opening in the middle of an action helps you get an idea of who a character is, right from the start. They could be in the middle of saving the day ... or cuttin' a piece of pie.

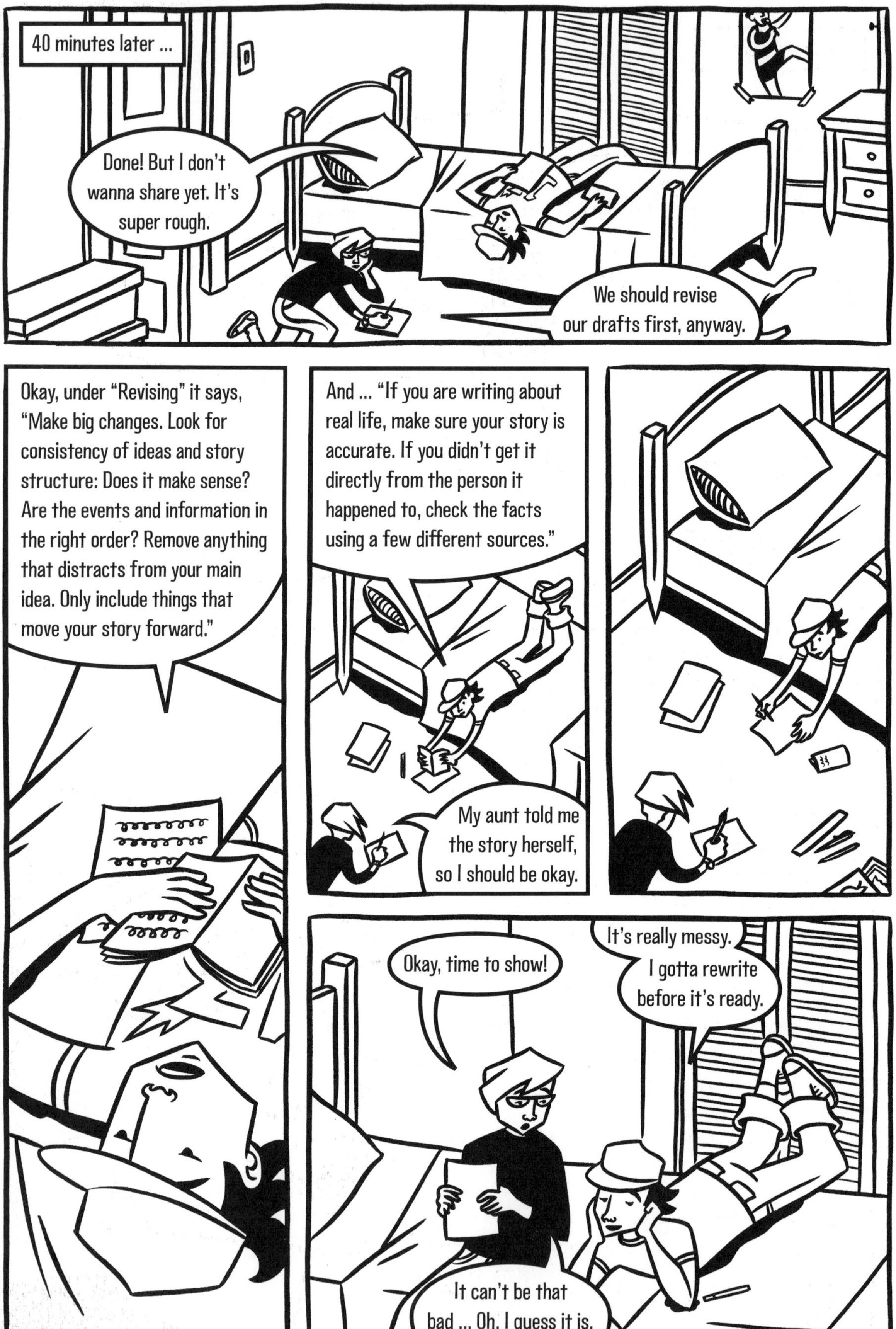
40 minutes later ...
Done! But I don't wanna share yet. It's super rough.
We should revise our drafts first, anyway.
Okay, under "Revising" it says, "Make big changes. Look for consistency of ideas and story structure: Does it make sense? Are the events and information in the right order? Remove anything that distracts from your main idea. Only include things that move your story forward."
And ... "If you are writing about real life, make sure your story is accurate. If you didn't get it directly from the person it happened to, check the facts using a few different sources."
My aunt told me the story herself, so I should be okay.
Okay, time to show!
It's really messy. I gotta rewrite before it's ready.
It can't be that bad ... Oh, I guess it is.

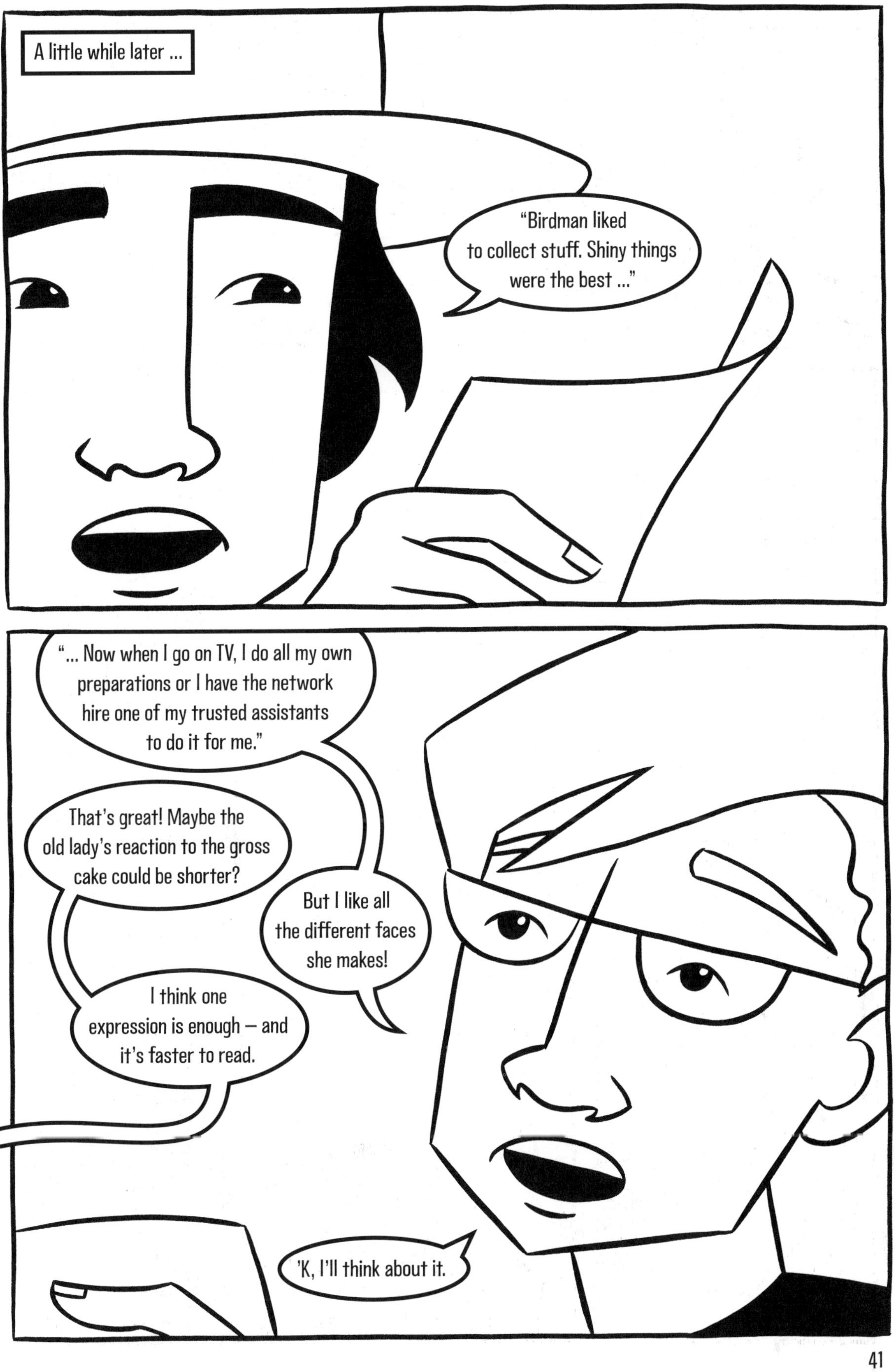
A little while later ...
"Birdman liked to collect stuff. Shiny things were the best ..."
"... Now when I go on TV, I do all my own preparations or I have the network hire one of my trusted assistants to do it for me."
That's great! Maybe the old lady's reaction to the gross cake could be shorter?
But I like all the different faces she makes!
I think one expression is enough – and it's faster to read.
'K, I'll think about it.

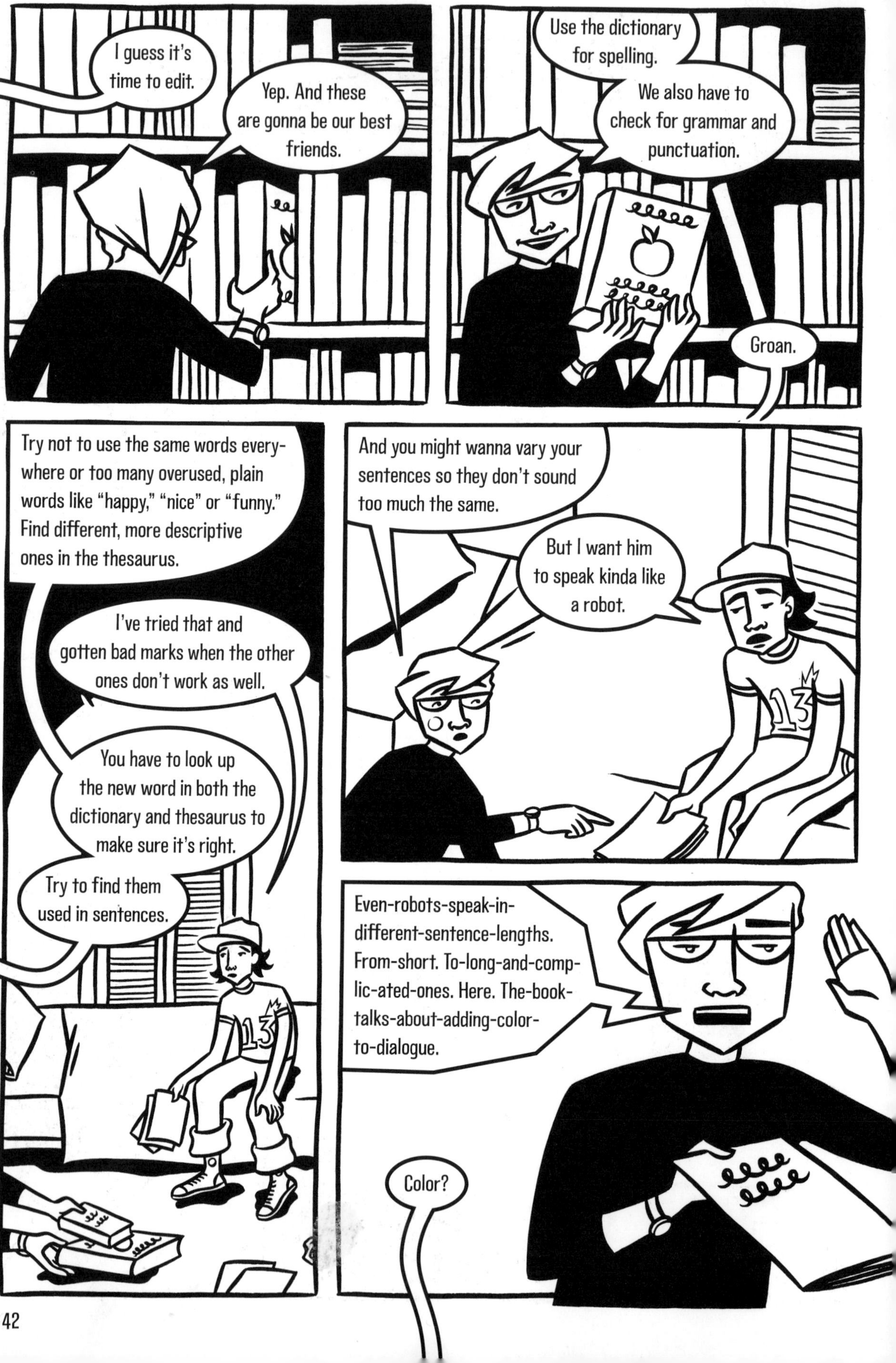
I guess it's time to edit.
Yep. And these are gonna be our best friends.
Use the dictionary for spelling.
We also have to check for grammar and punctuation.
Groan.
Try not to use the same words every-where or too many overused, plain words like "happy," "nice" or "funny." Find different, more descriptive ones in the thesaurus.
I've tried that and gotten bad marks when the other ones don't work as well.
You have to look up the new word in both the dictionary and thesaurus to make sure it's right.
Try to find them used in sentences.
And you might wanna vary your sentences so they don't sound too much the same.
But I want him to speak kinda like a robot.
Even-robots-speak-in-different-sentence-lengths. From-short. To-long-and-comp-lic-ated-ones. Here. The-book-talks-about-adding-color-to-dialogue.
Color?

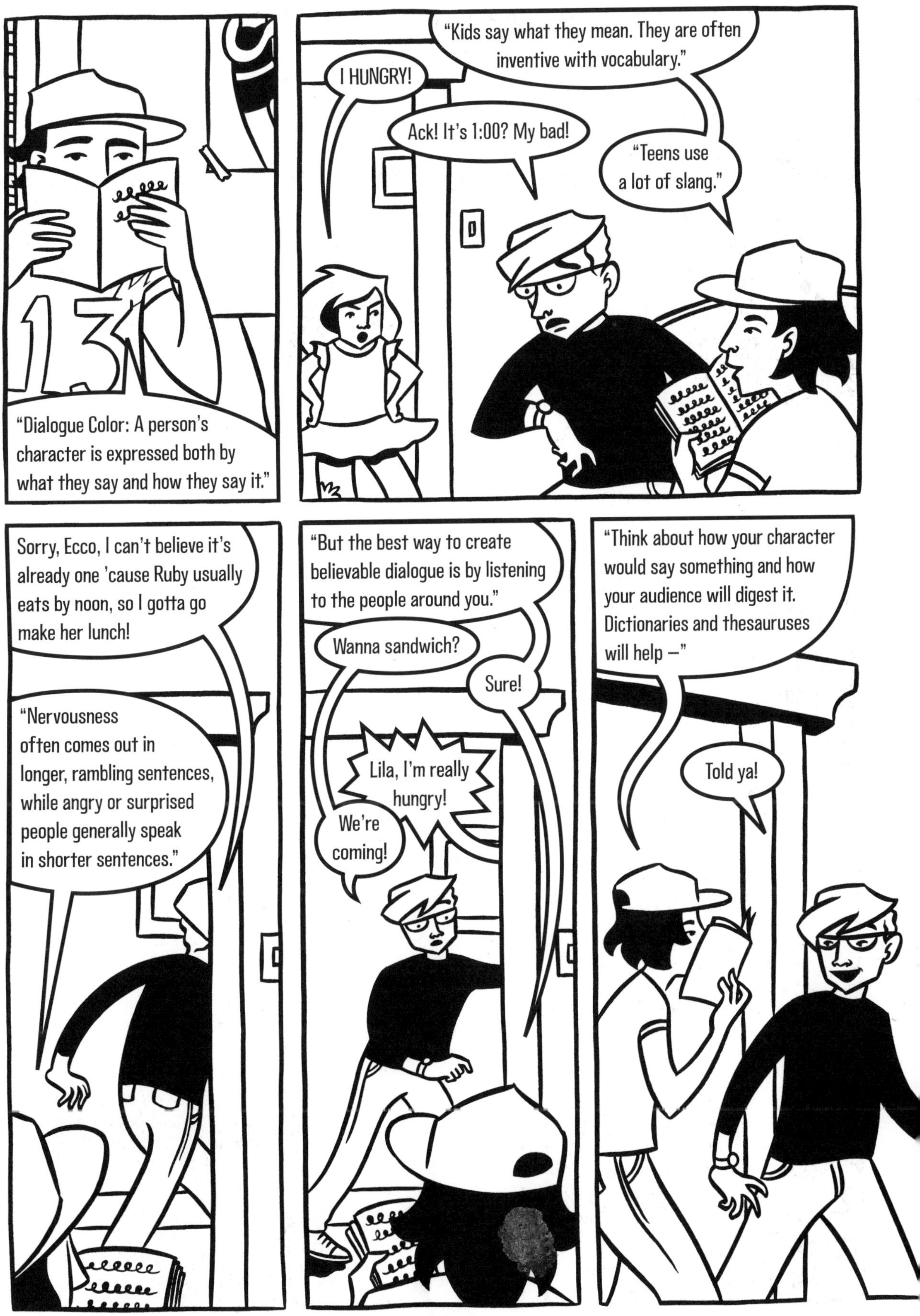
"Dialogue Color: A person's character is expressed both by what they say and how they say it."
"Kids say what they mean. They are often inventive with vocabulary."
I HUNGRY!
Ack! It's 1:00? My bad!
"Teens use a lot of slang."
Sorry, Ecco, I can't believe it's already one 'cause Ruby usually eats by noon, so I gotta go make her lunch!
"Nervousness often comes out in longer, rambling sentences, while angry or surprised people generally speak in shorter sentences."
"But the best way to create believable dialogue is by listening to the people around you."
Wanna sandwich?
Sure!
Lila, I'm really hungry!
We're coming!
"Think about how your character would say something and how your audience will digest it. Dictionaries and thesauruses will help –"
Told ya!

Script Formatting

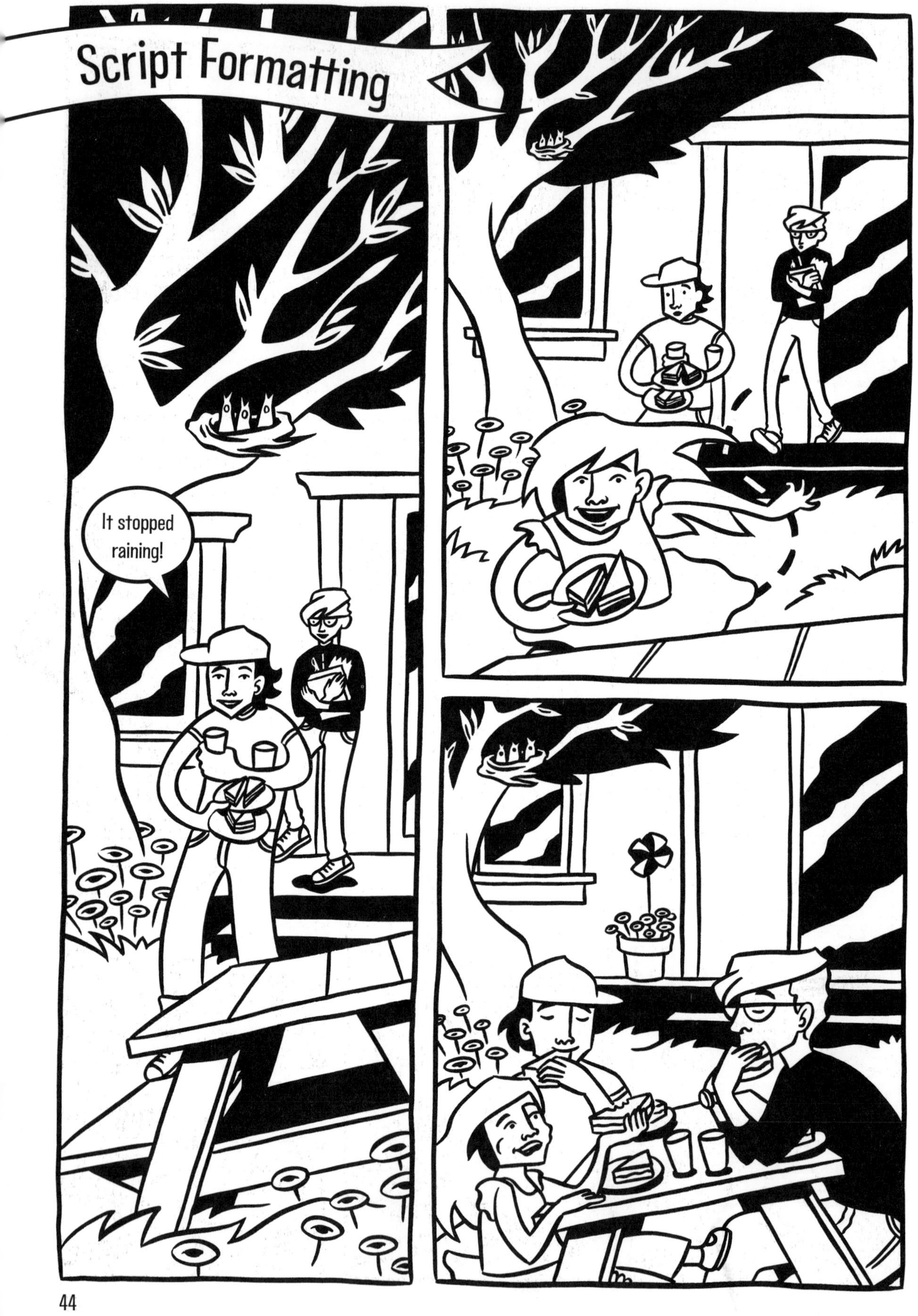
It stopped raining!

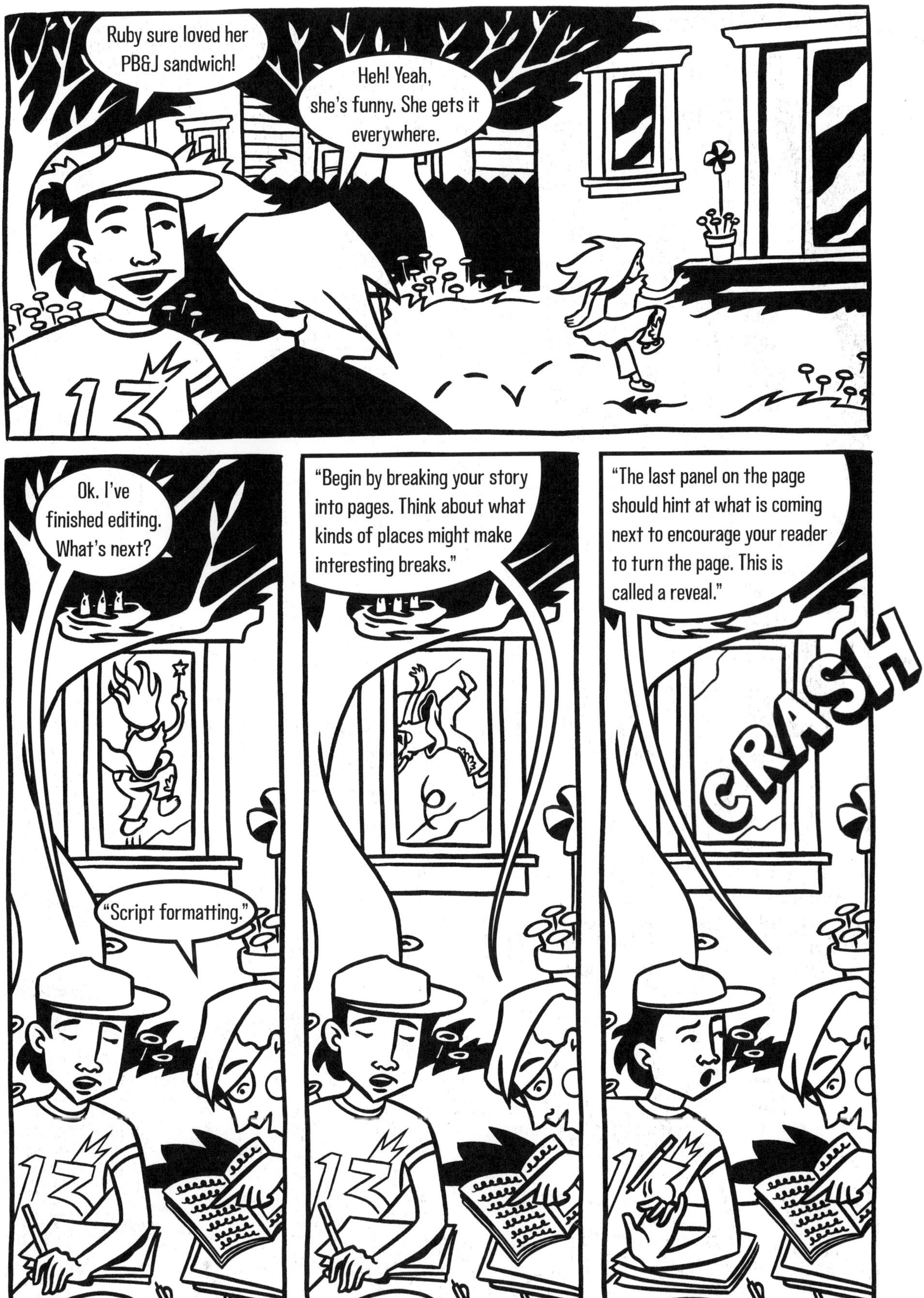

Ruby sure loved her PB&J sandwich!
Heh! Yeah, she's funny. She gets it everywhere.
Ok. I've finished editing. What's next?
"Script formatting."
"Begin by breaking your story into pages. Think about what kinds of places might make interesting breaks."
"The last panel on the page should hint at what is coming next to encourage your reader to turn the page. This is called a reveal."
CRASH

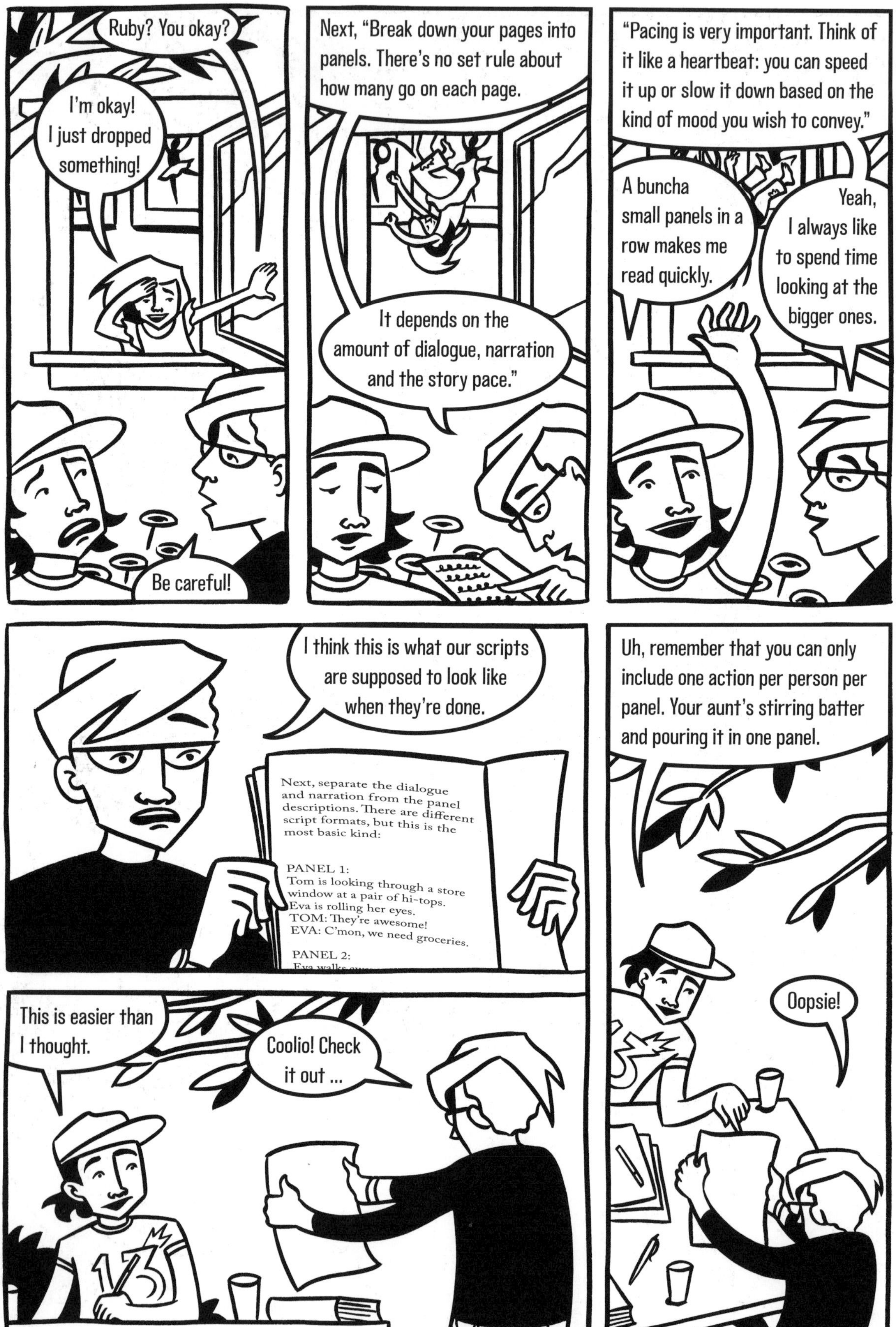
Ruby? You okay?
I'm okay! I just dropped something!
Be careful!
Next, "Break down your pages into panels. There's no set rule about how many go on each page.
It depends on the amount of dialogue, narration and the story pace."
"Pacing is very important. Think of it like a heartbeat: you can speed it up or slow it down based on the kind of mood you wish to convey."
A buncha small panels in a row makes me read quickly.
Yeah, I always like to spend time looking at the bigger ones.
I think this is what our scripts are supposed to look like when they're done.
Next, separate the dialogue and narration from the panel descriptions. There are different script formats, but this is the most basic kind:
PANEL 1:
Tom is looking through a store window at a pair of hi-tops.
Eva is rolling her eyes.
TOM: They're awesome!
EVA: C'mon, we need groceries.
PANEL 2:
This is easier than I thought.
Coolio! Check it out ...
Uh, remember that you can only include one action per person per panel. Your aunt's stirring batter and pouring it in one panel.
Oopsie!

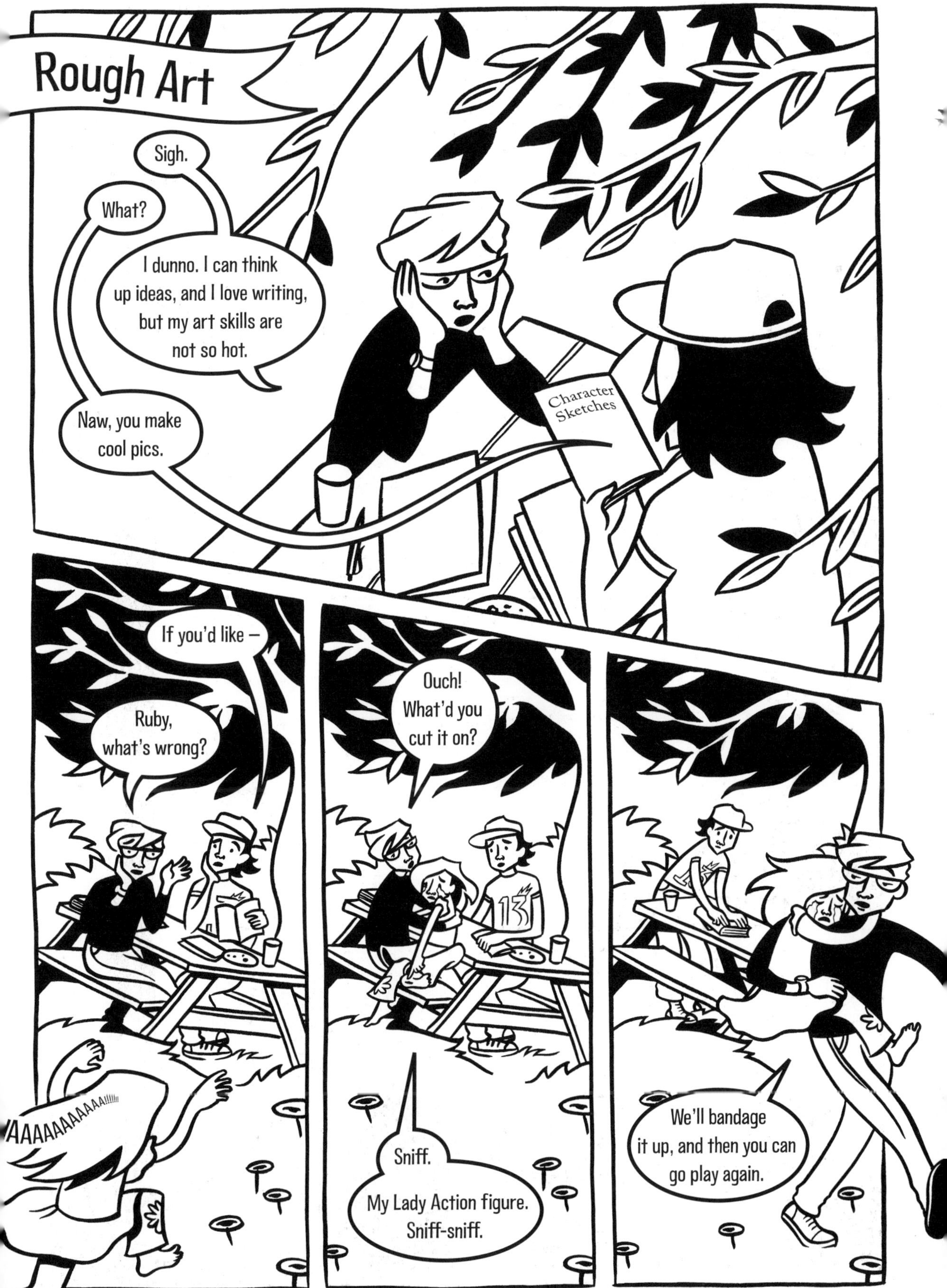
Rough Art
Sigh.
What?
I dunno. I can think up ideas, and I love writing, but my art skills are not so hot.
Naw, you make cool pics.
Character Sketches
If you'd like —
Ruby, what's wrong?
AAAAAAAAAA!!!!!
Ouch! What'd you cut it on?
Sniff.
My Lady Action figure. Sniff-sniff.
We'll bandage it up, and then you can go play again.

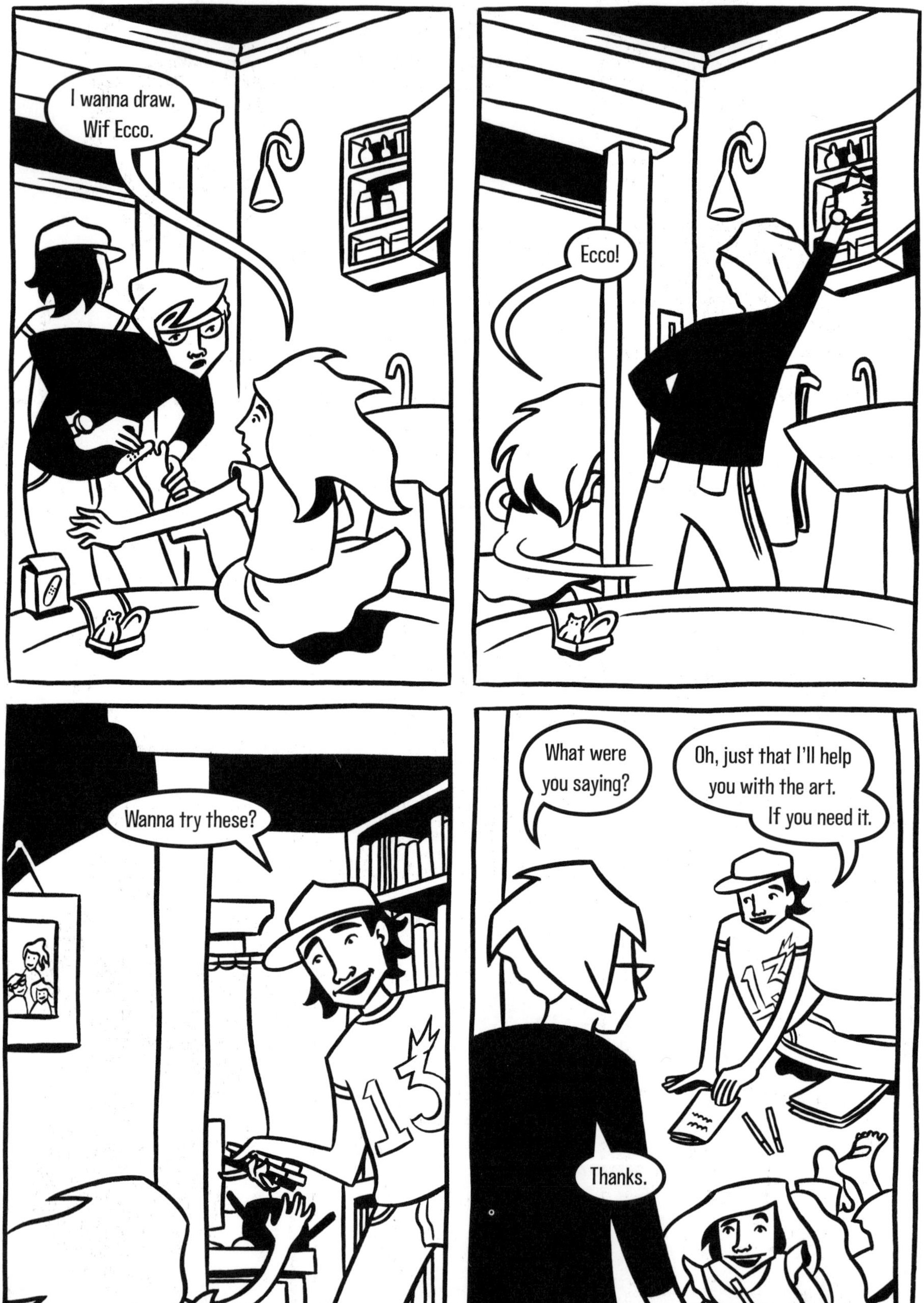
I wanna draw. Wif Ecco.
Ecco!
Wanna try these?
What were you saying?
Oh, just that I'll help you with the art. If you need it.
Thanks.

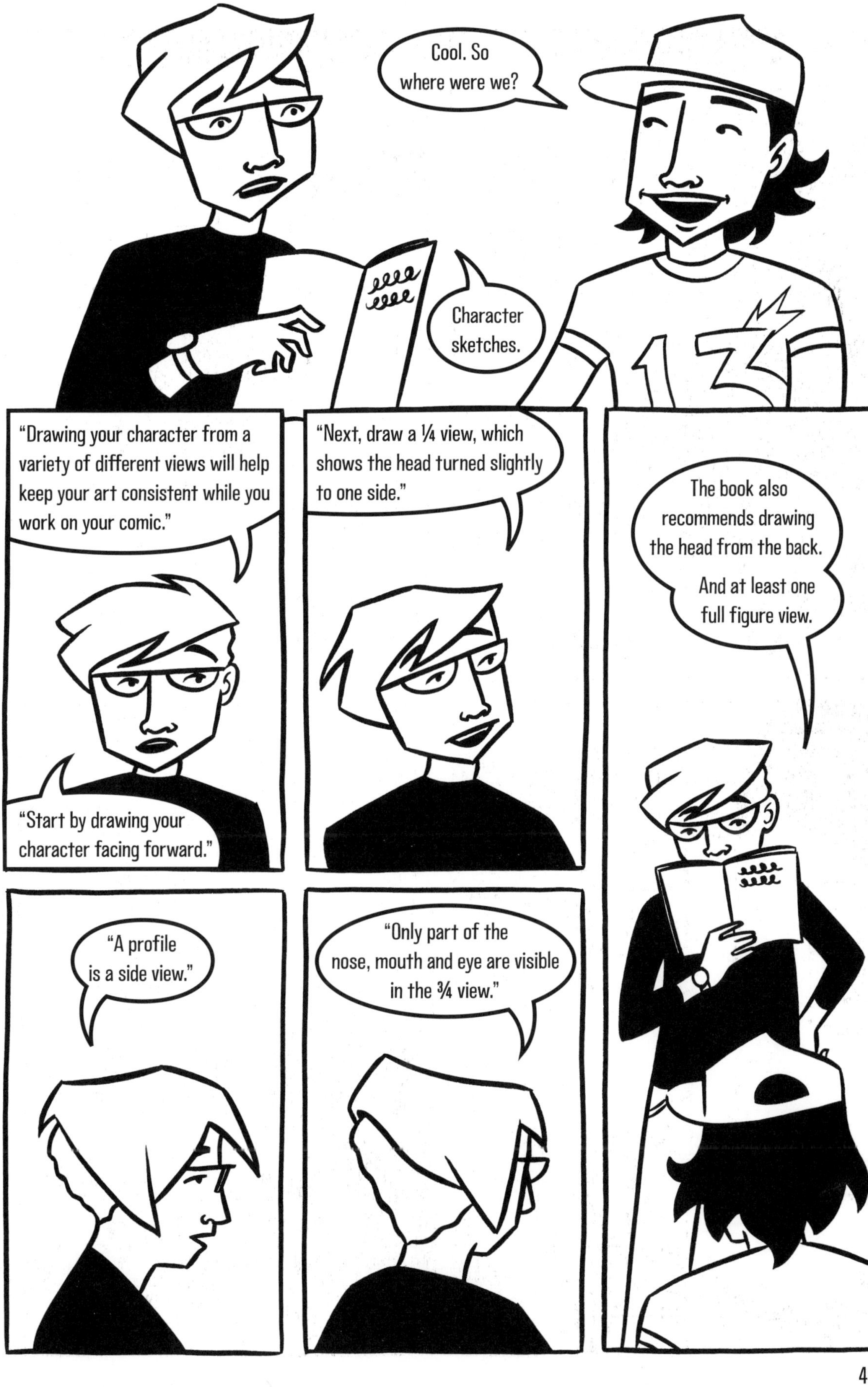

Cool. So where were we?
Character sketches.
"Drawing your character from a variety of different views will help keep your art consistent while you work on your comic."
"Start by drawing your character facing forward."
"Next, draw a ¼ view, which shows the head turned slightly to one side."
The book also recommends drawing the head from the back.
And at least one full figure view.
"A profile is a side view."
"Only part of the nose, mouth and eye are visible in the ¾ view."

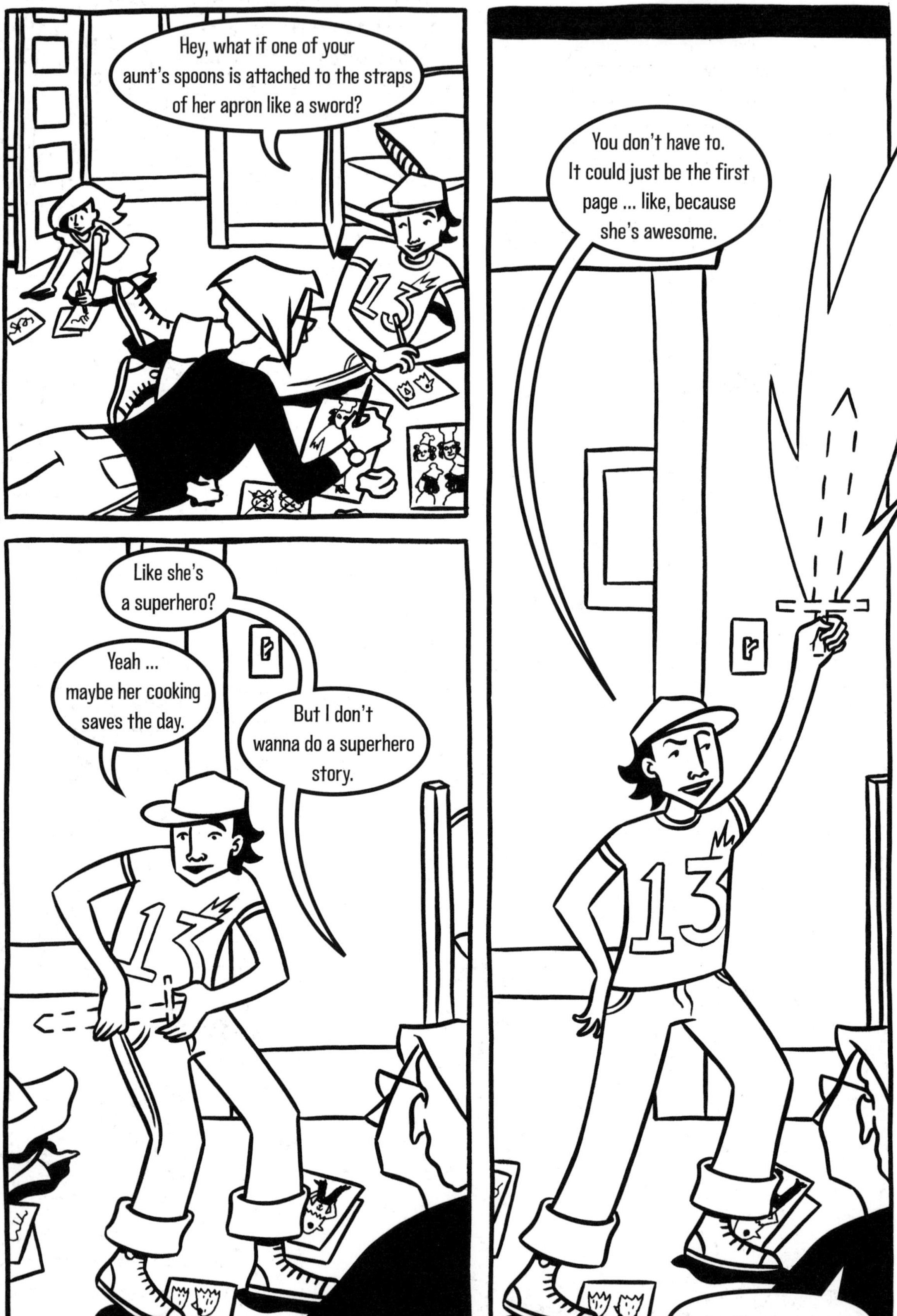
Hey, what if one of your aunt's spoons is attached to the straps of her apron like a sword?
Like she's a superhero?
Yeah ... maybe her cooking saves the day.
But I don't wanna do a superhero story.
You don't have to. It could just be the first page ... like, because she's awesome.
Ha-ha! She is pretty cool.

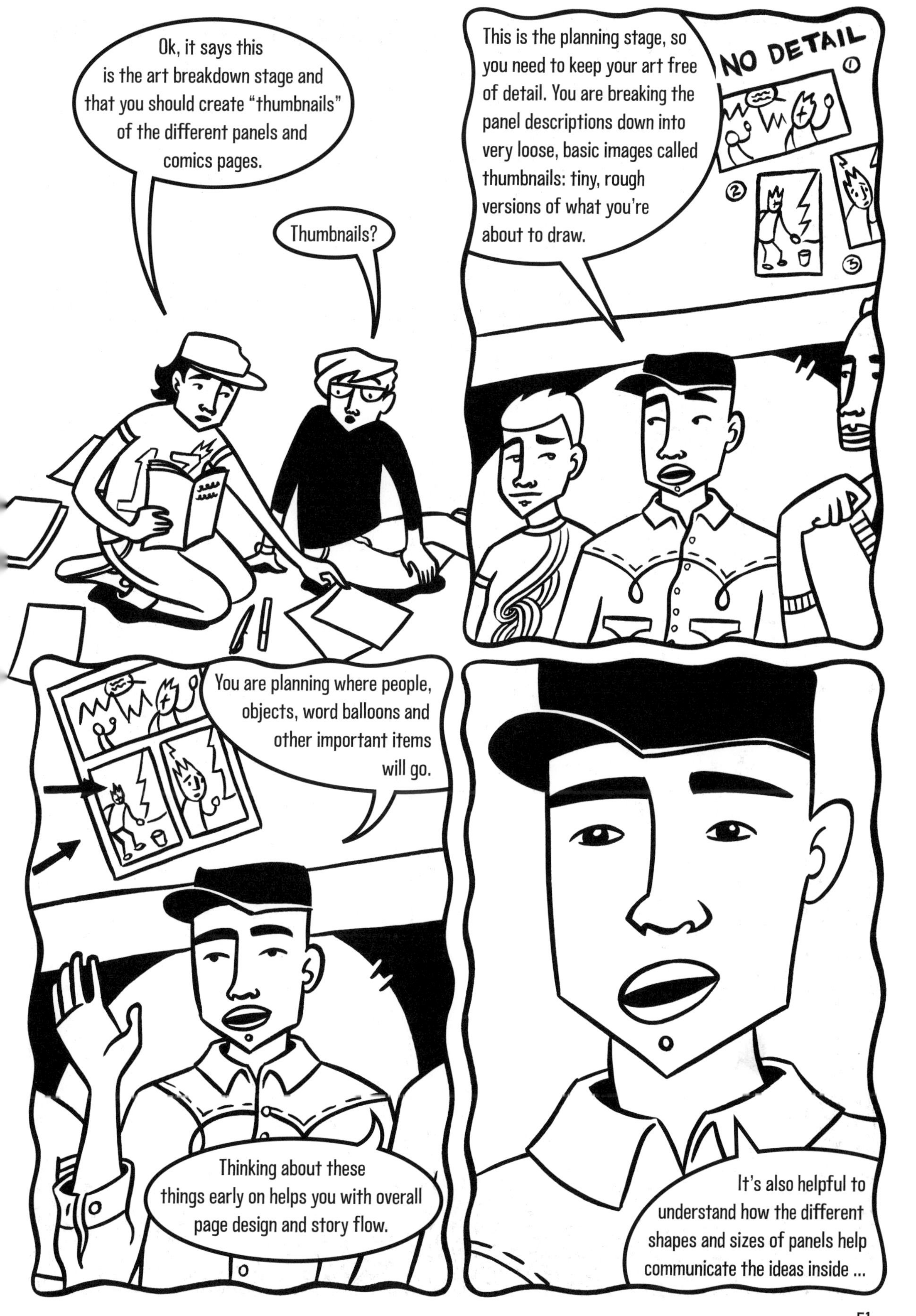

Ok, it says this is the art breakdown stage and that you should create "thumbnails" of the different panels and comics pages.
Thumbnails?
This is the planning stage, so you need to keep your art free of detail. You are breaking the panel descriptions down into very loose, basic images called thumbnails: tiny, rough versions of what you're about to draw.
NO DETAIL
You are planning where people, objects, word balloons and other important items will go.
Thinking about these things early on helps you with overall page design and story flow.
It's also helpful to understand how the different shapes and sizes of panels help communicate the ideas inside ...

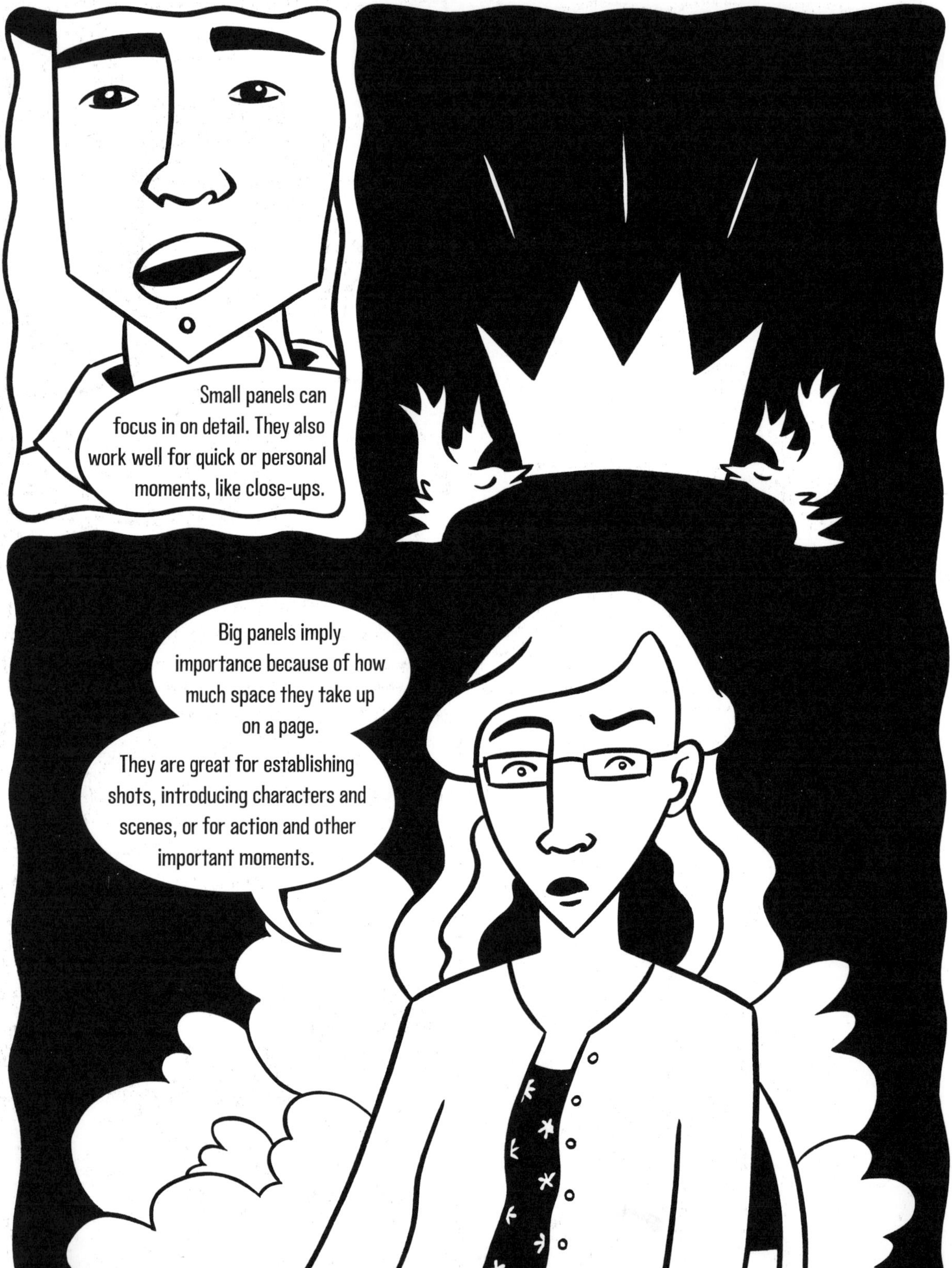
Small panels can focus in on detail. They also work well for quick or personal moments, like close-ups.
Big panels imply importance because of how much space they take up on a page.
They are great for establishing shots, introducing characters and scenes, or for action and other important moments.

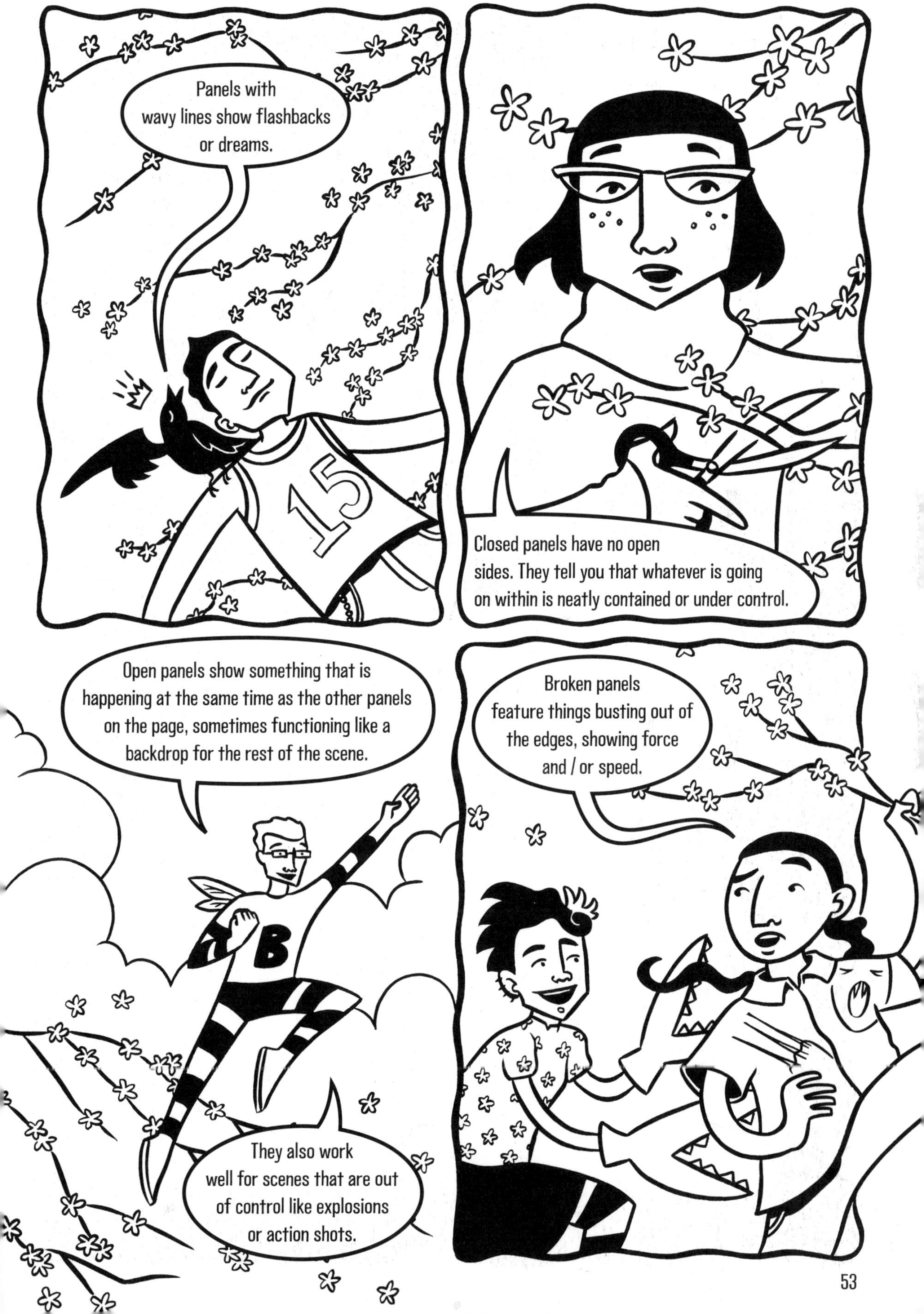
Panels with wavy lines show flashbacks or dreams.
Closed panels have no open sides. They tell you that whatever is going on within is neatly contained or under control.
Open panels show something that is happening at the same time as the other panels on the page, sometimes functioning like a backdrop for the rest of the scene.
They also work well for scenes that are out of control like explosions or action shots.
Broken panels feature things busting out of the edges, showing force and / or speed.

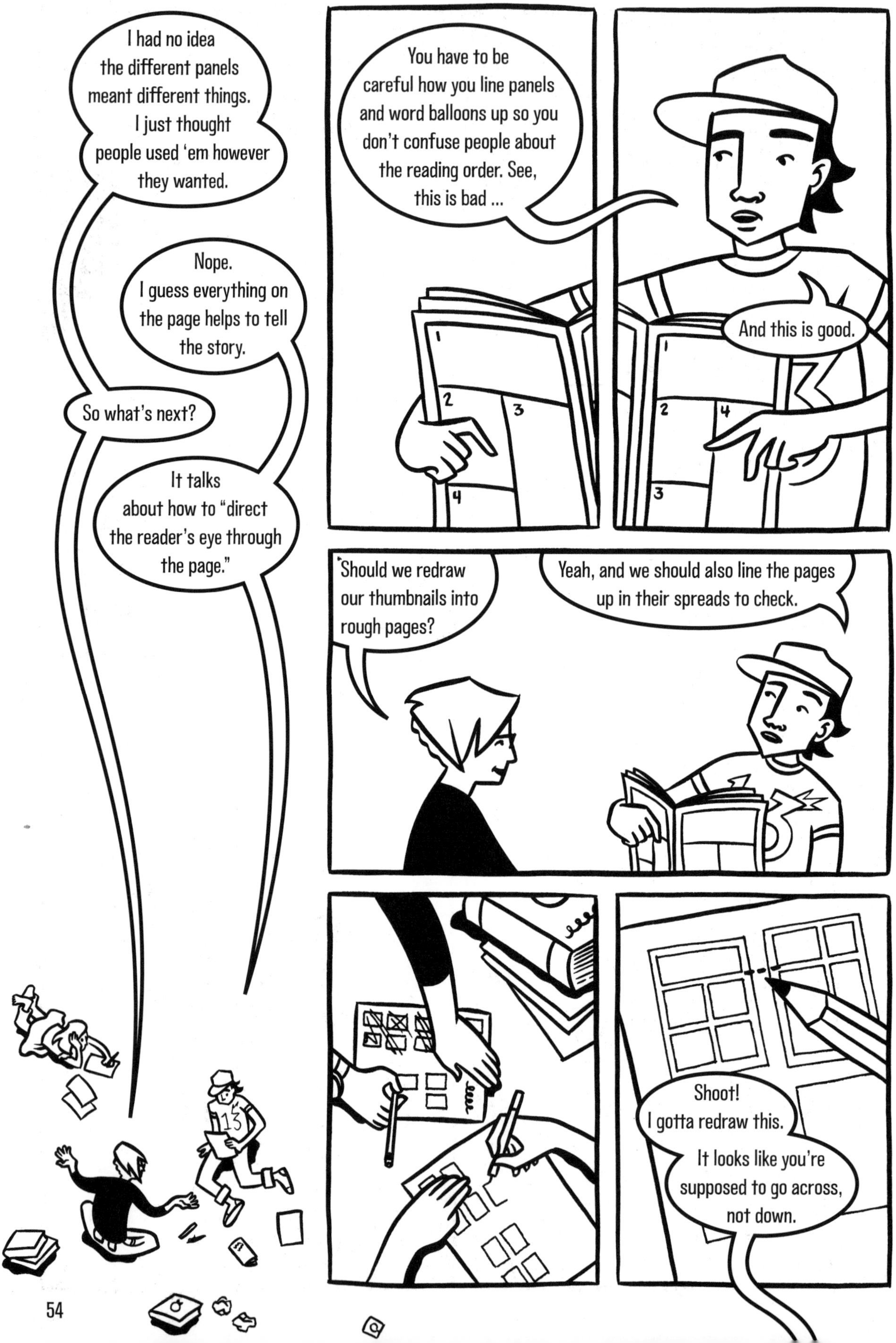
I had no idea the different panels meant different things. I just thought people used 'em however they wanted.
Nope. I guess everything on the page helps to tell the story.
So what's next?
It talks about how to "direct the reader's eye through the page."
You have to be careful how you line panels and word balloons up so you don't confuse people about the reading order. See, this is bad ...
1
2
3
4
And this is good.
1
2
4
3
Should we redraw our thumbnails into rough pages?
Yeah, and we should also line the pages up in their spreads to check.
Shoot! I gotta redraw this.
It looks like you're supposed to go across, not down.

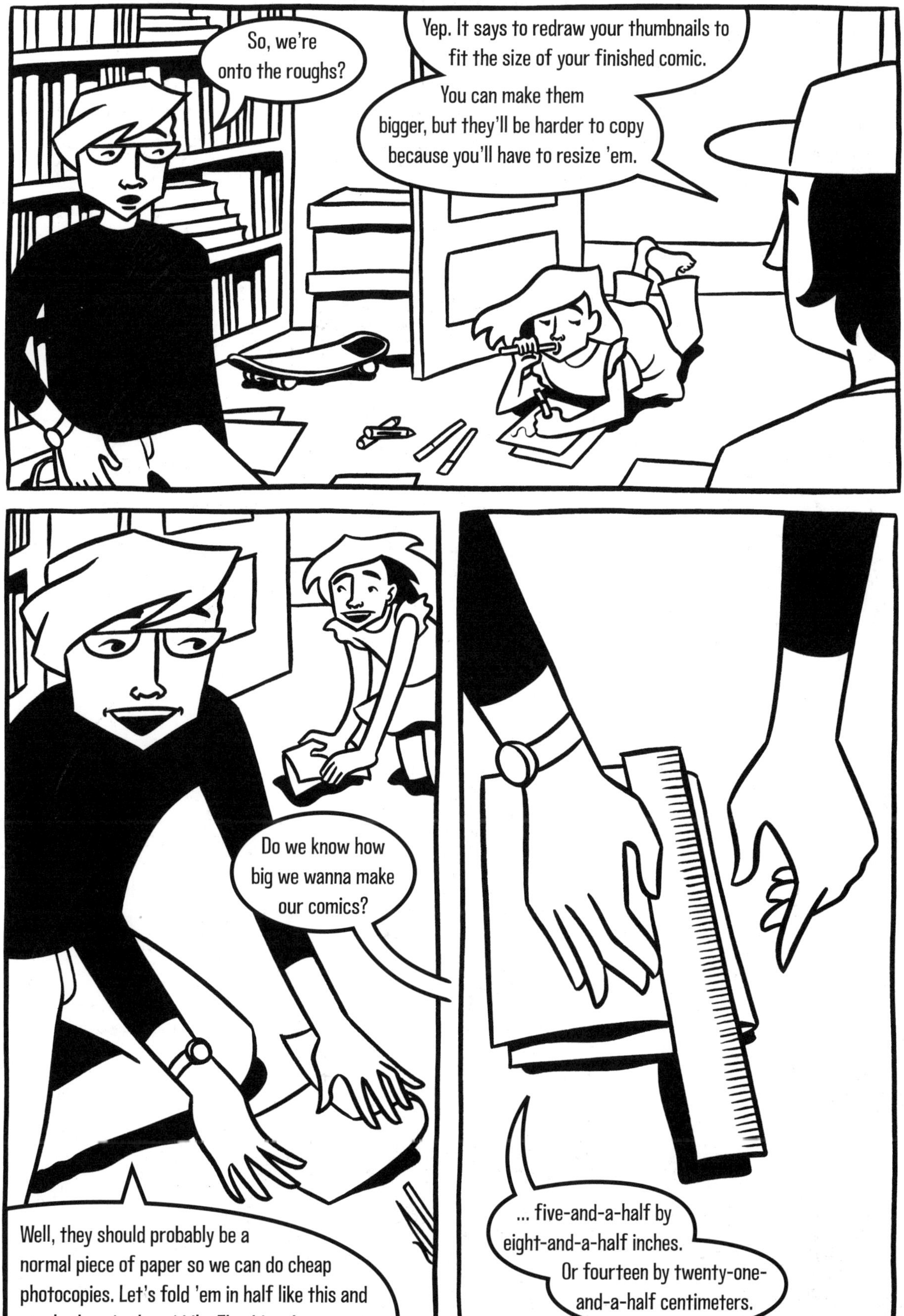

So, we're onto the roughs?
Yep. It says to redraw your thumbnails to fit the size of your finished comic.
You can make them bigger, but they'll be harder to copy because you'll have to resize 'em.
Do we know how big we wanna make our comics?
Well, they should probably be a normal piece of paper so we can do cheap photocopies. Let's fold 'em in half like this and staple them in the middle. That'd make our art ...
... five-and-a-half by eight-and-a-half inches.
Or fourteen by twenty-one-and-a-half centimeters.

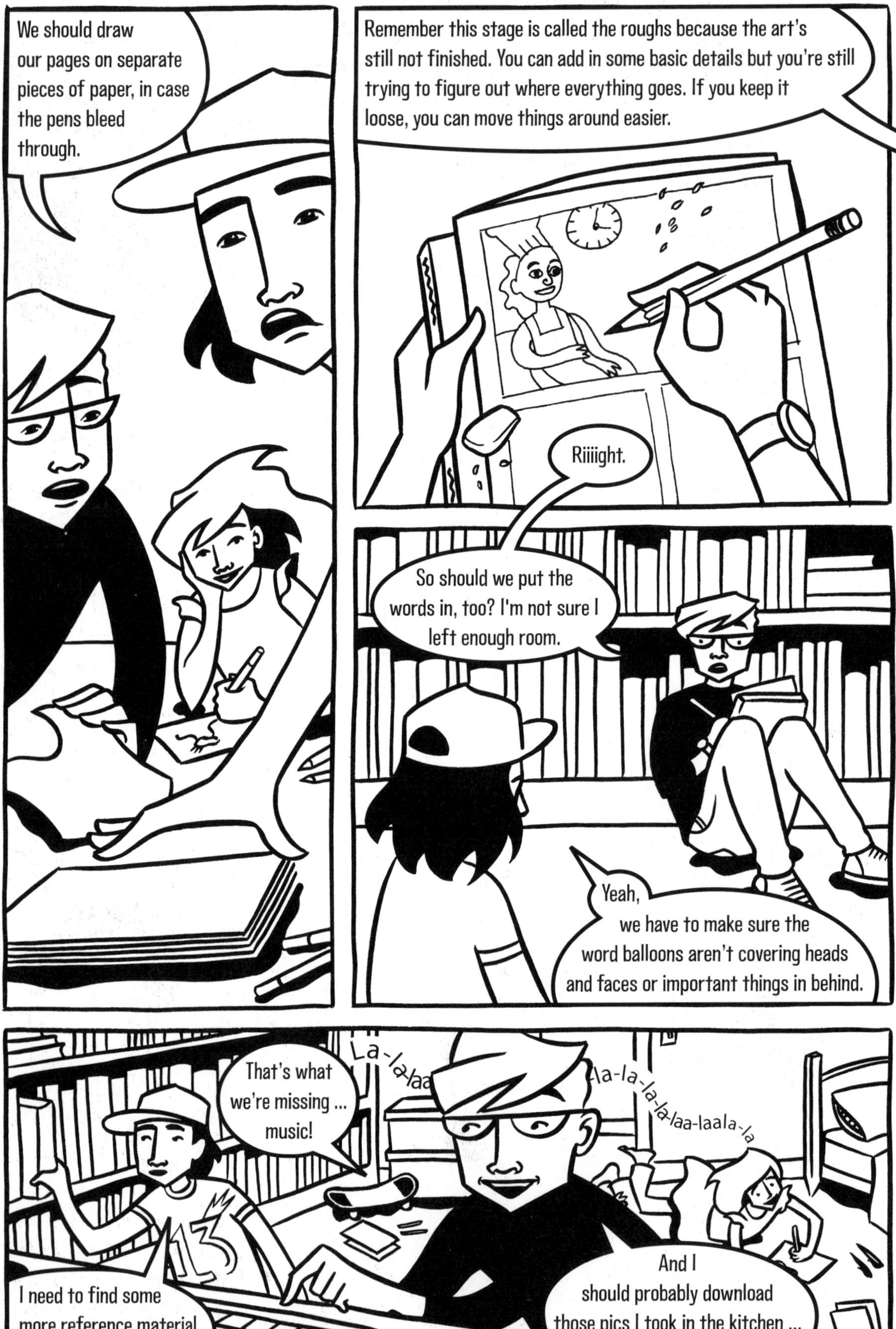

We should draw our pages on separate pieces of paper, in case the pens bleed through.
Remember this stage is called the roughs because the art's still not finished. You can add in some basic details but you're still trying to figure out where everything goes. If you keep it loose, you can move things around easier.
Riiiight.
So should we put the words in, too? I'm not sure I left enough room.
Yeah, we have to make sure the word balloons aren't covering heads and faces or important things in behind.
That's what we're missing ... music!
La-la-laa
la-la-la-la-laa-laala-la
I need to find some more reference material.
And I should probably download those pics I took in the kitchen ...

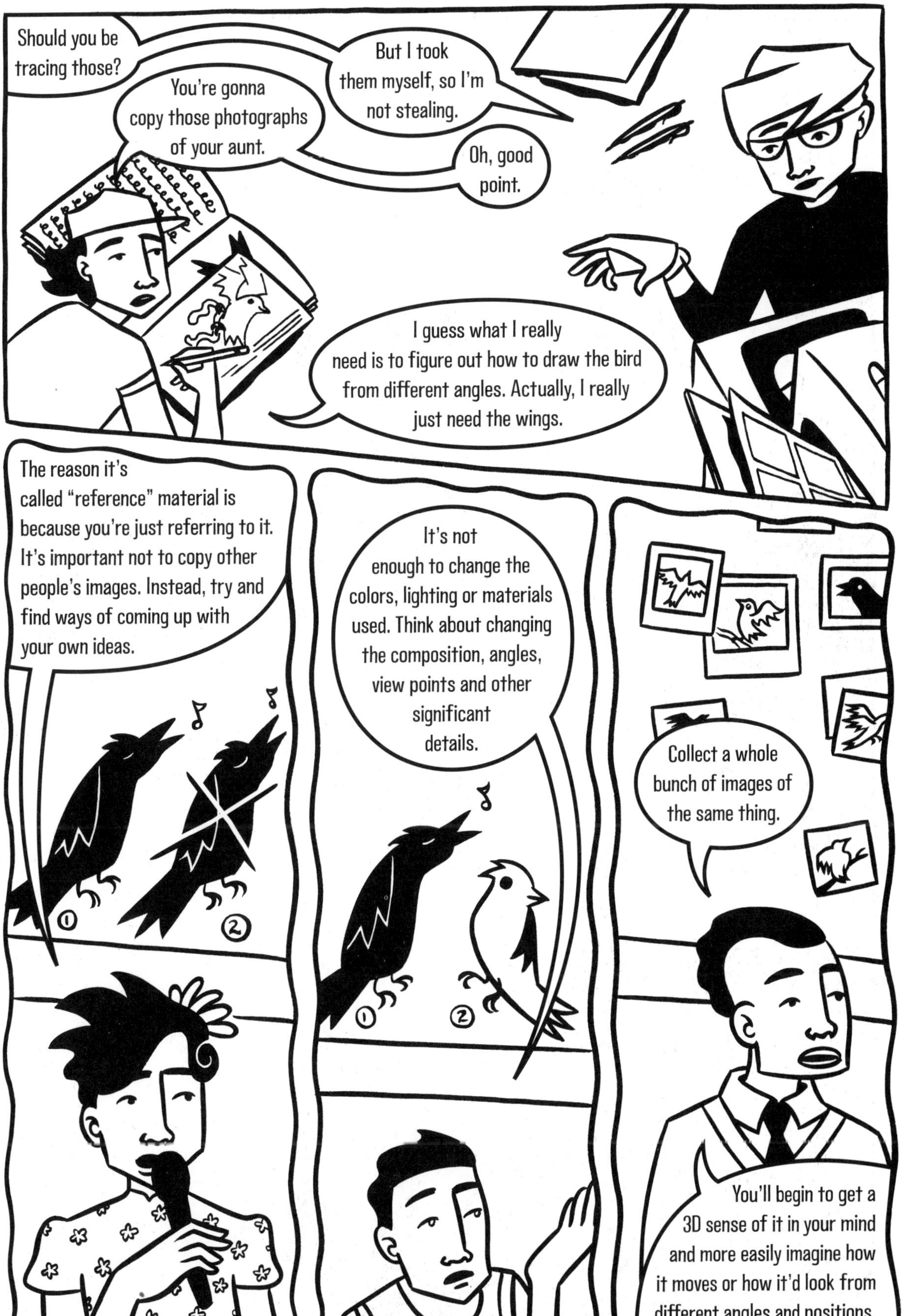
Should you be tracing those?
You're gonna copy those photographs of your aunt.
But I took them myself, so I'm not stealing.
Oh, good point.
I guess what I really need is to figure out how to draw the bird from different angles. Actually, I really just need the wings.
The reason it's called "reference" material is because you're just referring to it. It's important not to copy other people's images. Instead, try and find ways of coming up with your own ideas.
1
2
It's not enough to change the colors, lighting or materials used. Think about changing the composition, angles, view points and other significant details.
1
2
Collect a whole bunch of images of the same thing.
You'll begin to get a 3D sense of it in your mind and more easily imagine how it moves or how it'd look from different angles and positions.

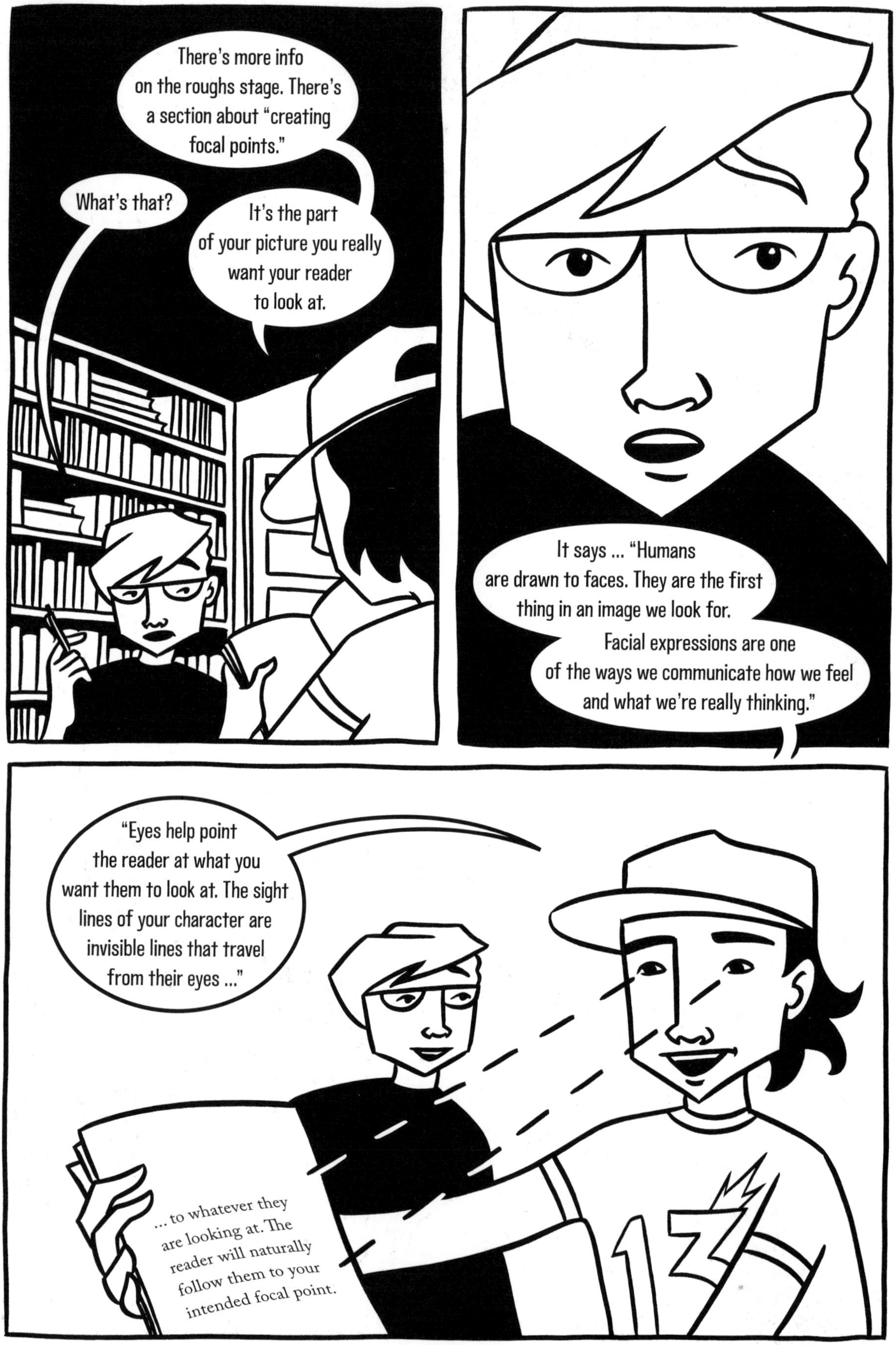
There's more info on the roughs stage. There's a section about "creating focal points."
What's that?
It's the part of your picture you really want your reader to look at.
It says ... "Humans are drawn to faces. They are the first thing in an image we look for.
Facial expressions are one of the ways we communicate how we feel and what we're really thinking."
"Eyes help point the reader at what you want them to look at. The sight lines of your character are invisible lines that travel from their eyes ..."
... to whatever they are looking at. The reader will naturally follow them to your intended focal point.

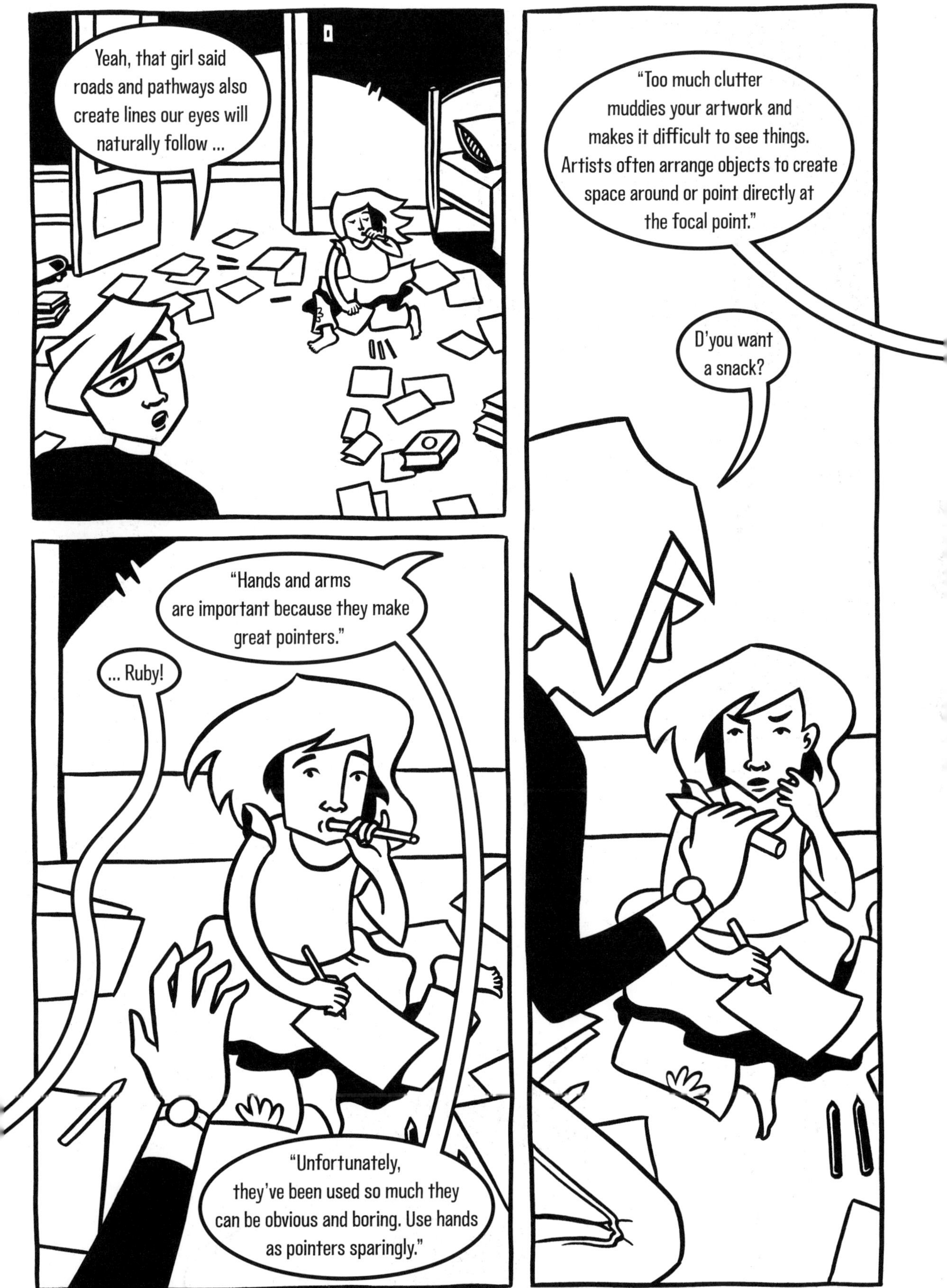
Yeah, that girl said roads and pathways also create lines our eyes will naturally follow ...
"Hands and arms are important because they make great pointers."
... Ruby!
"Unfortunately, they've been used so much they can be obvious and boring. Use hands as pointers sparingly."
"Too much clutter muddies your artwork and makes it difficult to see things. Artists often arrange objects to create space around or point directly at the focal point."
D'you want a snack?

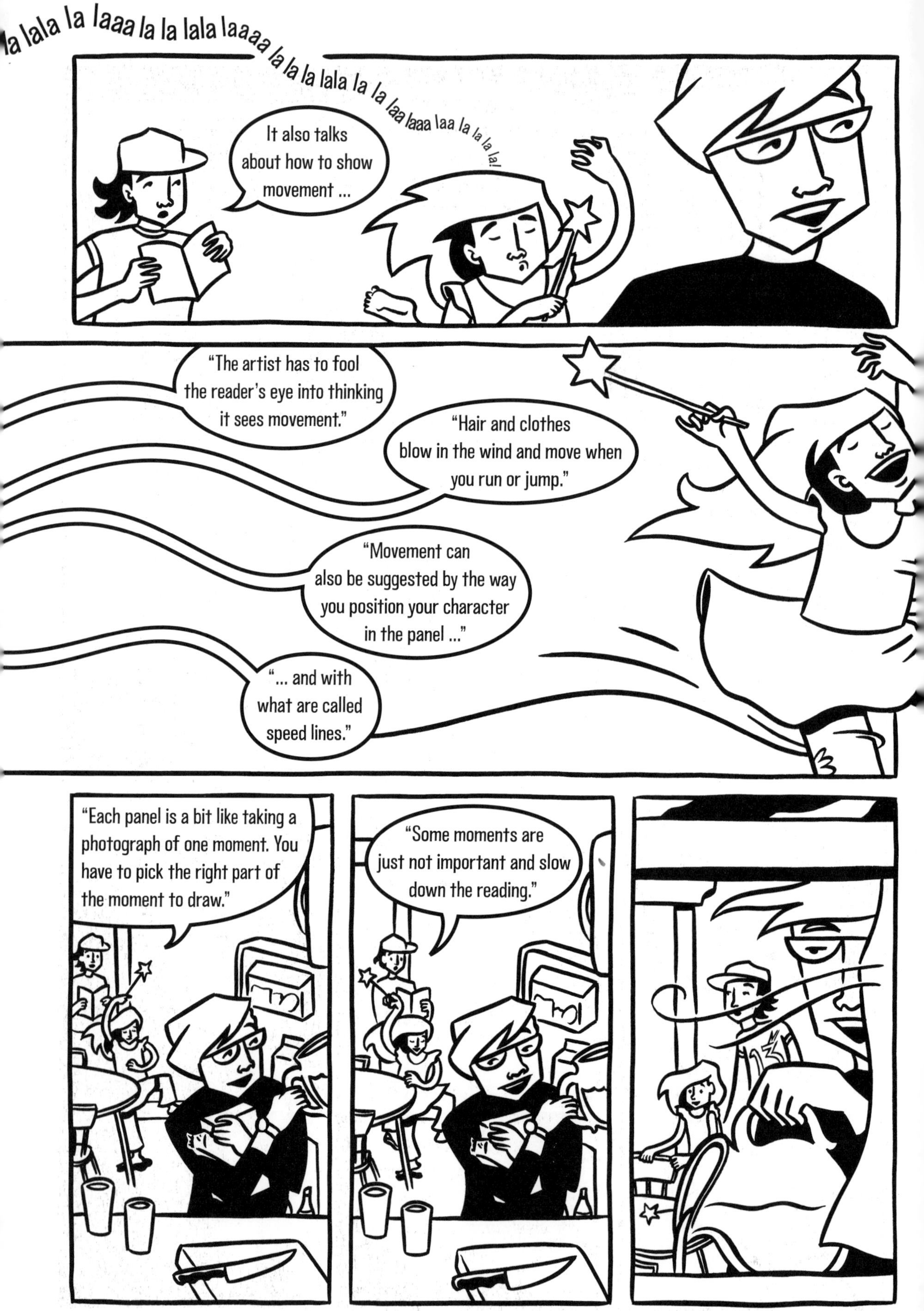
la lala la laaa la la lala laaaa la la lala la la laa laaa laa la la la la!
It also talks about how to show movement ...
"The artist has to fool the reader's eye into thinking it sees movement."
"Hair and clothes blow in the wind and move when you run or jump."
"Movement can also be suggested by the way you position your character in the panel ..."
"... and with what are called speed lines."
"Each panel is a bit like taking a photograph of one moment. You have to pick the right part of the moment to draw."
"Some moments are just not important and slow down the reading."

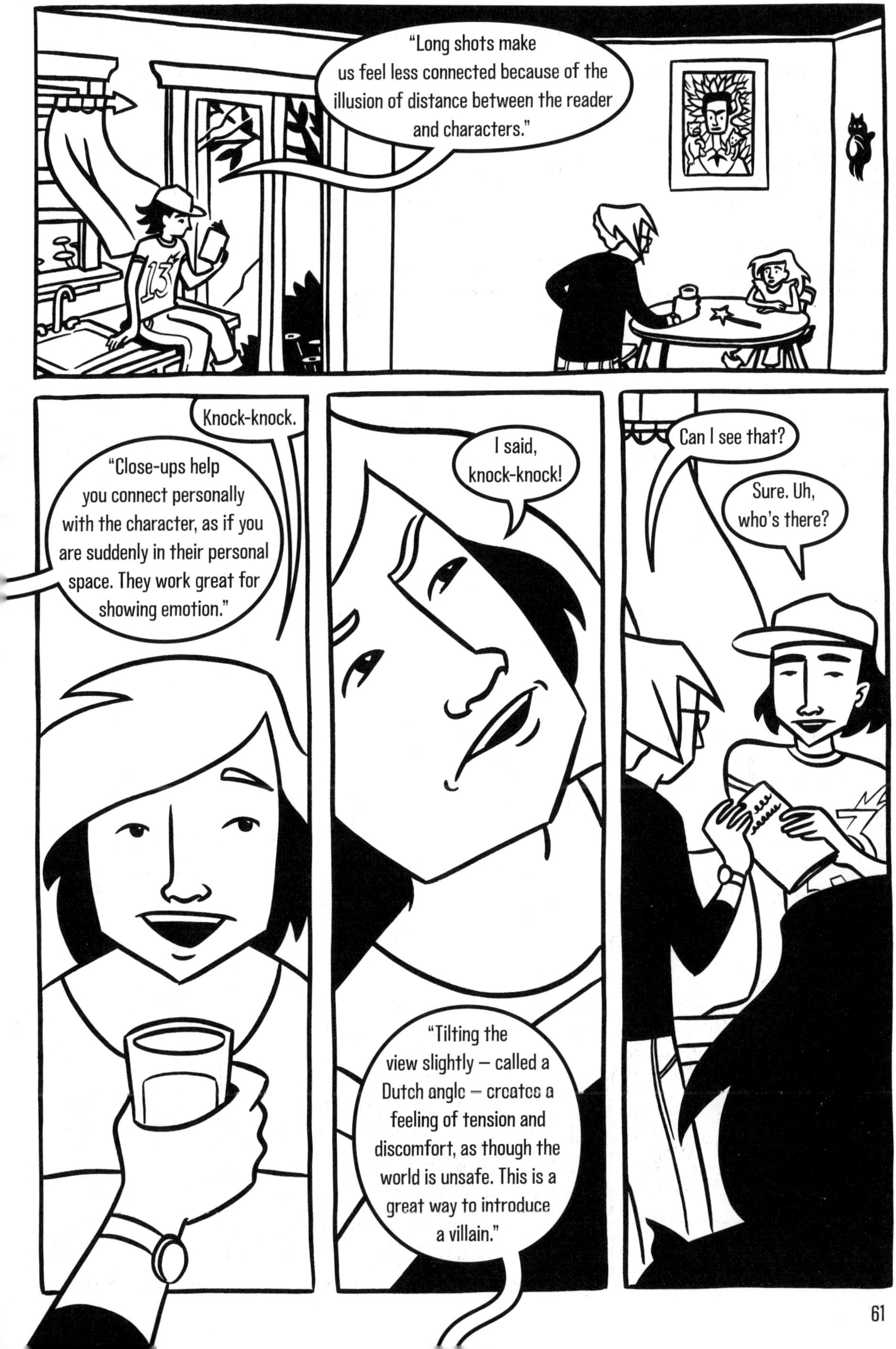
"Long shots make us feel less connected because of the illusion of distance between the reader and characters."
Knock-knock.
"Close-ups help you connect personally with the character, as if you are suddenly in their personal space. They work great for showing emotion."
I said, knock-knock!
"Tilting the view slightly – called a Dutch angle – creates a feeling of tension and discomfort, as though the world is unsafe. This is a great way to introduce a villain."
Can I see that?
Sure. Uh, who's there?

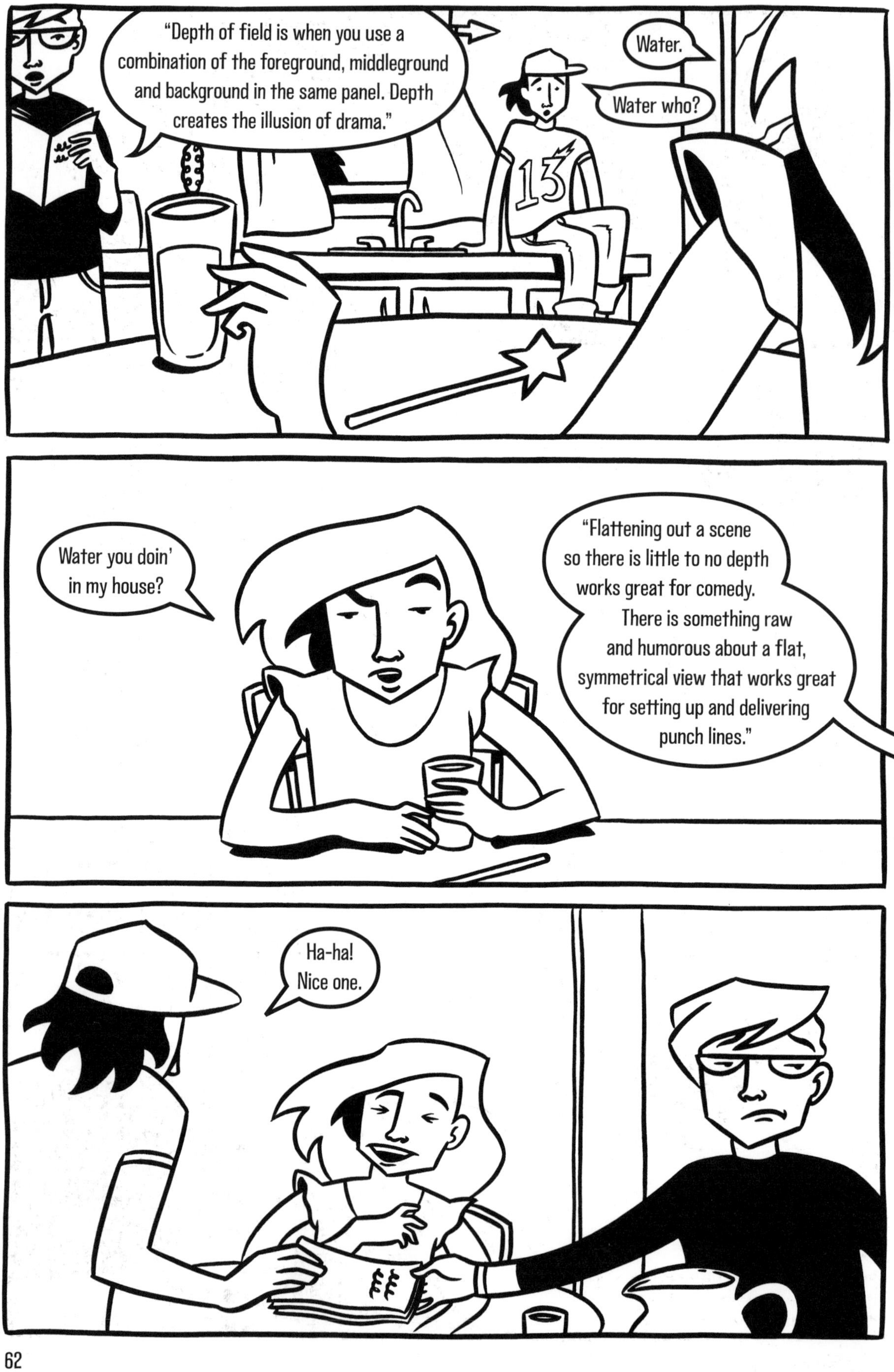
"Depth of field is when you use a combination of the foreground, middleground and background in the same panel. Depth creates the illusion of drama."
Water.
Water who?
Water you doin' in my house?
"Flattening out a scene so there is little to no depth works great for comedy. There is something raw and humorous about a flat, symmetrical view that works great for setting up and delivering punch lines."
Ha-ha! Nice one.

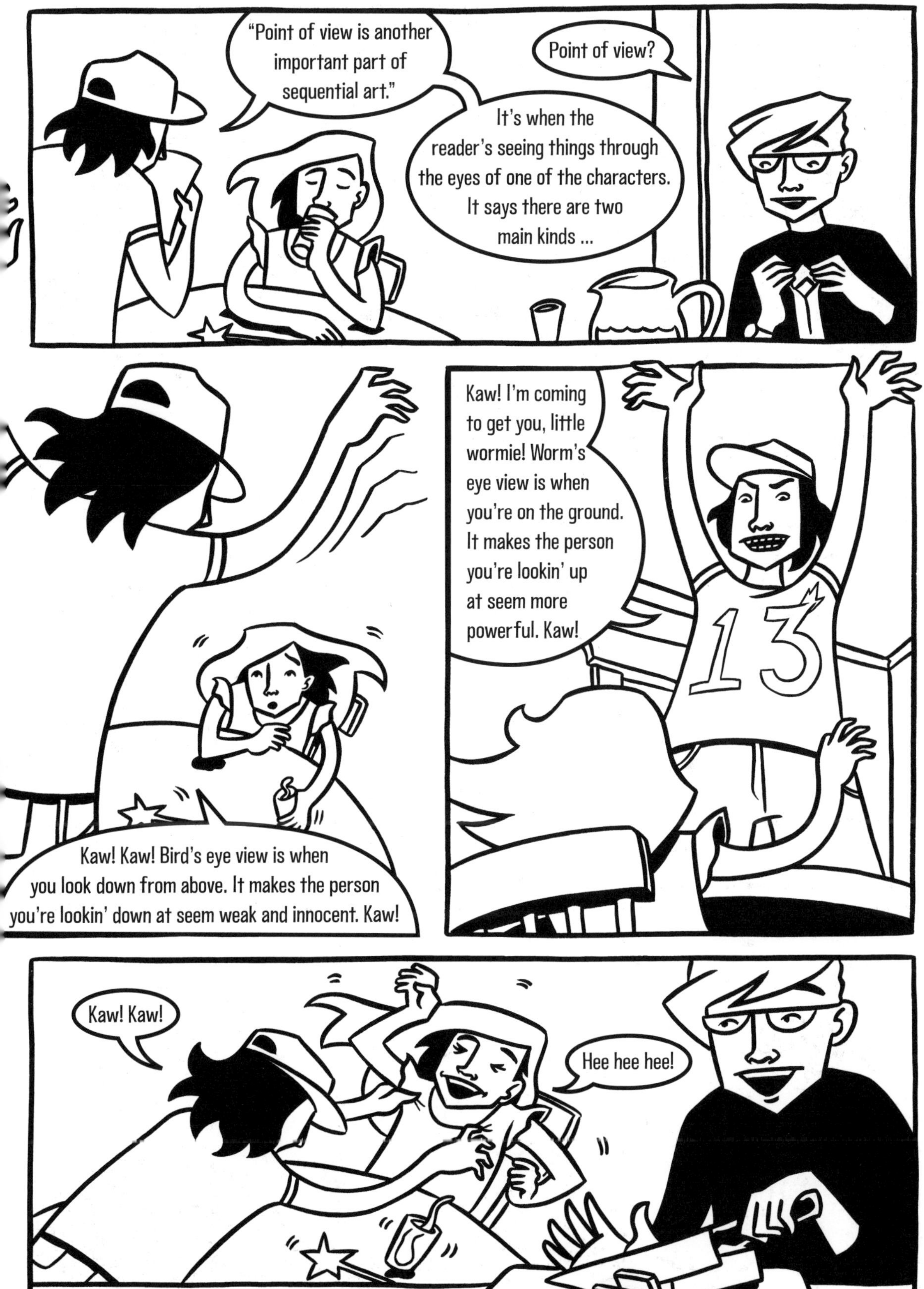
"Point of view is another important part of sequential art."
Point of view?
It's when the reader's seeing things through the eyes of one of the characters. It says there are two main kinds ...
Kaw! Kaw! Bird's eye view is when you look down from above. It makes the person you're lookin' down at seem weak and innocent. Kaw!
Kaw! I'm coming to get you, little wormie! Worm's eye view is when you're on the ground. It makes the person you're lookin' up at seem more powerful. Kaw!
Kaw! Kaw!
Hee hee hee!

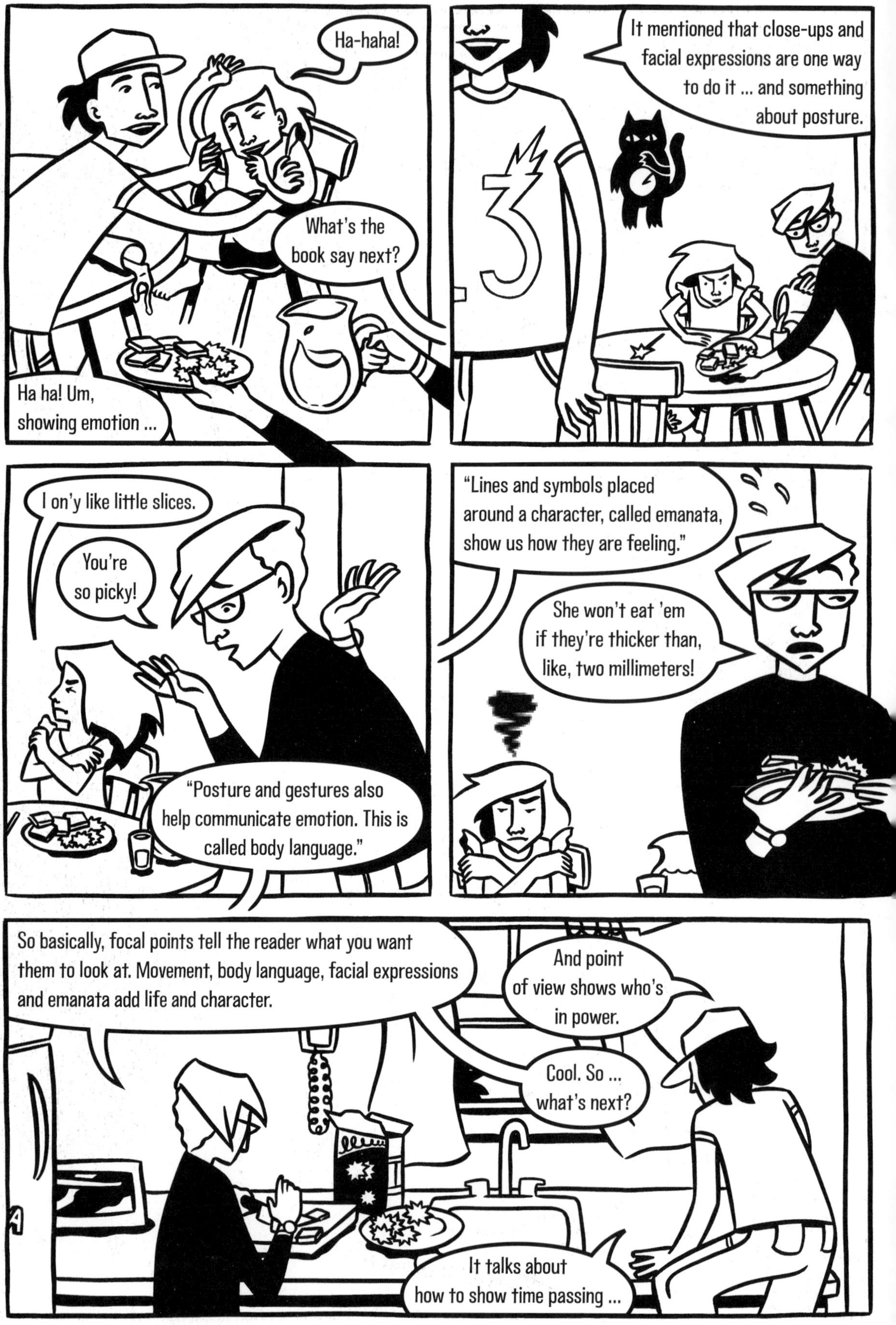
Ha-haha!
What's the book say next?
Ha ha! Um, showing emotion ...
It mentioned that close-ups and facial expressions are one way to do it ... and something about posture.
I on'y like little slices.
You're so picky!
"Posture and gestures also help communicate emotion. This is called body language."
"Lines and symbols placed around a character, called emanata, show us how they are feeling."
She won't eat 'em if they're thicker than, like, two millimeters!
So basically, focal points tell the reader what you want them to look at. Movement, body language, facial expressions and emanata add life and character.
And point of view shows who's in power.
Cool. So ... what's next?
It talks about how to show time passing ...

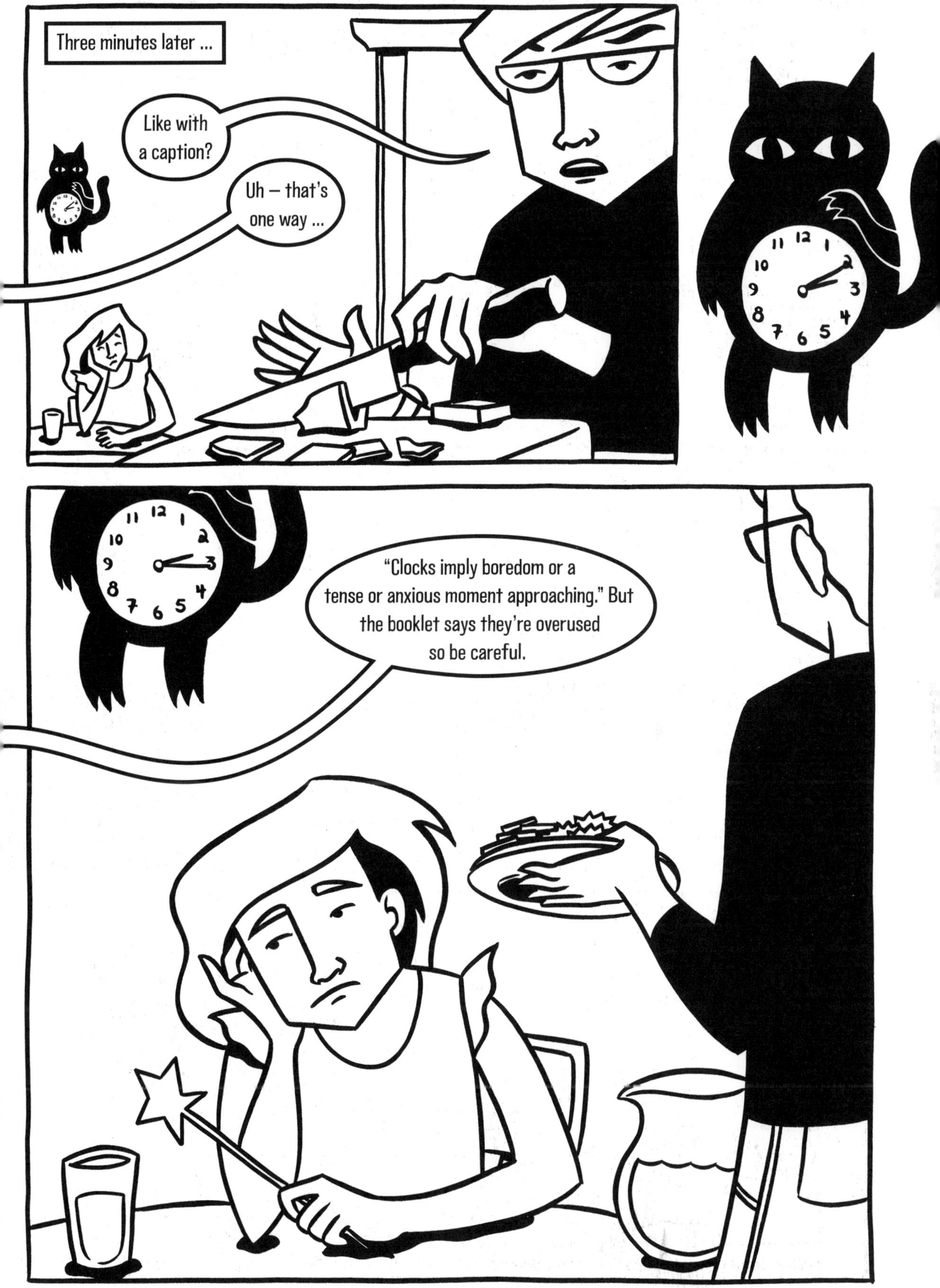
Three minutes later ...
Like with a caption?
Uh – that's one way ...
"Clocks imply boredom or a tense or anxious moment approaching." But the booklet says they're overused so be careful.

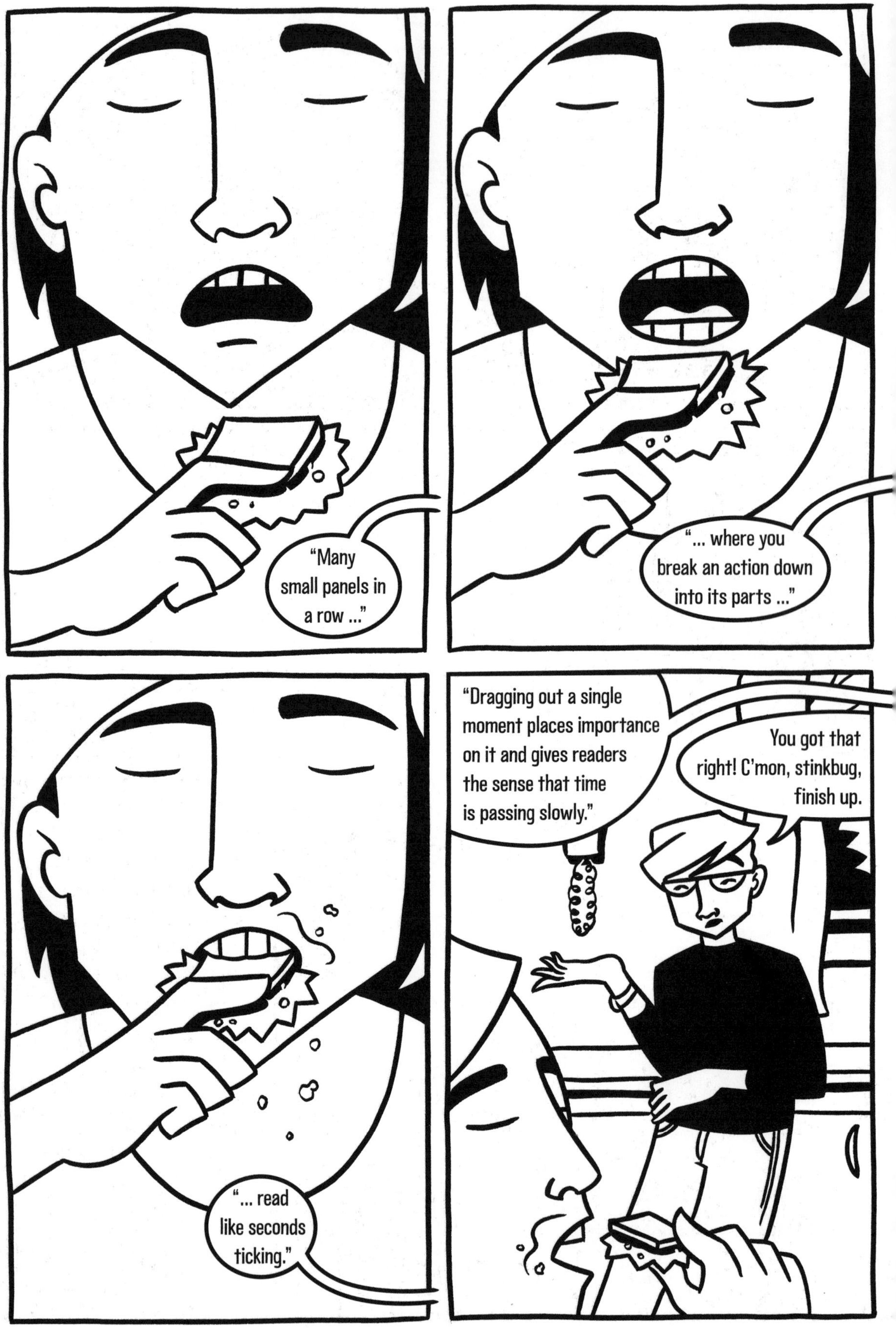
"Many small panels in a row ..."
"... where you break an action down into its parts ..."
"... read like seconds ticking."
"Dragging out a single moment places importance on it and gives readers the sense that time is passing slowly."
You got that right! C'mon, stinkbug, finish up.

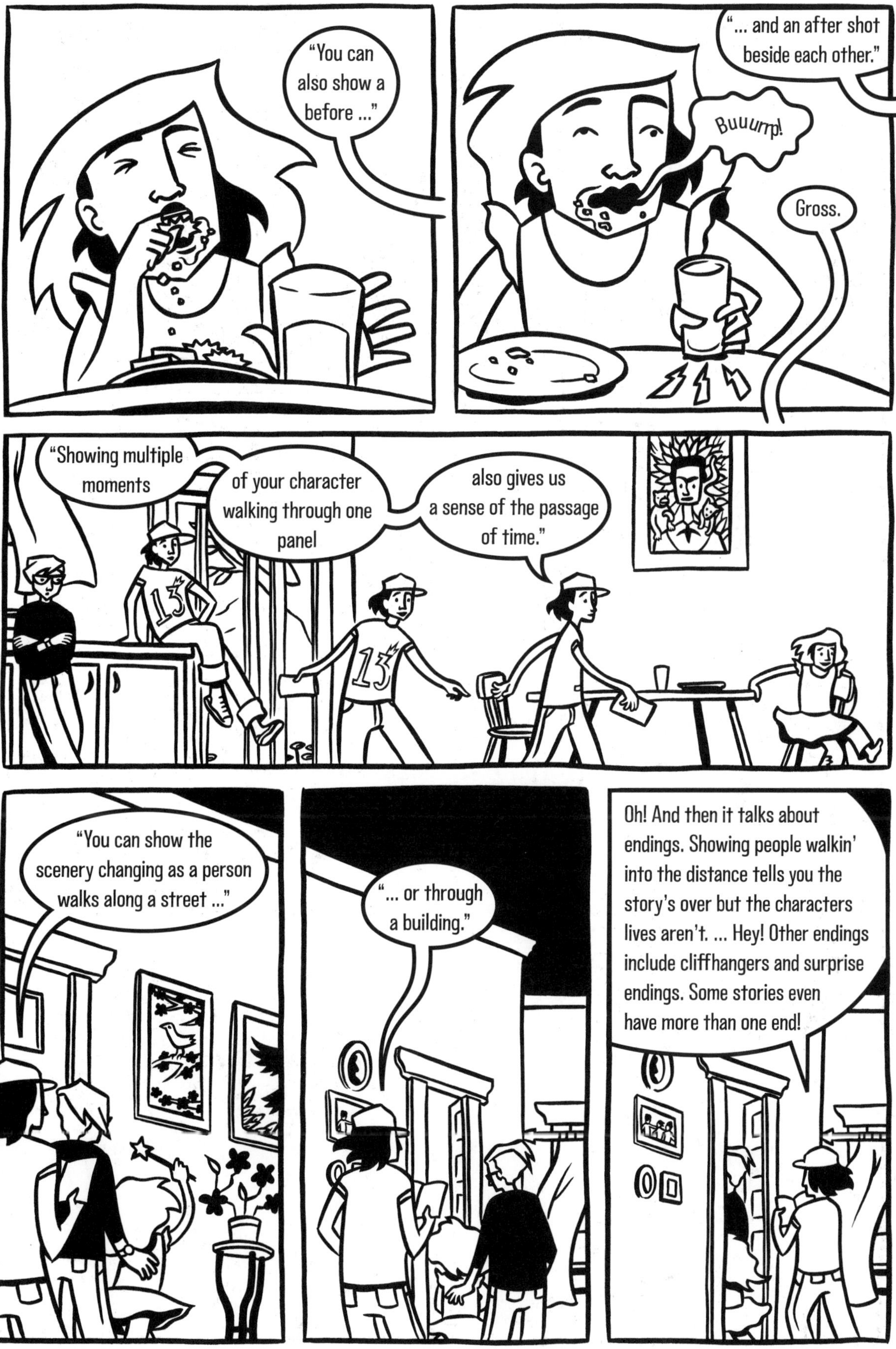
"You can also show a before ..."
"... and an after shot beside each other."
Buuurrp!
Gross.
"Showing multiple moments
of your character walking through one panel
also gives us a sense of the passage of time."
"You can show the scenery changing as a person walks along a street ..."
"... or through a building."
Oh! And then it talks about endings. Showing people walkin' into the distance tells you the story's over but the characters lives aren't. ... Hey! Other endings include cliffhangers and surprise endings. Some stories even have more than one end!

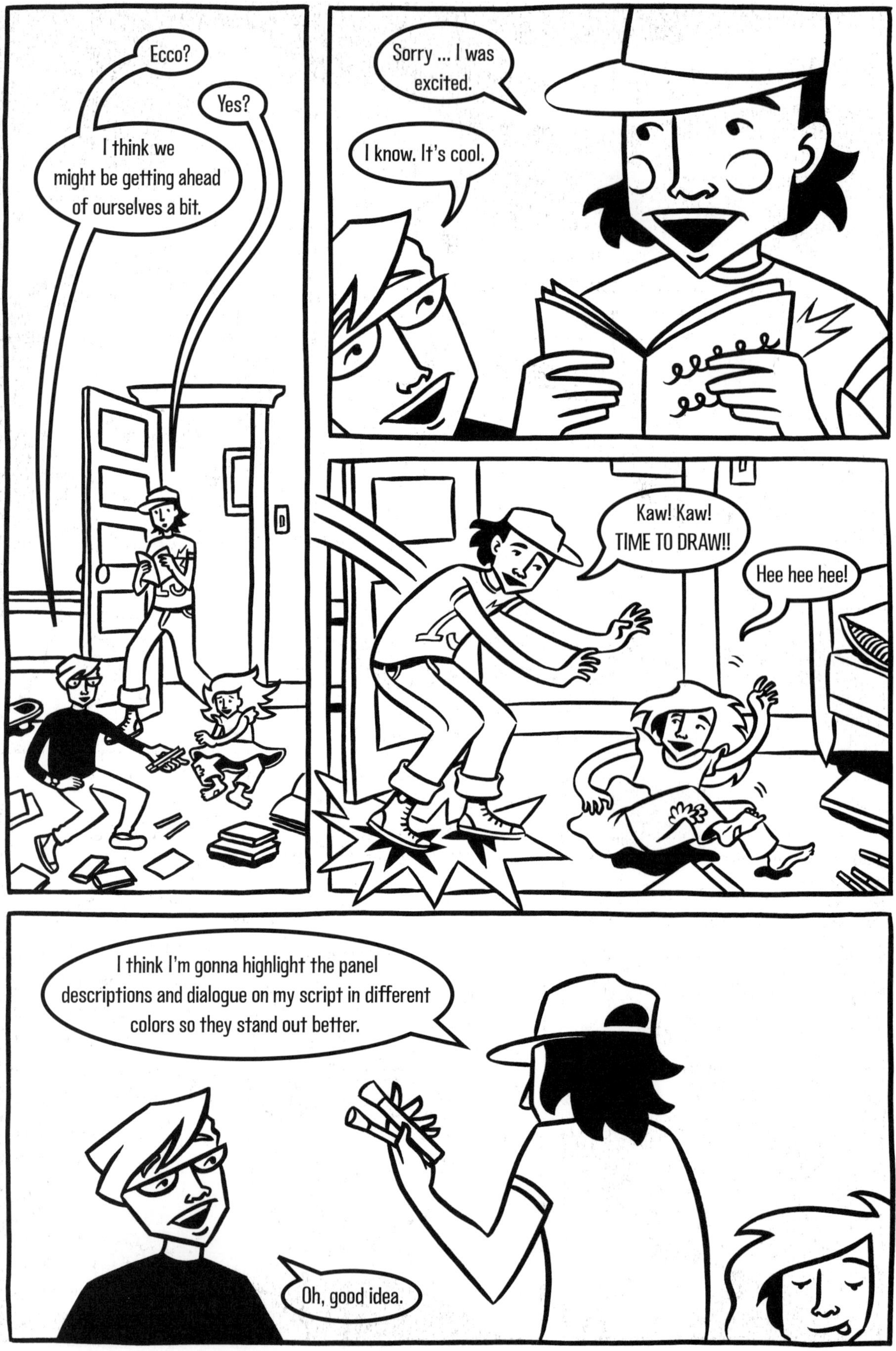
Ecco?
Yes?
I think we might be getting ahead of ourselves a bit.
Sorry ... I was excited.
I know. It's cool.
Kaw! Kaw! TIME TO DRAW!!
Hee hee hee!
I think I'm gonna highlight the panel descriptions and dialogue on my script in different colors so they stand out better.
Oh, good idea.

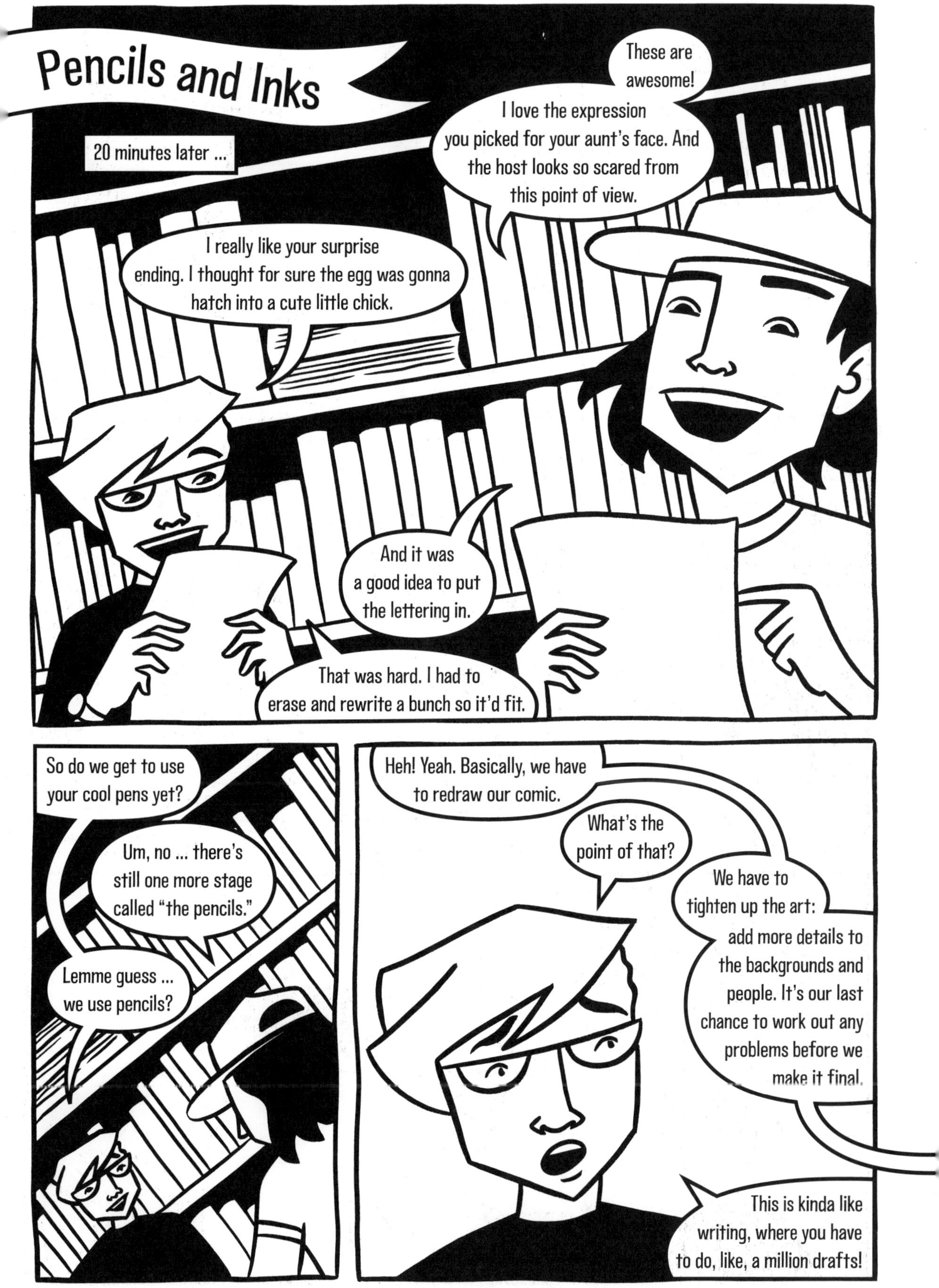
Pencils and Inks
20 minutes later ...
These are awesome!
I love the expression you picked for your aunt's face. And the host looks so scared from this point of view.
I really like your surprise ending. I thought for sure the egg was gonna hatch into a cute little chick.
And it was a good idea to put the lettering in.
That was hard. I had to erase and rewrite a bunch so it'd fit.
So do we get to use your cool pens yet?
Um, no ... there's still one more stage called "the pencils."
Lemme guess ... we use pencils?
Heh! Yeah. Basically, we have to redraw our comic.
What's the point of that?
We have to tighten up the art: add more details to the backgrounds and people. It's our last chance to work out any problems before we make it final.
This is kinda like writing, where you have to do, like, a million drafts!

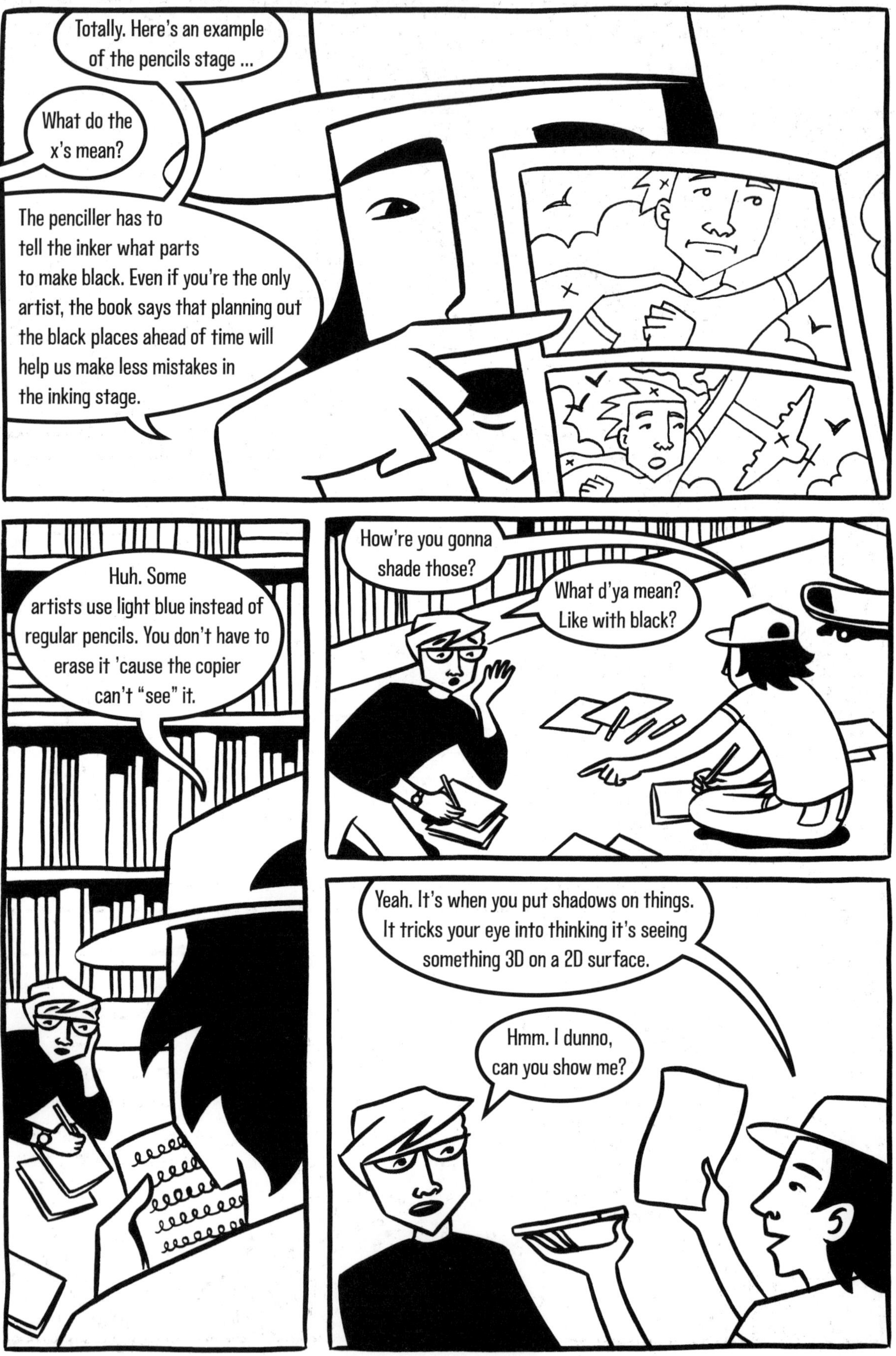
Totally. Here's an example of the pencils stage ...
What do the x's mean?
The penciller has to tell the inker what parts to make black. Even if you're the only artist, the book says that planning out the black places ahead of time will help us make less mistakes in the inking stage.
Huh. Some artists use light blue instead of regular pencils. You don't have to erase it 'cause the copier can't "see" it.
How're you gonna shade those?
What d'ya mean? Like with black?
Yeah. It's when you put shadows on things. It tricks your eye into thinking it's seeing something 3D on a 2D surface.
Hmm. I dunno, can you show me?

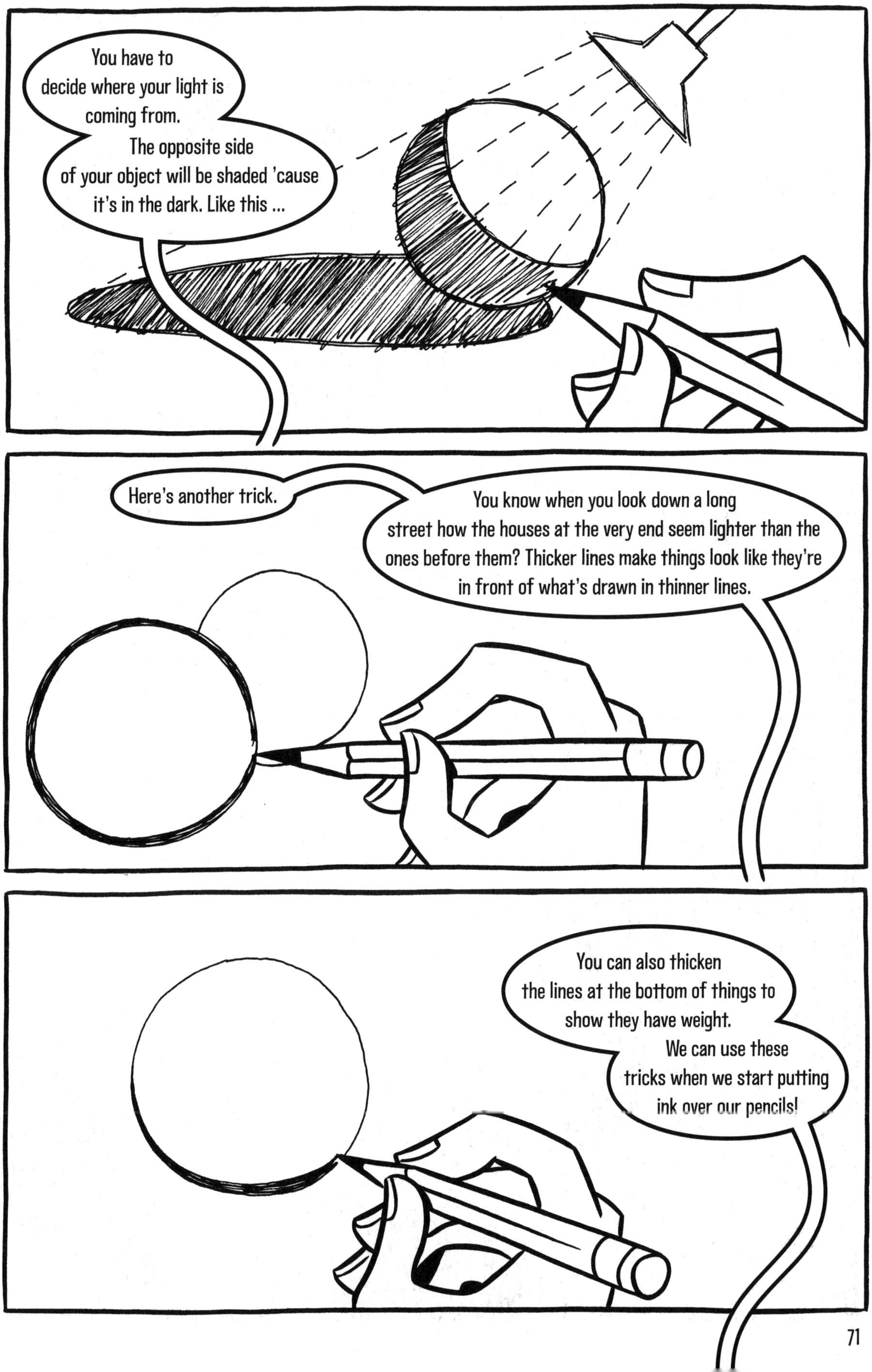
You have to decide where your light is coming from. The opposite side of your object will be shaded 'cause it's in the dark. Like this ...
Here's another trick.
You know when you look down a long street how the houses at the very end seem lighter than the ones before them? Thicker lines make things look like they're in front of what's drawn in thinner lines.
You can also thicken the lines at the bottom of things to show they have weight. We can use these tricks when we start putting ink over our pencils!

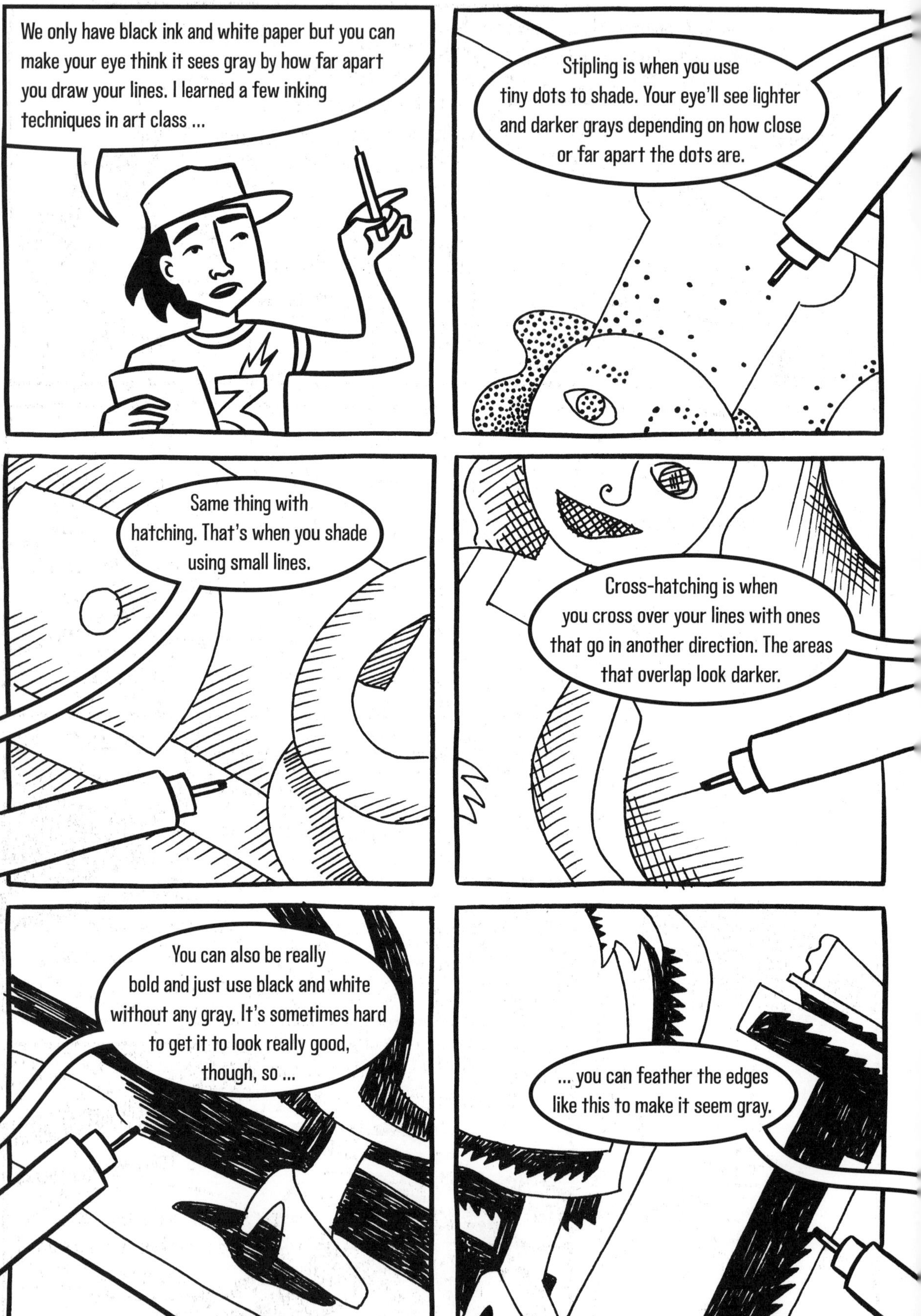
We only have black ink and white paper but you can make your eye think it sees gray by how far apart you draw your lines. I learned a few inking techniques in art class ...
Stipling is when you use tiny dots to shade. Your eye'll see lighter and darker grays depending on how close or far apart the dots are.
Same thing with hatching. That's when you shade using small lines.
Cross-hatching is when you cross over your lines with ones that go in another direction. The areas that overlap look darker.
You can also be really bold and just use black and white without any gray. It's sometimes hard to get it to look really good, though, so ...
... you can feather the edges like this to make it seem gray.

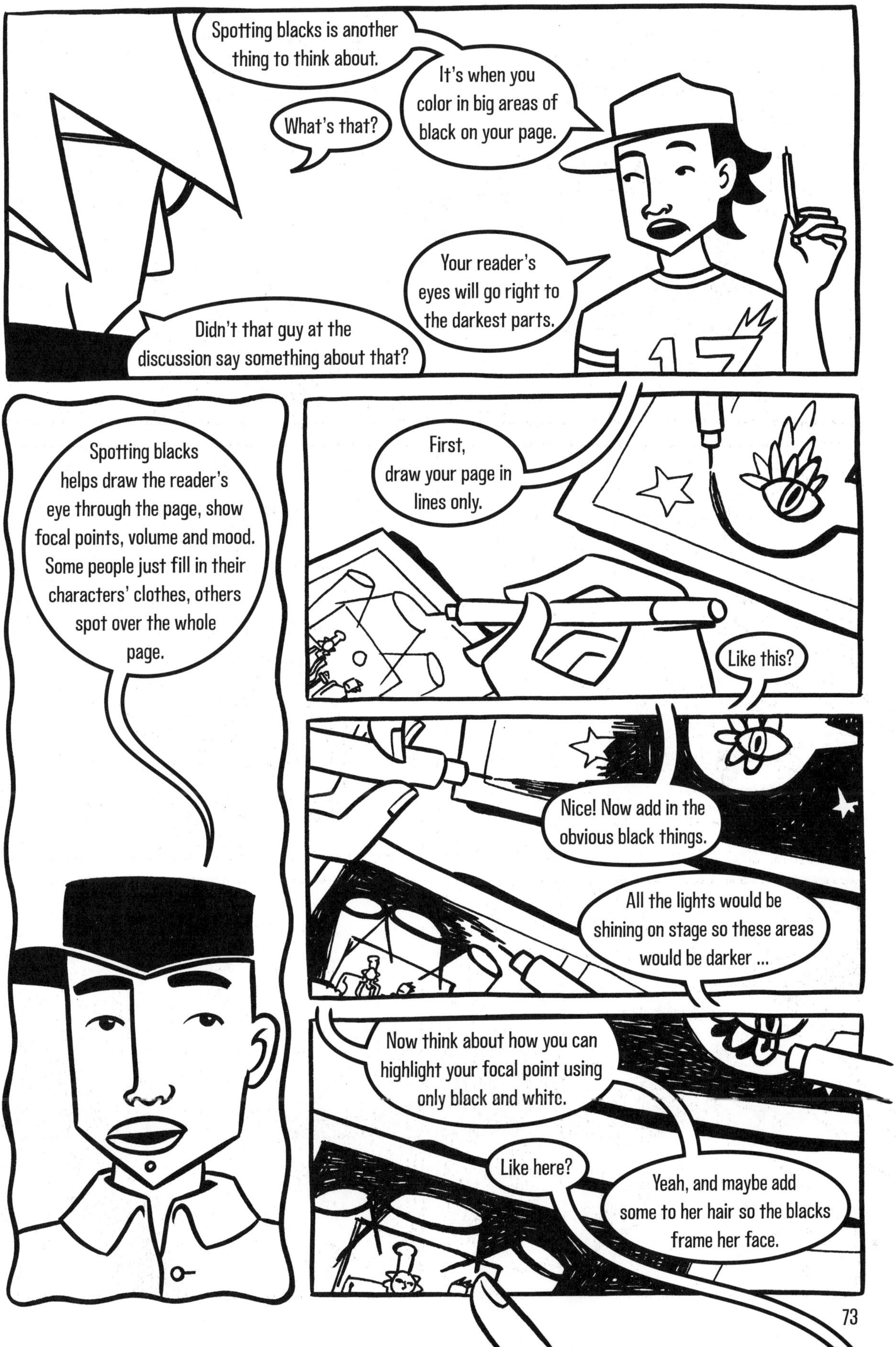
Spotting blacks is another thing to think about.
What's that?
It's when you color in big areas of black on your page.
Your reader's eyes will go right to the darkest parts.
Didn't that guy at the discussion say something about that?
Spotting blacks helps draw the reader's eye through the page, show focal points, volume and mood. Some people just fill in their characters' clothes, others spot over the whole page.
First, draw your page in lines only.
Like this?
Nice! Now add in the obvious black things.
All the lights would be shining on stage so these areas would be darker ...
Now think about how you can highlight your focal point using only black and white.
Like here?
Yeah, and maybe add some to her hair so the blacks frame her face.

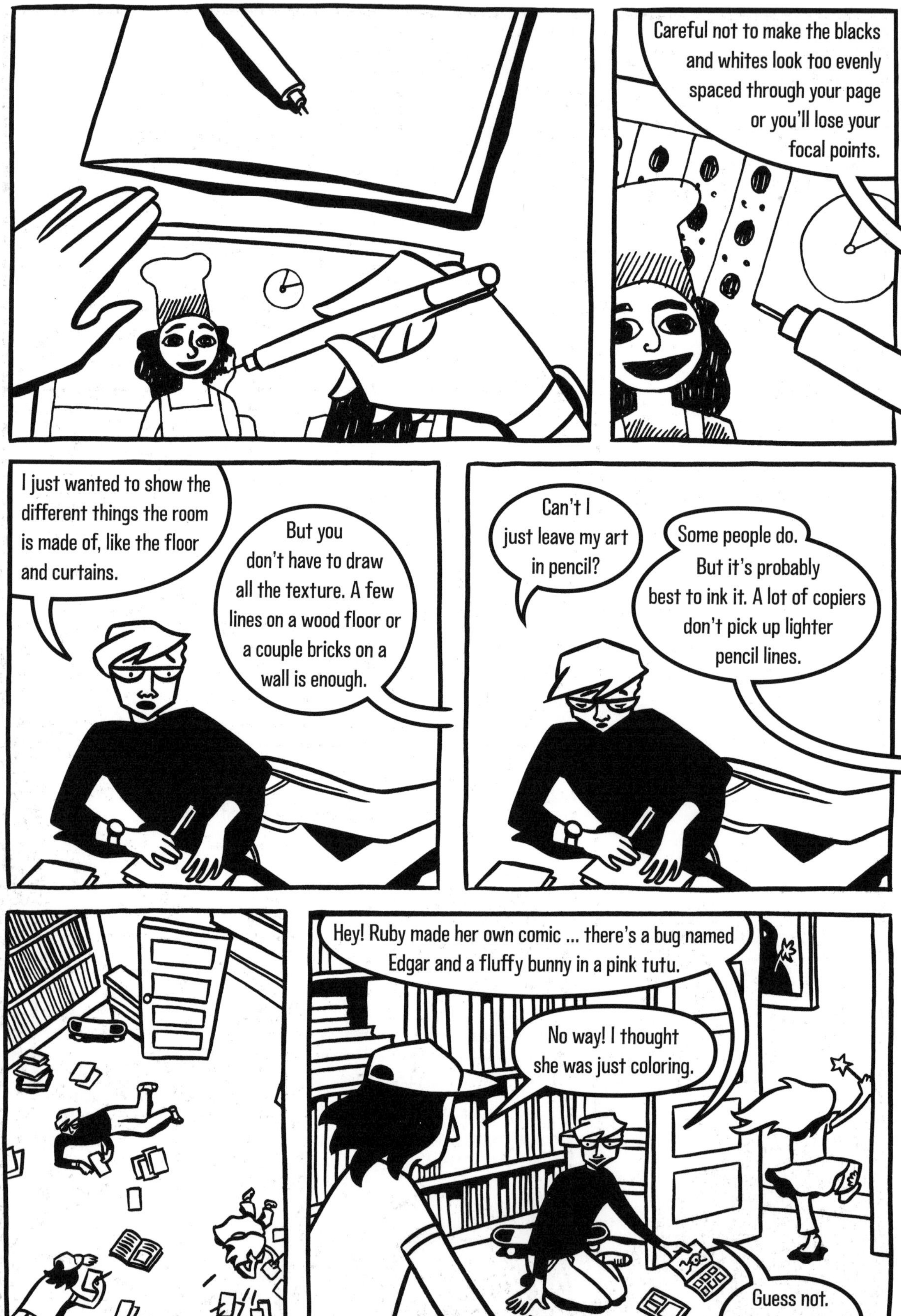
Careful not to make the blacks and whites look too evenly spaced through your page or you'll lose your focal points.
I just wanted to show the different things the room is made of, like the floor and curtains.
But you don't have to draw all the texture. A few lines on a wood floor or a couple bricks on a wall is enough.
Can't I just leave my art in pencil?
Some people do. But it's probably best to ink it. A lot of copiers don't pick up lighter pencil lines.
Hey! Ruby made her own comic ... there's a bug named Edgar and a fluffy bunny in a pink tutu.
No way! I thought she was just coloring.
Guess not. This is hilarious!

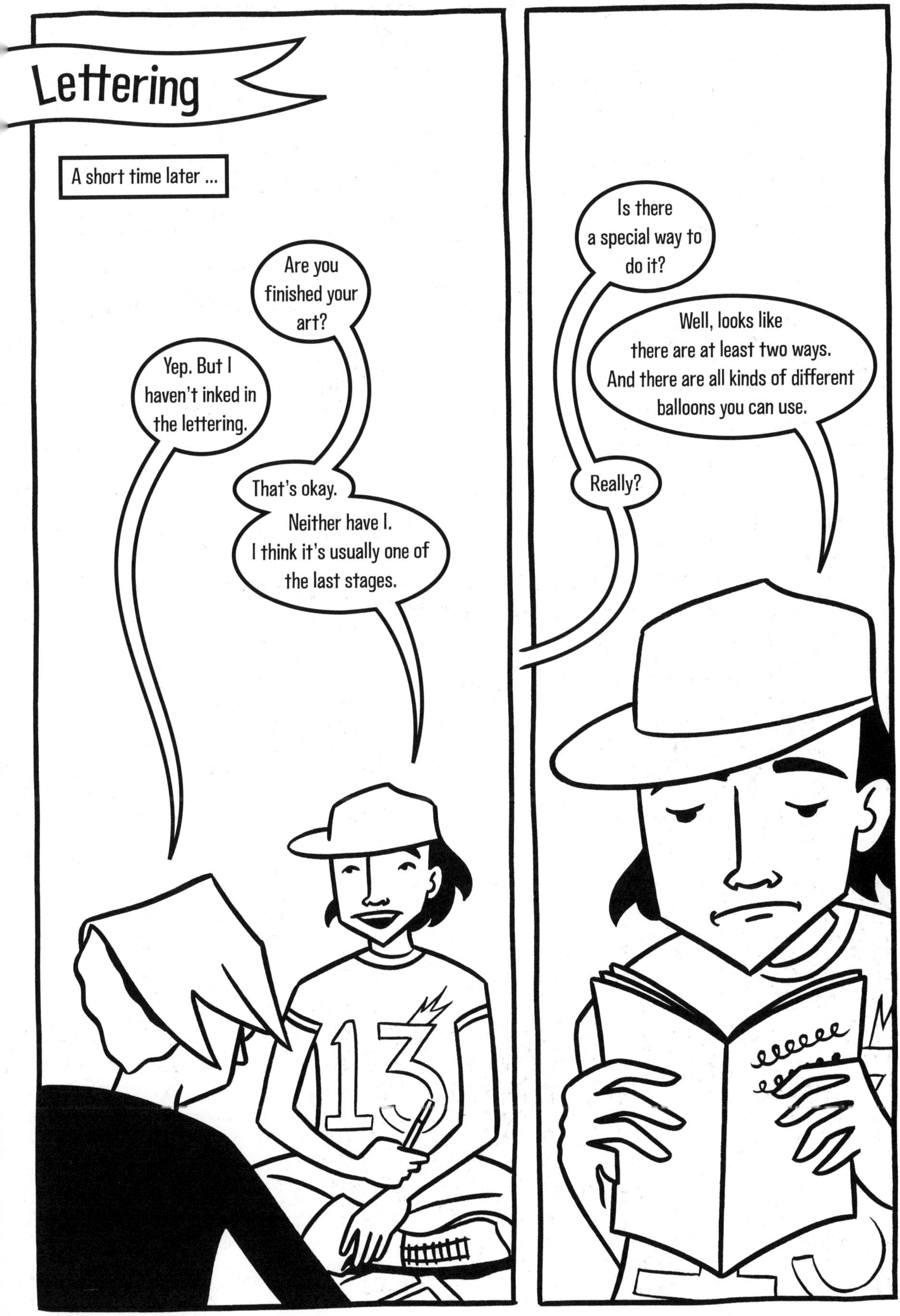
Lettering
A short time later ...
Are you finished your art?
Yep. But I haven't inked in the lettering.
That's okay.
Neither have I. I think it's usually one of the last stages.
Is there a special way to do it?
Well, looks like there are at least two ways. And there are all kinds of different balloons you can use.
Really?

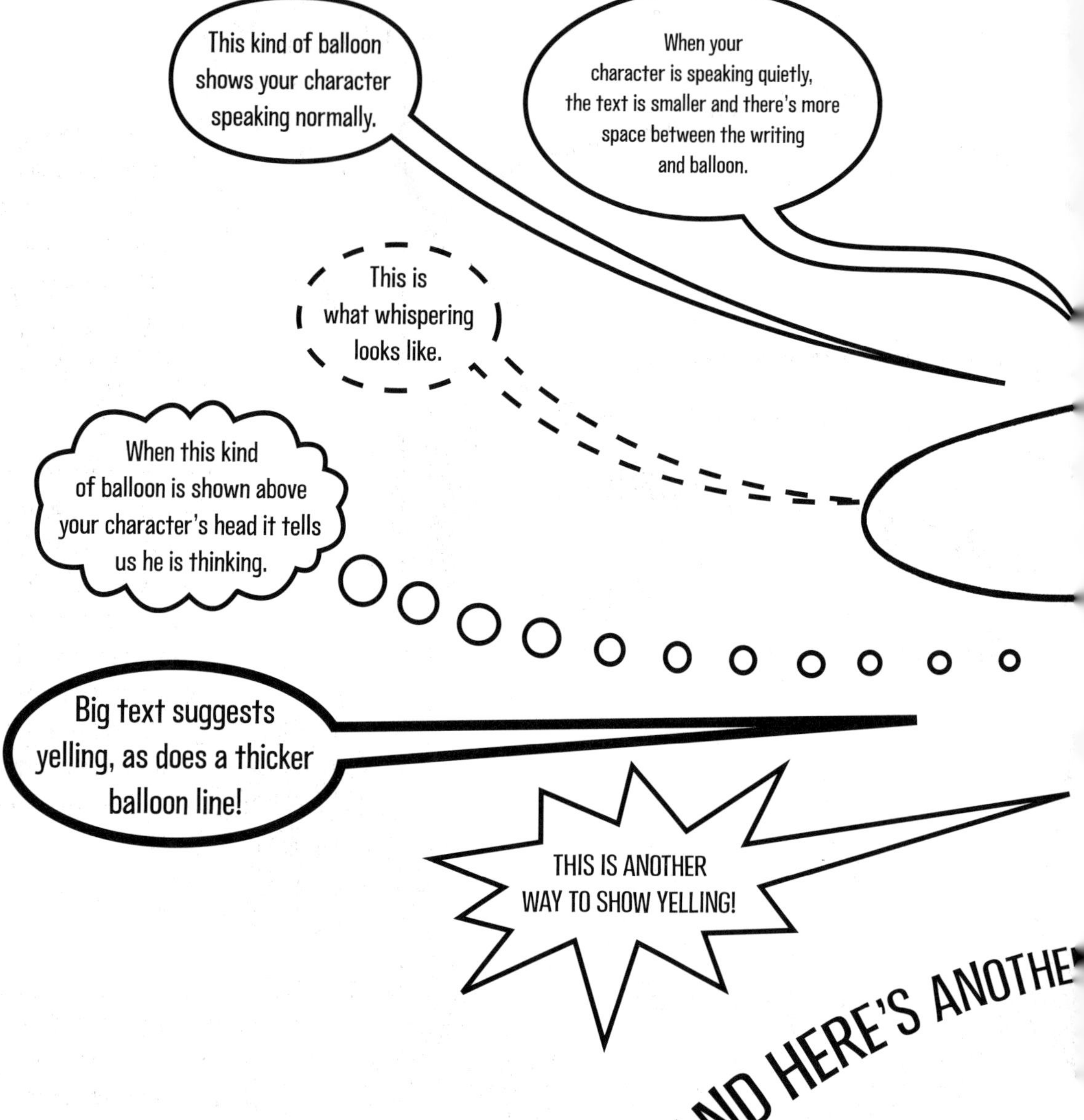
This kind of balloon shows your character speaking normally.
When your character is speaking quietly, the text is smaller and there's more space between the writing and balloon.
This is what whispering looks like.
When this kind of balloon is shown above your character's head it tells us he is thinking.
Big text suggests yelling, as does a thicker balloon line!
THIS IS ANOTHER WAY TO SHOW YELLING!
AND HERE'S ANOTHE

SFX – short for sound effects – are sound words like

KRUNCH

& BAM

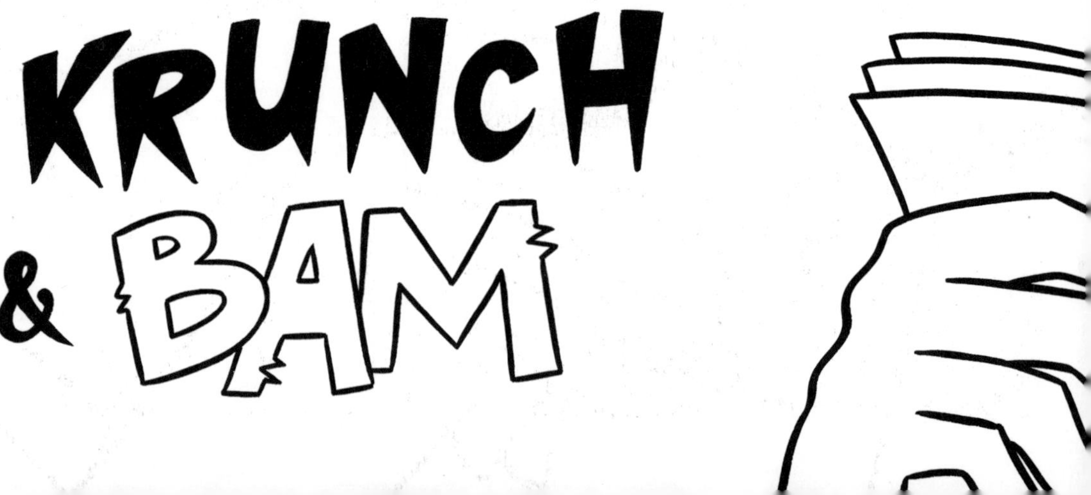

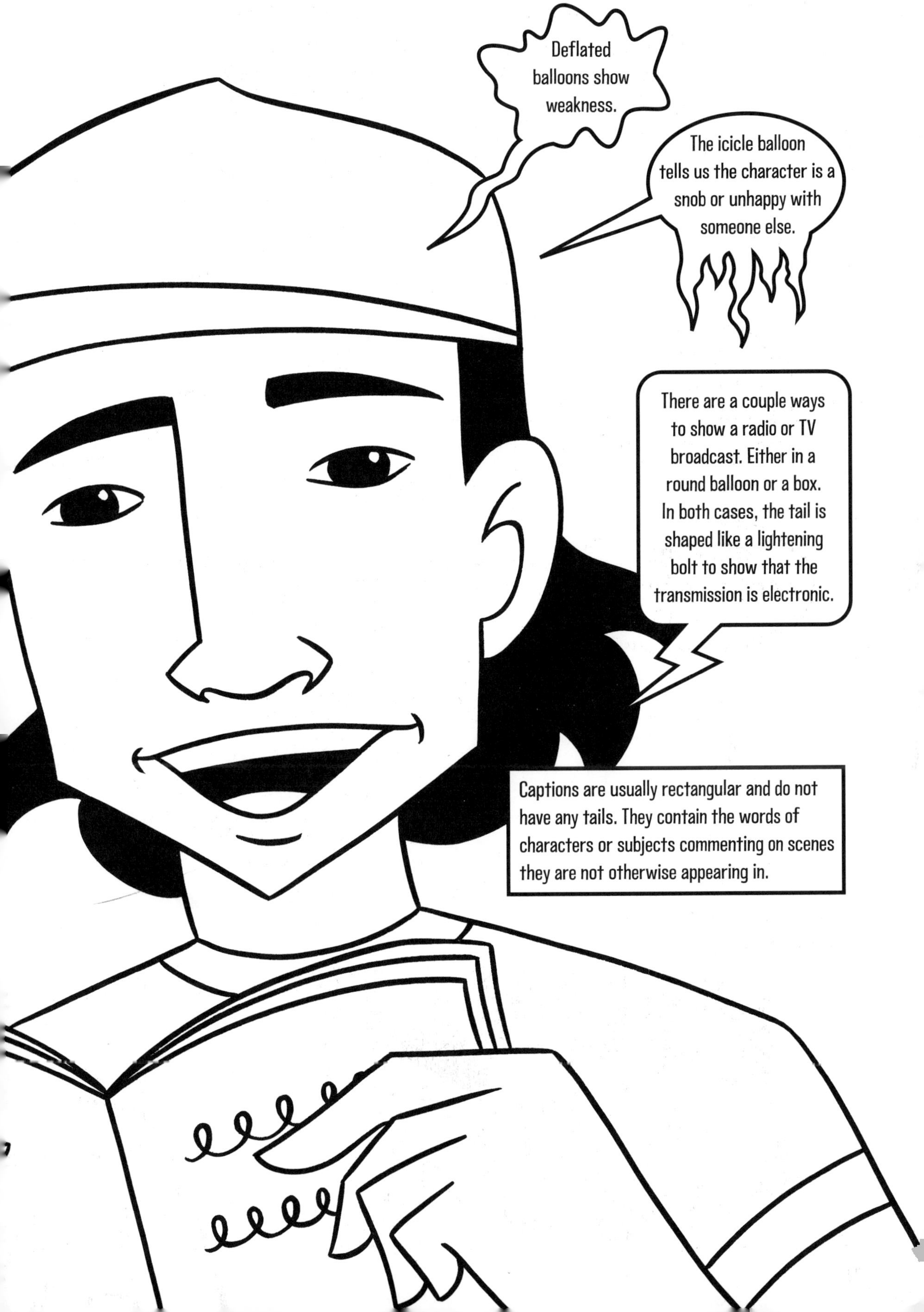
Deflated balloons show weakness.
The icicle balloon tells us the character is a snob or unhappy with someone else.
There are a couple ways to show a radio or TV broadcast. Either in a round balloon or a box. In both cases, the tail is shaped like a lightening bolt to show that the transmission is electronic.
Captions are usually rectangular and do not have any tails. They contain the words of characters or subjects commenting on scenes they are not otherwise appearing in.

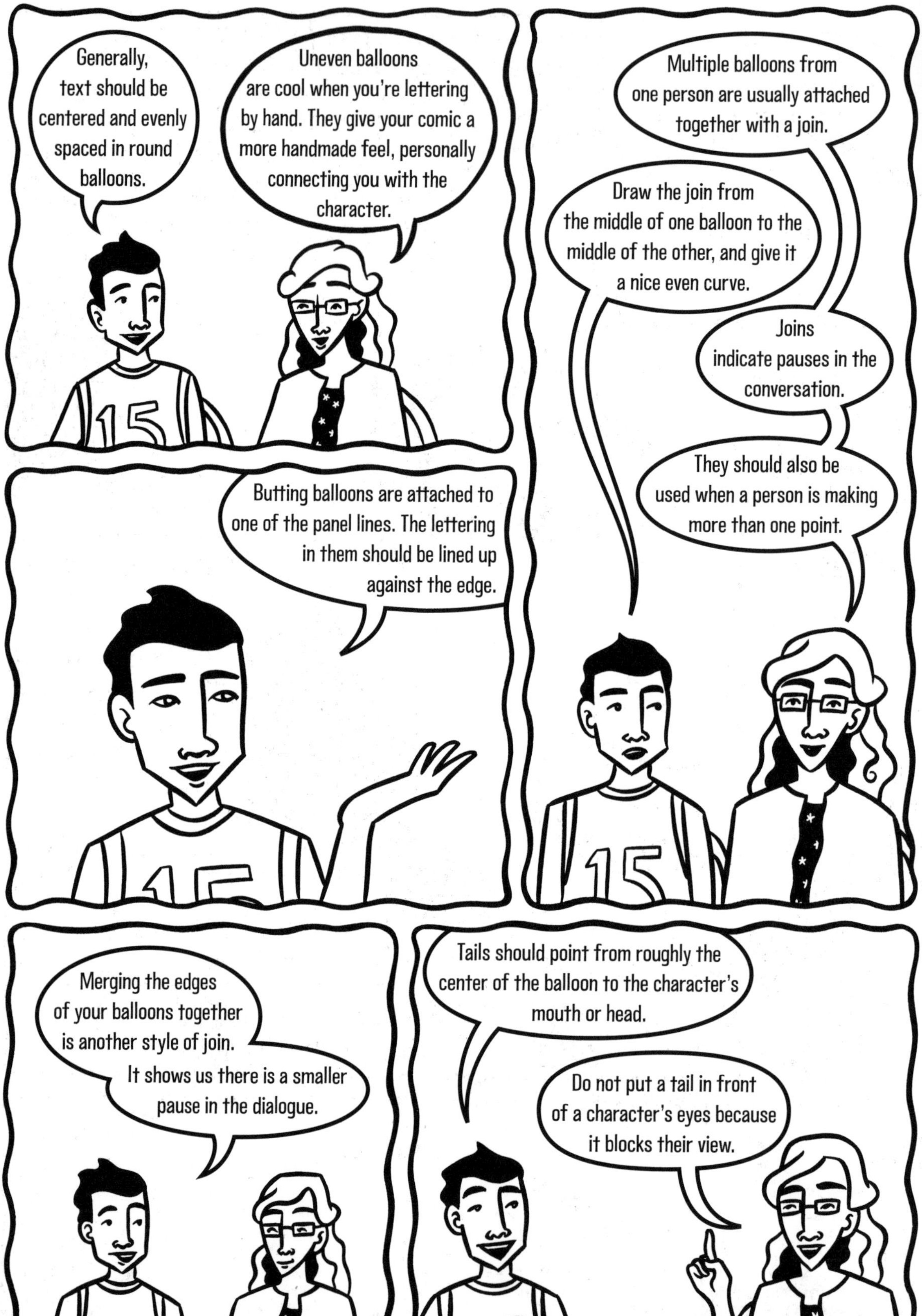
Generally, text should be centered and evenly spaced in round balloons.
Uneven balloons are cool when you're lettering by hand. They give your comic a more handmade feel, personally connecting you with the character.
Butting balloons are attached to one of the panel lines. The lettering in them should be lined up against the edge.
Multiple balloons from one person are usually attached together with a join.
Draw the join from the middle of one balloon to the middle of the other, and give it a nice even curve.
Joins indicate pauses in the conversation.
They should also be used when a person is making more than one point.
Merging the edges of your balloons together is another style of join.
It shows us there is a smaller pause in the dialogue.
Tails should point from roughly the center of the balloon to the character's mouth or head.
Do not put a tail in front of a character's eyes because it blocks their view.

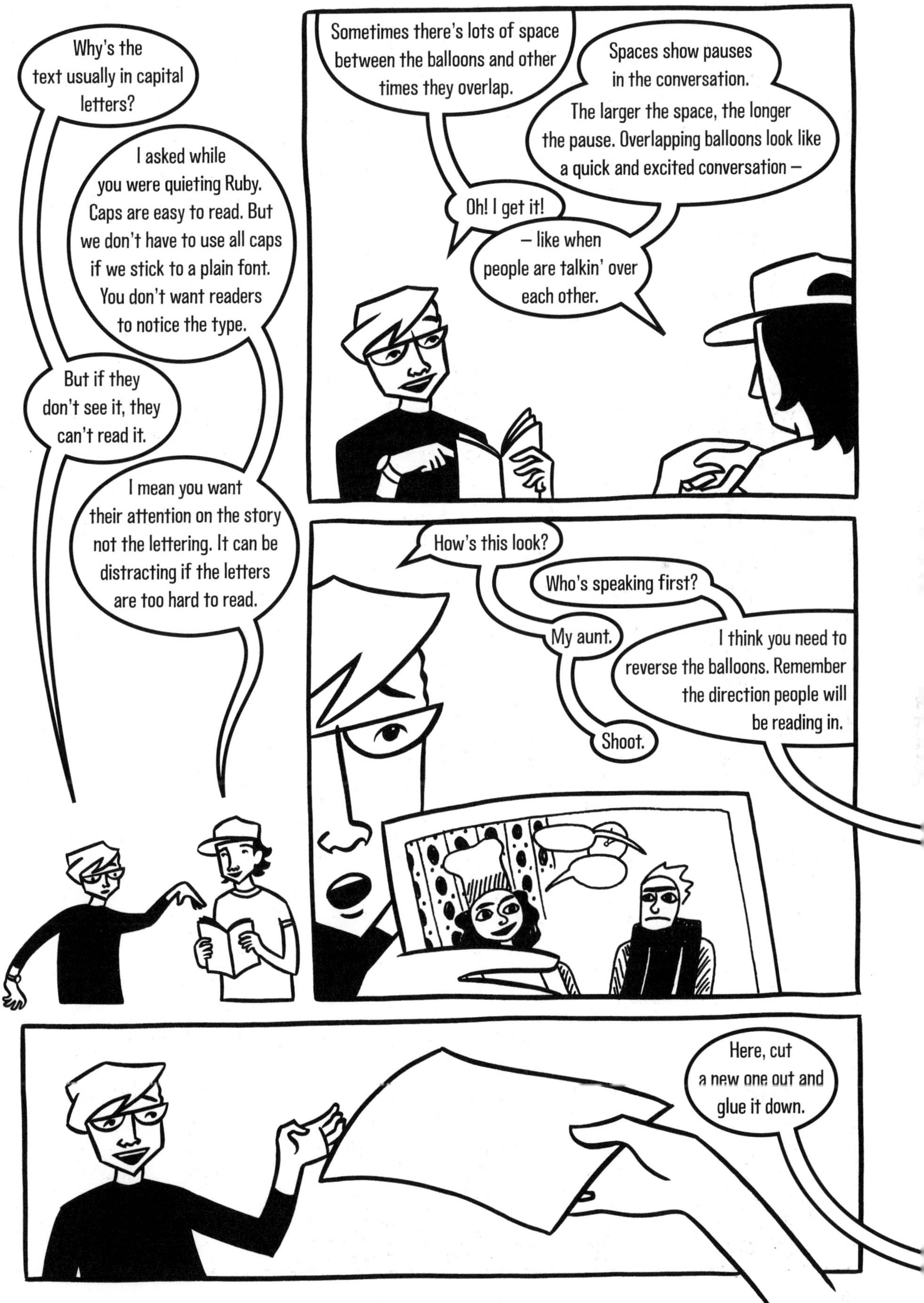

Why's the text usually in capital letters?
I asked while you were quieting Ruby. Caps are easy to read. But we don't have to use all caps if we stick to a plain font. You don't want readers to notice the type.
But if they don't see it, they can't read it.
I mean you want their attention on the story not the lettering. It can be distracting if the letters are too hard to read.
Sometimes there's lots of space between the balloons and other times they overlap.
Spaces show pauses in the conversation.
The larger the space, the longer the pause. Overlapping balloons look like a quick and excited conversation –
Oh! I get it!
– like when people are talkin' over each other.
How's this look?
Who's speaking first?
My aunt.
I think you need to reverse the balloons. Remember the direction people will be reading in.
Shoot.
Here, cut a new one out and glue it down.

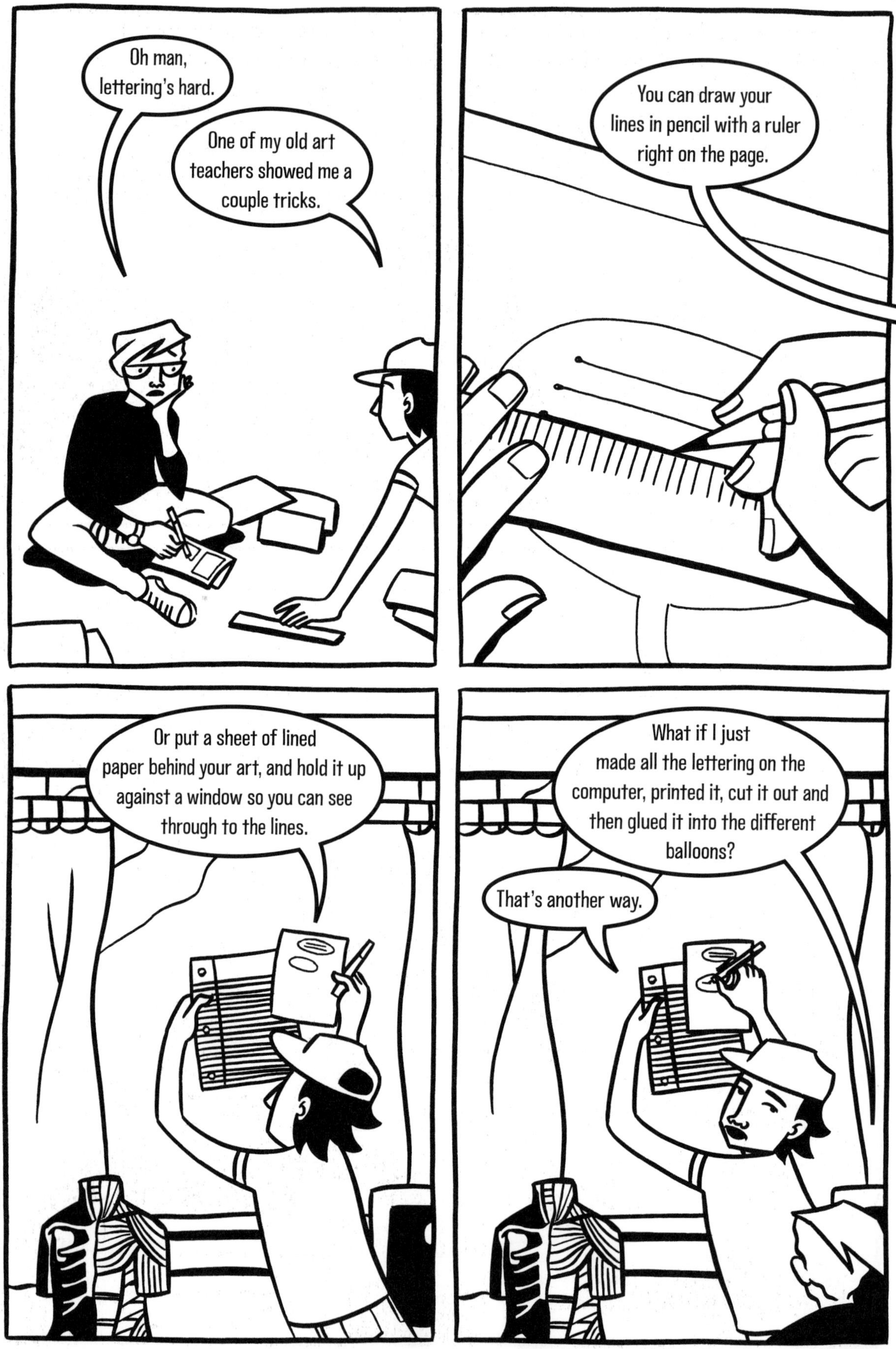
Oh man, lettering's hard.
One of my old art teachers showed me a couple tricks.
You can draw your lines in pencil with a ruler right on the page.
Or put a sheet of lined paper behind your art, and hold it up against a window so you can see through to the lines.
What if I just made all the lettering on the computer, printed it, cut it out and then glued it into the different balloons?
That's another way.

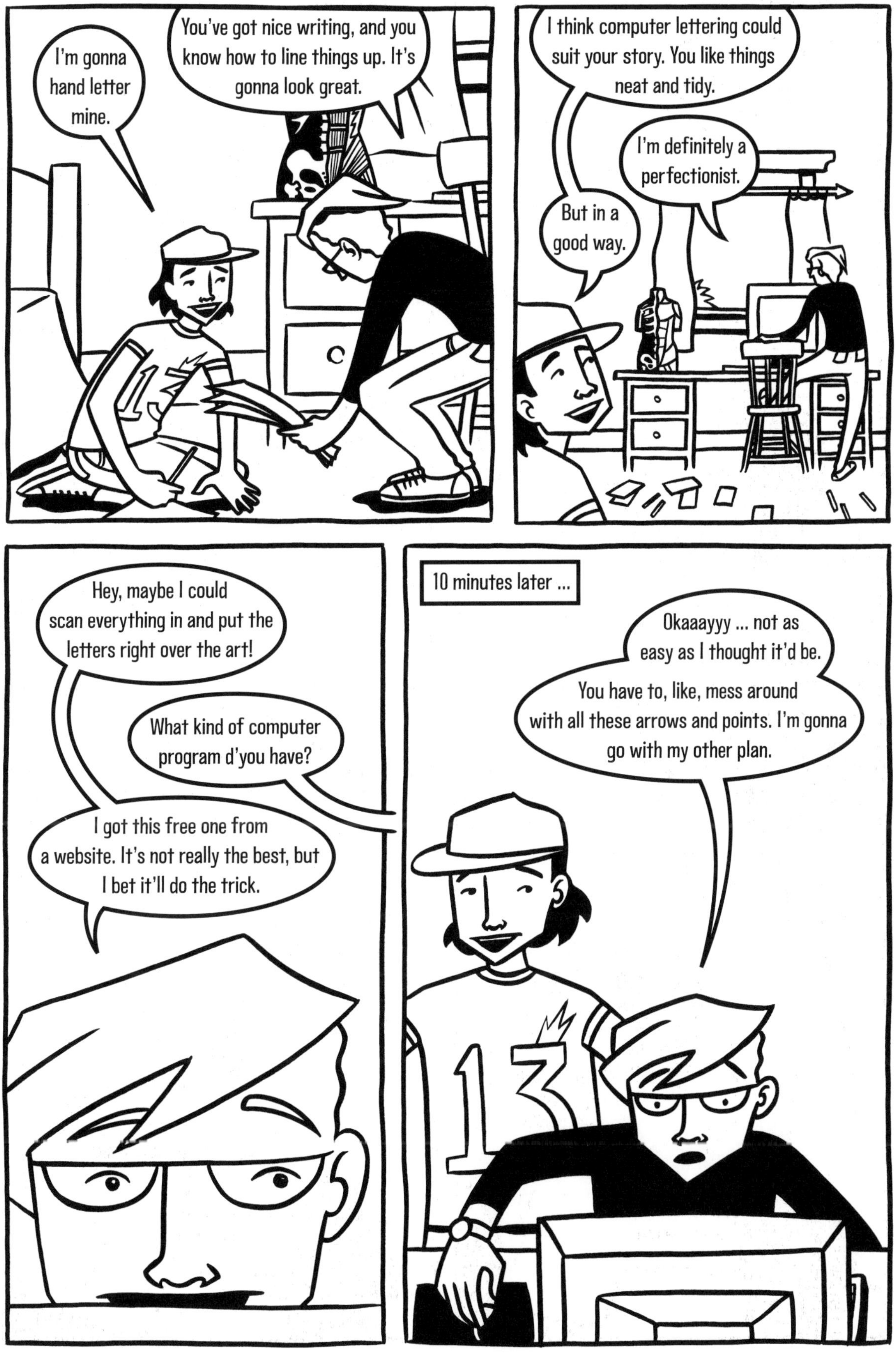
I'm gonna hand letter mine.
You've got nice writing, and you know how to line things up. It's gonna look great.
I think computer lettering could suit your story. You like things neat and tidy.
I'm definitely a perfectionist.
But in a good way.
Hey, maybe I could scan everything in and put the letters right over the art!
What kind of computer program d'you have?
I got this free one from a website. It's not really the best, but I bet it'll do the trick.
10 minutes later ...
Okaaayyy ... not as easy as I thought it'd be.
You have to, like, mess around with all these arrows and points. I'm gonna go with my other plan.

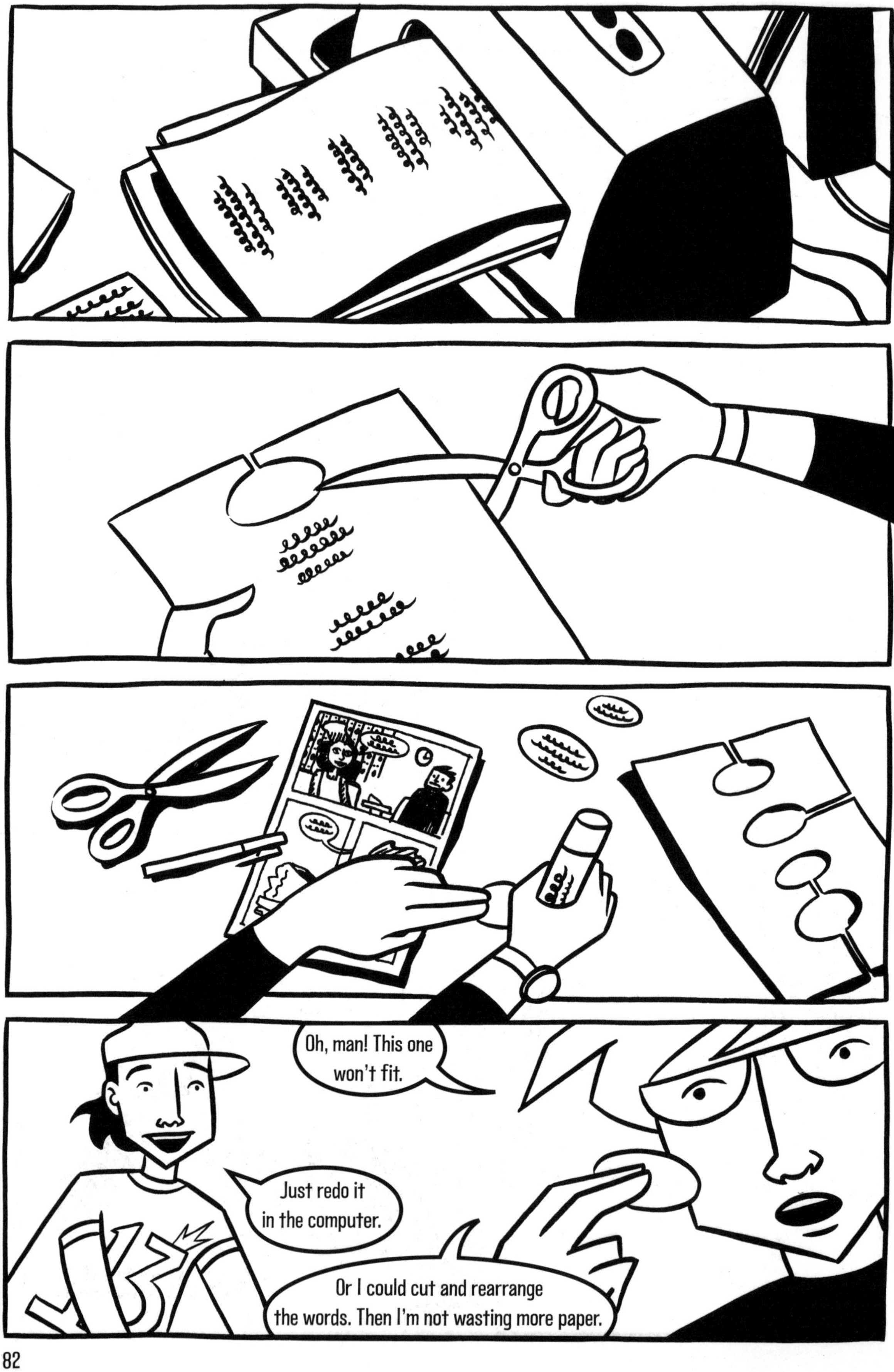
Oh, man! This one won't fit.
Just redo it in the computer.
Or I could cut and rearrange the words. Then I'm not wasting more paper.

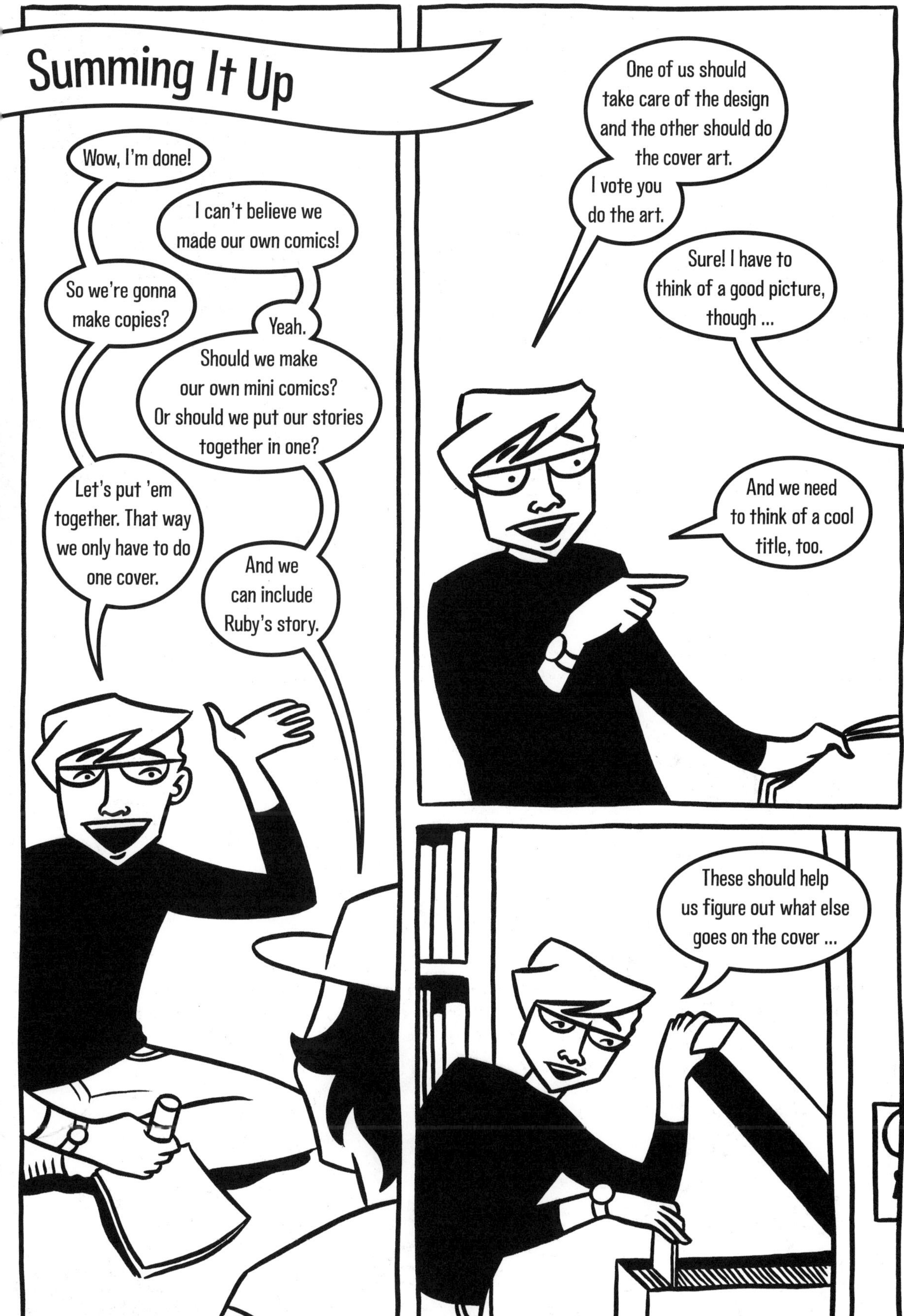
Summing It Up
Wow, I'm done!
I can't believe we made our own comics!
So we're gonna make copies?
Yeah.
Should we make our own mini comics? Or should we put our stories together in one?
Let's put 'em together. That way we only have to do one cover.
And we can include Ruby's story.
One of us should take care of the design and the other should do the cover art.
I vote you do the art.
Sure! I have to think of a good picture, though ...
And we need to think of a cool title, too.
These should help us figure out what else goes on the cover ...

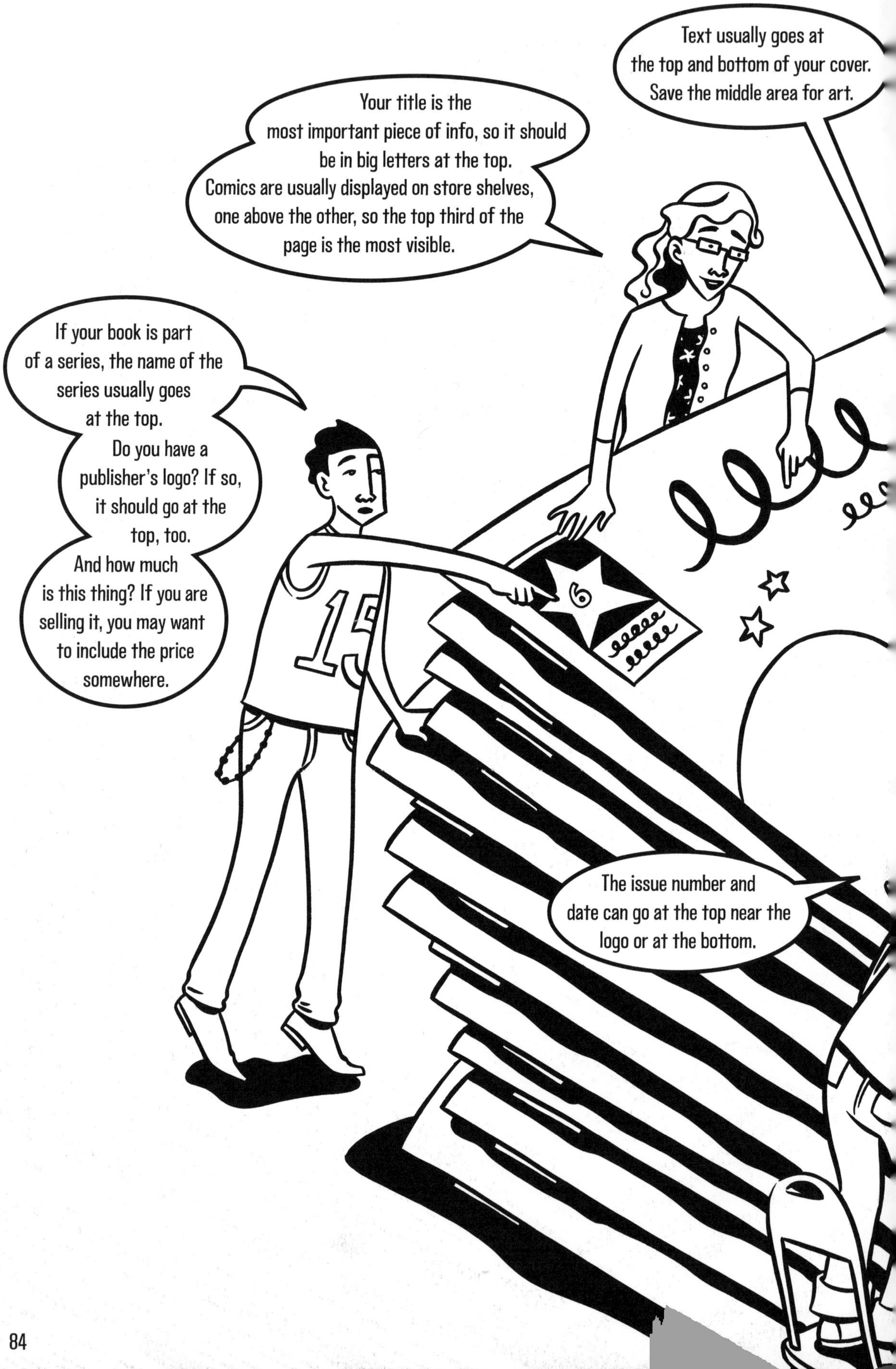

If your book is part of a series, the name of the series usually goes at the top.
Do you have a publisher's logo? If so, it should go at the top, too.
And how much is this thing? If you are selling it, you may want to include the price somewhere.
Your title is the most important piece of info, so it should be in big letters at the top. Comics are usually displayed on store shelves, one above the other, so the top third of the page is the most visible.
Text usually goes at the top and bottom of your cover. Save the middle area for art.
6
The issue number and date can go at the top near the logo or at the bottom.

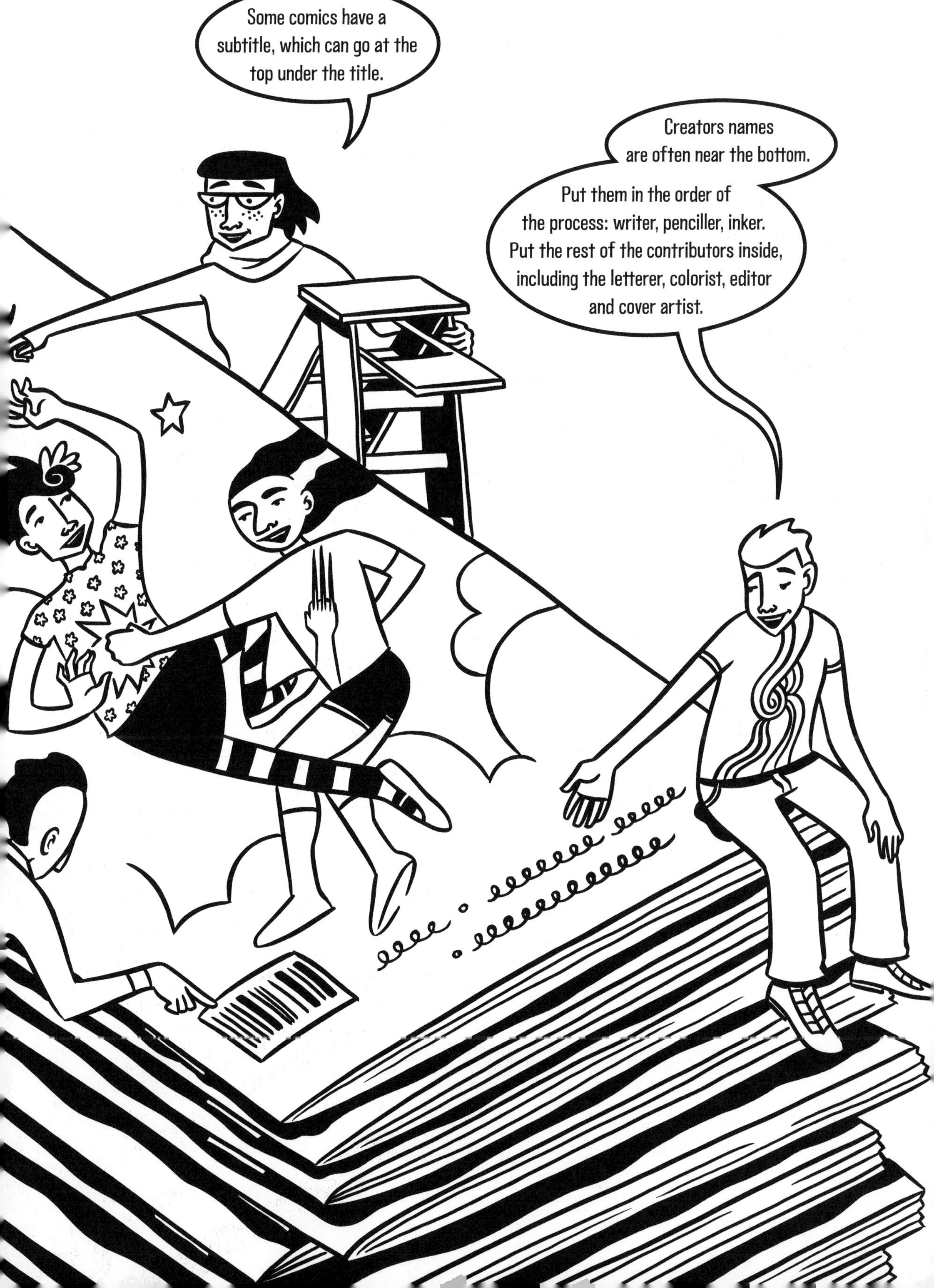
Some comics have a subtitle, which can go at the top under the title.
Creators names are often near the bottom.
Put them in the order of the process: writer, penciller, inker. Put the rest of the contributors inside, including the letterer, colorist, editor and cover artist.

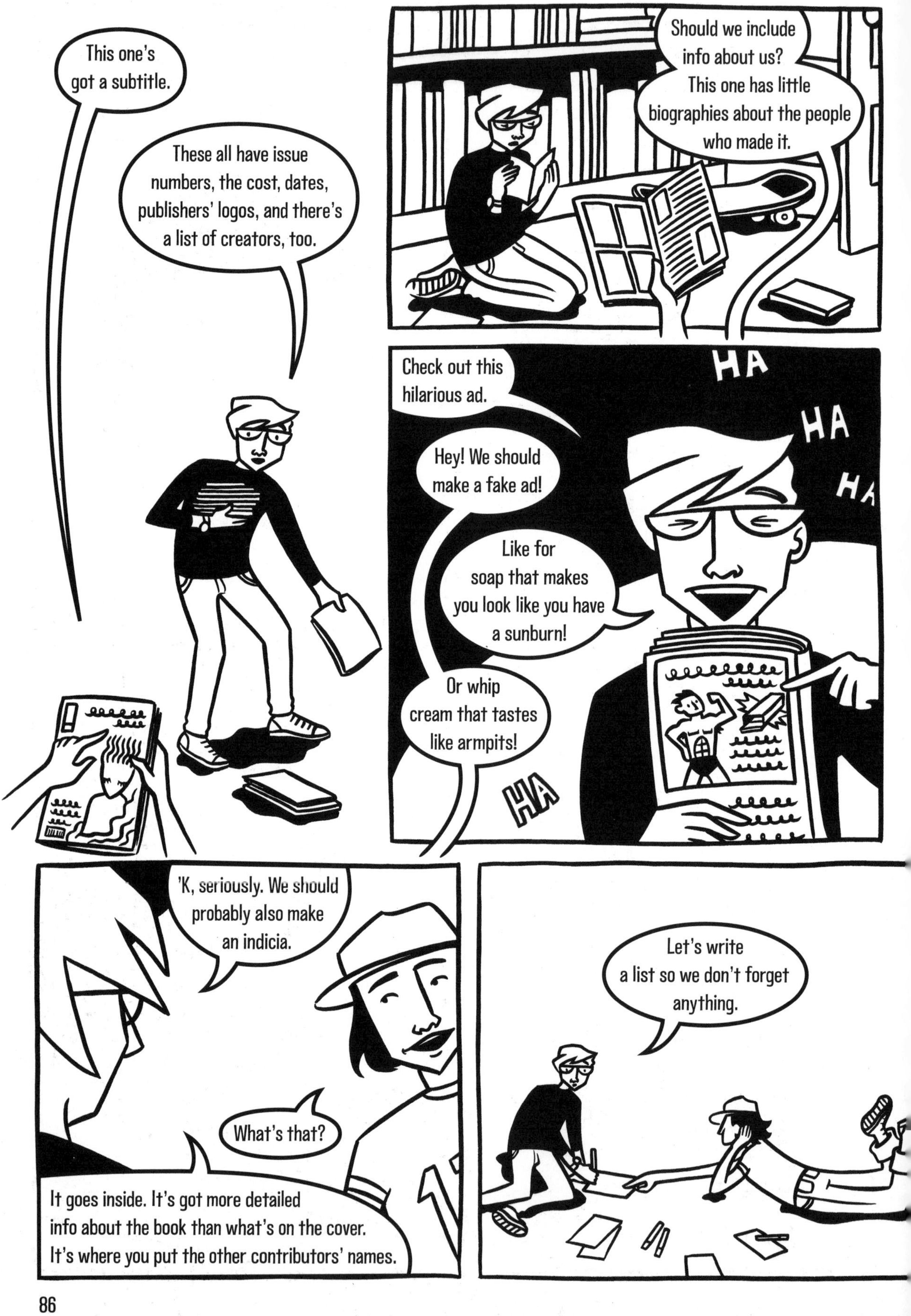
This one's got a subtitle.
These all have issue numbers, the cost, dates, publishers' logos, and there's a list of creators, too.
Should we include info about us?
This one has little biographies about the people who made it.
Check out this hilarious ad.
HA
HA
HA
Hey! We should make a fake ad!
Like for soap that makes you look like you have a sunburn!
Or whip cream that tastes like armpits!
HA
'K, seriously. We should probably also make an indicia.
What's that?
It goes inside. It's got more detailed info about the book than what's on the cover. It's where you put the other contributors' names.
Let's write a list so we don't forget anything.

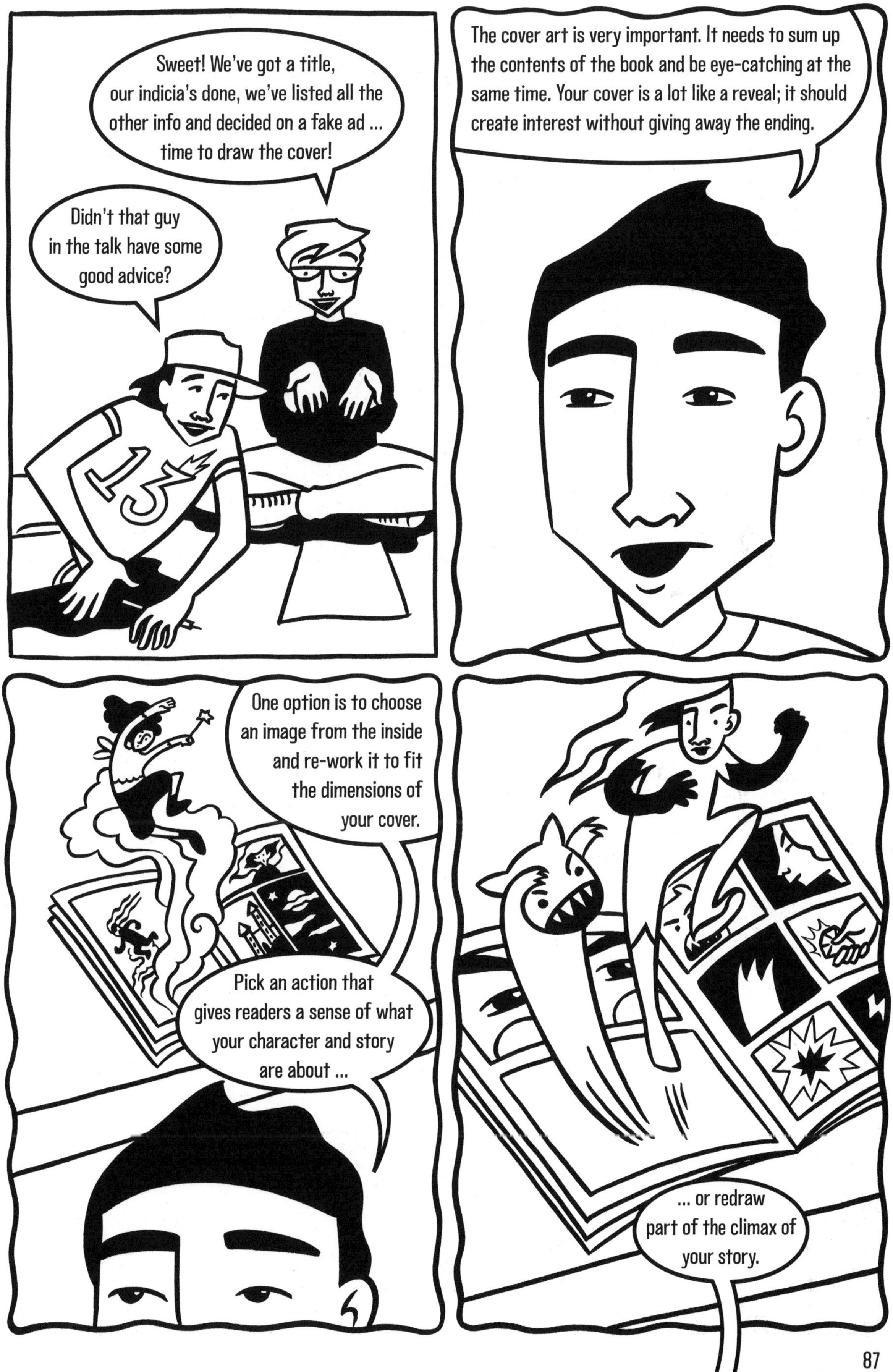
Sweet! We've got a title, our indicia's done, we've listed all the other info and decided on a fake ad ... time to draw the cover!
Didn't that guy in the talk have some good advice?
13
The cover art is very important. It needs to sum up the contents of the book and be eye-catching at the same time. Your cover is a lot like a reveal; it should create interest without giving away the ending.
One option is to choose an image from the inside and re-work it to fit the dimensions of your cover.
Pick an action that gives readers a sense of what your character and story are about ...
... or redraw part of the climax of your story.

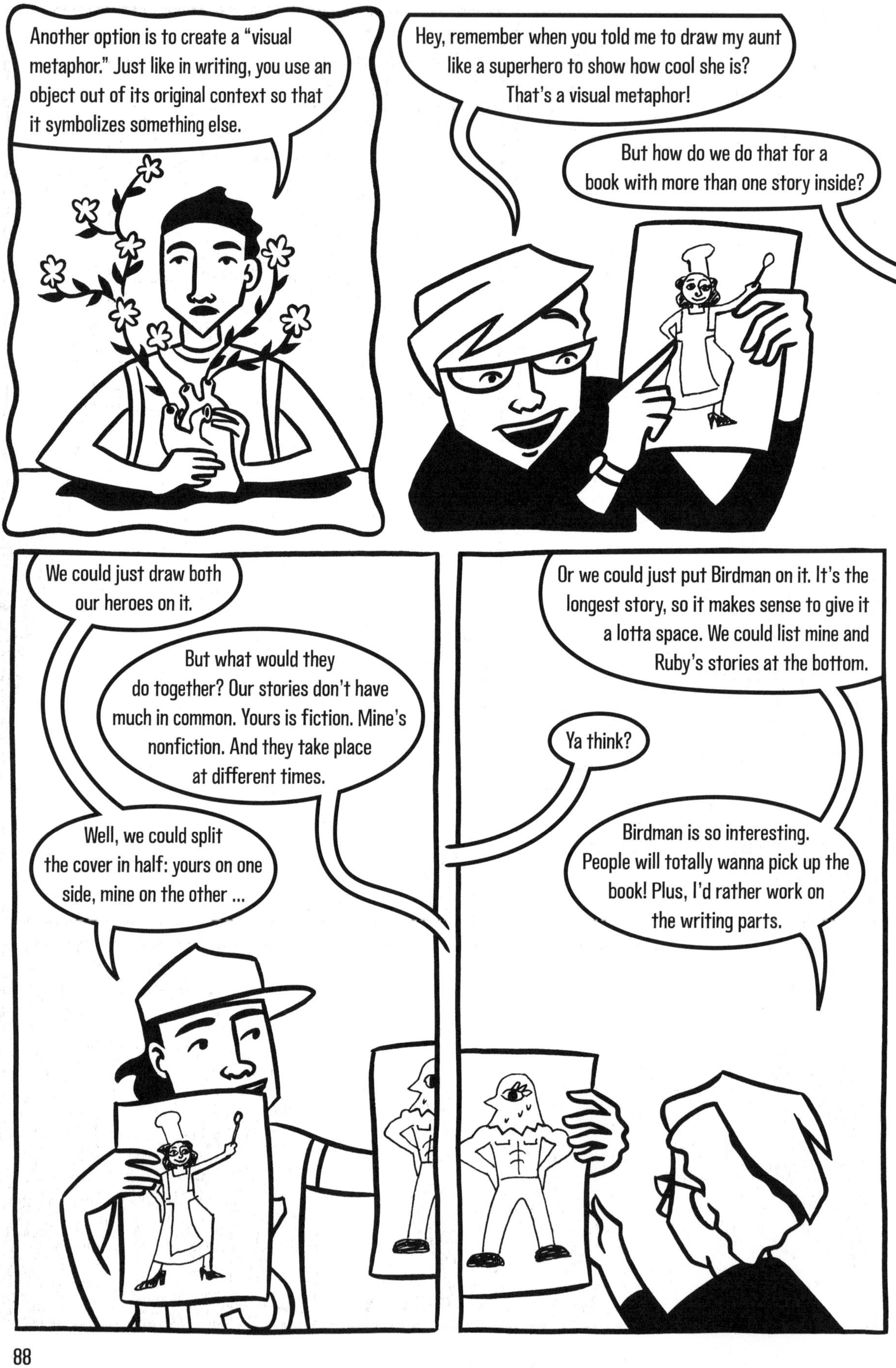
Another option is to create a "visual metaphor." Just like in writing, you use an object out of its original context so that it symbolizes something else.
Hey, remember when you told me to draw my aunt like a superhero to show how cool she is? That's a visual metaphor!
But how do we do that for a book with more than one story inside?
We could just draw both our heroes on it.
But what would they do together? Our stories don't have much in common. Yours is fiction. Mine's nonfiction. And they take place at different times.
Well, we could split the cover in half: yours on one side, mine on the other ...
Or we could just put Birdman on it. It's the longest story, so it makes sense to give it a lotta space. We could list mine and Ruby's stories at the bottom.
Ya think?
Birdman is so interesting. People will totally wanna pick up the book! Plus, I'd rather work on the writing parts.

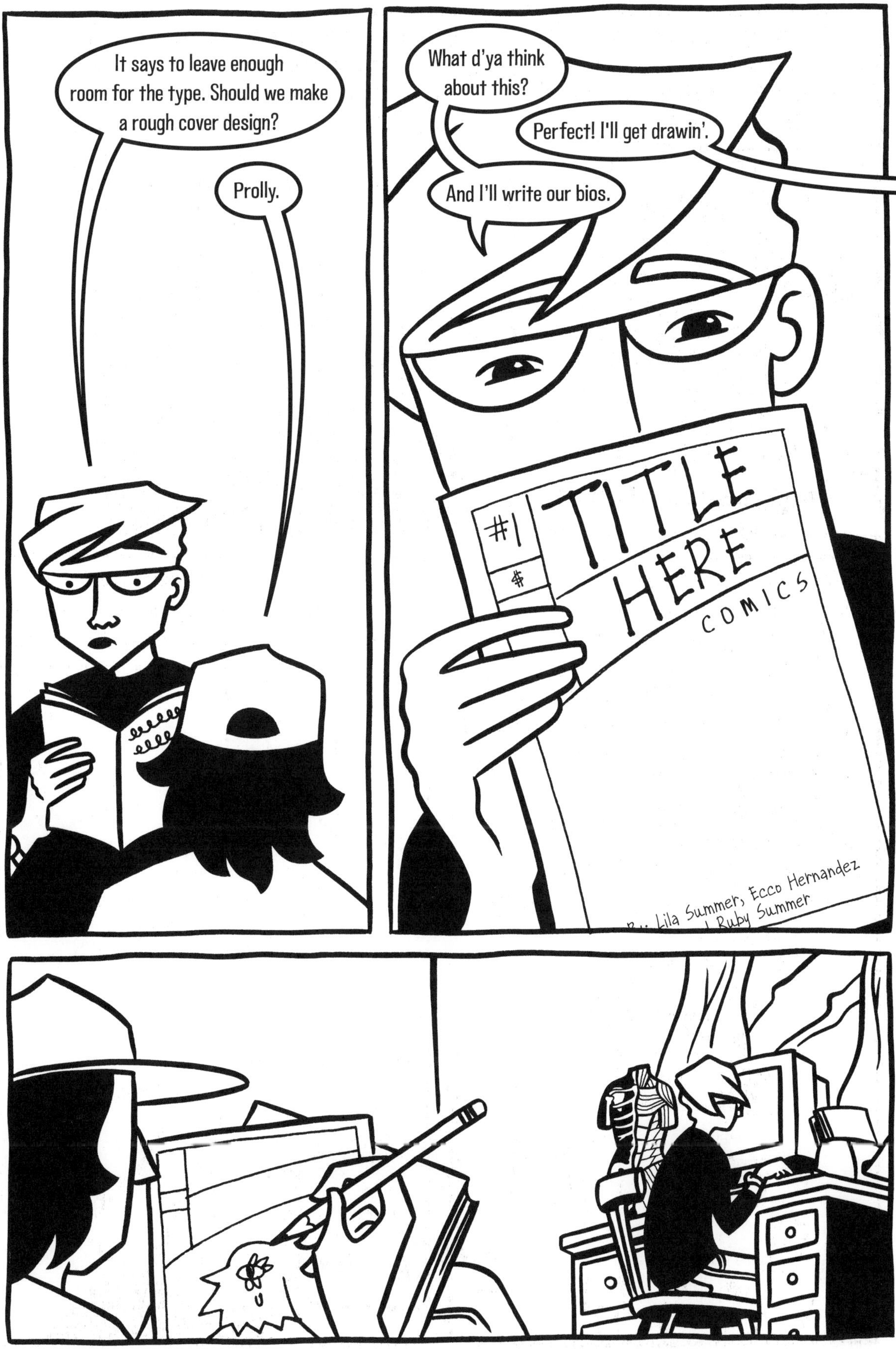

It says to leave enough room for the type. Should we make a rough cover design?
Prolly.
What d'ya think about this?
Perfect! I'll get drawin'.
And I'll write our bios.
#1
$
TITLE HERE
COMICS
Lila Summer, Ecco Hernandez
Ruby Summer

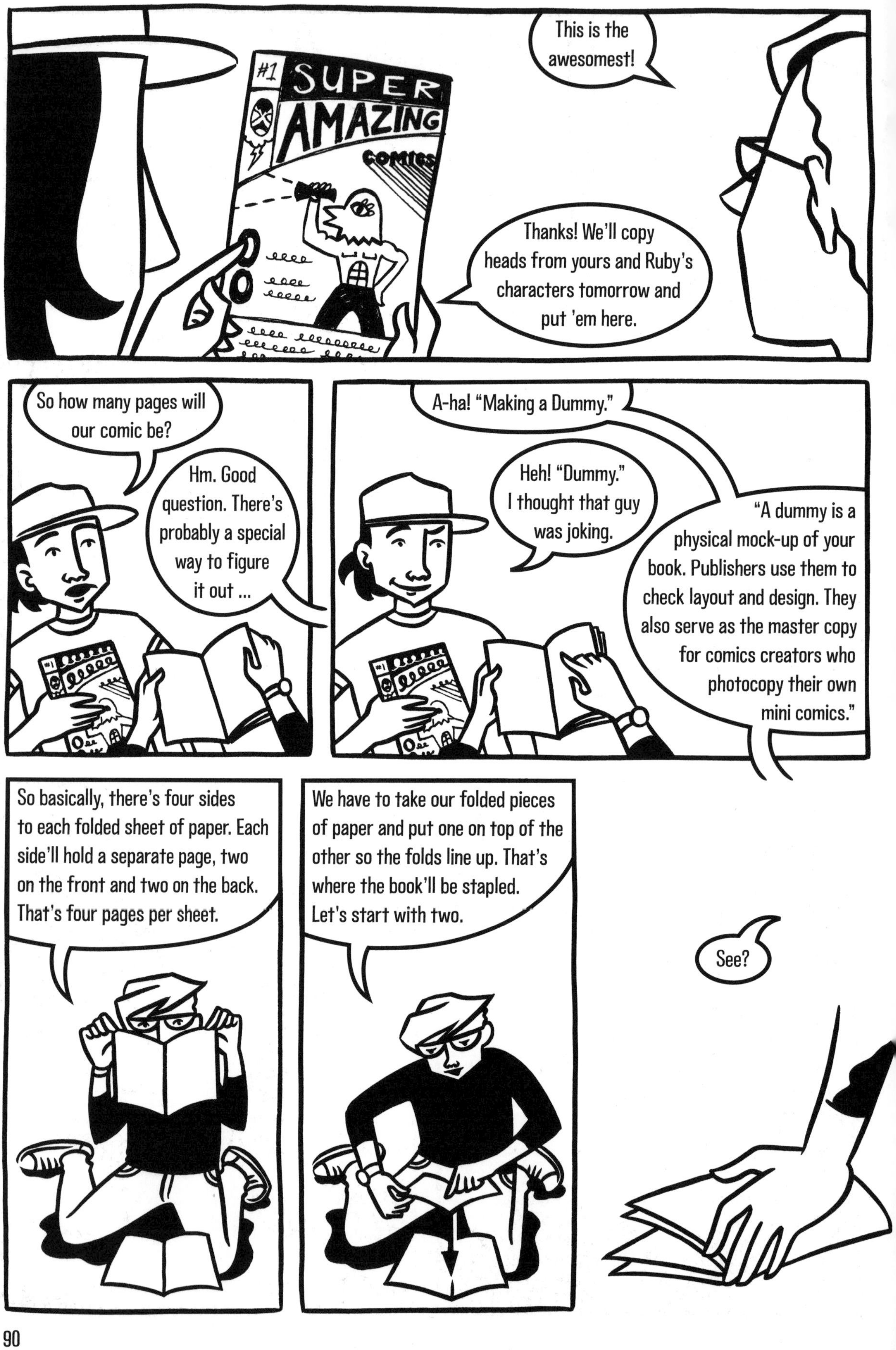

This is the awesomest!
#1 SUPER AMAZING COMICS
Thanks! We'll copy heads from yours and Ruby's characters tomorrow and put 'em here.
So how many pages will our comic be?
Hm. Good question. There's probably a special way to figure it out ...
A-ha! "Making a Dummy."
Heh! "Dummy." I thought that guy was joking.
"A dummy is a physical mock-up of your book. Publishers use them to check layout and design. They also serve as the master copy for comics creators who photocopy their own mini comics."
So basically, there's four sides to each folded sheet of paper. Each side'll hold a separate page, two on the front and two on the back. That's four pages per sheet.
We have to take our folded pieces of paper and put one on top of the other so the folds line up. That's where the book'll be stapled. Let's start with two.
See?

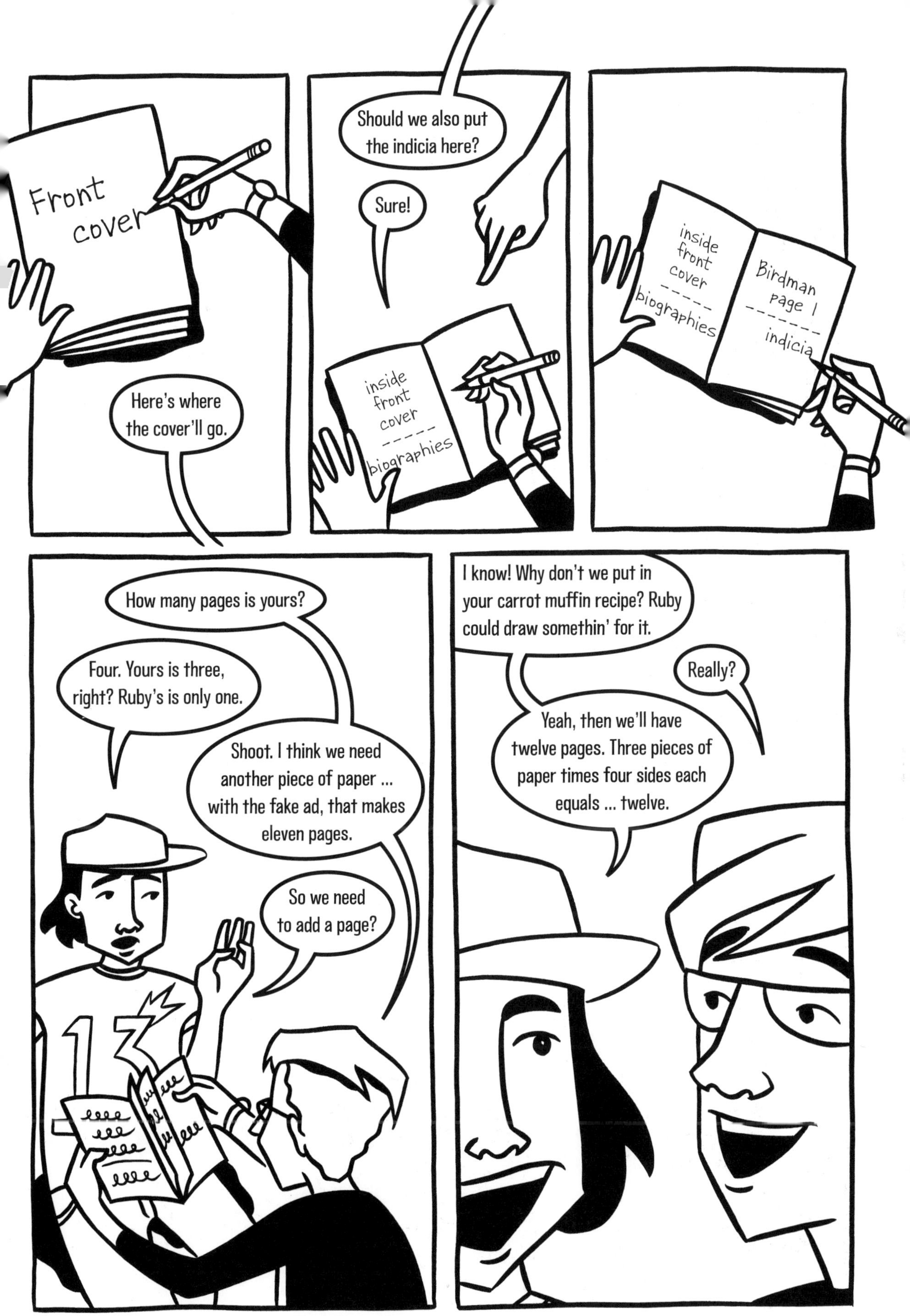

Front cover
Here's where the cover'll go.
Should we also put the indicia here?
Sure!
inside front cover
biographies
inside front cover
biographies
Birdman page 1
indicia
How many pages is yours?
Four. Yours is three, right? Ruby's is only one.
Shoot. I think we need another piece of paper ... with the fake ad, that makes eleven pages.
So we need to add a page?
I know! Why don't we put in your carrot muffin recipe? Ruby could draw somethin' for it.
Really?
Yeah, then we'll have twelve pages. Three pieces of paper times four sides each equals ... twelve.

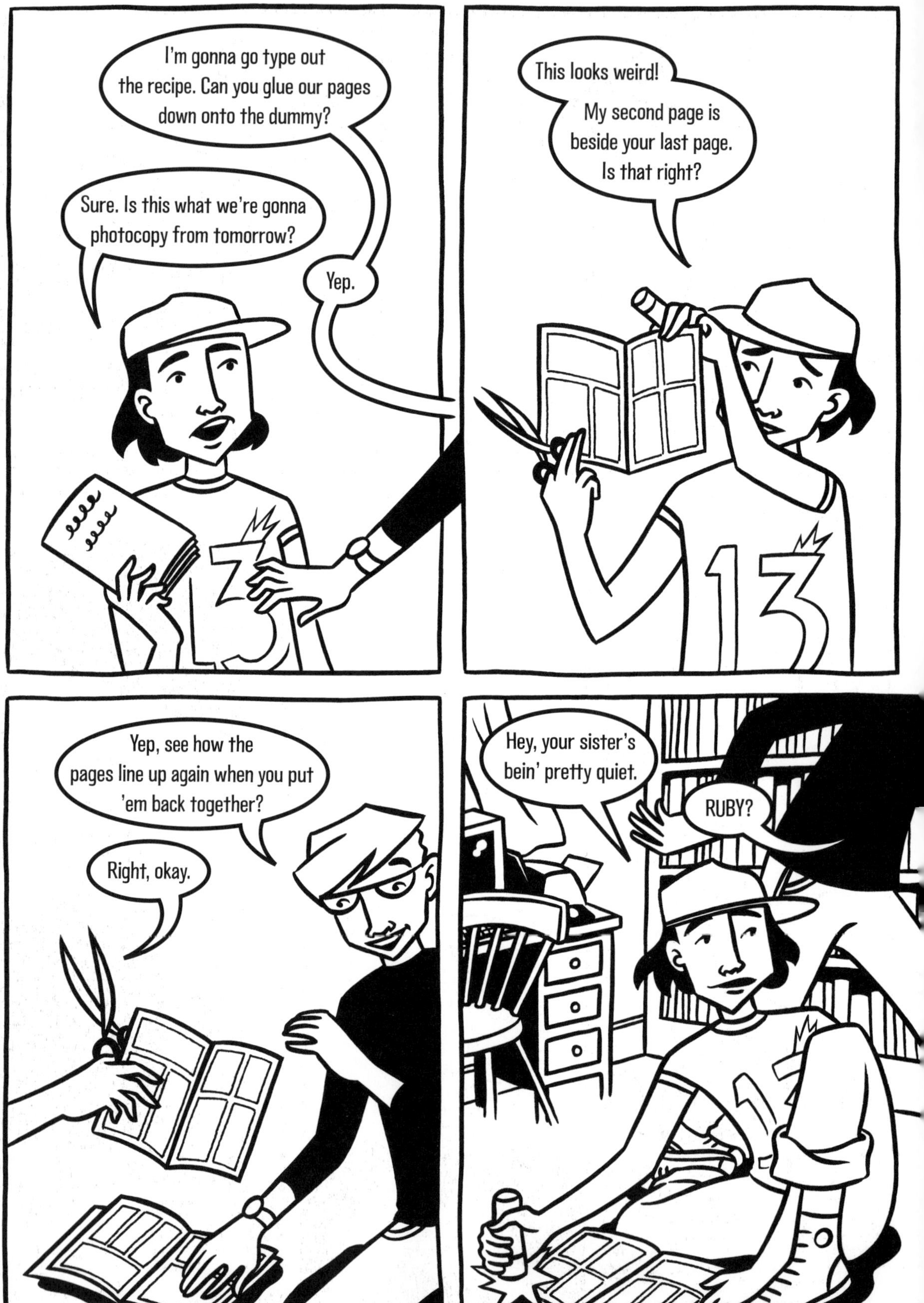
I'm gonna go type out the recipe. Can you glue our pages down onto the dummy?
Sure. Is this what we're gonna photocopy from tomorrow?
Yep.
This looks weird!
My second page is beside your last page. Is that right?
Yep, see how the pages line up again when you put 'em back together?
Right, okay.
Hey, your sister's bein' pretty quiet.
RUBY?

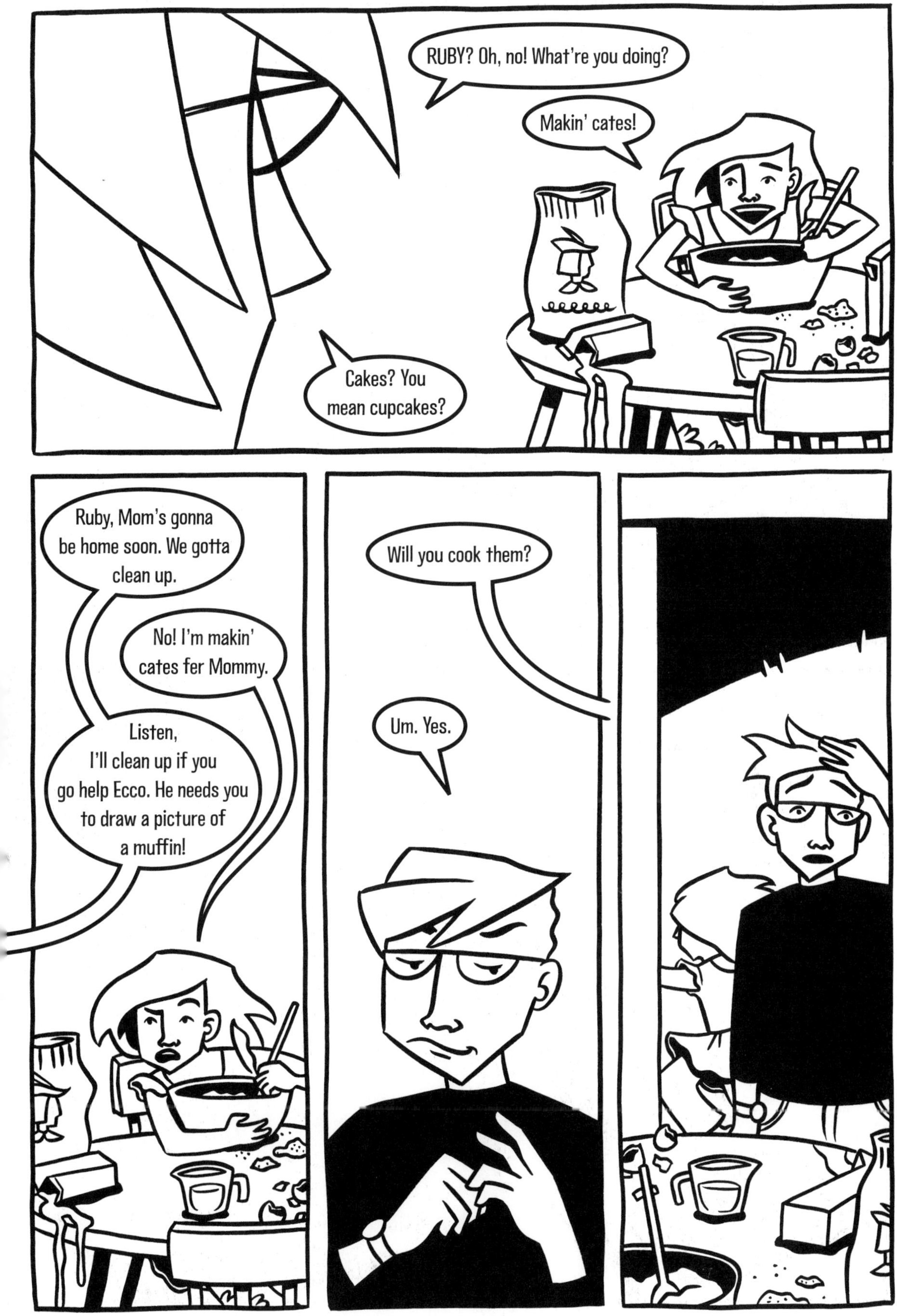
RUBY? Oh, no! What're you doing?
Makin' cates!
Cakes? You mean cupcakes?
Ruby, Mom's gonna be home soon. We gotta clean up.
No! I'm makin' cates fer Mommy.
Listen, I'll clean up if you go help Ecco. He needs you to draw a picture of a muffin!
Will you cook them?
Um. Yes.

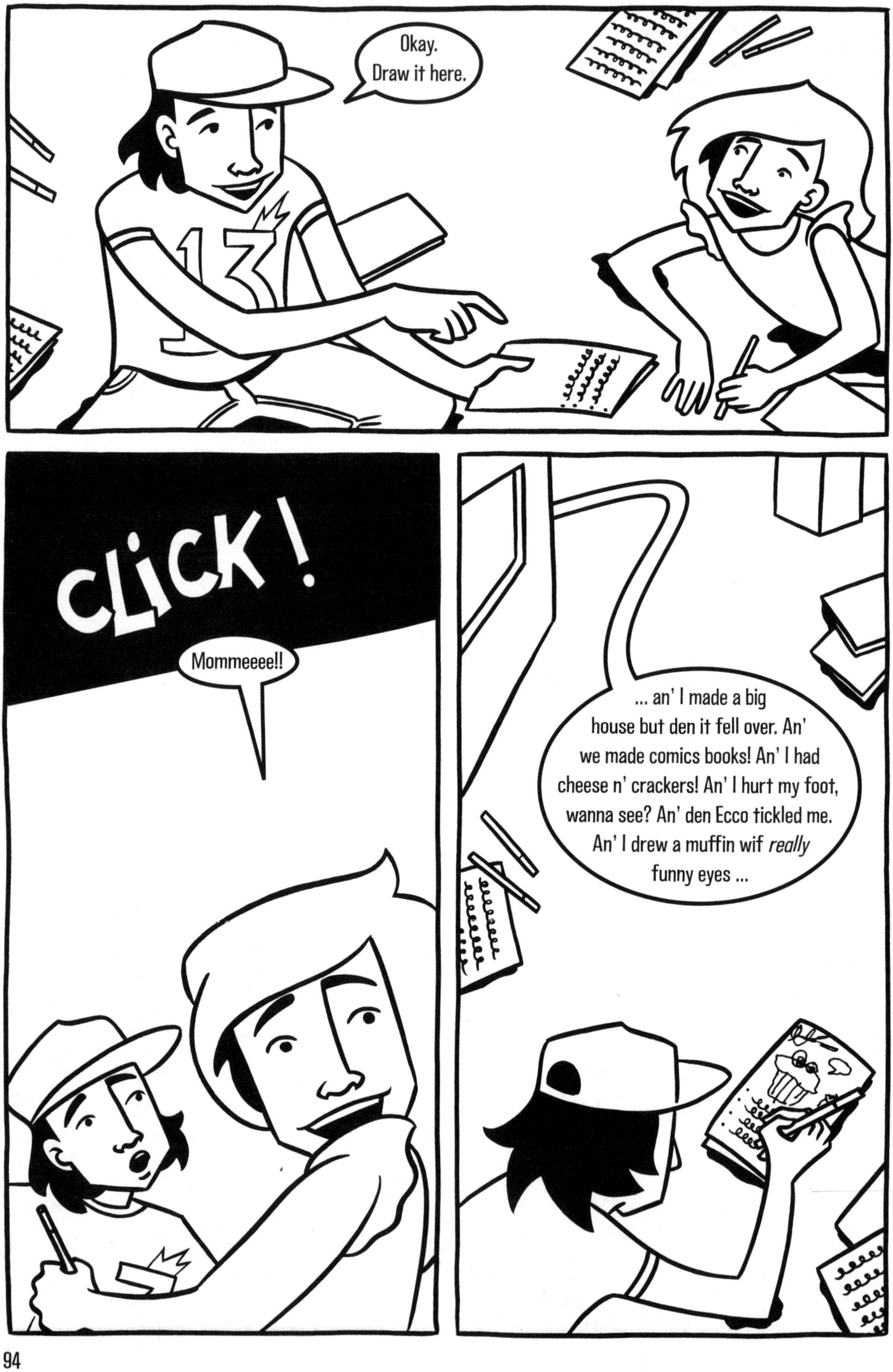
Okay.
Draw it here.
CLICK!
Mommeeee!!
... an' I made a big house but den it fell over. An' we made comics books! An' I had cheese n' crackers! An' I hurt my foot, wanna see? An' den Ecco tickled me. An' I drew a muffin wif *really* funny eyes ...

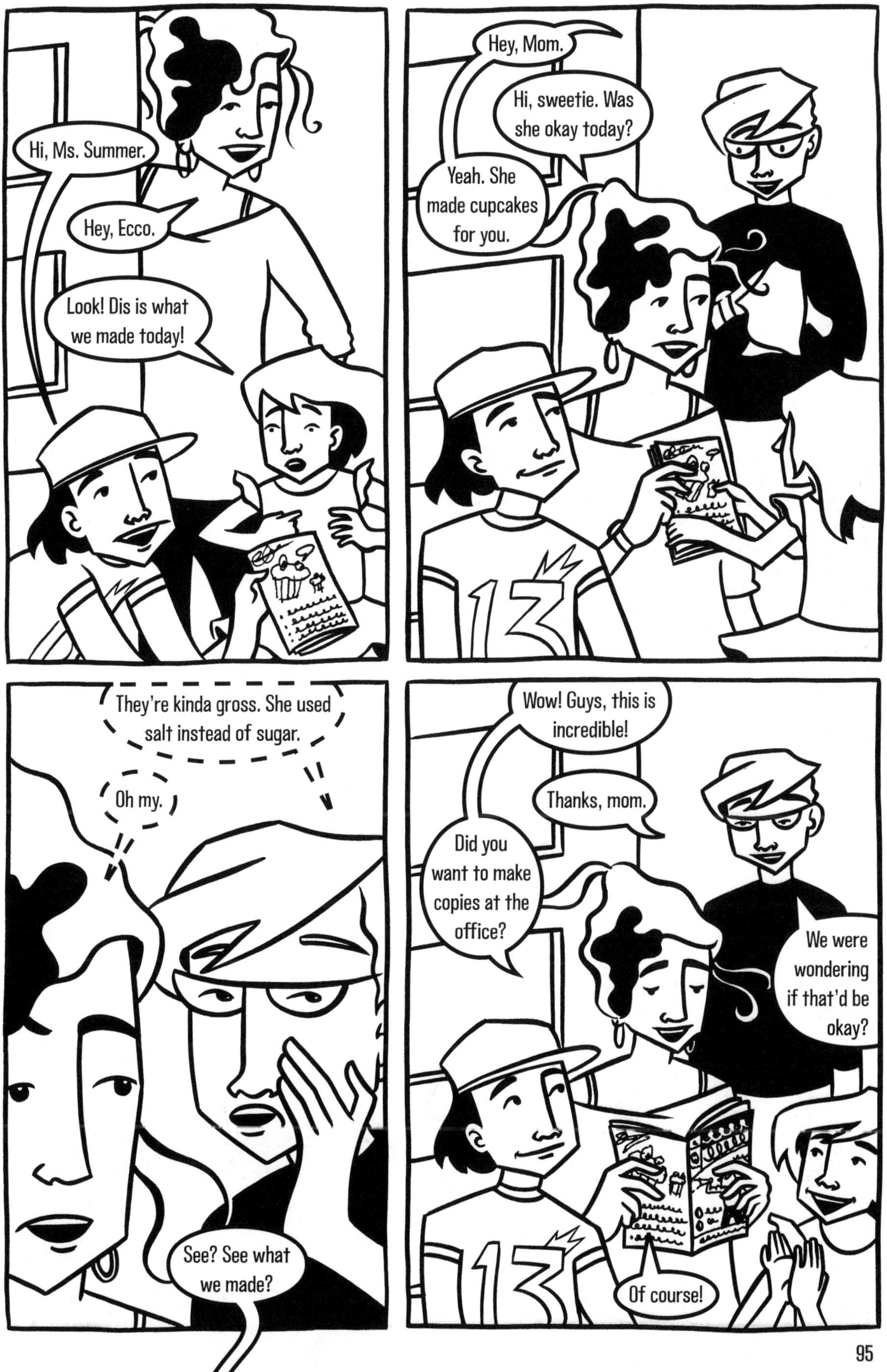
Hi, Ms. Summer.
Hey, Ecco.
Look! Dis is what we made today!
Hey, Mom.
Hi, sweetie. Was she okay today?
Yeah. She made cupcakes for you.
They're kinda gross. She used salt instead of sugar.
Oh my.
See? See what we made?
Wow! Guys, this is incredible!
Thanks, mom.
Did you want to make copies at the office?
We were wondering if that'd be okay?
Of course!

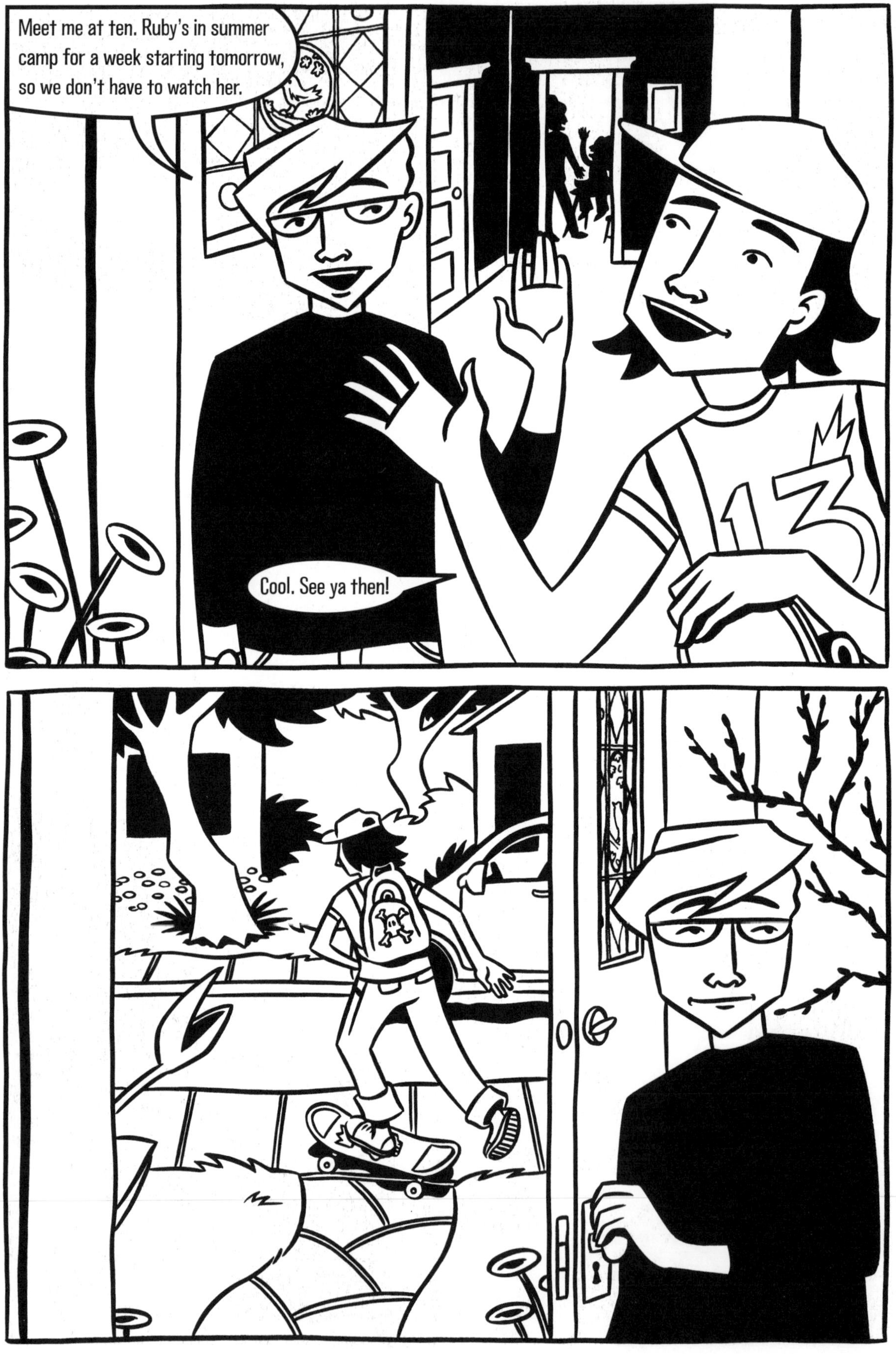
Meet me at ten. Ruby's in summer camp for a week starting tomorrow, so we don't have to watch her.
Cool. See ya then!

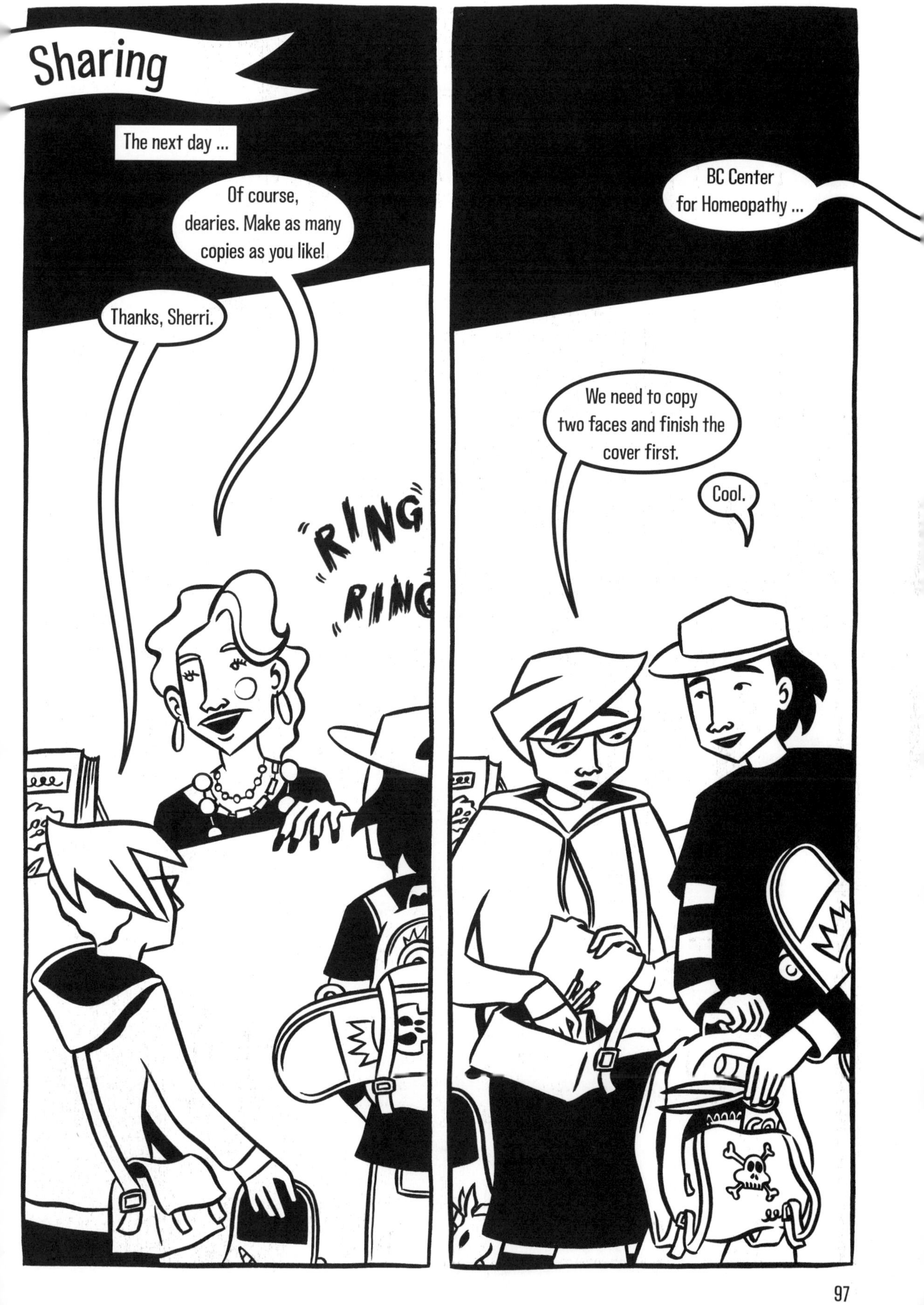
Sharing
The next day ...
Of course, dearies. Make as many copies as you like!
Thanks, Sherri.
RING
RING
BC Center for Homeopathy ...
We need to copy two faces and finish the cover first.
Cool.

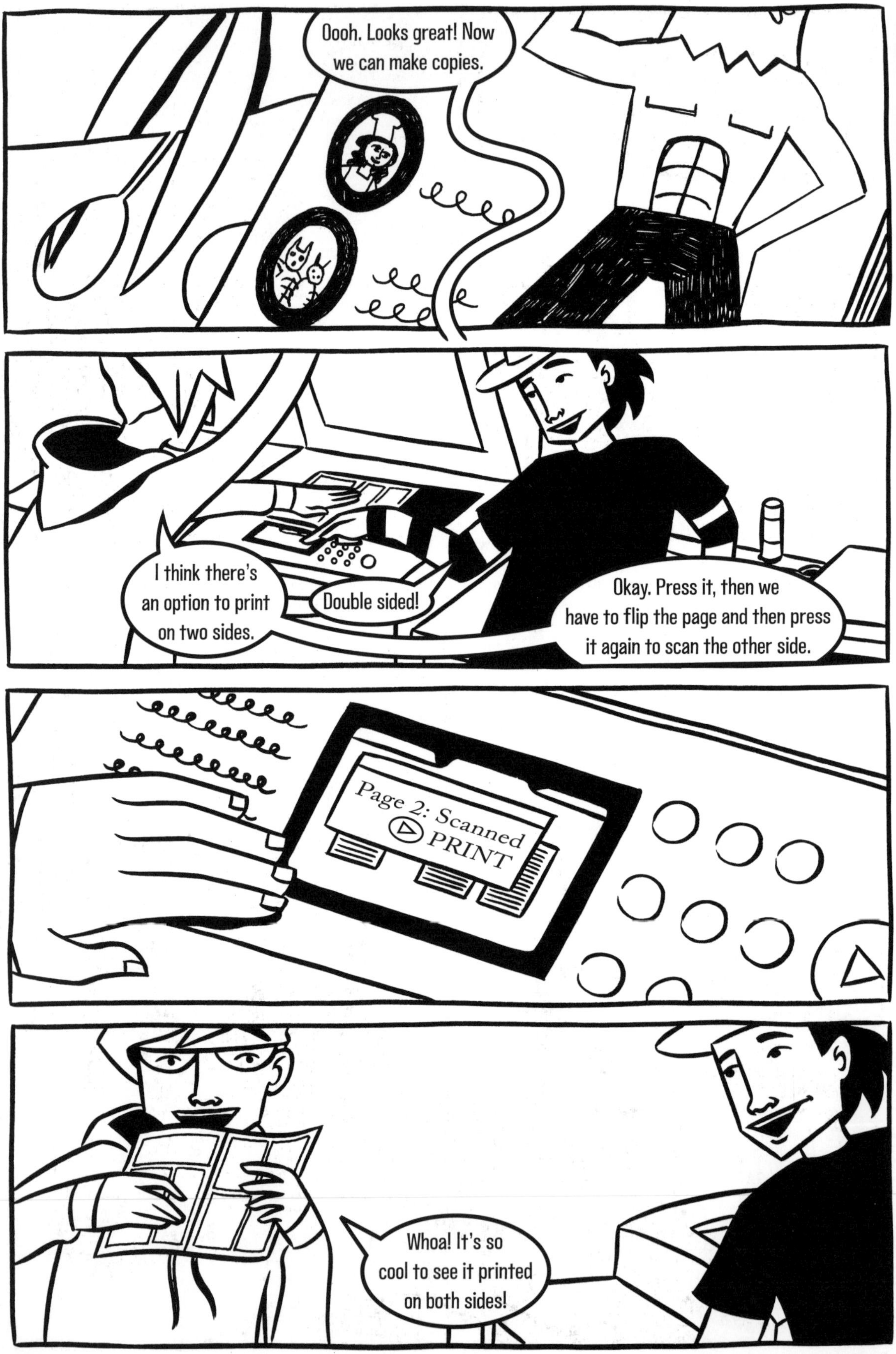
Oooh. Looks great! Now we can make copies.
I think there's an option to print on two sides.
Double sided!
Okay. Press it, then we have to flip the page and then press it again to scan the other side.
Page 2: Scanned
PRINT
Whoa! It's so cool to see it printed on both sides!

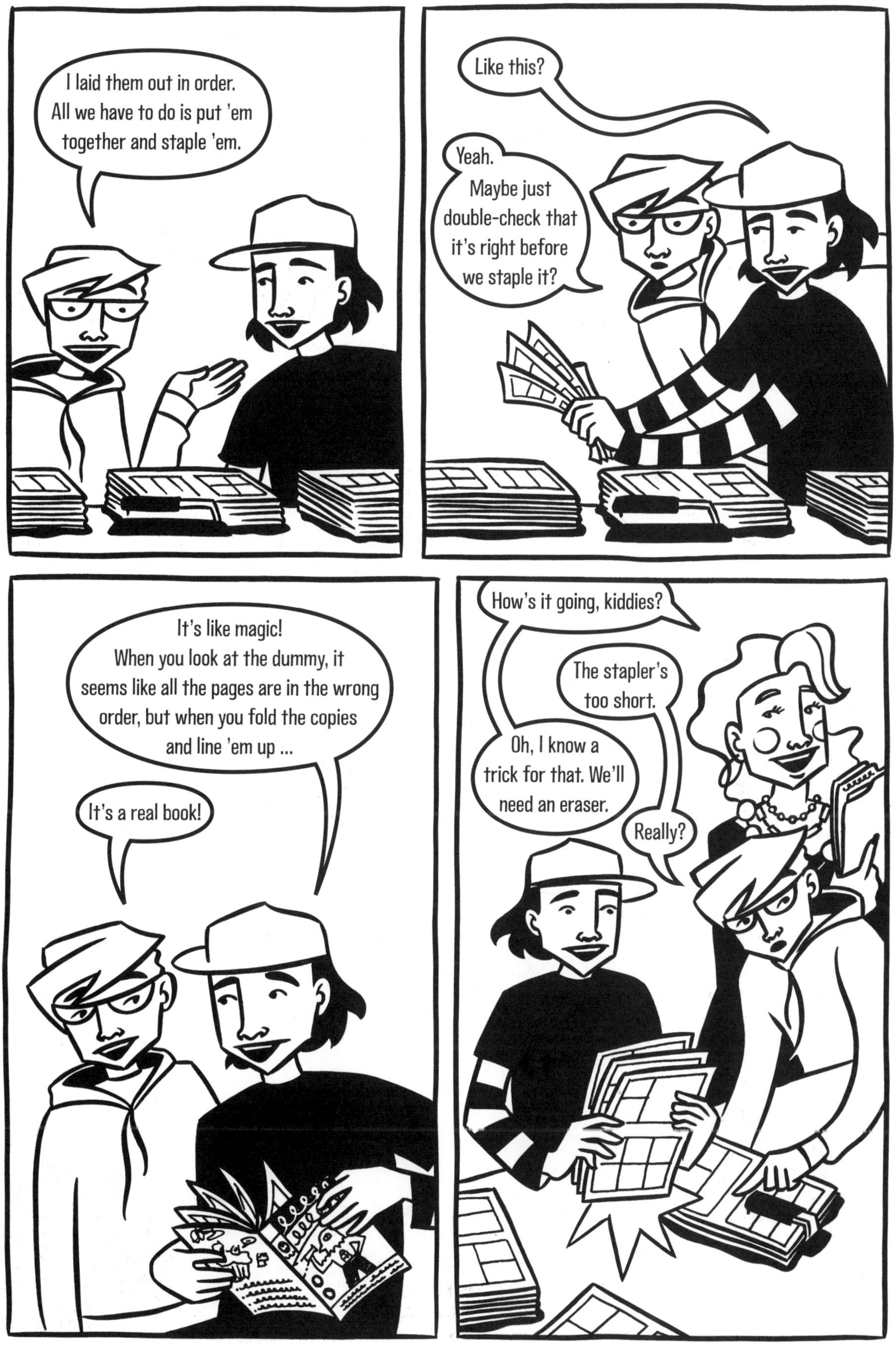
I laid them out in order. All we have to do is put 'em together and staple 'em.
Like this?
Yeah. Maybe just double-check that it's right before we staple it?
It's like magic! When you look at the dummy, it seems like all the pages are in the wrong order, but when you fold the copies and line 'em up ...
It's a real book!
How's it going, kiddies?
The stapler's too short.
Oh, I know a trick for that. We'll need an eraser.
Really?

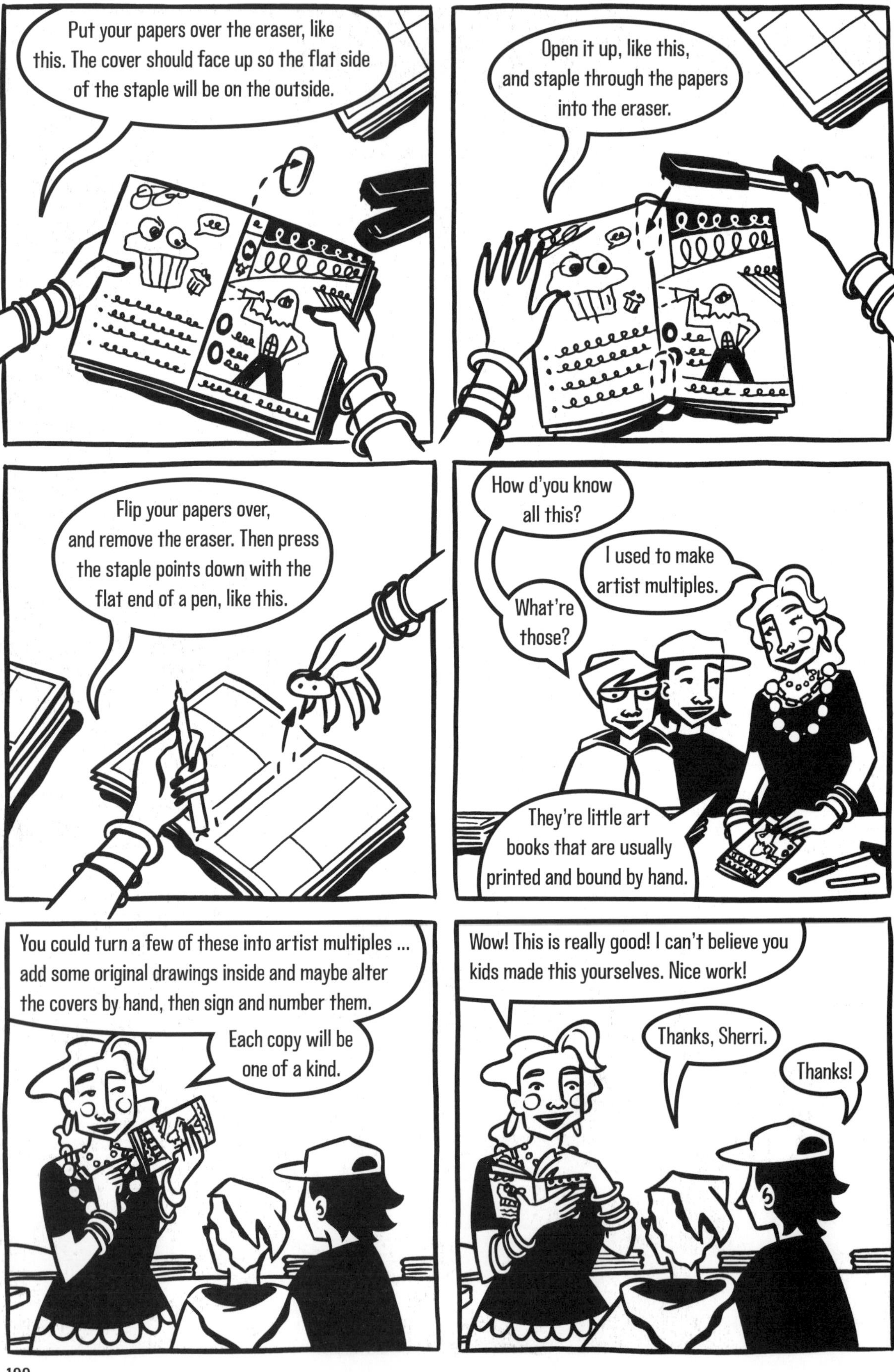

Put your papers over the eraser, like this. The cover should face up so the flat side of the staple will be on the outside.
Open it up, like this, and staple through the papers into the eraser.
Flip your papers over, and remove the eraser. Then press the staple points down with the flat end of a pen, like this.
How d'you know all this?
I used to make artist multiples.
What're those?
They're little art books that are usually printed and bound by hand.
You could turn a few of these into artist multiples ... add some original drawings inside and maybe alter the covers by hand, then sign and number them.
Each copy will be one of a kind.
Wow! This is really good! I can't believe you kids made this yourselves. Nice work!
Thanks, Sherri.
Thanks!

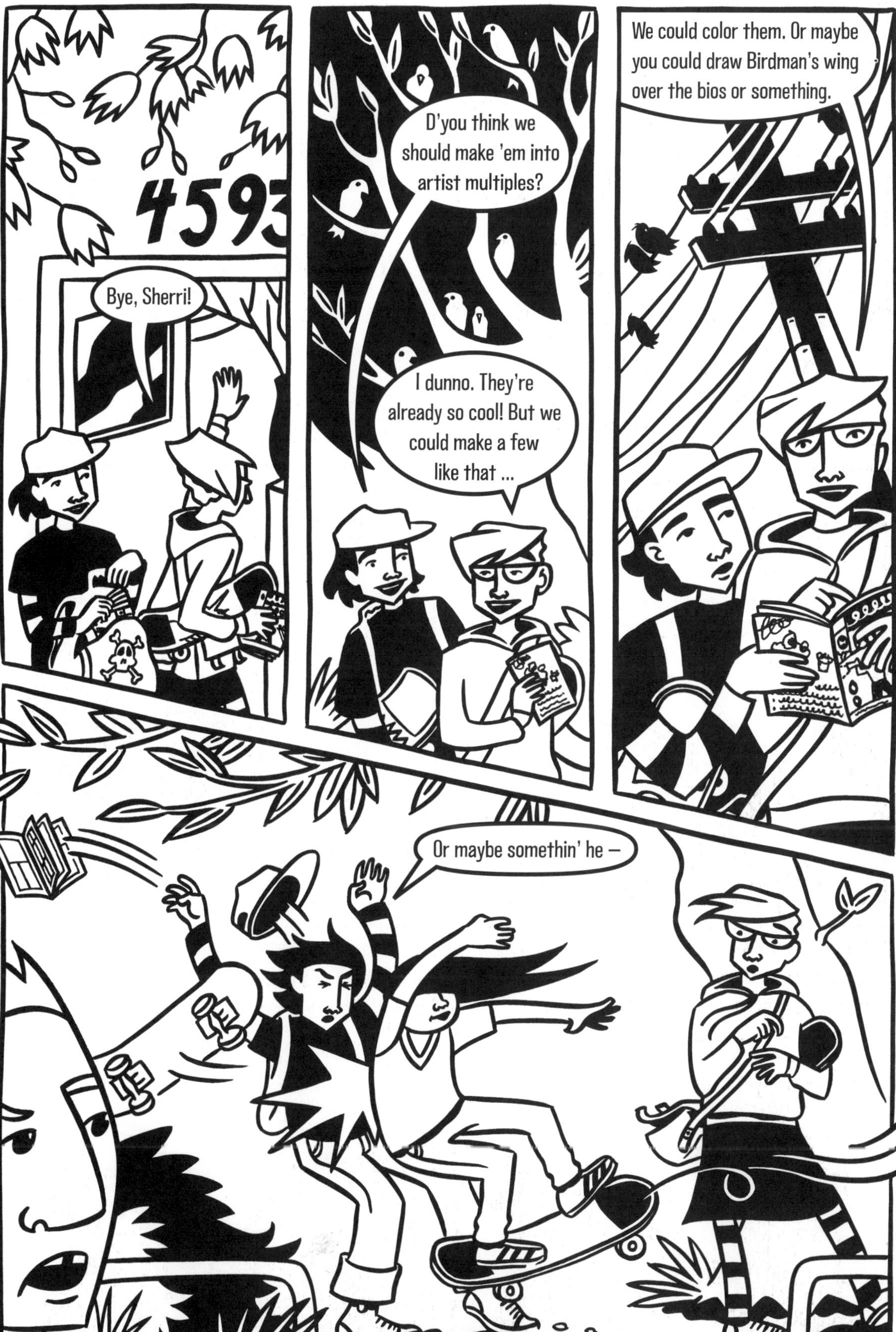
4593
Bye, Sherri!
D'you think we should make 'em into artist multiples?
I dunno. They're already so cool! But we could make a few like that ...
We could color them. Or maybe you could draw Birdman's wing over the bios or something.
Or maybe somethin' he –

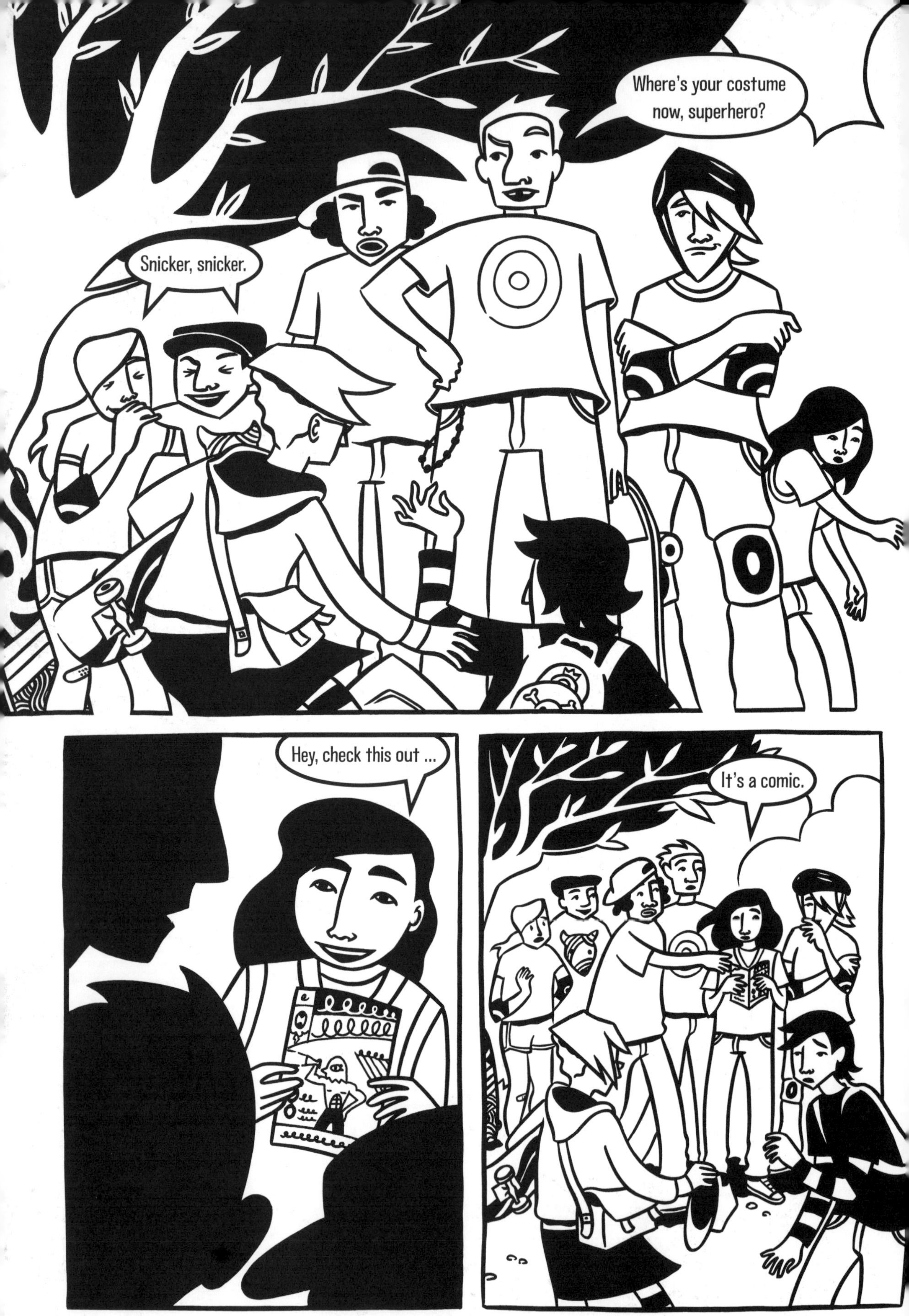
Snicker, snicker.
Where's your costume now, superhero?
Hey, check this out ...
It's a comic.

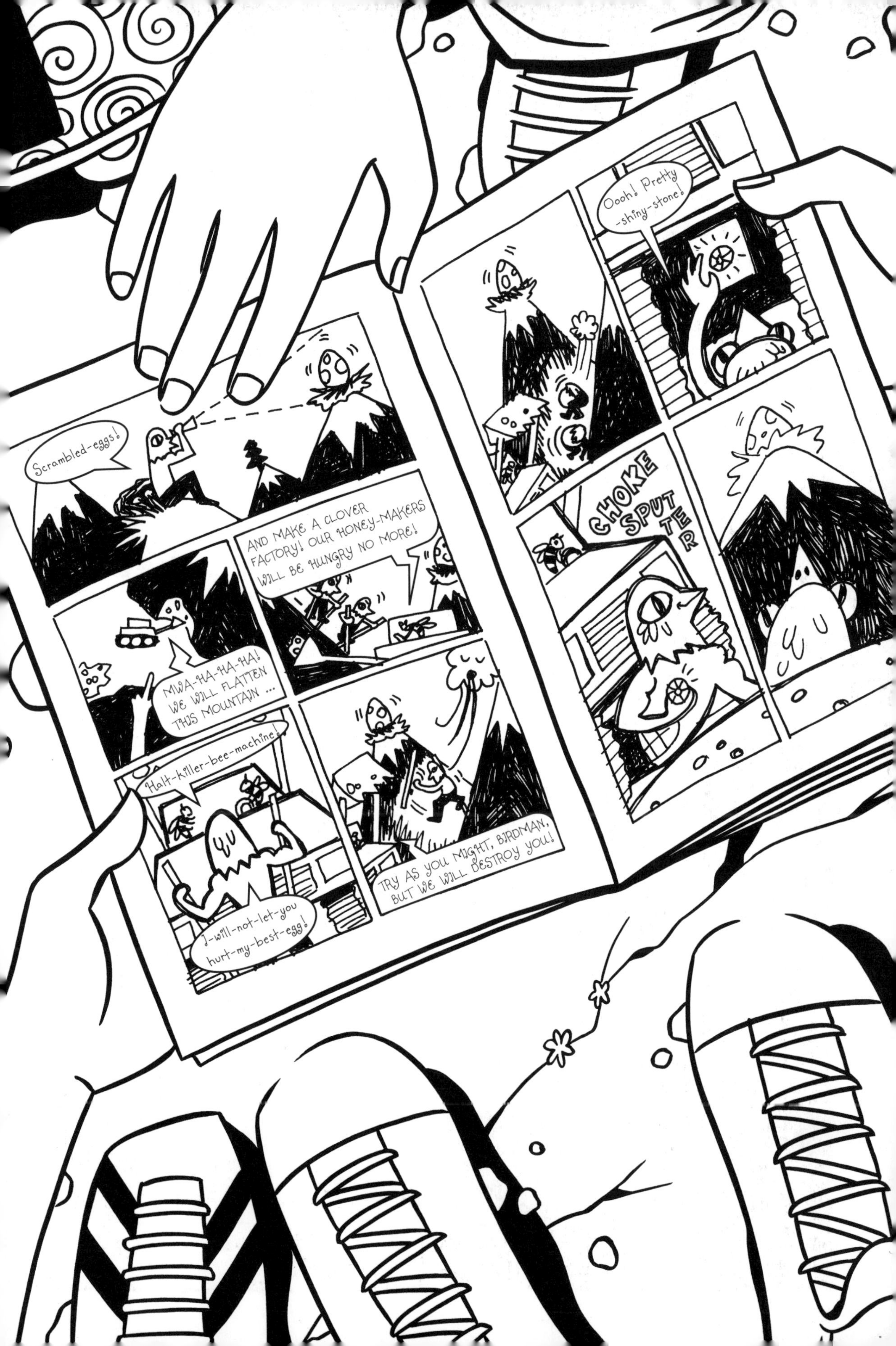
Scrambled-eggs!
MWA-HA-HA-HA! WE WILL FLATTEN THIS MOUNTAIN ...
AND MAKE A CLOVER FACTORY! OUR HONEY-MAKERS WILL BE HUNGRY NO MORE!
Halt-killer-bee-machine!
I-will-not-let-you hurt-my-best-egg!
TRY AS YOU MIGHT, BIRDMAN, BUT WE WILL DESTROY YOU!
Oooh! Pretty -shiny-stone!
CHOKE SPUTTER

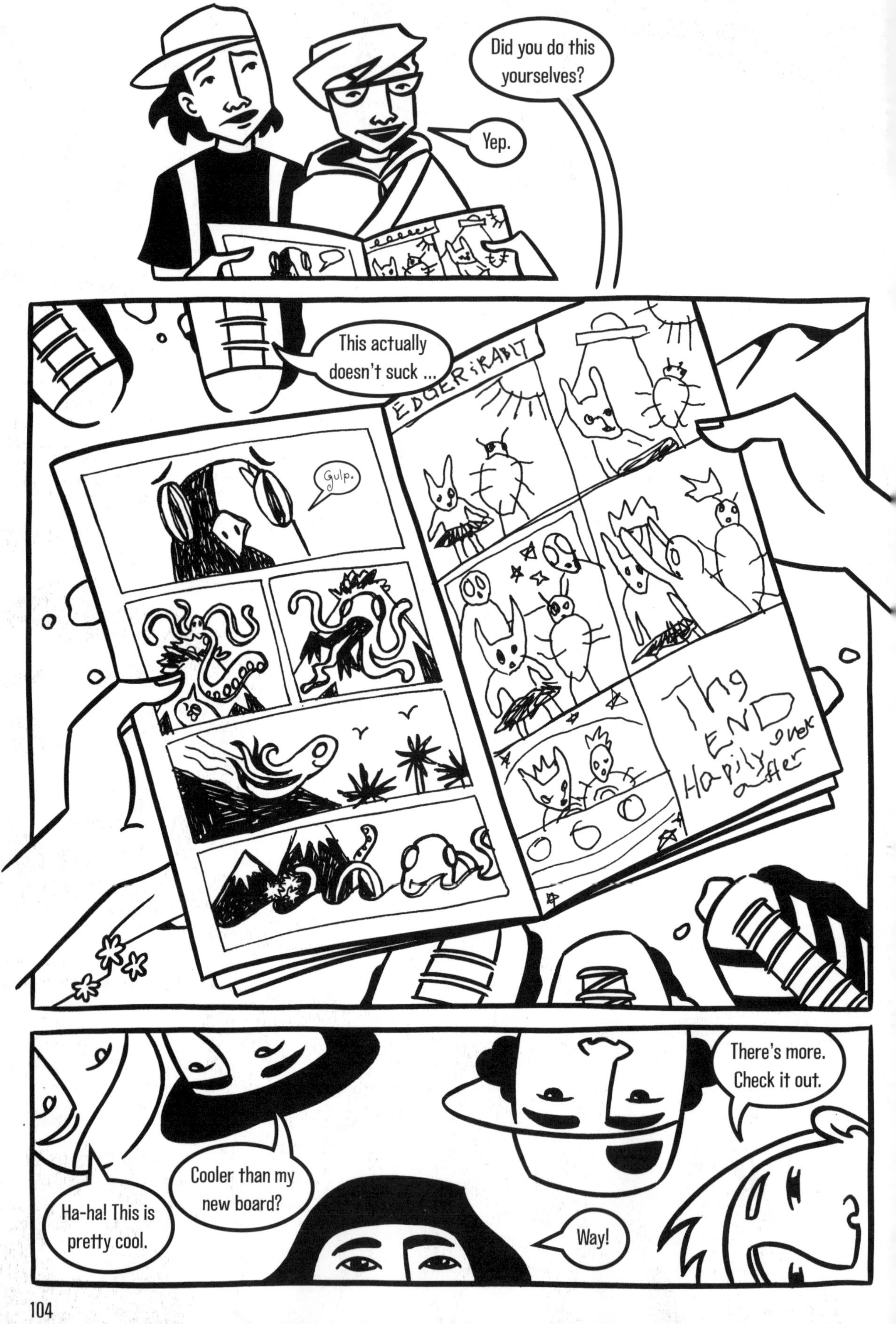
Did you do this yourselves?
Yep.
This actually doesn't suck ...
Gulp.
Ha-ha! This is pretty cool.
Cooler than my new board?
Way!
There's more. Check it out.

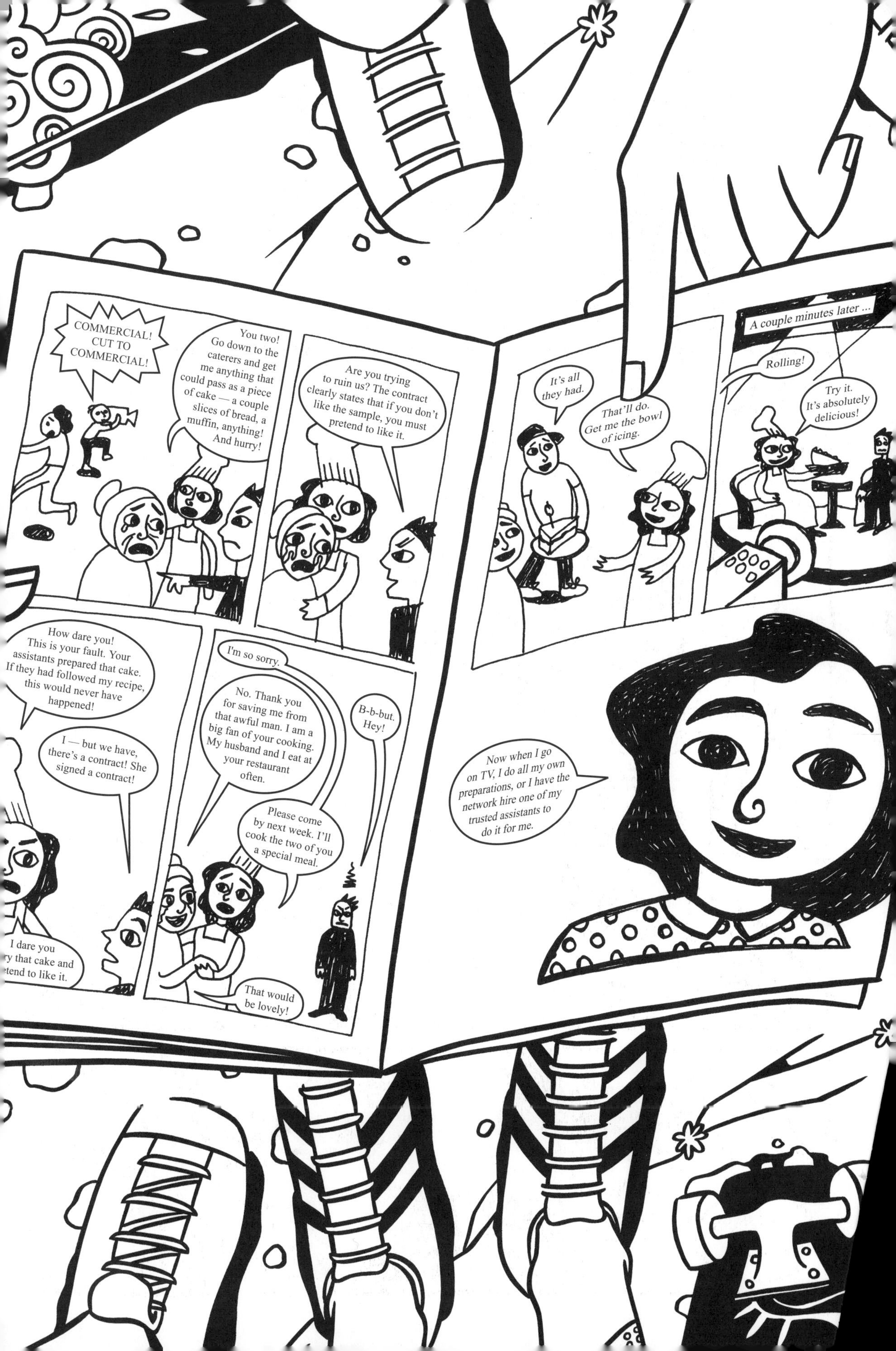
COMMERCIAL! CUT TO COMMERCIAL!
You two! Go down to the caterers and get me anything that could pass as a piece of cake — a couple slices of bread, a muffin, anything! And hurry!
Are you trying to ruin us? The contract clearly states that if you don't like the sample, you must pretend to like it.
How dare you! This is your fault. Your assistants prepared that cake. If they had followed my recipe, this would never have happened!
I — but we have, there's a contract! She signed a contract!
I dare you ry that cake and etend to like it.
I'm so sorry.
No. Thank you for saving me from that awful man. I am a big fan of your cooking. My husband and I eat at your restaurant often.
B-b-but. Hey!
Please come by next week. I'll cook the two of you a special meal.
That would be lovely!
It's all they had.
That'll do. Get me the bowl of icing.
A couple minutes later ...
Rolling!
Try it. It's absolutely delicious!
Now when I go on TV, I do all my own preparations, or I have the network hire one of my trusted assistants to do it for me.

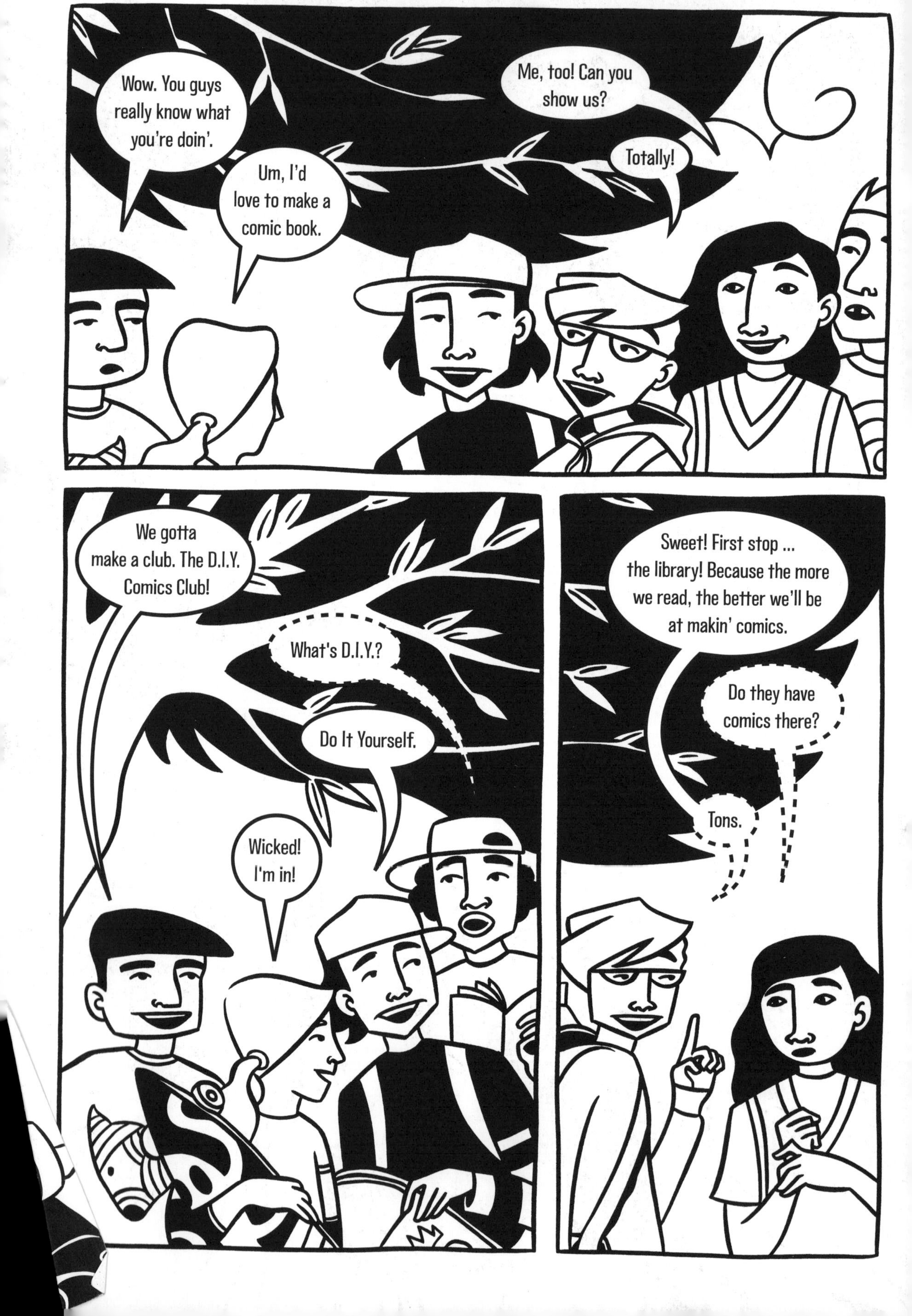
Wow. You guys really know what you're doin'.
Um, I'd love to make a comic book.
Me, too! Can you show us?
Totally!
We gotta make a club. The D.I.Y. Comics Club!
What's D.I.Y.?
Do It Yourself.
Wicked! I'm in!
Sweet! First stop ... the library! Because the more we read, the better we'll be at makin' comics.
Do they have comics there?
Tons.

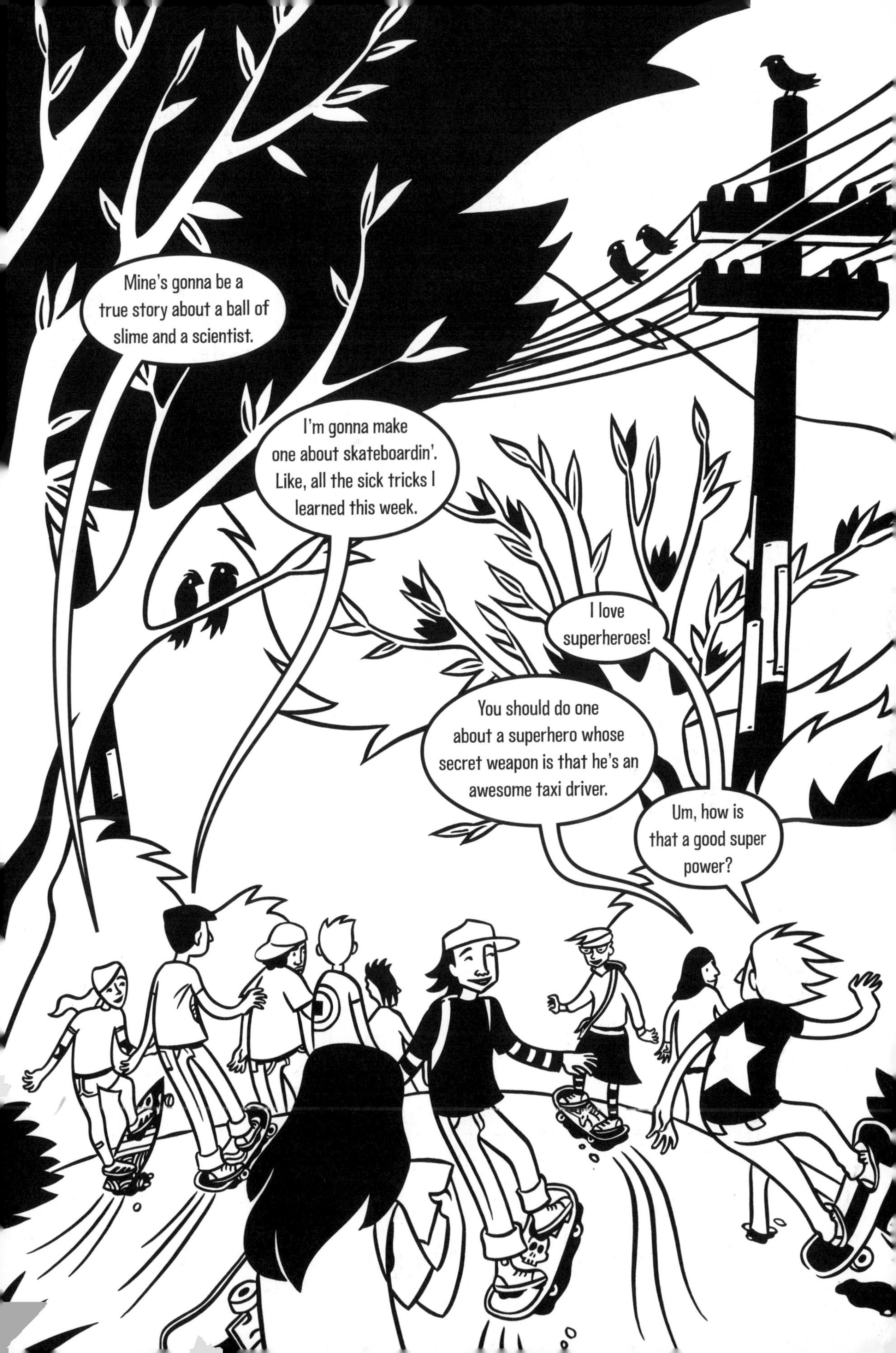
Mine's gonna be a true story about a ball of slime and a scientist.
I'm gonna make one about skateboardin'. Like, all the sick tricks I learned this week.
I love superheroes!
You should do one about a superhero whose secret weapon is that he's an awesome taxi driver.
Um, how is that a good super power?

Further Reading

Writing
Don't Forget to Write: 54 Enthralling and Effective Writing Lessons for Students 6–18
Learn how to become a better writer with this fantastic and fun book as your guide. Writing lessons by Jonathan Ames, Aimee Bender, Dave Eggers, Erika Lopez, Jon Scieszka, Sarah Vowell and more! Edited by Jenny Traig (826 Valencia, 2005).

Art
How to Draw and Paint Crazy Cartoon Characters: Create Original Characters with Lots of Personality
Learn techniques specific to comics and animation, including drawing and painting, anatomy, foreshortening, lighting and character development in this funny and insightful book. By Vincent Woodcock (Barron's Educational Series, 2007).

Perspective! for Comic Book Artists: How to Achieve a Professional Look in Your Artwork
David Chelsea teaches his hollow-headed student Mugg how to draw landscapes and insides of buildings in perspective. Recommended for older readers. By David Chelsea (Watson-Guptill Publications, 1997).

Comics

Understanding Comics: The Invisible Art
A detailed explanation of the special way in which comics communicate, including historical references and art theory. Recommended for older readers. By Scott McCloud (Harper Collins, 1994).

Drawing Words and Writing Pictures: A Definitive Course from Concept to Comic in 15 Lessons
Whether you like making manga, superhero or indie comics, this in-depth set of lessons will help you take your creations to the next level. Recommended for older readers. By Jessica Abel and Matt Madden (:01 First Second, 2008).

Lettering

Balloon Tales! Comicraft's Online Guide to Comic Lettering and Production!
If it's cool with your parents, hop online to check out this great resource on lettering and comic book production. Includes step-by-step instructions, tips and tricks, downloadeable fonts and an excellent glossary. www.balloontales.com. By John "JG" Roshell and Richard Starkings (Comicraft Studio, 2009).

Mini Comics and DIY

Whatcha Mean, What's a Zine? The Art of Making Zines and Mini-Comics
All you need to know about designing, printing and distributing your own zine. Recommended for older readers. By Mark Todd and Esther Pearl Watson (Graphia, 2006).

Glossary

And other comics terms!

anime: Japanese-style animation

background: what appears farthest from the central object or character / subject in the panel — usually the scenery

bandes dessinées: French comics, often referred to simply as "BD"

binding: how the pages of a book are attached together

brainstorming: a way of coming up with lots of ideas. Listing, mapping and webbing are all forms of brainstorming.

character: a fictional person in your story

cliffhanger: a kind of story ending where your character is left in the middle of a situation or hard decision

coloring: putting color on the final, inked artwork

colorist: the person who colors the final, inked artwork

comic strips: short, one- to three- or five-panel comics, usually published in newspapers and often funny — hence the term "funnies"

comics club: a group of people with the same interest in comics, who share information, resources and create comics together

comicon: a special event celebrating comic books for people who love them. Short for "comic book convention."

computer lettering: using computer programs and fonts to letter your comic

conflict: a struggle, fight or disagreement that propels characters or subjects through the story

cover: the front of your comic or book

cover art: the artwork that goes on the cover of your book

design: arranging all the elements on the page in a way that is pleasing, intentional and communicates clearly the ideas contained within

dialogue: what your characters and subjects are saying and thinking

directing the eye: designing the page — using panels, word balloons, focal points, point of view, sight lines and other graphic devices — to tell the reader where to look

feedback: other people's thoughts and comments about your story. Often referred to as "constructive criticism" since the goal is to help you improve your story.

fiction: stories that are made up, including fantasy, superhero and science fiction

flashback: a character or subject's memory of a past event or dream.

foreground: what appears to be closest to the reader in the panel

hand lettering: using pens, brushes and ink to letter your comic

indie comics: "indie" stands for independently created comics, which are self-published or published by independent presses. Often appearing only as graphic novels and rarely serialized as comic books.

inking: drawing over the pencils in black ink

inker: the person who paints over the pencilled artwork in ink

issue: a comic book that is not a complete story on it's own but is part of a series of comics that, together, tell a whole story

letterer: the person who puts the word balloons, dialogue, narration and sound effects over the final art

lettering: placing the word balloons, dialogue, narration and sound effects over the final inked artwork

location: where your story takes place

mainstream comics: North American–style superhero, fantasy and science fiction comics usually containing longer story arcs serialized about once a month in twenty-two-page comic books

manga: a style of comics that originated in Japan, read from right to left, top to bottom, which is the way Japanese is read and written

middleground: what appears to be in the middle of the panel, between the background and the foreground or reader

mini comic: small, self-published, handmade comics often photocopied in the style of a zine. Called "mini" for short.

mood: the overall feeling or atmosphere of your story or a scene within it

narration: the words of a character or subject who is commenting on scenes in which they do not appear, often represented in a caption

nonfiction: stories about real people and events, including biography, autobiography, history, journalism, educational and instructional comics

outlining: organizing your ideas or main points into the order you will follow when you write your story

pacing: how fast or slow the story progresses

panel descriptions: the writing in your script that describes what is going on in the panels

pencils: pencilled directly on the final paper, this is the drawing stage between the roughs and final, inked art

penciller: the person who draws the artwork in pencil

plot: what happens in your story

publisher: the person or company that makes and sells copies of your comic

research: finding information on your chosen subject including personality traits, location, time period and events. Research helps make your story, whether fiction or nonfiction, more believable.

revising: the part of the writing process where you make big changes to improve the consistency of ideas, story structure and in the case of nonfiction, to check for accuracy

script: the final written-version format, which includes pages, panel descriptions, dialogue and narration. Used in film, TV and comics.

series: several comics all on the same topic

sequential art: telling a story using a series of images and words in a specific order, or sequence

subject: a real person or topic you are writing about

subtitle: a secondary part of the title used to give more information about the content

tail: the part of the word balloon that points to the speaker's mouth or head

texture: the feeling or look of different surfaces

title: the name of your story or comic book. Chapters can also have titles.

type: printed letters

view: seeing something from a particular position, direction or location